THE INQUISITOR

"You are traveling with this Sorceress?" the farmer asked Thorn.

"Hellbog, no!" Thorn said. "I never saw her before in my life, Reverence."

"Then leave, Swordswoman."

Return to where I was hiding, Frostflower pleaded with her eyes. *Find Starwind. Keep him warm and dry. Even if you hate your son, save him!*

FROSTFLOWER AND THORN

Phyllis Ann Carr

PHYLLIS ANN KARR

FROST FLOWER AND THORN

BERKLEY BOOKS, NEW YORK

FROSTFLOWER AND THORN

A Berkley Book / published by arrangement with
the author

PRINTING HISTORY
Berkley edition / November 1980

ISBN: 0-425-04540-4

A BERKLEY BOOK ® TM 757,375

PRINTED IN THE UNITED STATES OF AMERICA
Text Designed by Michael Serrian

This book was born at George R.R. Martin's Clarke College Workshop, Dubuque, Iowa, in the summer of 1977. To the members and consultants of the workshop, and to my mother, who helped lick the story into shape, sincere gratitude.

FROST FLOWER AND THORN

Chapter 1

Thorn scowled at the morning sun coming through the shutter's broken slats. She sat up in bed, groped for one of her boots, and hurled it at a roach on the opposite wall. Then she picked up her other boot and used it to slap her latest bedpartner awake.

"Eeyy! What——"

"Out, Spendwell." Thorn felt sick again, and, for the moment, disgusted with men, especially pasty-faced merchants too proud of their new beards to shave them off.

"Out? I just fell asleep!"

"You've been snoring since middle watch." The swordswoman got out of bed and walked to the dented slop-pot in the corner. Damn morning sickness! She braced her head against the wall, and some crawling thing, probably another roach, wriggled into her hair. She slapped it out even before wiping her mouth. Behind her, Spendwell was moving around in his flappy slippers.

"Aren't you gone yet?"

"Don't take your temper out on me, Thorn. I wasn't the one who got you pregnant."

"Only because that damn weaver in White Orchard beat you to it." Or maybe it had been the smith at Eldrommer's Farm. At least it had not been a farmer-priest. Get pregnant by one of them, and a woman had to carry the brat full term so she could give it back to the farmer's family.

Thorn found her tunic, pulled it on, and belted it fiercely. The merchant was still looking for his gold-embroidered stockings. "If you're going to loll around here all morning," said the warrior, "do something to pay for your place. Tell me where I can find a borter in this stinking town."

1

Spendwell looked up and grinned. "Why not go ahead and bear the brat this time, Thorn? You can always give it away to the sorceri."

She found one of his stockings, looped it around his neck, yanked him to his feet, and pulled him, struggling and growing puffy in the face, to the door. She opened it, let go the stocking, and shoved him down the rickety stairs.

"Damn you, Thorn, you'll hang for hurting me!"

"Eat stones! You're breathing. You stumbled down over your own toenails."

"If my leg's broken—gods, I hope the brat splits you apart!"

Thorn started down the steps. Spendwell hurried to his feet, grabbed his stocking, and ran across the dirty brown tiles to the outer door. The swordswoman watched him fumble with the latch until he got it open and escaped. Then she chuckled and climbed back to her room.

After opening the window to let in some comparatively fresh air, she began her morning exercise. She jerked her knees up towards her belly with unusual roughness. Maybe she could cause a miscarriage and save herself the borter's stinking tongs. Warriors' God! She would rather fight in ten raids than lie down on a borter's table again. But so far the grub was stubborn.

She was squatting on the floor kicking on her legs when the innkeeper of the Golden Rye poked her head into the room. "Stamping around, slamming doors, shouting, throwing merchants down the stairs—gods! It's summer, warrior. Decent folk are still trying to sleep."

Thorn reached over and lifted Slicer from the floor near the bed. The innkeeper backed away. "I want you out before midmorning," she said as she closed the door behind her.

Chuckling at the innwoman's pitiable attempt to save face, Thorn jammed her sword point-first into the floor, digging up a few more splinters. Smardon's fingernails, but she would have loved to slice up an innkeeper, just once in her life! Unless you paid the night before, they left you to slop in the alley; and once they had your money, they looked for excuses to throw you out early. When Thorn remembered the restraint she had used with Spendwell . . .

But for slicing up innkeepers or merchants, a warrior would stink in Hellbog forever, even if she escaped being stoned or gutted first. Well, maybe she would still slice up an innkeeper if she ever got a good opportunity. Chances were she would stink in Hellbog anyway, and meanwhile she could probably dodge the townwarriors and escape to the other side of the Tanglelands.

Or maybe she would slice up the borter after he was through getting the grub out of her.

Thorn recognized the foulness of her mood by the foulness of these thoughts. At another time, they would not have occurred to her. Well, who wouldn't be sour-tempered in her present condition?

She finished her exercise and pulled on the rest of her clothes, shaking each boot first in case a roach had crawled inside. Someday she would cross-lace her trousers with velvet ribbons again, instead of hempstring. She emptied her purse into her hand: three coppers and a silver. For two or three goldens, she could hire a good physician to do the business, give herself that much chance. But even if she hired out to another farmer tomorrow, she might not have time to earn enough. Wait too long, and the physician charged five goldens and would not promise a woman's survival. So it had to be done soon, or she would be caught with a grub in her belly for thirteen times as long as a hen took to hatch an egg... more than half those days seeing her slim belly bulge out until she was waddling around with almost as much extra bulk as a criminal after swallowing the stones. Very few farmers or townmasters would pay a waddling, melon-bellied warrior. And afterwards, maybe she could find someone to buy the brat for about as much pay as she had lost during the final sixty or eighty days... gods! She would have to find a borter before another hen's-hatching had gone by.

Some warriors turned to robbery when they wanted money. Thorn would prefer to die with the borter's tongs in her. She looked for a moment at the sheen-amber in Slicer's pommel, the garnet in Stabber's. No, a physician was not quite worth robbing her sword or dagger. She had heard they did the same things the borters did, only a little better—usually. She had also heard that some physicians were drunken bog-bait; and how did a stranger know the good ones ahead of time?

She left the room, jerking the door shut, and descended the stairs, clumping as loudly as she could.

The time was an hour after sunrise on a summer day, and only three people were in the meal-room: a pair of stablemen throwing dice at the window table while they waited for their bread and beef, and a sorceress sitting at the small table beneath the stairs, drinking a bowl of milk in timid little sips. Her face was half-hidden by her black hood, and a big, mangy, brown mongrel lay at her feet, slowly thumping its tail against the floor.

Thorn pulled over a bench and sat at the dice-player's table. Stableworkers were not wealthy; but they were dicing for high stakes (for stablemen), and if the Warriors' God was generous this morning, she might win a couple of silvers.

The older stableman looked at her with narrowed eyes. "We don't know you, warrior."

She turned her purse upside down over the table. "Do you know the sound of money?"

"Let be, Father," said the younger man. "Room for three until the platters come. The game is Falling Doubles, warrior. A kip the round."

One copper the round was hardly worth rolling the dice. "Four kips the round," said the swordswoman.

The old man slapped his palm down on the table, but his son spoke first. "Our chances are two to one, Father. And stranger's money makes a sweeter game."

"Four kips the round, then." The old man shoved the dice to Thorn. "The roll is at threes."

Before the inn wench came with the stablemen's breakfast, Thorn's one silver and five coppers had dwindled to a single kip. Better save it for dinner. If she lived to eat dinner. Thanks to her bloody luck, she had better spend the day looking for a cheap borter who would loan his services for a witnessed pledge of double his usual price, to be paid before harvest.

"Breakfast, warrior?" asked the inn wench, setting down the platters of steaming beef and brown bread speckled with mustardseed in front of the stablemen.

Thorn growled a refusal and stood up, swinging her bench away from the table and banging it down again more or less where she had pulled it from. She glared once around the meal-room, then strode out of the Golden Rye before she yielded to impulse and broke something.

Rabbity townsfolk were beginning to loll around in the streets. A couple of merchants were going in opposite directions, each leading a donkey with sacks of merchandise. Probably one was taking blue cloth from the east side of Three Bridges to the west, while the other was taking green cloth from west to east. A smith was yawning like a hound as he hauled his anvil into the open space between his shop and his neighbor's, a tiler was lying on a roof beside the hole she would mend when her hammer would not disturb any sleepers, a stonecutter was lazily roughening pebbles for the next execution. Townsfolk were lazy bastards. On a farm, all the workers were hustling around before sunrise, even in summer.

Thorn crossed the street and headed for a fruitseller who was starting to bring out his stock for the day. Setting a basket of peaches on his window shelf, he eyed the warrior suspiciously. She scowled to show him she was honest. He yawned and turned back into the depths of his house for another load.

Someone was coming up behind the swordswoman. A person walking softly and an animal padding after. Had Thorn quarreled with anyone here in Three Bridges who might be stupid enough to try an attack by daylight in a town street? She waited until the unknown had almost reached her, then spun around and drew her dagger in the same instant.

It was the sorceress and dog she had seen in the meal-room of the Golden Rye.

The mongrel retreated behind its owner's black robe and waited there, whining and thumping its tail. The sorceress dropped her gaze at once, but otherwise did not flinch. "Swordswoman?" she said quietly.

Sorceri were scum, but if even half the tales about their powers were true . . . Thorn quickly returned Stabber to his sheath. "I don't think I know you, sorceress."

"My name is Frostflower. It is permitted here for sorceri to buy other folk food?"

The warrior shrugged. "I don't know. Probably not. I pay for my own meals anyway."

Frostflower sighed and looked at the half-filled window shelf. The fruitseller came and set out a bowl of cherries, frowned and shook his head at the sorceress, and returned inside. Frostflower tried to slip half a copper into Thorn's hand. "Fullorchard does not like to sell to us. You will buy a peach for me? I will wait around the corner to the right."

The dog had come out from behind the sorceress and was snuffling around Thorn's boots, still wagging its hairy tail. The warrior resisted the urge to kick its muzzle, and pushed away Frostflower's half-copper. "I still have money. Go wait." More to get away from the dog than to please the sorceress, she strode to the window shelf.

Suddenly she felt a longing for strawberries. She fought it. It was the damn grub inside her; she herself had never liked the blasted things. She began to look over the peaches. Fullorchard wanted a quarter-kip for a peach. The warrior refused to haggle, but she did insist on examining every piece of fruit and making her own choice. She took her time. Maybe if she took long enough, the sorceress would give up the wait. At last Thorn chose two of the largest peaches, one fully ripe, the other a little green. Plunging her dagger into the green one, she broke her last copper and tossed half to the fruitseller. He failed to catch it, and she strode away without waiting to see how soon he would find it.

Frostflower was waiting where she had said, her back almost touching a cheesemaker's thick wall, her fingers rubbing the mongrel's head. Thorn started to toss her the riper peach, but stopped and put it into her hand instead.

"Thank you. Now you must accept this." Again the sorceress tried to give her half a kip. Thorn, already devouring her own peach from the point of her dagger, shook her head. "Keep it. I don't need your damn quarter-kip. I need two goldens. Good-bye, sorceress."

She began to walk on. The sorceress kept pace with her. "You need the two goldens because you have a baby inside you?"

Damn that merchant to Hellbog for shouting it all over the inn. "That's my business."

"And the two goldens will buy a clean place to give it birth?"

"I said, that's my business." Thorn half-kicked at the dog, which was snuffling around her heels again. It avoided her foot, whined, and went on following her.

"You have still a long time to earn your two goldens."

"Eat stones, sorceress!"

Frostflower raised her head to look up into the warrior's face. She had one brown and one blue eye.

Thorn swallowed a bite of peach half-chewed. It was not wise to insult sorceri so openly to their faces. "I—that is, I've only got about two hen's-hatchings."

"Then you do not want the child?"

"No!" Whatever emotion the sorceress felt—confusion, eagerness, whatever the demon sorceri could feel—it did not seem to be anger at Thorn's insult. Relieved on that score, the swordswoman let out her frustration. "Big, awkward lump inside you, ugly trouble-making brat when it gets out—what kind of bloody load is that for a warrior?"

"You want the goldens for a physician, then, to bring it out before it grows too large?"

Thorn nodded, taking another bite of green peach and pushing the dog out of her way with one foot so that she could start walking again.

"And if you do not earn the goldens?"

"Then I'll have to find a borter to do it for a promise. Hell! Will you keep your—dog—away from me before I kick its teeth in?"

"Dowl!" said the sorceress. Whining, the dog returned to its owner. "Your pardon, warrior. Dowl helps a little, by his size, to discourage attack by folk who do not know he loves everyone."

"Unh." Thorn wondered if the creature would still love anyone who booted its hairy ribs in. She tried once more to stride away, but Frostflower laid one hand on her arm.

"I can help you, swordswoman. It will not be the same kind of help you would have from a physician or borter, but the result will be the same, for you."

"Yes? And what's your price?"

"Nothing. Only—"

"Only?"

Frostflower looked up at her again with those mismatched eyes. "Only the baby. And only if you decide to give it up."

Thorn slapped her hand against the nearest wall. "What the Hell would I do with the damn thing?" But what would the sorceress do with a bloody little grub like that? "You want it for some kind of sorcering?" the warrior asked suspiciously. "Or do you just want to eat it?" Frostflower was welcome to it for a meal—probably a lot better than the mold and dung sorceri usually ate in their retreats—but it was Thorn's grub, and she'd be damned if she would let it be used in any kind of weather-blasting or plague-spreading spells.

"We do not eat babies," Frostflower replied with a sad half-smile. "Only plants. And I want it for nothing ugly, nothing unlawful. It's not unlawful for us to raise children in our retreats, not in most parts of the Tanglelands."

"Raise it? It's a grub, sorceress. Not much more than two hen's-hatchings old!"

"Nevertheless, if I help you, it will live."

"Unh. I see. You'll help me the way a stinking priest would help me—shut me up somewhere for the next eleven or twelve hen's-hatchings."

"No. It will take longer than a physician's help, or a borter's, perhaps. I know little of their work. But no longer than a winter afternoon."

A winter afternoon's work done on a summer day like this, and Thorn would have time afterwards to earn a copper slaughtering a pig for somebody. "Quick enough," she agreed noncommittally, sucking on her peach pit.

"It will not be comfortable—"

"You think it's comfortable on a bloody borter's table? I don't give a blasted fart about comfortable, so long as it's quick. But if you're lying about that, sorceress, you'll wish the farmers were in charge of your scaffolding!"

Frostflower would not have time to wish that, actually. The only safe way to kill a sorceron was with a surprise attack from behind. Unless some fool could be found who would risk taking her virginity.

As if she had not heard the warrior's last insult, Frostflower bit into her peach, without sucking loudly or dribbling juice. She swallowed the bite before speaking again. "My retreat is ten days' journey from Three Bridges. We will do best to return there—"

"No!" A little sorcering Thorn would risk, laws or no laws, to get the brat out of her quickly and cheaply. But she would hang herself with a bellyful of stones before she would follow anyone into a retreat full of sorceri with their dung-larders and secret pits of crazed animals.

"It would be safest and most nearly comfortable. We have a cottage—"

"I've heard of your damn cottages. We'll find someplace here in Three Bridges, or I'll take my chances with a borter."

The sorceress ate more of her peach, slowly, keeping her gaze lowered so that Thorn no longer saw her eyes. "I can partly guess the things that are told of us. But whatever you have heard, our houses are clean and what few guests come to us in peace we treat with courtesy."

The warrior snorted, but Frostflower went on,

"The child can be little extra burden to you as yet. Travel with me for ten days, and we will both be safe. But for a sorceress to journey with a child whose existence none can explain—"

"Wrap it up in your blight-herb box and carry it in your sleeve."

Frostflower sighed. "Will you come with me as far as Frog-in-the-Millstone? I have friends there—not sorceri—a family of weavers who worship all your gods. They will lend us a place."

Frog-in-the-Millstone was half a day's walk from Three Bridges, but the weavers might share a meal or two, and the walk would give Thorn time to figure out how nearly she trusted this sorceress. Besides, it was that much closer to Maldron's Farm, and rumor said that Maldron was almost always ready to hire a new warrior or two. Thorn shrugged. "I'm getting sick of Three Bridges anyway."

The weavers' graincellar was cool and clean. Bunches of herbs hung from the ceiling beams to keep away insects, and a fragrant candle burned in a wall niche before a statue of the Wheat Goddess. Thorn lay on a slanted, makeshift bed near the wall, propping herself up on one elbow and watching Frostflower warily.

All the way from Three Bridges to Frog-in-the-Millstone, the sorceress had not only refused to answer, but had seemed not to listen to Thorn's questions about the animal pits and dung-stews of her retreat or the sorcerous tricks of blighting crops and stuffing the eyes of sleeping folk with mustard. But her friends the weavers, Brightweave, Yarn, and Small Spider, seemed honest enough— eight rooms to their house above, and a statue of one god or other in every room—and Small Spider cooked a good stew of cow brains and bacon. So here, dinner over, the swordswoman waited.

She intended to close her eyes and ears when the sorcering began, to get the thing done without letting it dirty her mind. So far, however, the sorceress might have been any midwife (for all Thorn knew of midwives), moving around with her basins of water, cool or steaming, and her armloads of clean rags, while her dog lay in one corner and thumped its tail against the bags of flour.

"You have not removed your belt yet?" asked Frostflower.

"I've loosened it. How much do you want?" The warrior felt naked enough already, with Slicer and Stabber out of reach on one of the foodshelves. The borter in All Roads West four years ago had made her take off nothing but trousers and sword; and, drunk as she had been for one of the few times in her life, she had kept Stabber at her waist and her fingers on his handle the whole time.

"Your belt must be off completely," Frostflower insisted, bending down and unbuckling it herself. "And your tunic . . ."

"I'm trusting you very far, sorceress."

"Your tunic is loose enough, if you truly wish to wear it, but it would stay fresher if you removed it for now. You have never given birth, Thorn? I think you do not understand—"

"No, and I don't want to understand your bloody sorcering! Just hurry up and get the grub out of me. No longer than a winter afternoon, you said."

"Yes; you are young, healthy—yes, it should take no longer, even though you will not—"

"Damn you!" shouted Thorn. "Do you know what the Hellbog you're doing?" In the corner, the dog whined and lifted its ears.

Frostflower met Thorn's gaze without blinking. "I have studied carefully for this, as only sorceri can study. Will you drink more wine?"

"I've drunk half a cup already," the warrior grumbled, subsiding a little. That was a bloody borter's trick, to get a woman drunk first.

The sorceress nodded, set down her last armload of rags, and knelt beside Thorn. "Lean back now. Do not let your tunic bunch under you—it must be loose. So."

The warrior lay back on the sloping mound of old sheets and cushions. She closed her eyes and spread her legs.

The sorceress touched her on the belly—unexpectedly, lightly, and left her hand there. Then, nothing. Not even a mumbled chant. Nothing but a few weak drafts in the air and a strange vibrating in the warrior's guts.

For a few moments Thorn kept her resolution not to watch any sorcering, even—especially!—any done to herself. But the silence . . . even the dog had stopped beating its mangy tail . . . the bloating in her stomach . . . what was Frostflower doing? What was the sorceress waiting for? Thorn opened her eyes.

Frostflower knelt above her, free hand quivering in the air, mismatched, unmoving eyes reflecting the candle flame, moisture glistening on the pale forehead.

Thorn glanced down from the sorceress to her own belly, stifled a gasp, and stiffened. Beneath Frostflower's hand, Thorn's body was swelling, growing before her eyes, mounding up like

a lump of warm yeast-dough. Frostflower had lured her here to
take vengeance for all the sorceri stoned, gutted, and hung up to
die! She was growing stones in her stomach—lumps of coal—
something to burst her open—set fire to her guts—and her weapons
on the other side of the room, out of reach—

It kicked! some kind of little monster—a baby mountain lion
to claw her insides, a cat-sized donkey kicking its way out.... Thorn
tried to speak, tell Frostflower she had never helped execute one
of her kind, had never— The sorceress remained still, fixing her
gaze on the candle, her strange eyes unblinking. In a panic, as
more kicks came from inside her belly, Thorn grabbed one of
Frostflower's wrists.

The sorceress turned her hand slightly and answered the warrior's grip. Otherwise, she remained unmoving, staring at the
candle flame. Her fingers were thin, frail, cold... but calm.

Suddenly Thorn understood. She lay back again, grinning.
Sneaky little bitch of a sorceress. No choice now but to wait it
out and hope Frostflower had the sorcering to get her belly flat
again as fast as she made it bulge out.

The kicks came quicker now, one after another. The grub was
trying to do some kind of stamping dance. Succeeding—it was
moving all around in her belly, peaking it up, wiggling it lower.
Maybe it was a damn pair of twins in there, humping already! It
was pushing hard enough now, hammering at her groin, squeezing
her lower guts.... Thorn rocked up and squatted on her hams,
looking for relief. The pressure was pulsing and fading with almost
every breath. Gods! She would get this thing out and be done with
it. She strained down fiercely. Something gushed out.

Water. Nothing else. She fell back with a grunt of disgust.

The sorceress bent and began to gather up the layer of soaked
rags.

"It's stopped," said Thorn. "It's not pushing any more."

Frostflower spread a new layer of rags beneath Thorn's body.
"It is wisest to allow the birth its normal speed now."

"Damn you to Hellbog, I want it out and over with!"

The sorceress tried to dab Thorn's face with a moist rag. The
warrior thrust her arm away. "I said I want it out!"

"I will hasten it as much as I dare."

Frostflower bent again and put her hand beneath Thorn's tunic.
She began to press and rub.

"What are you doing now?"

"I only try to learn its position. Shhh, now." Nodding, the sorceress removed her hands, returned to her kneeling pose, and touched Thorn's shoulder.

At once, the pushing started again, the bloody squeezing inside. Filthy little bugger! Thorn rocked back and forth on her arms, pushing back. Every few moments, the damn grub would give up, but Thorn kept on, straining hard enough to push out her guts, pausing only to catch her breath. By the gods, she would push it out of her whether it wanted to come or not—whether the sorceress was going to help or not!

"The rhythm is wrong!" cried Frostflower.

"Just—make it—faster!"

"This is too fast. You should push only with the child, rest between. You exhaust yourself this way—speed confuses us now."

The brat had stopped pushing again. Frostflower put both hands to Thorn's shoulders and half-shoved, half-lowered her to a reclining position on the rags. Thorn, already exhausted, accepted a moment of rest. Everyting seemed to be wet—the rags, her tunic, the smells of blood and hot body slush. It wasn't a brat, it was a bloody lump of mush leaking out in spurts and dribbles. What was the sorceress doing about it? Nothing. Fussing with the rags again, wiping Thorn's face with wet cloth. . . .

The brat started pushing once more. With a cry, Thorn rocked forward and strained. The thing was not trying to get out, it was trying to grind her guts loose. She squatted, hands on the floor to steady herself, fighting the brat to push it out and away from her bowels, until it gave up again and she fell back panting. "It's trying to kill me! What the Hellstink are you doing?"

The sorceress seemed to be pressing around Thorn's undermouth with her fingers. "Soon now," she said quietly. "Very soon, and in its own time. No!" as the grinding began again and Thorn started forward. "Lie back now. Push, but lie back."

The warrior obeyed. She felt numb between her legs, but she also seemed to be a field's length wide down there, and crammed up with something. She was vaguely aware of Frostflower's fingers adding to the pressure. Something burst out—a big hard lump. Her leg muscles jerked in reflex, but the sorceress was between, holding the thighs steady. Thorn opened her eyes and looked down. It took her a minute to realize that the dark lump Frostflower was fussing with between her legs was the brat's head. She was amazed it was so small.

The sorceress glanced up, met her gaze, and smiled. "The hardest is over. Lie still . . . do not try to sit up next time. Let it come straight."

"Stink in Hell," mumbled the warrior. Frostflower was more concerned about the brat than about Thorn. Well, the swordswoman remembered groggily, she had wanted it for her pay. Let it come the rest of the way out, and Thorn could stop bothering about it. Already it was squalling. Stop squalling, you little bastard, and push!

It pushed. Not so hard as before, but hard enough, with Thorn's efforts added, to get it all the way out.

"It is born," said Frostflower, above its wails. "Ah, what a fine child! You will want to keep him . . ." she added wistfully.

"It's a grub," said Thorn, glancing at the slimy, purplish, wrinkled thing. "What do I want with it? Is that one of my bowels it's pulled out with it?"

Frostflower turned the grub so that Thorn could see the intestine was growing out of its own navel. "You have never seen a young animal being born?"

"I'm not a stableworker. Its navel cord?"

"Yes. The cord that joins mother and child."

"Then cut it. Unjoin us. Get rid of it."

The brat had stopped squalling at last and lay wiggling. Frostflower watched the long gutlike cord for a few moments until it stopped pulsing. Then she twisted a couple of knots in it, close to the brat's belly, and sliced it between the knots with a silly little dagger. "Can't you do anything simply?" said Thorn.

"Shhh." The sorceress was fussing with the brat, putting it in a basin of water and rinsing it off as carefully as if it were an eggshell blown hollow. As she worked, she hummed. The dog was thumping its tail again. Thorn felt both the humming and the thumping through the pillows when she turned her head.

She shivered in her wet tunic, and sat up to peel it off, then fell back once more, naked and sweaty, on the rumpled sheets. Messier than my first man, she thought foggily. She drowsed for a while, until yet another pushing started inside her. A small one this time, but annoying. She tightened her muscles, and felt a hot gush. "Anything else left to come out?" she asked, glancing with disgust at the big, spongy bloodclot lying between her legs.

"No." the sorceress had finally finished with the brat and put
it somewhere for a while, leaving her free to clean up the afterbirth.

"Then how soon before my belly's flat again?"

"It's flattening now."

Thorn tried to tighten her stomach and abdomen. It was not
comfortable, and they still felt flabby. "Can't you hurry it up, the
way you hurried the grub?"

Frostflower began to wipe the warrior's face and body with
warm, damp rags. "Rest now. It is nearly time for supper. Sleep
here tonight. In the morning, if you are still dissatisfied with your
body's own speed, I will hasten the muscles. Will you suckle your
child?"

Let the brat get on her chest like a bloody leech? "Hellstink,
no!"

"I think it would help pull your womb tight once more."

Rolling over to let Frostflower change the rags and sheet beneath her, the warrior somewhat nervously felt her breasts. Were
they swelling up? The last thing she needed was a sucking baby
for a year or more, but if she was going to have a sore, swollen
chest otherwise—Damn the sorceress! At least with a borter Thorn
would not have had this worry. "I suppose if I don't let it leech
me, I'll be going around like an unmilked cow?"

"I do not think so. I concentrated on your womb and the infant.
Your breasts may not have kept pace; and even if they have, your
milk will dry within a few days without suckling. Indeed, your
milk may never come."

The warrior grunted in relief. "Then don't let the grub near
me. I'll take care of my own belly in the morning." The graincellar
seemed chill now that she had stopped working. Frostflower spread
a couple of thick linen sheets over her.

The sorceress removed her black robe, sat down in her white
smock on a pile of meal-sacks, unlaced her bodice and bared one
breast. Carefully she picked up a bundle of linen and held it to
her little bump of a nipple. Thorn watched lazily for a few moments before she realized what Frostflower was doing. "You don't
think *you're* going to suckle it?"

"Perhaps."

"I thought you sorceri were supposed to be virgins."

"Sometimes even one of our men can suckle an infant." The
sorceress did not take her gaze from the baby. "It will be several
days, and in the meantime we must feed him goats' milk from a

spoon, but if he will continue to suck, milk may finally come even from my breast."

"*You'll* feed him from a spoon," said the warrior. "It's your worry now, not mine." She closed her eyes. A night to spend in the weavers' house, gods knew how long to work her belly back as flat and tight as it should be (how could such a tiny grub have bulged her up so high?), days, maybe, of tender, swollen breasts . . . well, probably it had still been preferable to a borter with his stinking tongs and scrapers. But . . . "Damn it, short as a winter afternoon, you said," Thorn muttered as she fell asleep.

Chapter 2

"I think I will call him Starwind," said Frostflower, gazing down at the little one who was nuzzling with his soft, insistent mouth at her breast.

"Quite a name for an ugly little bugger like that," said Thorn, lounging back on the trunk of the fallen tree. "Just call it Grub or Stinkbeetle until it grows up."

Frostflower shook her head and touched one of the infant's cheeks with her free hand. "We who are raised among the sorceri always keep our child-names."

"Unh! So did I!"

Dowl, with his head on Frostflower's lap, pricked up his ears and whined questioningly at the swordswoman's laugh, but Starwind did not even blink. All sensations would still be much the same to the infant: either equally strange or equally prosaic. Perhaps he did not as yet even connect his diligent sucking with the milk he should draw; perhaps that was how he could continue to work so trustingly at a dry breast.

"You, Thorn?" asked the sorceress. "You kept your child-name?"

"Well, almost. The whole thing was Rosethorn, and I never did like the Rose, but the rest of it seemed to fit well enough. You really think you're even going to wetnurse the grub?"

"Perhaps." She had only been trying for two days. The infant's sucking brought her pain; but the young sorceress thought her sore nipples were enlarging somewhat, her tissues swelling. Sometimes she seemed to feel a small trickle, even an occasional tiny spurt, deep within. God grant it was not her imagination, pricked on by hope. Imagination was a dangerous thing to sorceri, who must see reality if they would use their powers without twisting it.

16

"How much longer are we going to sit here like turds in the shade?" asked the swordswoman as Frostflower shifted the infant to her other breast.

"Not much longer."

"Not much longer. That's what you kept saying the whole damn time you were messing around getting the grub out of me. Not much longer! Now you'll let it play around at that tit until it finally gives up and starts bawling, then you'll still have to get half a skin of goat's milk into it with your silly spoon.... Ten days to your blasted retreat? We'd walk it in five if we weren't always stopping to play with the bloody brat."

"You are good to come with me." It had not taken so much effort as Frostflower had feared, persuading the warrior to escort her; Thorn had even agreed to do it cheaply, at the payment of one dreamberry for every day spent on the trip. But she still insisted she would bring her only within sight of Windslope Retreat and come no further.

The warrior pulled her sword out of its sheath and began to polish the sheen-amber in its handle. "It'd be easier if I'd come with you while the grub was still inside me. But then you wouldn't have needed so much protection—ironic, eh? Why don't you just grow the damn brat big enough to gnaw carrots and walk on its own two feet?"

"We are unwise to manipulate time except when necessary. Already Starwind will learn slowly, because his brain did not keep pace with his body's growth. He could not meditate fully on all that happened to him within the womb."

"Meditate! A grub like that meditate!"

"All creatures meditate, Thorn. Many of us believe that the very corn and beans we grow meditate. That is one reason we grow only enough for our needs. Even a carrot is better for maturing in its own unprodded time."

That was not the only reason. Manipulating time for any creature, living or inanimate, required full concentration to channel the power. Quickly as sorceri could grow an individual plant, they could not have supplied any considerable part of the Tanglelands with food. There were not, had never been and surely never could be enough sorceri to feed the whole population, while even the attempt to supply a single village would have brought down on them a full attack from the farmer-priests. But to say more than necessary would break Frostflower's vow of prudence. She must

know the swordswoman longer before she could judge how fully
to take her into confidence.

"Your carrots taste as good as farmers' carrots to me," said
Thorn. "And I'll eat stones if a lump of a two-day-old grub med-
itates. What about those dreamberries you're going to grow me
for getting you through safe? I suppose there'll be something
wrong with them, too."

"I have several of my own growing, if you wish to sample
one."

"Hellbog, I wouldn't know the difference. Never touch the
things myself—worse than wine for scrambling your brain. But
I'll find plenty of folk ready to pay good coins for them, no
questions. Wake me when you're ready to move on." The warrior
closed her eyes and was soon breathing evenly. Dowl got up and
padded over to stare up wistfully at her sunburned face, wagging
his tail but keeping at a careful distance from her foot.

The infant at last let go Frostflower's nipple and began to
wrinkle up his small face. At his first wail Thorn woke, snorted,
muttered "Damn brat," and shut her eyes again.

Frostflower sighed and reached down for the skin of goat's
milk and the small tin spoon. If she had actually borne Starwind
herself—indeed, if she had ever borne any child—it might have
been possible to speed time for her bosom, to bring milk faster.
But in that case, she herself could no longer have manipulated
time. She would have lost her sorcerous power along with her
virginity. Milk could not be hurried in her breasts; if it came, it
must come in its own time, through the infant's sucking. Yet it
might come. Silverflake had nursed children. So had Wren, and
so had the old sorcerer Moonscar.

There was another reason Frostflower would not have speeded
Starwind's growth. Any person whose time was speeded lost the
equivalent number of days or years from the end of the natural
life span, unless put into the trance of cool breathing to adjust the
balance. Frostflower had not yet told the swordswoman this—she
would also have had to explain that the good sleep Thorn had
enjoyed that first night in the weavers' house had been the trance.
She guessed, however, that if she told Thorn how four years'
growth now might cost Starwind four years from the end of his
life, the warrior would respond, "What difference do the first three
or four years make to a stupid grub?"

When Starwind had fed, the sorceress changed his breechcloth and buried the soiled one. It was safer to carry only clean, old rags and conceal the wet and smelly ones.

Then she awakened Thorn and they returned to Straight Road North. On the other side of Weldervrise Forest, on the edge of the marshy land just south and west of Maldron's Farm, they came to a gibbet—two upright ladders, each twice as high as a tall man, with a third ladder nailed crosswise atop them. From the top ladder hung a warrior, the thick rope that was passed around her back pressing deeply into her armpits and shoulders, her head slumped forward, her hands tied together in front of her with the fingers strapped together. A few outlaws some years ago had managed to untie themselves during the night, so that farmer-priests and townmasters now took precautions. The warrior's feet were only handsbreadths from the ground. The unstained rags bound tightly around her midriff and abdomen suggested that her scaffolding had been the commonest one, that of being forced to swallow small, sharp pebbles. Had she been disembowelled for the quickest death, the rags would have been bloodstained; had she been hung without scaffolding for the slowest death, there would have been no rags.

"Hellbog of a place for a gibbet," Thorn remarked. "Marsh bugs stinging the poor bitch to a pulp before she dies."

The hanging wretch groaned, twitched, raised her head for a moment to cry out a few half-coherent words before slumping forward again. Frostflower stopped. She could not leave the woman like this.

"Take him, Thorn. For only a few moments. Please?" She held Starwind out to the swordswoman. Thorn shrugged and took the infant, not happily, but with reasonable care.

One hand on Dowl's head, to steady herself against the sight, Frostflower walked the score of paces to the gibbet.

The hanged woman lifted her head again, very slightly, and stared at the sorceress with glazing eyes. Then she screamed and tried to clutch at her waist with her bound hands.

"Stones?" whispered Frostflower.

"Sixty—seventy—help me!"

There was no hope for life, then. "You would die quickly?"

"Gods!—stab—something!"

Unable to bear the sight of the distorted, insect-bitten face, Frostflower closed her eyes and twisted her fingers into Dowl's shaggy coat. "You would die quickly?" she repeated. How could the woman *not* wish it? Yet the sorceress must have a clear answer.

"Yes!—Damn you—gods, yes!"

The sorceress sighed, breathed deeply, and stretched out one trembling hand to touch the hanging warrior. Then she concentrated, finding the heartbeat of the woman before her, gripping it in her mind and making it race faster and faster until the separate throbs melted together into a steady hum. . . .

The hanging warrior shrieked, jerked, uttered a quick, hiccoughing rattle. Then Frostflower sensed by the quieting of the air drafts that she now hung still. Beside the sorceress, the dog whined a little and then started to howl. Frostflower opened her eyes, glanced up once more at the motionless warrior who stared unseeing downwards, then turned and walked back to the road. She was suddenly aware of Starwind's wail.

"Well," said Thorn, handing back the infant, "why did Maldron hang her?"

"What?"

"What was her crime? Farmers don't usually gibbet poor bitches just for practice."

"I don't know." Shaken from the effort, Frostflower hugged Starwind close and started to walk down the road once more.

"You didn't ask her? What were you talking about?"

"I asked her if she wished to die quickly."

"Warriors' God! Couldn't you figure that out for yourself?"

"Despite all, even in pain, a person may desire life as long as possible," replied Frostflower after a few steps. "I could not act without her assurance, and she was not . . . completely coherent."

"I'd like to know how damn coherent *you'd* be! Look here, sorceress, if you ever find *me* dangling from a gibbet with my belly full of stones or my guts hanging out, don't fart around asking me if I want to die! Just kill me and get it over with."

It took little imagination—too little imagination—to see the swordswoman's tall body dangling, tawny golden head slumped forward, green eyes beginning to glaze . . . Frostflower's mind recoiled from the image. "You will not let me find you like that, Thorn?"

"Well, I couldn't run away if I saw you coming." Thorn grinned, as if they were not speaking of torment and execution. *She has more perfect detachment-in-unity than I*, thought Frostflower, *more acceptance of the limitations of her own awareness* and the little difference her comfort or pain makes to the rest of her fellow creatures.

"But it would have been handy," the warrior went on, "to know what that poor bitch back there did. Once in a while you find a farmer with some strange laws for his territory. You sorceri should know that even better than us warriors."

"Still, I think they do not often form a law without reason." At least, the sorceress thought, not without such excuses as they considered reason—but the rule of the farmer-priests was still preferable to the rule of some others who had held power in the Tanglelands and elsewhere in ancient days, as sorceri learned from the old writings.

Thorn pulled out her dagger, tossed it up spinning in the air, and caught it deftly by the blade as it descended. "A sorceress praising the farmers! What is an innocent like you doing out in the open?"

"Allowing you to bring me back safely to my retreat."

"Unh. Well, I suppose you have to get out of those stinking places sometimes for a little fresh air, hey?"

Frostflower did not answer. Despite her effort to talk lightly, the gibbeted warrior still echoed in her mind. After walking a few moments in silence, Starwind's weight a comfort in her arms and Dowl brushing against her robe from time to time, she said, "I did not kill her, Thorn. I quickened time for her body. She died as she would have died, but much sooner."

The swordswoman tossed up her dagger again, caught it, and shrugged. "Whatever you did—if I could do it, I wouldn't need Slicer and Stabber. Why do you want me along with you?"

"We must not use time for a weapon."

"Hunh." Thorn sounded unconvinced. She would have heard many tales, some of them based on truth. "Well, if you have to be a damn virgin and eat vegetables, I wouldn't qualify anyway."

The warrior put her dagger back in its sheath and began to whistle as she strode along. Dowl pricked up his ears and sidled a little closer to Thorn, hopefully but cautiously. She had been pushing him aside since their first meeting.

In normal circumstances, sorceri usually preferred to journey alone. The same rumors and tales which caused them to be hated, despised, and cursed in muttered tones throughout the Tanglelands also caused them to be feared and generally left to themselves. The protection of a warrior, when one could be found willing to hire herself to sorceri, had its own inherent dangers. During the first ten days of her journey, Frostflower had relied on the evil reputation of her kind. Mutterings and rudeness had sometimes grown loud, perhaps because she was smaller than most sorceri who ventured abroad, and because she cultivated the inoffensive rather than the menacing appearance; but she had found that a sudden stare from her mismatched eyes would silence the jeers when they became too threatening. In Windslope Retreat, her eyes, the left brown and the right blue, were a matter for affectionate pleasantry; but here among the worshippers of the farmers' many gods, folk seemed to find these eyes things of superstitious horror. Even Thorn had faltered on first seeing them.

Starwind had changed Frostflower's circumstances. Throughout the Tanglelands, it was a mortal crime to steal a child. A sorceress with an infant was an immediate object of suspicion, and the suspected offense was so abhorrent that folks' indignation might outweigh their fear. Nor would she dare try to explain the child's presence, as she might have if she had merely bought him. By farmers' law, such sorcery as she had used for Thorn was unlawful for all of them—sorceress, woman helped, and even, they said, for the child.

The very presence of a warrior at her side, however, would do much to allay suspicion and discourage attack. Already, by walking openly in daylight, they had passed a party of merchants and two drivers of fruit-wagons on Straight Road without arousing more than a few glances of surly surprise and distaste.

Thorn waved her hand toward a high stone wall ahead to the right. "Maldron's Farm, probably. Too bad we can't take cover there."

Sorceri could generally find lodging for a night in towns, but they never went into farms.

"We could dress you up like a craftswoman, maybe," Thorn went on.

"That would be a lie, Thorn."

"Um. Besides, you've been this way, coming south. They'd know you by your blasted eyes. Well, let's hope we get to Gammer's Oak before those clouds build into something." Thorn cocked her head toward the northwest. "I was thinking of hiring out to Maldron, too. They say he's a decent farmer to work for, usually planning a raid on somebody."

"Elvannon does not send his warriors on raids, but he pays generously." Frostflower was glad to mention the nearest farmer-

priest to Windslope, a comparatively mild lord, gentle in his use
of superstition.

"Sounds like the kind that expects a warrior to help herd the
bloody cows when she's not fighting. Well, your dreamberries
should bring me enough money to take my time and scout around
a little on my way back."

Maldron's Farm was large, but its length lay east and west,
so that the travellers soon passed the part of his wall bordering
Straight Road. The marshland was still to their left, as treacherous
if not quite as malodorous as the Hellbog of the farmer-priests'
mythology; but now Beldrise Forest, a wood of oak and ash, had
replaced the wall to their right.

According to records and speculations preserved in Windslope
Retreat, a farmer-priest of many generations ago, perhaps when
warriors were still the fighting members of the farmers' concu-
binaries, had filled in the land east of Straight Road, using the
sturdy, ancient pavement as a retaining wall. The work had been
extensive, reaching north until the land began to rise naturally at
the Rockroots. When first completed, probably it had all been
farmed. But in the following generations, as the original farmer's
descendants lost power and drew in their fortifications, the northern part of the filled area had reverted to the wild. No doubt the
oldest of these trees had first been planted to retain the soil, but
the forest had long been reseeding itself. Moonscar, the oldest and
chief sorceron of Windslope, could remember how, before he had
come to the Retreat as a newly-converted lad of thirteen, Beldrise
Forest had been so dense with undergrowth that a person could
not walk in it without a sickle to cut the way.

Maldron's grandmother Arrana, a widowed farmer-priestess
of almost legendary determination, had instigated the family's
return to power in the higher politics of the farmer-priests. Her
son had begun the work of clearing the undergrowth north of the
Farm, so that today Beldrise was a pleasant wood to walk in.
Maldron, it seemed, preferred to increase his lands by raiding his
neighbors on the east and south, than to work at filling in un-
claimed marshland west of the road as his distant ancestor had
filled in marshland to the north.

Starwind was crying again for food, Gammer's Oak was still
almost an hour's walk, and the forest offered secluded places.

"Well, all right," said Thorn, glancing again at the sky on their
left, above the marshland. "But don't mess around poking your
tits at the grub. Just feed it with the spoon right away. You can

play with it to your heart's content when we're snug and dry with that baker friend of yours in Gammer's Oak."

The sorceress studied the western sky. She had no wish to expose the infant to a storm; but she did not consider the threat as imminent as Thorn seemed to suppose. As yet they felt no hint of cool winds, and the slowly massing clouds, though dark, were still far in the distance. Sorceri had reason, perhaps more reason than warriors, to study weather; and Frostflower judged they would have time to feed the infant—provided she did not linger too long—and still reach Burningloaf's home before the rain.

They found a fallen ash not far from the forest's edge, but far enough to be hidden from the road. Whenever they stopped to care for the infant's needs, Thorn was either lazy or restive. This time she was restive. She buried Starwind's wet rags herself, grumbling that they had to think about saving time. Then, after watching Frostflower ease two spoonfuls of milk into the child's mouth, the warrior said, "I'm going to look for toadstools. I'll probably find a silver's worth before you're ready to burp the brat."

Frostflower nodded. Thorn would not wander far; she was too impatient to resume their journey. The sorceress thought she would be back before Starwind had swallowed his last spoonful.

She was not. The infant pushed the last spoonful away with tongue and lips, gurgling in satiation; and Frostflower held him at her shoulder and patted his back until the belches came. Still the swordswoman had not returned. Beldrise Forest seemed suddenly very quiet. The birds were twittering, the small animals rustling and scurrying, Dowl thumping his tail against the fallen tree; but there were no human footsteps, no whistling or stamping.

The sorceress waited, cooing the baby to sleep. Sometimes, when he was well asleep before she rose, she could walk with him a considerable distance before he woke.

Now a west wind was beginning to stir through the trees, and Frostflower herself was growing more concerned about reaching Gammer's Oak before the storm. She had noticed, out of the corner of her eye, which direction Thorn had taken. As soon as the infant slept, Frostflower rose and followed the swordswoman. She went slowly, watching for the newly-scuffled moss, the fresh-tramped humus and crushed grasses that marked Thorn's path deeper into the woods. She expected at every step to meet the warrior coming back to scold her for not waiting near the road.

Somewhere ahead and slightly to the left, she began to hear a low chanting. It was quiet, one deep voice joined at intervals by a second, higher voice. There was nothing openly sinister in it, yet it caused her to shiver. It was not sorcerous chanting—it was in a minor rather than a major scale; the rhythm was not even, but varying between short and long holds; and it seemed, as she neared it, to be in a strange language. Could this be the chanting of farmer-priests? She had never heard it, never witnessed any of the rituals they used to spread their myths of many gods. Yet did not the farmers conduct their rites in large halls, for large groups of people, rather than deep in the forest?

She paused, half fearful and half curious. The chanting continued, rising and falling. Beldrise Forest was not likely to have an open place large enough for a farmer-priest's congregation. One of the voices seemed to be a woman's. Perhaps Thorn had met a man among the trees? Could these be the sounds lovers made while mating? All the more reason the sorceress should not go on.

But the cool wind was blowing in advance of the approaching storm, and the woman's voice seemed higher and lighter than Thorn's husky contralto.

If the swordswoman's trail had not led in the direction of the chant, Frostflower could have followed her with a clear con- science. But Thorn apparently had moved toward the chant. The sorceress laid one hand on Dowl's head, hoping he would un- derstand the need to remain quiet. Then, holding Starwind close, ready to turn back at the first whine from baby or dog, or at the first alarming sign from ahead, she moved cautiously forward.

She saw the three warriors well before they had seen her. Thorn was leaning against a tree, an expression of bored annoyance on her face. The other two were standing on either side of her, also looking bored. One of them leaned against another tree, the second propped herself on her spear. All were carefully facing away from what appeared to be a small glade just beyond them. The chant came from this glade.

Frostflower shrank back, trying to hide herself better among the trees. Thorn seemed in no danger. Apparently she had merely chanced upon whatever was happening, and been made to wait until it was over. But why had she been made to wait instead of being sent away? And if she was in danger, would she not scorn to show it?

Ah, God, guide me! thought the sorceress. Do I truly need to know what is happening in that glade, so as to judge whether or not the situation is dangerous? Or am I merely seeking an excuse to satisfy my own curiosity?

She stooped and gently pushed down the dog's hindquarters, making him sit. When he began to whine, she held his mouth closed for a moment until he stopped, then left him, praying he would wait in silence. Starwind still slept peacefully in the crook of her arm.

She circled softly until she could glimpse the clearing between the trees. Someone and something were within; but Frostflower waited until she was almost directly opposite Thorn and the other two warriors before she ventured nearer.

The thing in the center of the glade was a stone altar, recently erected. It was carved of mountain granite, its hewn surfaces unweathered, its edges sharp and even. It stood about waist high, and around its base were niches, every one with its statue of some god, every statue still unchipped. On the altar knelt a woman; beside it, facing her, stood a man. Both were in profile to the sorceress who watched from her hiding-place among the trees.

The man and woman were in the long white gowns of the farmers, and wore wreaths of metal wheat-heads in their hair, the man's wreath golden, the woman's silver. Then the man must be Maldron, the woman one of his wives or sisters. He was of medium height, stocky, with streaks of gray in his dark brown hair; she was tall and slender, with a long oval face and copper-colored hair braided high on her head. They had apparently come here arrayed in layers of ceremonial garments and weighted with jewelry, for on either end of the stone altar lay a pile of brightly-colored cloth and glinting metal; but now only a few necklaces and bracelets, and their gold and silver belts, remained on their bodies to offset the stainless white of their gowns.

They were chanting, gazing deeply into one another's eyes as they chanted. At certain intervals, they would extend their arms and each remove some piece of jewelry from the other's body, bend down (still gazing at one another) and add it to one of the piles already on the altar. Then each would pick up a golden cup and hand it to the other. They would drink, return the cups to the altar beside the piles of removed clothing and jewelry, and resume their chant.

So this was a ceremonial of the farmer-priests? Thus far, it seemed graceful and harmonious—indeed, harmless, but for the base of falsehood on which it rested and which it helped to further. And yet, how could it further the superstitious religion the farmers used to control the common folk? Here were none but two farmers, alone together. Even the warriors who had accompanied them to this glade were waiting outside, with their gaze averted. Since they were not wanted in the ceremony, and since no one would dare attack the person of a farmer-priest, the warriors must be stationed here to prevent anyone from witnessing the rites, as they were preventing Thorn. Then what purpose could such a ceremony have? Did the farmers themselves believe their own mythology?

Frostflower moved back a little, looking toward the warriors. If her surmise was correct, one of them should make a round of the trees enclosing the glade, to be sure no wanderer approached from another direction. But it seemed they must be confident that wanderers would come only from the direction of Straight Road. Yes: to the south were Maldron's own fortifications, to the east and north was a far deeper stretch of woodland.

When the sorceress slipped closer once more to the glade, Maldron and the priestess were removing the wreaths from each other's hair. Their gowns were already unbelted, the last of their jewelry removed. For the first time since Frostflower had been watching, they took their gaze from one another, lifting their faces and arms up toward the sky, then down toward the earth. They hooked their wreaths together, and Maldron touched them reverently to the woman's abdomen, then knelt and laid them before one of the statues. Priest and priestess drank, looking again into one another's eyes, and afterwards poured what remained of the dark purple beverage from their cups onto the ground on Maldron's side of the altar. Then, silent now, they reached forward and began untying the neck ribbons that fastened each other's white robes, slipping the unbound garments down around each other's shoulders.

Frostflower turned away and slipped back through the trees. So this was nothing more than farmers' love-making. Who would have thought they shrouded it with such ritual, even when alone together? Or that they would come so far from their own bed-chambers? Those few sorceri who chose to sacrifice their vow of virginity and their powers for the sake of marrying and bringing children safely into their retreats used love-making as a simple wonder, requiring no more ceremonies than did the resulting childbirth—at least, so far as Frostflower knew. But perhaps all other folk of the Tanglelands followed such preliminary rituals as she had just witnessed through her foolish curiosity? Dared she question Thorn? No—such knowledge would be useless and perhaps dangerous to her. Besides, despite her embarrassment, she smiled at the mental image of the sunbrowned, tumble-haired warrior kneeling docilely on an altar and permitting some tradesman to strip her of weapons and clothes.

Dowl was waiting where Frostflower had left him. He rose and came toward her. She cupped her hand round his mouth just in time to keep him from barking.

And now? Should she retreat at once, or wait here until she saw Thorn permitted to return? They must certainly release Thorn; and the sorceress had already strained her vow of prudence to the limit. Yet what reason could they have to hold the swordswoman this long? Frostflower crouched beside Dowl, her left hand stroking his head while her right arm cradled the sleeping baby. Before her, a few faint grunts and moans came from the glade. Behind her, the first thunder rolled faintly in the distance. Dowl pricked his ears, but her stroking kept him silent. The sorceress began to count her heartbeats.

At about the eight-hundredth heartbeat, the farmers began to chant again. This time it lasted only a few moments. Then, after a few more moments of silence, Maldron came out to the three warriors. He was again dressed in his white robe, belted with the gold chain. His wreath was on his head, a single gold necklace around his throat, and he carried one of the golden cups.

"The senses must be purified, of all who have witnessed these mysteries," he intoned, in a voice that seemed meant to call forward anyone who, like Frostflower, had wandered near the glade. The sorceress shivered and kept her hand clamped round Dowl's mouth.

The first spearwoman turned, stepped forward, and knelt before the farmer-priest. Having dipped his forefinger into the cup, Maldron touched her ears, each in turn. He dipped his finger again, bent, and touched her eyelids, afterwards handing her the cup. When she had drunk a little, he took it back, dipped his finger a third time, and sprinkled her. Finally, he motioned for the next warrior.

So this was all! Or would it be all for Thorn? Frostflower watched while the farmer touched and sprinkled his second war-

rior. Then Thorn advanced, knelt like the others, and underwent
exactly the same process.

The sorceress allowed herself a sigh of relief, then silently
upbraided herself for having followed the swordswoman at all.
Dowl might have betrayed her—he tried to obey, but was much
too friendly to understand that some people were enemies. Or Starwind might have awakened at any moment. Frostflower considered
slipping back again the way she had come . . . but best not try it
yet. Here, she was in a small depression, well screened by several
large trees. Better not to risk leaving her cover until Maldron and
his party had gone. The wind was strengthening, the thunder coming nearer; but the storm was less threat to her than discovery by
the farmer-priest. Why did they not leave?

Maldron stood between his two oak trees, slowly gazing around
the forest. Could he suspect? Frostflower shrank a little deeper
into her hiding place.

"You will shelter with us for the night. Will you not, swordswoman?" said the farmer. The tone of ceremony had not quite left
his voice.

"All gods keep you, Reverence. But I'm expected at Gammer's
Oak."

"I doubt you can reach the town before the storm."

"Then I'll get wet." Thorn shrugged. "I've been wet before."

A single clap of thunder sounded, close enough to be distinct
rather than muddled. A few steps to Frostflower's left, some small
animal suddenly broke cover and bounded away. Dowl strained
to get up, his muscles twitching for the chase, but she kept her
hand tight around his mouth and he subsided, thumping his tail
once in perplexity.

Maldron and his warriors looked toward the sound. Surely they
must know it for a forest creature?

"A rabbit," said Thorn. "With your Reverence's permission,
I might still give that storm a decent race."

"Not yet, swordswoman." Maldron transferred the cup into his
left hand, while with his right he removed the gold chain from
around his neck and dipped it into the liquid. His manner had
once again become completely ceremonial, completely solemn.
He lifted the chain, held it dripping for a moment, then tossed it
to the ground in front of him. Looking down at it, he raised his
arm and pointed towards the area where Frostflower crouched,

where the rabbit had broken cover. "Some other has witnessed our mysteries."

"I'll search the middle," said Thorn. "Clopmule, you take the left, Wasp—"

"You are not in my hire, swordswoman, nor raidleader of my warriors," said the farmer-priest. Then, lifting his voice, "Unknown witness, come forward now! You will have seen the rite of purification—it is nothing to fear."

Aye, nothing, for a common person. But for a sorceron, who might be hung for a night for so much as listening with one ear against an outer wall to hear a farmers' chant . . .

"Be it as you will," said Maldron after a pause. "Wasp, Clopmule."

The two strange warriors touched fists to lips and started forward, the swordswoman limping.

They would come slowly until something moved, then they would rush toward the movement. As soon as the spearwoman saw a figure in the black robe of the sorceri, she would hardly scruple to throw; and although there were many trees which might deflect the spear . . . If nothing moved, they would continue to search until Maldron were either proved right, or until he himself called them back with some excuse for his augury having been mistaken. Since Frostflower was too near the glade to hope they would not reach her, Maldron's guess would be proved correct.

Her best chance, then, was to come forward. She knew little about Maldron, after all—and some farmer-priests could be merciful. If he did not question her so that she must confess actually having seen part of the mysteries, she might escape comparatively easily. Ah, but to step forward with Starwind, to add the weight of that suspicion to the offense of having heard the chant . . .

She must choose quickly, while Wasp and Clopmule were still far away. Feeling as if she were tearing out her own heart, she laid Starwind softly on the layers of old leaves and whispered to Dowl, "Protect!" He would give no protection against any human who approached, but he would lie by the child to keep it warm and to frighten off any chance forest creature.

Frostflower tried to cry out that she was coming, but her throat was constricted. She stroked Dowl's head one last time, then stood and took several hasty steps forward.

"Damn!" said Thorn.

Frostflower looked up and saw Maldron's spearwoman taking aim.

"Lower your spear, Wasp," said the farmer.

"But a sorceron, Reverence—"

"If she was going to blast us, she'd have done it by now," said Thorn.

Maldron glanced at her. "Keep your thoughts to yourself, warrior. I am judge here. Sorceress, come forward."

Common folk usually showed their fear of sorceri. Farmer-priests did not. Frostflower came forward with arms crossed over her breast and head lowered, an attitude calculated to reassure farmers' folk, who seemed to think sorceri could not use their power when holding their arms thus. She glimpsed the spearwoman moving to one side, keeping her in range for a sudden throw; she heard the uneven stride of Maldron's swordswoman moving in at her back, no doubt preparing to strike quickly from behind at the first suspicious move. They credited sorceri at once with so much power, and so little! The storm would soon be near enough, and then Frostflower could direct a charge of lightning before they realized she had begun concentration. But, please God, it might not be necessary.

"What have you seen and heard, sorceress?" asked the farmer.

"Enough to know this was a private ceremony, Reverence." Frostflower kept her head bowed. A glimpse of her eyes would not incline Maldron to believe her.

"So you came no closer?"

He was shrewd; already she was pressed to find answers that would appear to lessen her guilt without being untruthful. "I was closer for a time, Reverence, but I retreated again."

"Close enough to see?"

"She couldn't have been," said Thorn. "We never saw her."

Maldron frowned at the swordswoman, then at his own two warriors. "Nor did you suspect her presence when she was as close to you as the sixth tree in an orchard is to the first. Sorceress, what did you see?"

The thunder grumbled, a little closer yet.

"What difference does it make what she saw?" asked Thorn. "I saw a few things myself, before your women turned me around. Purify her and let us go, Reverence."

"Do you try to command a priest, warrior?" said Maldron.

"More than wine is needed to purify a sorceron. There must be pain also, and blood mixed with the wine. . . ."

"Well, how long will it take?" Thorn demanded.

The farmer turned towards her. "You are traveling with this sorceress?"

"Hellbog, no! I never saw her before in my life, Reverence. I just want to leave before the storm hits us."

Frostflower felt a twinge of envy for Thorn's freedom to lie quickly and easily.

"Then leave, swordswoman. You are purified."

The sorceress risked a glance at Thorn—the angle was such that she hoped Maldron would not see the colors of her eyes. "Do not wait to be rained upon, warrior," she said respectfully, trying to send a silent appeal: Return to where I was hiding. Find Starwind—keep him warm and dry. Even if you hate your son—save him!

"Get out of here, Thorn!" said the swordswoman behind Frostflower. "His Reverence told you to leave!"

"He gave me permission to leave, Clopmule. It happens I'm curious to see this."

"Then silence your impudent tongue!" said Maldron.

Thorn reddened and touched her fist to her lips. The farmer turned back to Frostflower and lowered his voice again. "There must be pain in the guilty senses to purify them."

Frostflower trembled. "Will you deafen me, Reverence?"

"I would not be overly harsh. . . . We will do best to return to my hall while I think of this."

To be taken inside a farmer's dwelling—held prisoner there, more at his mercy than most common folk suspected—subject to some unknown purification which threatened her hearing and sight—perhaps even her power! To risk the horrors of a farmer's dungeon! Yet she might have gone meekly—she thought she might have been willing to go—if she could trust Thorn to remain behind and recover the infant.

But Thorn seemed determined to remain near her. The sorceress knelt before the farmer-priest. "I beg your Reverence, if it is possible, purify me at once, here beneath the trees. Even if you must be more harsh."

He might choose the surest and quickest way—signal Clopmule behind her to use the sword. Or he might stab her ears and eyes at once, without trying to devise a gentler rite. But the storm was almost near enough now, almost above them. If she could delay Maldron only a little longer, she might soon be able to catch a bolt.

The farmer sighed. "Well, then, a small slit in the skin just below each eye, just inside each ear, on the tip of the tongue; then a few drops of wine poured over slit and organ. There is the pain and the blood. Best add a time of lying in the rain afterwards, until the stain is washed away. We will leave you to guard the sorceress, Thorn."

"Will you pay me a silver or two for standing guard in the rain, Reverence?"

"You will do it in piety and in repayment for being permitted to remain and watch."

The wind had dropped. Soon the first, large drops of rain should fall.

"We must not wait longer," said Maldron. "Lift your head, sorceress."

She lifted it a little, and caught sight of the priest's dagger. Maldron had slipped it from his belt and held it ready. The silver blade was almost as long as a quill pen, very thin, etched with symbols of wheat and rye, and honed at the tip to a needle point. She closed her eyes and tilted her face further back. Pushing away her hood, the farmer placed one of his hands on top of her head as if to hold it steady.

"Remain perfectly still. A sudden movement may cost you an eye."

Moments ago, she had been waiting eagerly for the storm. Now that the farmer had fixed such a mild punishment for her, she wanted only for no chance bolt to startle him during his rite. Breathing slowly, she began to concentrate on keeping this area clear of thunderbolts and rain. She raised her eyelids very slightly and, through the haze of her long lashes, glimpsed Maldron's knife coming toward her left eye.

Somewhere at the western edge of the forest, beyond the reach of her power, lightning struck. A howling started behind her— mixed wails of infant and dog.

Maldron's hand slid from the top of her head to the back of her neck and clamped tight. She gasped, jolted into opening her eyes. His face was twisted with sudden anger.

From within the glade, the priestess called out, "A child!"

"Lie still, Inmara!" There was no anger in the farmer's words to his wife.

But immediately he held the thin knife to Frostflower's cheek. "Lying sorceress!" Louder: "Wasp! Find the infant!"

"I'll find it," said Thorn, bounding forward out of Frostflower's range of vision.

The sorceress heard thudding, cursing, grunting. Thorn must have run into Wasp to prevent her from reaching Starwind. Frostflower could not turn her head—she could only kneel frozen in Maldron's grip. The farmer-priest struggled visibly with his wrath. Dowl barked wildly, begging for some human to come and help.

The priestess appeared behind Maldron, panting a little, clutching her loosely-draped robe about her, staring eagerly ahead. She did not glance down at Frostflower—she did not seem to see even the struggling warriors somewhere beyond. Her large gray eyes gazed as if entranced toward the sound of the baby. "An infant! Maldron—an omen!"

"Inmara! Rest—dearest, you must rest the full time—"

"Husband, it is an omen! The goddess has answered our prayers—"

"It is a child stolen by this cursed sorceress!"

"What? Ah!" The priestess glanced down at Frostflower, seemed for the first time to notice the fighting. "Then we must save it at once."

Inmara began to run toward the wails. Frostflower had a glimpse of bare feet and fluttering white silk. Lightning struck, nearer yet. The thunder came in great cracks, and the sound of rain began on the leaves above.

"No!" shouted Maldron. "Clopmule, help Wasp! Are all of you impious fools?"

Clopmule must have been about to strike me from behind, Frostflower thought. She closed her eyes again, trying desperately to regain some quiet in the midst of fear and confusion. The farmers would cherish Starwind and care for Dowl . . . they treasured lost infants and liked dogs. That thought helped her to ignore her own danger—Maldron's dagger pricking at her cheekbone, the trickle running down her face, the shouting and blows of metal on metal.

One of the warriors screamed. Thorn shouted, "Now, Clopmule, damn you!"

Maldron pulled away his dagger and thrust Frostflower to the ground, holding her with one foot in the small of her back. "Throw down your sword, impious warrior!"

Struggling for breath, the sorceress twisted her neck. Thorn and Clopmule were circling, striking at each other with their swords. Maldron's spearwoman—Wasp—lay twitching on the ground.

Beyond them, Frostflower glimpsed Inmara's white form, standing perfectly still, holding the infant in his blanket, while Dowl barked and jumped around her.

"Throw down your sword, damned one!" cried Maldron. "It is a priest's command!"

Thorn paused. Clopmule started to jump closer, swinging her weapon. Thorn leaped back and struck it away, barely in time. "Call off your own cow and let us go!"

"The gods will rot your fingers on your hand, Thorn!" In his anger, Maldron pressed his foot deep, causing such a sudden increase of pain that Frostflower screamed.

Thorn cursed in rage and started towards the farmer. Clopmule, moving rapidly despite her limp, came between them. For a few heartbeats, the swordswomen crouched, glaring at each other, their blades swaying.

"You will stink in Hellbog!" cried Maldron.

"I'm damned already!" Thorn leaped forward. Frostflower closed her eyes. She heard the clash of their swords and looked again to see that Clopmule had beaten Thorn off.

"Throw down your sword, damned warrior." Suddenly Maldron sounded almost calm, although he had to raise his voice above the storm and the barking dog. "I can break this child-stealing creature's spine."

"She could wither you dead first!"

"A priest does not fear a sorceress." He ground his foot down deliberately, releasing the pressure only after he had forced another scream from Frostflower. God! Would he truly break her spine?

Thorn turned and began to run. Clopmule limped after her, but halted midway. Thorn had stopped and seized the priestess by one arm.

"Let her go, Reverence, or I'll—"

"You do not dare! You do not dare touch a priestess, warrior! Release my wife, or Azkor and Smardon will stuff your living bowels down your own throat in deepest Hell!"

Thorn seemed to shudder—she was too far for the sorceress

to read her expression. But she kept her grasp on Inmara. "That's whenever I sink to Hellbog! Meanwhile, I'll kill your lady, Maldron! I swear it!"

"Thorn! No!" Frostflower cried, and then screamed again as Maldron's foot clamped down.

"Let her go, farmer! By all the gods and demons! I'll do it!"

This was like the fury that sometimes made common folk forget their fear of sorceri—Frostflower had never guessed it might also turn against their own farmer-priests. But Thorn must not harm Inmara! Not a completely innocent woman!

The priestess stood quiet, unmoving. Another crash of lightning, very close. Thorn glanced up toward the sound. Clopmule sprang at her. Frostflower screamed and shut her eyes.

When she looked again, Clopmule was staggering back, bent over and clutching at herself. She fell and lay writhing. The infant was wailing again. Inmara still stood motionless.

"I mean it, priest!" shouted Thorn.

"Then feel the anger of all the gods!"

Maldron's foot was agonizing; but now he seemed to push down forgetful of the sorceress, lost in his own struggle and anguish. Frostflower thought, I must not scream—I must not remind him of myself, I must not arouse Thorn to strike. There is one chance—

"All you gods of the storm!" Maldron's voice rose in the sound of a farmer's chant. "By your solemn names I call you! Eajandur, lord of the thunder! Meactira, lady of lightning! Alrandru, ruler of the whirling storm-winds!"

Digging her nails into her palms, blinking back her tears, Frostflower twisted her neck to look upwards. She saw the farmer-priest raising his thin silver dagger over his head, holding it in both hands, blade pointing straight upward. Oh, God! He would attract the lightning down on himself! But his effort to cow the maddened swordswoman might help Frostflower.

Where could she direct the next bolt? God, strengthen my eyes—show me a point! They are standing so close, Thorn and Inmara—and Inmara holding Starwind! It must be close enough to terrify, but it must not hurt—oh, God, none of them must be hurt. . . . There! The tree a few steps behind Thorn, that large branch half an arm's length above her head—

"All you mighty gods, nourishing the worthy and destroying

the unworthy! All you brothers and sisters of Jehandru of the Seven Secret Names, great Giver of Justice!"

The sorceress tried to shut her eyes to Maldron's meaningless chant, breathed as deeply as she could with her back and stomach so pressed. She had been taught how to enter the trance quickly under conditions almost this unfavorable. Fixing her gaze on the chosen branch, she thought only of thunder and waited for the next bolt near enough to snatch with her mind.

The charge was gathering—she felt it, in the sky above the glade. Good—it would come from behind the farmer-priest.

She caught it! Rode it, an instant that seemed to her trained power several moments. The bolt tried to swerve down to Maldron's silver blade—she forced its energy back, made it curve up again to compensate for its early descent—drove it at last against the branch, down through the living trunk, off through the moist, root-filled earth safely away from warrior, infant, and priestess.

At the explosion, she felt Maldron's leg waver. She rolled. He fell heavily. She rolled further, away from his legs, pushed herself up, ran towards Thorn and Inmara.

Maldron screamed at her. A sorceress owed no obedience to a farmer, and the time for humble submission was past. Thorn was on her knees—they could not have been hit after all? But Inmara was still standing.

No, Thorn was not hurt, but she was babbling in terror. Clutching at Inmara's robe, she was pleading, "Lady! Forgive me! Oh Gods! Lady, pray to the gods "

The farmer-priestess stood dazed, looking from the warrior at her feet to the child wailing in her arms. Then she looked beyond them, toward her husband, and gasped.

Frostflower glanced back and saw that Maldron had been able only to half-rise. He held one hand to his shoulder, and a dark stain spread down over his white robe. His own ceremonial dagger—he must have fallen on it somehow.

"Lady," said Frostflower softly and urgently, "the child is mine. I feared to bring him forward, because of the suspicions, but he is mine. Truly."

The priestess glanced at her, so quickly that Frostflower forgot to drop her gaze. Then . . . Inmara pressed Starwind almost absently into Frostflower's arms, and began running toward Maldron.

The gambit had worked! Frostflower hugged the infant close to her breast and fought down a feeling of triumph.

But Thorn was still moaning on the ground in a state of terror and shock. And the rain was falling faster, starting to beat down steadily through the leaves.

Frostflower stooped and shook the warrior's shoulder. "Thorn! Thorn, it was only a warning."

The wind rose and the rain increased to a sudden torrent. The sorceress sheltered the child as best she could with her robe, turning her back against the wind. She would not hold the rain and wind away from herself, not now. Thorn must continue to believe, for a time at least, that her own gods had sent the warning bolt. Again she shook Thorn's shoulder. "Thorn—it did not strike you, it missed you. We must hurry, Thorn." Dowl left Frostflower and tried to lick Thorn's face.

The swordswoman rose, quiet now, but still dazed, and stared at the sorceress through the rain. Merciful God, thought Frostflower, have I broken her mind? If the farmers' superstition has this strong a grip on her, how did she defy it long enough to threaten Inmara? "Your sword," she urged aloud. "You must not forget your sword." She wished she could remember its name.

The warrior nodded, looked down, and retrieved her sword from the wet humus. Frostflower saw with relief that Thorn wiped the blade without urging, and that she felt of her own accord to be sure the dagger remained in its sheath at her belt.

Then, uttering a single loud shout, Thorn seized Frostflower's arm and began to run.

Sorceri learned to run well, and Frostflower kept pace with the swordswoman; but it was a dash of slipping in sodden leaves and bumping against trees, with rain striking like sleet against her skin, Starwind a squirming weight in her arm, and Dowl forever jumping out of their way at the last moment. Not until they paused to rest, when the rain had slackened somewhat and they had found shelter beneath a huge old oak with dense foliage, could she sort her thoughts.

She had felt a rush of triumph when she rolled from beneath Maldron's foot and felt him fall. That was bad, very bad—must it not be the emotion a warrior felt on cutting down her enemy? It was a heady feeling, this battle-triumph—dangerous for sorceri. And then when she had looked back and seen he was wounded and could not follow ... no, surely then it was relief she felt; and fear, also, for his sake, was mixed with it? Surely there had been fear for him, and even remorse. She was to blame for his injury—no, it was his own choice to hold his dagger as he had held it, and to stand with his foot on her back. And had she not guided the lightning, he would be dead; even though it had not been her first purpose in seizing the charge, she had saved him. Then, when she told Inmara that Starwind was hers, she had not lied. Had not Thorn given him to her?

But Thorn . . . ah, if only I had not followed her, not yielded to my filthy curiosity! Now Thorn will be hunted by the farmers. If they take her alive, they will scaffold her and hang her like the poor wretch we passed—was it only today? Because I could not wait for her.

The sorceress looked timidly at her companion, who stood shivering and poking up clumps of moss and humus with the point of her sword. "Thorn . . . forgive me?"

"What? Oh. All right, you're forgiven. My own damn temper. My own damn, fathermilking temper." The swordswoman shook her head and turned to study the moss on the tree trunk. "Better find the road so we know where we are. At least they won't get too damn close to us in this bloody rain. He's got to get back to his hall first, to—oh, Hellbog!" She started to put her sword away in its leather sheath, then stopped and kept it in her hand. "Well, come on!" Straightening her back, she strode forward.

Frostflower readjusted her robe and blankets around Starwind, pulled up her hood over her own head, and followed, with Dowl shuffling at her side. She should have felt sad and frightened, for, while earlier they had been merely objects of suspicion, now they would be hunted outlaws. Yet she was filled instead with a strange, victorious joy.

Chapter 3

"We should've gone south." Thorn stared down Slicer's blade to his point, which she was jerking back and forth in the floor boards. "Maldron knew he we were heading for Gammer's Oak."

"And so he will reason that we would not continue on here."

"What do you know about how a farmer's mind works, sorceress?"

Frostflower glanced up, with her damned everlasting smile, as if she knew everything in the whole bloody world and was just a little too sly to say so aloud. "I know something, at least, of how their punishments work." The fresh scab on the cheek below her brown eye looked almost like a mole in the candlelight.

"Oh, Hellstink! What bloody difference does it make?" The swordswoman got up from the bed and started to pace the baker's small upper room. "He'll be sending his warriors out in all directions, anyway." Unless he was dead. "Frost."

"Yes?"

"You think maybe he's dead?"

"No. It was not a large knife."

"Long enough to hit some vital places."

"Surely, if it had, he would have died at once? But he rose on his knees and cried out to us." The sorceress seemed to think she was comforting Thorn.

"Maybe he jabbed a vein and bled to death."

"Inmara was there to tend him."

Damn! Even if the farmer did die out there in the rain, the priestess also had gotten a good look at Thorn. Probably that Demon's turd Clopmule was going to live, too. Maybe she should have killed them all. She could hardly have it much worse in

40

Hellbog for finishing the job than she would already have it for threatening a priestess. What a Hell of a thing for a warrior to carry around the rest of her life into every raid, every gaming-house—it was one thing to expect you would *probably* end up in Hellbog sweltering forever just beneath the surface—it was something else to *know* you were going to end up as living sausage-meat for Smardon's torture toys.

The best Thorn could hope for was to postpone it forty or fifty years. And to do that, she had to get to the other side of the Tanglelands and hire out to some small farmer or townmaster who did not much care what happened in the north.

Sooner or later she would have to double back and slip past or circle around Maldron's farm; and it should have been sooner, before he had the chance to get back to his hall and alert his women. Damn! thought the warrior, why wasn't I thinking clearly? What possessed me to come on north to Gammer's Oak? All right, maybe we did need someplace warm and dry to get out of the storm—you can run better if you stay healthy. And who else would have risked taking us in like this? Those weavers in Frog-in-the-Millstone, maybe. Warriors' God! What kind of damnfool idiots not only made friends with sorceri, but took them in and hid them when they came knocking and saying they were probably being hunted?

The same kind of damnfool idiots who got themselves damned to the slimiest tortures of Hellbog for a bloody sorceress.

It was almost dark outside. The storm was only a drizzle now. Any moment Maldron's bitches might come hammering on every door in Gammer's Oak. And there the sorceress sat, letting the bloody grub play with her tits again!

"Hellbog!"

"Shhh, Thorn. You've frightened him." The grub was yowling, and the mangy dog was whining again, and even if the sorceress did not care a damn what happened to herself—gods! She ought to care what happened to a hard-working bitch of a swordswoman fool enough to befriend her!

Thorn sat down and began polishing Stabber to keep herself busy. "Why the Hell don't you shunt the brat off on one of your friends? The mongrel, too. How can we hide with that pair of bloody noise-horns sounding off all the time?"

"Burningloaf is unmarried and would be questioned if he were found with Starwind."

"Nothing like he'll be questioned when they find him with us above his blasted ovens."

"Dowl was also seen with us and might be recognized as ours."

"As *yours*, you mean. Don't give *me* part possession of the mangy demon's-mop!"

The dog whined and put its head in Thorn's lap, banging its tail against the floor. Thorn raised her dagger menacingly. The dog moved its head from her lap and lay down at her feet, still swinging its tail.

"We are as safe here as anywhere within a night's walk, Thorn. Safer than we would be outside."

"No, we're not. We'll be trapped up here like rotten maggots when they come looking. We'd be a Hell of a lot safer outside in the woods—but, oh, no, we can't let the damn grub get damp and uncomfortable, can we? Or miss a chance to let him try to suck blood out of a dry tit?"

Frostflower quietly transferred the brat to the other side. "Thorn, you have not yet forgiven yourself for threatening the farmer-priestess?"

"Forgiven . . . myself? Forgiven *myself*? What the bloody Hell good would that do? Ask—ask . . ." She dared not say even the title of the God of the Seven Secret Names, great Giver of Justice. She gestured upward with her dagger. "Ask the One Who sent the lightning to forgive me. See how bloody far you get."

"Thorn . . . if you think—Aljandru, was it?—sent the lightning, can you not think he sent it to stop you before you had gone too far?"

"What do you know about it, sorceress? 'Aljandru'—hah! There's no such god." (At least, she did not *think* there was.) "You can't even keep their names straight."

"You rarely use their names, only 'Wheat Goddess,' and 'Lightning God,' and so on. I think I never heard that they had other names until today."

"Unh." Their names were for the priests to use. "And you're going to tell me what they can and can't do."

"I am sorry. I was guessing by what we believe of our God."

"Your God! Your stinking pile of—no, forget it. Look, let's just forget the whole bloody mess for a while."

"But you would not really have harmed Inmara."

"I said, let's forget it." *Would* she have killed the priestess? Not in her saner moments . . . but the battle-rage had been on her, or she would never have made the threat—and she had never made an idle threat in her bloody life. Warriors' God! "Damn you, sorceress, I don't know! I think—I would have killed her!"

Frostflower pulled the brat gently away from her tit and began spooning goat's milk into its mouth even before retying her bodice. "But the lightning stopped you. You are not guilty of her blood, Thorn."

"I might as well be."

"You cannot believe that your gods sent it to save you from sinning?"

"He sent it to save her Ladyship. Can't you get it into your stupid head? I was already damned. Hell, sorceress, I—look, let's just forget it." Thorn slipped Stubber back into his sheath and began polishing Slicer.

"You truly believe in such unforgiving gods?"

Damn it to Hellbog! Did she have to put up with Frostflower's blaspheming pity, too? Damned little bitch of a sorceress, sitting there acting compassionate and superior, as if she was going to end up lying in silk and fondling kittens forever. Damned . . . yes, Frostflower was damned too—all sorceri were damned, and why the Hell should Frostflower sit there acting safe and smug? "Maybe you think you're going to have things soft and comfortable," Thorn said cruelly, "but you're going to end up only a couple of levels above me, sorceress, with the demons playing stretchrope with your guts."

The sorceress finished feeding her brat, set it down long enough to lace her bodice, then picked it up again and held it over her shoulder, patting its back. She seemed subdued, more thoughtful even than usual.

Thorn clamped her sword flat between her thighs and dug her nails into her arm. What good did it do her to tell Frostflower where she was going to end up? Because you have to live with it hanging over your death, do you want to make her suffer the same way, warrior?

Frostflower wrapped up the grub and laid it in an old kneading trough the baker had given them for a cradle. She knelt over it a few moments, humming softly. Then she got up and came over to sit on the bed beside the swordswoman.

"Look," began the warrior, "I'm sorry I said that. Go on and believe whatever you like, Frost. It's none of my bloody business what you believe."

"Thorn . . . your Lightning God did not send that bolt."

Gods, it was like telling a snail to fly! Thorn rammed Slicer's point into the floor. "You want us in Hellbog tonight? Damn it, sorceress, believe whatever you want to, but don't blaspheme the gods while I'm around to get blasted with you!"

Frostflower waited a moment, then laid one hand on the warrior's arm. "We have a second power."

Thorn gazed into the lump of polished sheen-amber on Slicer's pommel. "Just don't use it on me."

"I . . . already have, Thorn."

The swordswoman lifted her head and stared at the sorceress. "What the bloody Hell—when?"

"Forgive me, Thorn, I . . . it was necessary, to save us all."

"What in the names of all the gods and demons are you talking about?"

Frostflower's fingers tapped softly and nervously on the warrior's frayed sleeve. "We can manipulate the weather, Thorn."

The dog was asleep and twitching in its dreams. The candle was flickering in its wall niche in front of the statue of the Yeast Goddess, and the last of the rain was dripping off the roof outside. The floor was warm under their feet—it was just above the baker's oven.

"What?" said Thorn.

"Oh, we cannot bring storms or fair weather. But when a storm comes near enough . . . we can catch the lightning, and aim it."

Yes . . . yes, there were stories, but—Hell, she had gotten the idea that all Frostflower ever did was go around speeding up people's time when they asked her, growing plants, and never hurting a gnat! Silky-mouthed little bitch, acting almost too soft to chew up her vegetables! "*You* almost knocked my head off!"

"I could not let you harm the priestess, Thorn."

"You—you— Damn you!" Thorn yanked her arm from the other's touch and began to stamp around the room. "Damn your stinking guts to Azkor's teeth!"

"Thorn—it is necessary! Inmara was not trying to hurt us—"

"Eat stones! Well, what are you going to do? Blast me again? Go ahead—finish the job. Can't miss at this distance, can you?"

"Thorn! I can't. . . . You know I could not. . . ." The sorceress actually got off the bed and knelt in front of the warrior, trying to catch her hands.

Thorn jerked back and raised Slicer. Frostflower cringed away.

"You cannot see why I told you, Thorn? Your gods—they are only idle stories! You have no Hellbog to fear—"

"Nothing to fear but you blasted sorceri and your stinking powers, eh? Come on, sorceress, blast me down! Shrivel me up! But by all the gods, I'll take you with me." Thorn was getting her rage under control now, feeling it harden into cold, disgusted purpose. She drew her dagger in her left hand, balancing the sword in her right. "Make your move, sorceress. Come on, make your blasted move, and I put Slicer through your guts and Stabber up your chin! The gods love a sorceri-killer."

Frostflower rose and backed away, watching her fearfully. The dog was awake again, probably woke up a long time ago, and just sat there looking from sorceress to warrior and whining. For a few moments Thorn could almost have sworn Frostflower was whining, too.

But when Frostflower spoke again, it was in the same old honey-edged voice, low and patient like a humble little priestess. "Our God loves no kind of killing, Thorn. I could not have harmed you. But I could not see you harm an innocent woman. I would have lost my powers."

"You would have . . . you would have . . . You stinking bitch, I get myself damned to Hellbog to save your life and you blast my head off to save your bloody power?"

"But you are not doomed to Hellbog—"

"What about the farmer? You're so damned handy with your lightning, why the Hell didn't you blast the bloody farmer?"

"We must not harm anyone, Thorn. Not even to save our-selves."

"You rotten liar!"

"No! We do not lie. We lose our power if we lie."

Thorn grinned and walked towards the sorceress. Frostflower shrank back against the wall, but did not run. The warrior put the point of her knife against Frostflower's belly. "Now—if I start pushing in, you won't blast me?"

Frostflower attempted a smile. "I could not strike you with lightning when there is none above us for me to snatch."

"And you won't turn my heart upside-down or grow a nest of wasps inside my guts?"

"Those are idle tales, Thorn. No sorceron can do such things. No sorceron would wish to."

"And you won't wither me into a weak old crone?"

"No."

"Bloody liar! I met a spearwoman in West-of-the-Marsh—gods, she was a lustier cow than I am! The townmaster caught a sorcerer someone saw robbing a chicken coop."

Frostflower gasped. So the story bothered her? Good. Thorn would not shorten it. "They tied him down on one of the townmaster's beds, tore off his clothes, and sent that spearwoman in to tickle him up and milk him."

Frostflower closed her eyes and turned away her face. Relentlessly, Thorn continued. "There wasn't a gray hair on her head when she went into that room, sorceress. When she came out, she might as well have been eighty years old. Now—look at me and tell me a sorceron never hurt anybody!"

The sorceress did not open her eyes. "If we are trapped, as . . . as he was, if we are to lose power and life whatever we do, and there is no hope . . . then we strike back once, as strongly as we can."

"Very pretty. Very, very pretty. Gentle and humble and kind-to-everyone, and then you just forget all about it at the end. You damn sneaking bastards!" Thorn raised her knife from Frostflower's navel and put the blade against her throat. "Well, you can start aging me any time now, and we'll see who works fastest."

"No."

"What?"

"I do not believe you will harm me, Thorn. No more than you would have harmed Inmara. But in any case, I will not harm you."

"Why the Hellbog not? I've got a bloody knife at your throat, don't I?"

This time Frostflower completed the smile—her usual sad, step-on-me-again smirk. "We are here alone. Burningloaf can hardly spread the tale; he must not be known to have sheltered us. The only reason a sorceron has for striking back with the last charge of power is to spread the tales."

"To spread the tales."

"You do not understand? The more we are feared, the fewer folk are willing to attack us."

"Then in the names of all the gods, why tell me all this? You bloody fool, you know you've just explained there's no damn reason in the world I shouldn't kill you right here?"

"Is there not, Thorn?" Again the hangdog smile. "Even so, I cannot lie to you."

"You cannot lie." The warrior took her knife from Frost-flower's throat and slapped him back in his sheath. She stepped back, waved Slicer once or twice at the sorceress, and then returned him, also, to his sheath. The sorceress was not worth killing. "You can't lie, but you can wither us senile—if you want to. You can't hurt anybody—but you can scare your friends senseless when they try to help you! You damn bitch, you want us to think you wouldn't step on a roach, and then you try to make us think you'll blast us all to Hellbog! You throw lightning at a poor idiot who's damning herself for you and pretend you didn't have anything to do with it—you can't do anything *but* lie! You couldn't live the truth if you wanted to."

She turned, kicked the dog out of her way, and strode to the trapdoor. She yanked it open, glanced down to satisfy herself that the baker was alone in his oven room below, thrust the dog out of her way again, and dropped the rope ladder.

"Thorn?" said the sorceress timidly. "Thorn—you will not leave us? How can I bring Starwind to safety without you?"

Worth killing? Hellstink, she was not even worth spitting at. "Stay here and rot," said the warrior, and climbed down.

Burningloaf was braiding loaves for the oven. He was a shrivelled old runt who must once have had a sense of humor, to choose the name he had. "Any sound of warriors in the street?" Thorn asked him.

"If there were, do you think I would have let you go on shouting?"

"Heard us through the floor, hey? Thought you told us it was solid."

"I heard *you*, warrior. Nobody else—not Frostflower, not the baby, not the dog, just you."

"Save your sour looks, baker. I'm leaving—taking my chances in the open before I get trapped like a damn roach."

"If they catch you, warrior, I never saw you in my life."

"Don't worry, bogbait. I never heard of you, either. I don't go around betraying people who've helped me." Thorn picked up a couple of rye buns from a pan not long out of the oven and bit into one. "You'd better watch out for the sorceress, though. She'll tell the first bugger who asks. Sorceri never tell anything but the bloody truth, you know."

The baker was looking from the empty places in his pan to the limp purse at Thorn's waist. All right, you damn pricker, she thought, I wasn't going to cheat you. She took out her last half-copper and put it down on the edge of the table, then took another look at Burningloaf. Shifty. Probably not much better than a sorcerer himself. "Thought I'd try cutting through the marshlands to Sludgepocket or maybe West-of-Nowhere," she said.

"You'll never make it through the marshlands," he said, as if he was proud of the pricking bogs.

"How'd you like to go with me?" She grinned, crossed to the back door, and slipped out.

It was a good night for escaping—just enough moon coming through the clouds to keep a warrior from breaking her neck, more than enough darkness to find a nice thick shadow at the first suspicious noise, just enough fine drizzle to keep the mud oozy and fill in her tracks. She headed southeast; only a fool would try to hide out in unfamiliar marshlands. She was not sure how far she could trust Burningloaf. Or that Hell-bitch of a sorceress. Let the baker tell Frostflower, and she would probably blab it all over the Tanglelands. Good—let her tell everyone that Thorn was hiding in the marsh. Let Maldron lose five or ten warriors in the bogs and quicksands before deciding she had sunk. Meanwhile, she would be making a nice, wide circle back around the southern edge of the Rockroots, slipping down to the east of Maldron's Farm, and on south to Nedgebottom.

That was a good, open town where the townmaster gave farmers no more respect than he had to, and people made it a habit not to recognize anybody. In Nedgebottom she could find some way to earn a few more coppers, and until she got there she could live off the forest and riverland. Maybe not so well as when she had traveled with a sorceress and had fresh grapes and squash and so on, grown in a few moments whenever they felt hungry. . . .

Warriors' God! She had traveled with Frostflower a day and a half all together, not counting the day they spent resting in the weavers' graincellar getting Thorn back to normal after the grub. Gut me and hang me up if I ever make friends with a blasted sorceron again! she thought. Well, she was sick of vegetables anyway. She wanted meat, and if she judged she could not risk a fire, she was ready to eat her kill raw.

Chapter 4

Frostflower knelt on the floor with her face in her hands, the tears wet on her cheeks and palms, and a hard pressure in her head, neck, and chest.

A harsh, foul-mouthed warrior, cruel, loud, and evil-tempered. Then why can I hardly breathe except in sobs? And why can I not straighten my back? I had not thought she could be so cruel. I knew her temper, knew her tongue, but to hear her say . . . and cold—a woman who did not want her own child, who would not even stay to see her own child safe . . . and cruel! I had not thought she could be so cruel.

But Starwind was crying. Numb and guilty, Frostflower crawled to the improvised cradle and lifted him from it. She could not trust her voice to sing or hum; she could only hold the infant close and sway back and forth on her knees in silence. Still, he quieted almost at once, gurgled, and went back to sleep.

The ends of the rope ladder creaked again on the floor planks. Frostflower looked up eagerly. But it was not Thorn. It was Burningloaf climbing up to her.

"What happened up here, Frostflower?"

"She is gone?"

"Gone and good riddance. What was the trouble?"

What had been the trouble? Anger? Pride? Outraged superstition? Frostflower returned the infant to his cradle. What had been the trouble? She turned her palms outward in a gesture of helpless confusion.

"Unh. Well, I'll bring you up some fresh bread. And wine. You'll want a few cups of wine."

"Thank you. You are kind. And perhaps you will bring me . . . no. No, nothing."

"Well? What else?" He spoke kindly, but shortly. Had there always been that slight, that very slight hint of suspicion in his tired voice and withered old face?

"A little pot of earth, old friend. Only a little pot of earth."

"I feed you well enough, Frostflower. Whatever spices you want, I can put them in your vegetable stews."

Yes, he would feed her and shelter her, for the sake of her grandmother, his childhood friend. But he wanted no sorcering under his roof. Nevertheless, she must know..... "Only one small cup of earth? I will leave no traces."

"You need rest, Frostflower. Lie down and take a nap while I get your supper."

She reached up and pressed his powdery hand. He helped her to her feet. For a moment she thought she would cling to him, finding comfort in his thin old arms and stooped shoulders, hardly taller or broader than her own. "Friend," she said, looking into his eyes. "Old friend..."

He looked away and began easing her toward the bed. "Lie down and sleep, Frostflower. I'll bring you some heated wine."

He, too, was avoiding her eyes. Even Burningloaf distrusted her mismatched eyes. Thorn had not been afraid of them. At first she had, but not later.

The sorceress lay down, still holding to the baker's hands. "There are warriors?"

"If there are, they haven't gotten to Gammer's Oak yet."

"She will escape? Do you think she will escape without meeting them?"

"That swordswoman can damn well look out for herself."

He twisted his hands from her clutch, then stroked her forehead with his dry, dusty palm. "Don't worry, Frostflower. They won't find you here."

He left her. Shuddering, she closed her eyes and tried to relax. Was the bed still a little warm beneath her shoulders, where Thorn had sat polishing her weapons? A swordswoman who took such care of her sword and knife, who would not sell the gems from their handles even when her tunic was fraying and her trousers laced with old hempstring, and when she needed money for a physician... or an aborter....

Dowl came and rested his head on the mattress near Frostflower's leg. She began to stroke him, slowly and gently. Thorn had kicked Dowl, too. Yes, but never hard enough to injure him.

Burningloaf, her old friend, her grandmother's friend, avoided looking at her eyes, would not call her 'sorceress,' did not wish her to practice the most harmless skill beneath his roof. Thorn would call her 'sorceress'—after a day, it had no longer seemed an insult from the warrior's mouth, but a title of common respect, like "merchant' or 'friend.' Thorn used to look into her eyes. Thorn had not feared her, had even threatened her. . . .

And might—oh, God!—might have killed her. Might have killed Inmara. . . . Yes, if I had truly been sure she would not hurt the farmer-priestess, why would I have directed the lightning so near her? Why not near Maldron? God, ah, God, is it true? I have lied . . . it is so hard, here in the middle Tanglelands, outside our retreats, to balance the vow of Truth and that of Prudence, and I have failed, I have lied! Not in speech, but in silence.

But if I had continued silent, if I had not tried to comfort her— too soon—she would still be brooding over the tortures she expects, the tortures the farmers have taught her to expect. But she would still be here with me.

That is why I wanted to keep her with me, then—for the pride of calling a swordswoman my friend. To be another Mockingbird, another sorceron who traveled with a warrior as friend and not as suspicious, reluctant, fearful hireling.

Dowl put his front paws up on the bed and whined, staring at Frostflower with his round, whiteless eyes. Dowl did not turn away from her gaze. The dog's consciousness had no room for doubts and motives, only for hope and acceptance. She stroked his ears. Eagerly, he clambered onto the bed, pawing her shoulders, licking her hands and cheeks, trying to play.

She got her arms around his neck, laid her face in his shaggy hair, and wept unthinkingly.

"Here," said Burningloaf. She had not heard him return. She glanced up to see him standing at the room's one, small table. Quickly she looked away again, to spare him her eyes.

"I must leave," she said.

"They won't look here, Frostflower."

"No—you are kind, but I cannot stay and endanger you."

"I tell you, so long as you keep your dog and that baby quiet, they won't even think to search my house. Gods, the whole town knows I'm no lover of your people."

"I will stay . . . only a little longer. Only to let Starwind sleep a little longer."

"Safer to have you stay, than maybe get seen leaving here. Look, I'm not going to slop around outside in the drizzle for your cup of mud, but I brought you a bowl of floor-dirt I swept up. I don't know what you're going to do with it, and I don't want to know, but I hope you have the mess cleared up by the time your stew's cooked."

"Thank you. You are very kind."

After he had descended, she pulled up the rope ladder and closed the trapdoor. Then she went to the table and examined the floor-dust, flour, dried mud, gnurr and a few dead insects in the bottom of the small, brown-glazed bowl. She smiled. How little he understood of sorcering.

She could not use the floor-dirt, but she could use water instead of earth. She emptied the bowl neatly on the corner of the table, wiped it clean with part of her skirt, and filled it with water from the pitcherful Burningloaf had given them when they came here earlier this evening. Thorn had carried the pitcher up in one hand as she climbed the wood ladder which could be raised from below.

Putting down the pitcher, Frostflower brought out her pouch of seeds. Was it such a harmless thing as a seed-pouch that had given rise to stories of—what was it Thorn had called it—a box of blighting herbs? She shook out a number of seeds onto the table, selected a dried bean and dropped it into the bowl of water, then returned the other seeds to their brown linen bag.

She was moving slowly, hesitant to make the trial. What would be left to her if she had indeed broken one of her vows? What in all the world?

The infant. The child Thorn did not want. Frostflower returned to Starwind, rocked the kneading-trough cradle on the pillows that supported it, gazed down at the sleeping child. She let her thoughts wander. Yes, she would take Starwind back to Windslope Retreat, raise him in one of the cottages . . . perhaps the little cottage beneath the three pines, where Hopelost had lived her last years. If she could no longer train him in sorcering, there would still be much she could teach him: all the small daily things every child must learn, all the additional cautions a sorceron must know, and the love of the One God, so simple. Thorn! Will you in twenty-five years meet a strong young sorcerer and guess him to be your son? When the thought of such a meeting caused Frostflower to smile, she knew she was calm enough to stop delaying the test.

She rose and went back to the table. The bean waited, dunnish

white, beneath water which quivered slightly from the vibrations
of her feet on the floorboards. Taking a deep breath, she put one
forefinger down through the water. Good; she touched the bean
at once, despite the water's refraction of light and the new ripples
made by her hand. It was not an omen—only farmers' folk believed in omens—but it argued well for her steadiness and concentration.

She brought her hand back to the water's surface, resting her
palm on the edge of the bowl, her fingertips just covered by the
liquid. She fixed her gaze on the candle flame and breathed with
conscious rhythm. Vegetable things were harder than animal; they
had no heartbeat of their own on which to concentrate. But they
had a dormant life. The sorceress projected her consciousness into
the plant that lay curled in embryo beneath the dun-white seed
skin and layers of nourishment. She waited until the feel of cool
moisture seemed to spread over her whole body, then forced her
own heartbeat into the seed.

She breathed faster now, as quickly as she could breathe and
still expand her lungs to their fullest. There was a giddiness in
her head . . . she should not need to force her mind, it should flow
more easily than this. She should not tremble—she was splashing
the water a little—but she thought she had hold of the plant's own
time . . . she hoped that the swelling she felt was the shell loos-
ening, soaking in water, distending the plant fibers. It was harder
than it should be, for she had begun in nervousness; but she would
not stop. . . .

Tendrils touched her palm! She felt them . . . she was sure it
was not mere movement of the water. No, these could only be
the new green shoots, tender, yet strong in their growth and per-
sistence. But she would not glance down, not yet. She spread her
fingers wider; the tendrils found their way between, into the air.
She felt them wave and straighten again, felt small moist folds
of membrane uncurl on the tops of her fingers.

Then, at last, she looked down to see the new plant, grown
from a dry seed in a few moments, already half-covering her hand.

"Dowl!" Laughing in relief, she slipped her left hand beneath
the bowl, lifted it, knelt and set it on the floor, her right hand
remaining the whole time partly in the water, between new roots
and new leaves. "Dowl!"

The dog trotted over and sniffed eagerly at the new plant. Still
laughing, stroking Dowl's neck, she lifted the plant from the bowl.

He ate it quickly, nuzzling her hand, sucking up the roots from beneath her loosely-held fingers, licking her palm when sprouts and roots were devoured, finally lapping the water left in the bowl.

She had not broken a vow; she had not lost her powers.

But she had lost her warrior, and with nine days' journey remaining to Windslope. That thought sobered her as she sat once more beside the sleeping infant.

How much safer had she really been with Thorn? Had the swordswoman not gone into battle rage, Maldron might have been content to purify the sorceress and let her go on her way. No, that was not just. Starwind's crying had brought the worst of the trouble. Yes, but if Thorn had not been impatient and gone deeper into Beldrise Forest instead of waiting nearby while the baby was fed... ah, but if I had not been equally impatient and followed, or if I had not been blamably curious and slipped close to see the forbidden rites of the farmer-priests...

Frostflower was weary of soul-searching and useless regrets. Thorn's presence at her side had warded off three possible attacks by farmers' folk, who would always suspect a lone sorceron carrying a child. But that had been earlier. Now they would be hunted. If pursued, Thorn would have to fight; and even to witness bloodshed could threaten a sorceron's power. They might in any case be slightly safer apart, now that they had been marked as together.

Burningloaf tapped on the floor six times with a long stick. Frostflower opened the trapdoor and let down the rope ladder. It was slightly more difficult for him to climb than the wooden ladder he kept below; but the wooden one was heavier for him to haul into place. He ascended, carrying the end of the cord by which, after reaching the top, he would pull up the basket of food.

"You see," she said, "I have left no trace of my sorcering."

He peered around the small room. "Good. Don't tell me what you did. Or why you suddenly had to do it."

"I will not. But I am truly grateful, old friend." For his thought, at least—for his overcoming his repugnance.

"Well, at least you look happier now." Having left the food on the table, he turned back to the trapdoor. "I suppose you people have to get it out of your minds sometimes, like the rest of us have to have a nightmare now and then."

"We rarely suffer nightmares," said Frostflower. "I will leave your house tonight, after I have eaten."

He stopped and glanced back. "I thought I told you you'll be better off staying."

She felt a little of her old, irrational mischief. "Suppose this sorcering fit you have described should come upon me again under your roof?"

"Then I'll sweep the floor again for you."

"I must leave eventually. Better for me to leave now, than wait for the search to come to Gammer's Oak and beyond."

"You can go when the search dies down."

"I would rather try to outrun it."

Burningloaf looked down at the trapdoor, then up again towards her. "Stop worrying about the search. Four years ago I hid my niece and her worthless husband—the one they caught a year later in Three Bridges and gutted for stealing a pig. The warriors never even asked to look up here."

"The search may be more thorough for a sorceress with a child. We endanger you, old friend."

"I'll take the chance." He was avoiding her eyes again. "Safer for all of us if you stay here."

She rose and crossed the floor to him. "Old friend, what is the true reason you do not wish me to leave your house?"

"You're safer here."

"But you are not." She touched her right hand to his chest, over his heart.

The old man's glance flickered up to her face, then back down to her clean, black-sleeved hand resting on his stained yellow apron. "I didn't want to say this, Frostflower. But if you were caught and . . . questioned, you'd tell them about hiding with me."

She withdrew her hand, nodded, and turned away.

"Eat your food while it's hot." Burningloaf descended the rope ladder. Again she pulled it up and closed the door after him. She began to unpack the basket. Below, she heard faint, thumping sounds, but paid little attention. They were not warriors. Warriors would have come with shouting.

She had begun her meal when the baker signaled again. More surprised than alarmed, she rose to open the door and lower the rope ladder. This time he did not use it. Instead, he propped his long wooden ladder against the opening, climbed up, untied the ends of the rope ladder, and let it fall to the floor below.

"Do you fear so much," she said, "that I will tell them you helped me?"

He did not look in her direction. "They can make anyone answer their questions, Frostflower. And you people don't lie."

He climbed down hastily. Sighing, she closed the trapdoor and returned to the table. Scarcely had she eaten three bites, when she heard a new sound, a hammering immediately below the trapdoor. As she watched, a small point appeared through the wood.

Burningloaf was driving nails into the bottom of the trapdoor. Why? He must be pounding in hooks: the heavy, angled hooks smiths made to support half a cow or the equivalent weight hanging from the ceiling. A baker could hang baskets of dried fruit, smoked meats, strings of garlic and onions—anything that a baker might use or an ordinary householder want close at hand. It would make excellent camouflage for a trapdoor. It might also make the trapdoor much too heavy for a small sorceress to lift from above.

She had not expected such treatment from the friend of her grandmother and mother. She wondered at herself for accepting his actions with so much calm. Perhaps Thorn's angry leavetaking had hardened her somehow . . . or made so large a hole in her emotions that only a little edge remained for Burningloaf to crumble. She ate slowly and leisurely, listening to his work, trying to guess by the sounds what kind of heavy supplies he was hanging from his new hooks.

Probably he did not mean to betray her to Maldron. She hoped he did not, for both their sakes. A farmer-priest might grant such a betrayer full pardon, or punish him as severely as if he had not delivered up the one betrayed.

Probably, also, Burningloaf did not mean to starve her. He had left her a large crock of vegetable stew, a large jug of wine, a full loaf of bread, and almost half a small cheese, besides a full skin of goat's milk for Starwind and a large dish of table scraps for Dowl. More than enough for supper and breakfast, but not so much as to suggest he did not intend to bring up more tomorrow. Had he meant to starve her, surely he would have brought either less food this evening, or more.

Almost certainly, then, his only motive was fear for himself. He planned to keep her safely, but he would not allow her to leave until he himself judged it safe. For a time she wondered, why not? Why not trust him? Whom could she find between here and the mountains more worthy her confidence? They could remain here quietly, Starwind and Dowl and herself; and no doubt they would be at least as safe here as anywhere else between Nedgebottom

and Windslope. She could abandon all fears and worries, all efforts and anxieties, to Burningloaf—yes, that would repay him
sufficiently for mistrusting her—while she waited tranquilly, pow-
erlessly, for the search to die down, or for the warriors to search
this upper room. She would have several days, perhaps a hen's-
hatching or longer, to rest, with no responsibility save keeping
Starwind and Dowl quiet. She would have ample time to let the
infant's sucking arouse milk in her breasts, ample time to heal the
wound Thorn had given her.

She had known the warrior scarcely three days. Thorn should
not have been able to hurt her so.

Perhaps it was fear of Thorn's memory festering rather than
healing if she sat idle above Burningloaf's oven; or perhaps it was
annoyance that the baker, who had known her family since his
own childhood, should mistrust her—but Frostflower soon realized she could not remain here. Had he contented himself with
argument, she might have yielded at last; but to shut her in—
musing on this, Frostflower found she was close to indignation.
After years of practice, she was able to discard that emotion.
(Why, then, was it so difficult to discard the earlier pain?)

She finished her meal, eating enough to fill but not bloat her.
Starwind woke and began to fuss. She changed his breechcloth,
leaving the soiled rag in the chamberpot, and then allowed him
fully as long as he wished at her breasts, while she found comfort
in the pain his sucking caused her dry nipples. At last she fed him
leisurely, burped him, and hummed him back to sleep with the
Dreamwine lullaby.

By now Burningloaf's noises below had long ceased. Frostflower drank a few swallows of goat's milk and considered how
best to escape.

The room was about six paces at its longest. It had no regular
window; but there was a small ventilation grate, high under the
eaves so that rain seldom blew in. The grate was carved directly
out of the long hardwood planks that formed the wall. The fancy
fretwork covered an area large enough for Frostflower to crawl
through. The only other way out was the trapdoor.

Unless she waited for another thunderstorm, which might come
before morning or not for several days, she would have to manipulate the time of inanimate materials—the hardest skill of all
time manipulation. Nevertheless, she had done it before. Had she
not developed the two standard powers almost as fully as possible

in a sorceron only twenty-seven years of age, she would not have been permitted to journey in the outer Tanglelands.

Whatever way she chose, she would need a rope or ladder. She could always tear and knot her blankets. She would need to find the best way, also, for bringing Starwind and Dowl safely to the ground. She wished to destroy as little as possible. A lightning bolt guided through the wall would leave Burningloaf with the need to make extensive repairs; it might, besides, cause a fire; and it would of course terrify the infant and the dog. As for the grate, it had been beautifully carved, in a pattern of stylized pumpkin vines, and she thought it would be a pity not to allow it to rot very slowly in its own time. That left her the trapdoor.

She smiled, realizing that she had probably intended all along to strike back at Burningloaf with the weapons he himself had nailed up against her. She might not even need to tear his blankets.

Five iron tips she counted slanting up through the trapdoor; others, perhaps, had not poked up quite so far. Burningloaf was taking no chances. The sorceress almost giggled to think of the forest of supplies hanging below, more likely to arouse suspicion than turn it away.

Some water still remained in the bowl which had held the sprouting bean. Frostflower poured it over the trapdoor, wetting all visible nail points. Then she settled herself comfortably on the floor, leaned forward, and touched the tip of a nail with either hand.

There was, of course, no life at all to grasp in the metal. She must first project part of her own consciousness into the nails, feeling as iron might feel if it were capable of feeling. Identification with metal might take whole seasons from her own life, unless she rested afterwards in the trance of cool breathing; but only through identification could she put into the unliving material any substance with which to meld the sense of passing time.

She closed her eyes, groping for a vague pseudo-memory of melting and hardening, of warm coals and cool water, of hammers, tongs, and files. Forged, polished, sharpened, driven up into wood, with the splinters clutching, mildly ticklish, around the metallic body. Then the wood splinters softening and swelling with a slow ooze of moisture . . . Yes, now she had the identification she needed. Into the iron's simulated consciousness, she projected her own heartbeat.

For a time her heart slowed between her lungs, held by the

sluggishness of metal; but her will was stronger. First she brought the heartbeat back to its normal speed, both in her own chest and in its echo in the nails. Then faster, faster, like a drummer beating quickdance. She could not bring it to the speed of a steady whir, as she could do with living things—old Moonscar could race his projected heartbeat to a high-pitched whine even in soft metal and sandstone, but as yet Frostflower must be content with a rhythm no faster than a treehopper's legs on a summer evening.

Fortunately, this was fast enough. Even in its own time, wet iron began to rust within half a day; and, with unliving metal, even a person's normal heartpace would greatly speed its own natural processes. Within moments, Frostflower felt both nails weaken, crumble, snap—almost simultaneously—with the weight below. She heard the crash—one of the hooks, at least, must have supported heavy metal utensils. She glanced with satisfaction at the spots of rust on her two fingertips, then reached for another pair of nails before her concentration could break entirely.

She had not yet begun to project her heartbeat into the next set, when Burningloaf's voice reached her from below. "Frost-flower! What—What have you—"

"Stand away from beneath your weights, old friend!"

"You fool! You—you sorceress!"

"I regret sorcering in your house, old friend. But you yourself suggested that the fit comes upon us sometimes."

"You'll wake the town! You'll—"

"It was you who hung the weights for me to play with. Stand away."

"No! Wait—Frostflower—friend—I'll take them down! Give me time to take them down."

She lifted her hands, folded them in her lap, and waited, chuckling as she listened to his hasty thumps below. Poor Burningloaf! So much work to undo again. When at last he tapped six times on the trapdoor, she stood and lifted it for the last time, amused that he had gone back to the former signal instead of simply calling to her.

He put the wooden ladder to the opening and climbed up, angry, shaken, and trembling, in his nightdress. She felt some remorse, but not overmuch, to see the terror beneath his wrath.

"Here!" he began. "What did you mean, causing this noise?"

"I meant to make the trapdoor light enough for me to lift."

"I worked longer than it takes to bake two ovenfuls, hanging those things to hide the trapdoor for you!"

"Did you? So long? Forgive my ingratitude." She realized she was beginning to badger him with words. As Thorn had badgered her? Or as Thorn had accused her and all her kind of doing? She must speak plainly. "When you imprison sorceri, even for their own protection, you make them very anxious, old friend. I mean to leave your house."

"You're mad, Frostflower! You'll be caught—raped, power-stripped—give us all away—"

"If I remain, my presence here will condemn you more surely than anything I might say of you if I should be taken outside."

"You won't go, sorceress! I'll find some way of keeping the door shut."

A second time he had called her sorceress, after so long avoiding that word in seeming consideration for their friendship. "Would you lose an outer wall the next time?" she said.

He glanced at her, glanced quickly away to other things—his wall, his window grate, the baby in his kneading-trough, the dog whining interestedly on the floor. "Stay the rest of tonight and tomorrow. You can start as soon as it gets dark tomorrow night."

"I will do better to start at once. By tomorrow, Maldron's search may have reached as far as the Rockroots and beyond."

"I suppose you'll try to go through the marshes, like that idiot swordswoman?"

"Thorn has gone into the marshlands?" Inwardly, the sorceress moaned. Did Thorn know them well enough to escape their treachery? "No. Why should I risk my Starwind in the marshes? My way lies north. I shall try to slip through the northern reaches of Beldrise."

"Maldron's own forest?"

"Would he not be as incredulous as you to think it of me?" Frostflower smiled. "Now, old friend, you will bring me the rope and basket to lower my dog?"

Sullenly, the baker climbed down. When he reached the oven-room floor, he hesitated, then put his hands on the ladder and glanced furtively upward.

The sorceress had been watching his moves. "You may leave me ladderless again, but this time I will not replace the trapdoor." She half-pointed her finger at him—a harmless and meaningless gesture, charged only with the exaggerations and superstitions of farmers' folk. Burningloaf jumped away from the ladder and hurried to find the large basket and bring it up to her.

Thorn had pulled Dowl up in this basket unaided. Frostflower needed Burningloaf's help to lower the heavy dog, who sat patiently cramped and wagging his tail for most of the way down, until, when within a few rungs'-lengths of the ovenroom floor, he jumped out, to station himself beside the ladder. Frostflower would not entrust Starwind to the basket. She carried him down secure in her arm. Once, while descending, she glanced up to see Burningloaf, who was still in the upper room, glaring down at her. For a moment she felt as he must have felt to see her gazing down and pointing her finger at him. God! He would not push the ladder with her and the child on it? She had not so thoroughly destroyed the trust and friendship of years, in this one evening? Holding Starwind closer, she returned the baker's stare until he turned his head.

Then she hurried down the last rungs, chucked softly to Dowl, and slipped out the back door before Burningloaf could descend.

The night had largely cleared. Clouds still blotted many of the constellations, but the moon showed Frostflower that the time was after midnight. She circled north and east around Gammer's Oak, thankful that it was too small and poor a village to be walled. The mud was soft and oozing, ready to melt her tracks and Dowl's as it must earlier have melted Thorn's.

On the western side of Straight Road, the sorceress hesitated. Beldrise loomed dark across the embankment; would her safest plan really be to slip north through Maldron's own woods? Yet this part of the forest was far removed from the farmer's walls, and the very shadows and wood noises that seemed to menace her would help hide her movement.

She hurried across the road and among the trees. A low branch brushed her face and she shrank back, holding down a gasp. Then she smiled. Would any farmers' folk believe that a sorceron could be as timid of dark woods as other people? Did they not believe sorceri to be creatures of darkness, at home in such places on nights like this? Frostflower kissed the infant, who was beginning to cry, and hummed him back into tranquillity. She stroked Dowl's head for a few moments, then began to pick her way slowly and carefully between the trees, keeping near enough the forest's edge so that she could make out the line where woods thinned on the border of the road.

When day broke, she moved further into the woods, so as not to be glimpsed from the road. She was by now very tired. She had not slept for a day and a night, had not truly rested since just before her castigation by Thorn, had eaten nothing since leaving the baker's house except a piece of her dinner loaf, which she had carried away in her deep pocket. She stumbled often; and sometimes, when for a moment her mind let go the thought of her danger, she began to doze on her feet.

Nevertheless, she continued. They would not expect to find her in Beldrise; hence, they would not search here. But the general search would move in all directions, and might be waiting to seize her somewhere on the other side. She had set out with the determination to outstrip Maldron's warriors. Long before she reached the Rockroots, she knew she could not succeed in this aim. Her muscles would not carry her far enough and fast enough. Nor would Dowl's strength outlast hers; the dog was keeping pace with her only through loyalty and because her own steps were unsteady, her own speed flagging. If she attempted pushing herself too far, she might fall on top of the infant.

She decided to aim no further than the Rockroots. Somewhere in those outcroppings of stone and crag, jagged and riddled like a miser's teeth, she could surely find a small cave or other shelter. She would hide in the nearest boulders to Beldrise, thus keeping the protection of being in the unexpected place. And she would rest there several days, growing small vegetables for herself just before sunset and just after sunrise, hoping that her breasts would fill by the time she had run out of goat's milk for Starwind.

About mid-morning she came to the first of the Rockroots. She had to search several of the piles before she found a formation with a crevice that might be suitable. It was not a good hiding place. While searching for it, in her weariness she accidentally broke some of the bushes that grew before the opening, and had to cut down a few more wild shrubs and drag them over to help screen her refuge. And it was scarcely large enough for all three of them. Once inside, she had no room to hold Starwind to her breast nor feed him with the spoon. Fortunately, there was a small natural ledge on which she could place him and thus avoid the danger of pressing or overlaying him; without this ledge, she would have rejected the crevice even as a temporary shelter, for she had no space below the ledge to roll from side to side. She must lie on her stomach, head resting on her folded arms. Her feet pressed into the narrow angle where two boulders met, while her elbows brushed the leaves at the opening; and Dowl had to sprawl on her back and learn painfully that he could not lift his head too high. No, they could not hide here several days. They must leave as soon as possible and find a better hiding place, deeper among the Rockroots. But first, she must sleep.

She thought of entering the trance of cool breathing, and regaining the time she had lost from the end of her life by identifying with iron in order to rust it. But Starwind depended on her. Even now, through simple weariness, her sleep would be too sound for safety . . . moreover, to enter the trance, the mind should be more clear.

She woke to hear Starwind crying. Somehow it seemed like a wail that had been going on a long time. The weight was gone from her back, the loose bushes knocked down from in front of the opening. Clearly Dowl had taken his dog's rest and jumped outside to hunt small animals for his food.

"Hush, hush," whispered the sorceress, reaching up one hand to soothe the infant. The movement of her thin, lithe fingers, fluttering and forming into designs of light and dark above his face, seemed to hold his attention for a few moments. While he was quiet, she listened carefully, and heard no suspicious sound, nothing but woodland noises from the edge of Beldrise, and the soft whining of her dog somewhere on top of the rocks. She peered cautiously out. The setting sun cast long shadows eastward through a golden atmosphere, tranquil and lonely.

In spite of Dowl's escape knocking away the screening bushes, in spite of the baby's crying, the hiding place had not been discovered. The sorceress edged her way out of the crevice. Peering around once more, and still seeing nothing to fear, she turned, bent, and gathered Starwind from his ledge. He began to cry again, and for a few moments she heard nothing but his wails, her own hushing murmurs and, as a background, Dowl's baying.

Starwind in one arm and the goatskin of milk in the other, she backed a few steps away from the rock. Dowl was barking eagerly, as if to welcome her out of hiding. Strange, that he had not bounded down to her by now. Taking another step backward, she looked up.

Sitting on top of the boulders with Dowl was the farmer-priest. Frostflower spun round. A warrior had appeared at the edge of the woods—a tall, broad-shouldered spearwoman facing the sorceress almost directly across the rocky meadow. Frostflower was not sure how far a warrior could hurl a spear, but guessed she was within range.

Other warriors were slipping out from between the trees on either side of the first—spearwomen and swordswomen. Not only from the trees—they were also coming from behind the nearest boulders. Turning again, Frostflower saw a huge, scar-faced axe-woman standing beside the very rocks which formed her crevice.

There was little moisture in the air, little play of hot and cold currents, not a cloud nor a stirring of wind strong enough to manipulate with any effect. Caught without weather resources, she was surrounded by a circle that cautiously drew tighter—obedient, no doubt, to signals from the farmer-priest who sat above, holding and stroking Dowl. Eight warriors . . . no, nine. They were shy of her—yes, though they despised sorceri and obeyed their farmer, they still feared tales of sorcerous evil. Frost-flower dropped the goatskin and lifted her hand, pointing at one of the spearwomen. The warrior faltered, fell back a step, and raised her spear.

"Stop!" ordered Maldron. The warrior lowered her weapon, but stood reluctant to take another step. Her companions glanced around at each other.

"She cannot throw her spells at you with a child in her arms," the priest went on. "Nor are you to risk injuring the babe."

As long as she held Starwind, and the warriors obeyed their farmer, so long was she safe. But that could not be long. And at any moment fear might overcome obedience and one of the spear-women, or even the axewoman nearly at her shoulder, might strike her down—such things had happened, and the farmer usually punished the disobedience mildly, with one or two lashes of a light ceremonial whip.

Frostflower's only chance for escape was to set Starwind down and run for the opening between two warriors now, while the circle was still wide enough. Probably their spears would strike her down, but that would be better than what might follow if she waited. Yet she would have to lay the infant down quickly—too quickly—and abandon him without seeing whether he escaped accident. So she stood and waited, holding him closer to her with both arms.

The warriors were coming no nearer, at least for a while. They stood warily, hate and anger in their faces, blotted out now and then by a recurrence of fear.

"You have yet to be purified, sorceress," said Maldron.

Could this have been his purpose in tracking her down? "You have brought nine warriors after me so that you could purify me for witnessing a part of your ritual, Reverence?"

"It was a solemn and secret rite, even though you blaspheme it in your mind, sorceress."

"I could trust you more readily if you had brought two or three warriors, instead of ringing me in with nine."

"You slipped away once already from two warriors."

Frostflower did not remind him it was Thorn, and not herself, who had defeated Wasp and Clopmule. "You have not changed the purification rites from those you fixed before?"

"Have you spoken to any person of what you saw and heard?"

"I have not." Not even with Thorn had she discussed the farmers' ritual.

"Then your purification remains what it would have been."

The sorceress looked from face to face. It was still light enough for the warriors to see the colors of her eyes, and they glanced quickly away, but stood in their places. "Send away your warriors, Reverence," said Frostflower, "and I will submit with all good will."

"You will submit while my warriors look on, sorceress. You have no choice."

One of the spearwomen muttered something. Frostflower caught the words: ". . . blasts us all."

"Silence!" Maldron, too, had heard the warrior. "The sorceress knows she has nothing to fear in the rite, unless any mischance should cause my knife to slip. Obey my commands, and she will blast none of you."

Frostflower shivered. She could hardly believe Maldron had come merely to finish his silly and superstitious rite of purification . . . yet she saw no men except himself among his party, no brawny young smiths or stablehands such as came with their copper bars and sprunging-sticks to second the warriors on a sorceress hunt. And never had she heard that a farmer-priest used his own body to take a sorceress' power. So, her back against the rock, she hugged Starwind and waited unmoving for Maldron to descend.

The farmer disappeared from the top of the boulders and

climbed down somewhere in back. When he reappeared, on the side where his axewoman stood, Frostflower saw that he held Dowl by a light leash. The farmer walked carefully, keeping his left shoulder stiff; and she remembered the blood flowing from it yesterday. A woman in gray smock and kerchief, carrying a large basket, followed him—an old, comfortable-seeming creature who must have been waiting behind the rocks.

The dog bounded forward and jumped up on Frostflower, planting his front paws on her thigh while his tail swayed violently. Maldron came close behind, untwisting the leash, which was tangled between Dowl's legs. When the farmer had the cord straight once more, he hooked the end to his silver belt, then stretched out his arms as if to take Starwind.

Frostflower held the infant tighter. "He is mine, Reverence."

Maldron nodded. "So Inmara told us you claimed. But you cannot hold him during these rites."

The sorceress glanced beyond the priest to the old woman, who was taking things from her basket and arranging them on the rocks. Flask, goblet, and a kind of silver beaker stood ready. The woman found a niche for a small stone jar, set down her basket, and turned. She had a kind face.

"We may trust Cradlelap to hold him," said Maldron. "She has nursed my sons and daughters, and myself before them."

The old nurse smiled. Frostflower kissed Starwind on the forehead and permitted the farmer to take him from her arms. At once she bent and fondled Dowl's head and neck passionately. She felt as if she were gambling with Starwind's life and as if she were risking her own vow of prudence . . . yet what else could she do?

Starwind began to cry when the farmer took him; but, once in Cradlelap's arms, the infant quieted again. Now Maldron took Dowl by the collar and pulled him away from Frostflower. Patting him affectionately, he led him to one of the swordswomen, who touched her fist to her lips in a salute and then accepted the leash, afterwards squatting and stroking the dog's head.

Frostflower knelt, closed her eyes, and tilted up her face. Again Maldron pushed back her hood; again she felt his fingers on the back of her head. For several heartbeats, while she inhaled slowly, nothing further happened. Then she felt his other hand touching her left cheek, finding it wet. Another pause, and a soft cloth wiped her cheeks dry.

She waited, motionless, moderating her very breath. Surely

Maldron should not require this much time? Too great delicacy, too much deliberate slowness, often brought about the very accidents a person was taking such pain to avoid. . . . He was chanting something in the occult language of the farmers' rituals. She dared not look, dared not let her eyelids waver even a little. Her only hope lay in Maldron's sincerity and her own humble submission to his foolish rites. Submission was not acquiescence. She was no more guilty of his superstition than were any of his other tools, the silver of his knife, or the wine in his goblet. His ceremonies would flow around her and leave her dry and undirtied while she knelt passively, unreceptively. . . .

Was someone else moving close behind her? The thrums of stealthy footfalls, the stirrings of breath and body-warmed air at her back . . . two more, she thought. Warrior-acolytes, perhaps, hovering near to witness or assist in some arcane pretense. She must believe, incredible as it seemed, that Maldron would let her go with Starwind and Dowl after he had finished this ritual—she must believe it, or panic. But why did he chant so long?

At last the point of his knife came to rest just above her right cheekbone—God, so close to her eye! Almost in the same instant, hands seized her arms and pulled them behind her.

The knife was resting just above her cheek, on the surface of the skin, or slightly below the surface—she could not protest, could not pull against the hands that were now clamping metal gauntlets about her wrists. Ah, God! Their own movements might cause the knife to slip upwards, though she knelt unresisting.

It was done. The clamps were fastened, the warriors removed their hands from her, Maldron completed his tiny slit and lifted his knife away. The sorceress felt a warm trickle start down her right cheek. "You need not have bound me," she said.

"I trusted to your meekness once before. Do not interrupt the rites a second time."

He began to chant again. Frostflower felt a stinging in the new wound—tears rolling down to mix with blood. She had lost the gamble. Maldron had deceived her.

No doubt the gauntlets were made of copper. It was the metal farmers' folk had learned to use against sorceri: unrusting, and strong enough to hold securely. All she could have done in the available time was thicken its layer of patina, and that would shorten her life without helping her escape.

Maldron's knife touched her other cheek, just above where it had left the scab yesterday. And again it rested there, while she fought down a desire to thrust her own eye onto the blade in anger and suspense. This time his warriors inserted a long, flattened rod between her upper arms and her back, fastening it in place with chains between shoulder and elbow. Elaborate precautions they were taking to secure her. It would not help the priest if he meant to take her virginity—another human was the easiest of all creatures to capture in its own time; and with the angry closeness of the touch, and the burst of power that might come to all persons in emergency, a skilled sorceron could add half a century to the attacker's age between first touch and final loss of power. Their copper chains and bars could not save their priest.

Breathing deeply, she tried to gather her reserves in readiness. She could begin to age him even now, while he touched her head. But not so quickly as in the ugly passion. And there was yet a hope that he did not mean . . . that he had some other reason for this binding—reassurance to his warriors, perhaps.

He made his second slit—tears stung at once in the wound— and took away his knife. She opened her eyes. He was stirring the blade in a goblet held by one of his women; and beyond him two more were handling a long copper rod, forked at its visible end.

Forked at its other end also—she knew it—she had never seen one before, but she had heard of them, the things farmers' folk called sprunging-sticks. Her last hope gone, she panicked.

"No!" She tried to get up.

The farmer pushed on the top of her head and she fell forward. She struggled to bring her legs back under her, to lift her body straight again . . . if only she could rise, break through the circle— better to die with a spear through her stomach, better to die alone in the forest with arms copper-chained behind her—but the metal lay so heavy on her back. . . .

Maldron's hand was on her head again, thumb and fingers gripping almost from temple to temple. The thin flesh over the skull, the skull bone itself, throbbed with the force of his grip. Slowly he turned her head to the left. "Do not interrupt the chant a third time."

His warriors were pushing down on the ends of the rod, crushing her breasts and lungs to the ground. They still feared her— she felt the quiverings of fear in the pressure they exerted—but she had harmed none of them yet, and they took courage from their priest.

The point of his knife rested inside her left ear, touching, she thought, the bit of flesh and cartilage that guarded the passage to inner ear. A tiny pricking just inside the passage—the least movement, and her hearing would be punctured, her ear deafened.

God! Maldron—treacherous farmer-priest, lover of pain and torture—I will wither you to the edge of senility, I will leave you just time enough to watch yourself dithering on the edge of your farmer's grave, your farmer's hellbog—

So these were the thoughts, this the rage, that enabled her kind to blast their enemy in the last moment of power.

Dowl was whining, scratching the ground with his paws. The sound came clearly to her right ear, pressed to the earth. Hearing in her left was clogged as if by water. Only moments ago, Maldron had stroked Dowl like a person with fellow-feeling for animals.

If she withered him now? That would destroy her own powers, as surely as the thing he planned to do to her. Aye, it might frighten off his warriors . . . and leave her to die weighted down, perhaps unable even to rise. Could she trust the old nurse not to drop Starwind and run?

They were drawing her legs apart, catching her ankles in the forks of the sprunging-stick.

Why have I not aged him already? With my legs free, I might have had some hope. . . .

He removed the knife, swished it, no doubt, through his goblet of wine, turned her head to the other side, inserted the blade into her right ear, made his little stab. Slowness was no longer needed. Both her ankles were chained tightly in the forks of the sprunging-stick, held more than a stride apart by the length of copper.

So easy it was to capture a sorceron. Yet they feared her still; after Maldron lifted his hands and stepped away, the warriors turned her over on her back and retreated at once, as if afraid she might spell-blast them even now. And if there were a storm cloud, or so much as a strong wind, even now she would not be so completely helpless . . . aye, perhaps they had cause to fear.

Maldron knelt astraddle her, taking her jaw in his left hand, pulling open her mouth. Her tongue—even that needed his "purification."

"Reverence," she said, "I will harm no one—I swear it. Do not—"

"Even if I trusted you," he muttered, "my women would not. Put forth your tongue."

They were weighting the rods down, seemingly with pierced stones or metal. She could feel weights sliding onto the ends of the bar that pinioned her arms, weights being notched over the middle of the stick between her ankles. She had not realized farmers' folk dreaded sorceri as much as this. Closing her eyes, she put the tip of her tongue between her lips.

The knife pricked it, and involuntarily she drew it back, tasting the blood in her mouth. Maldron remained above her. After a moment he pulled apart the lids of her right eye. She saw the gold cup tilting above her, tried to blink as a dash of wine stung her eye, to be followed—thank God!—a heartbeat later by a sluice of pure water. The farmer did the same to her left eye, then washed her ears in turn with wine and water; but she hardly noticed it now. His warriors were ripping the garments from her lower body . . . black outer robe, undertunic . . . now only her light linen trousers remained.

Maldron lifted her head and poured the last of the wine, and afterwards water, perhaps half a cupful, into her mouth. She swallowed thirstily, her throat working as if unconnected with her mind; but her stomach contracted as if to churn the stuff back up. Probably that would have amused the priest and his creatures.

"You have done purifying me?" She spoke clumsily, her tongue stiff and pain-clogged. "Leave me, then. I will not spellcast you, any of you."

"From whom did you steal the infant?" said Maldron.

Starwind—as she had feared. They were doing all this to her for Starwind's sake.

"I did not steal him. He is mine—given to me freely."

"Who are his parents?"

"A warrior who did not want him. I think even she was not sure of the father."

"Who is this warrior?"

What she had said so far could harm no one. To say more . . .

"Thorn, was it?"

He must already want the swordswoman for her defiance of him, her threats against his wife. "What would you do to her?"

"What need I do to her? She has gone into the marshlands. The marshlands do not let two strangers a generation escape unguided."

The sorceress had tried to forget—Burningloaf, also, had told her Thorn was going into the marshlands. Perhaps she had hoped Thorn would change her plan . . . that tall, broad-shouldered woman, with her green eyes, browned skin, and free speech . . . sucked down into the marsh bogs. . . . "He is Thorn's child!" said Frostflower with a sob.

Maldron shook his head. "Clopmule has told us of fighting with Thorn in Eldrommer's unsuccessful raid against Arun, barely three hen's-hatchings ago. She wore a tight belt then. She could not have given birth to this child since. The truth, sorceress."

To explain . . . it could not hurt Thorn now, but would it not endanger Starwind? Farmers prized children and lauded fertility— if Maldron could find no parents, he himself would care for the infant. But would not a farmer consider a sorcer-grown child to be a thing tainted and cursed somehow? A creature—ah, God!— to be destroyed?

He kneaded her abdomen with one hand. "Who are the child's parents, sorceress?"

"A warrior who does not want him—a father who does not know of his birth. We do not lie, farmer!"

He put his knife to the waist of her trousers, slit cord and seam, and ripped the cloth apart.

"Torture me as you will, Reverence. I will not use my power— but do not take it!"

He brushed his hand once over her bare abdomen. Come then, farmer-priest, she thought—touch me again—touch me firmly— come and let me blast you to the edge of your grave!

But he rose and stepped away from her. "Bring the merchant."

One of his swordswomen saluted with fist to lips, and stepped behind the rocks.

Frostflower had thought, at least, that Maldron was showing himself one priest who took his own risk in this. Why had she not withered him while he was touching her? Now she must age some common merchant . . . aye, some merchant, no doubt, who had sold his services for a high price. Yes, she could wither such a man. If only she could wither Maldron as well!

The swordswoman returned, pulling a very young man by one arm. He walked stumblingly. Lifting her head a little, Frostflower saw that his ankles were hobbled. His hands remained behind him despite the warrior's tugging. His face was almost white, the eyes dilated, the thin light-brown beard a pitiable attempt to hide his youth. She had seen him before, somewhere.

The swordswoman drew her dagger and apparently cut the cord binding the young merchant's hands. "Drop your trousers, cloth-peddler."

Instead, he began dazedly to rub his wrists, staring down at Frostflower not as if he recognized her, but as if she were some deadly viper. As she would be to him. He was so young . . . the forty or fifty added years which would have brought Maldron to his grave would leave this merchant still with time to doze in the sun and dandle small children on his knee. . . .

"Your trousers, Spendwell." The warrior slashed his braided-silk belt with her knife, pulling his garment down to his knees. Immediately Frostflower stared up again at the merchant's face.

"Reverence," he was stammering, "please—not me!"

The sorceress drew a deep breath. "You are wise, young com-moner. Touch me, and I add fifty years to your body's age."

"And I will give you another fifty goldens for every year," said the farmer. "You will serve the gods and their priest—a work of piety for which you will be well rewarded both here and in the Glorious Harvest."

"And you will go to your 'Glorious Harvest' fifty years the sooner!" cried Frostflower.

"Reverence—I—I can't! I—I'm impotent!"

"Impotent?" said Maldron. "Did we not find you lying among your own merchandise with a dairywoman who seemed well sat-isfied?"

"Reverence—I—I—a sorceress—"

"Look at her, man! Her body is but a woman's. And such a woman's!" Maldron stooped and ripped apart Frostflower's upper garments, laying her bare from neck to ankle. It was done so quickly that she only realized her lost chance when his fingers were no longer on her breasts, when he had stepped back again.

"You see, man? Has she added a year to my age? Or can your clabbery dairy wench compare with her? Work quickly, and she will not age you so much as thirty years. Your name is Spendwell? Thirty years spent well, puncturing such a maidenhead as that."

Frostflower released a sob and let her head fall back. She heard one of the warriors say, "We'll stiffen him up, Reverence." When next she opened her eyes, she saw two of the swordswomen crouching down rubbing and massaging the young merchant. Quickly she looked again at his face. Yes, she must wither it— for the safety of the rest of her kind, she must show one more example of how much power remained in a sorceron even weighted down, naked, and unable to move. But she must not think of it too much, or she would pity the youth—he, too, was being forced. . . . She concentrated on trying to remember where she had seen him. A pale young man rolling down the stairs, shouting up in anger at a boisterous swordswoman, then bolting from her in fear . . . Spendwell had been Thorn's lover in Three Bridges! For a moment the recognition brought a kind of irrational relief; in the next instant came an irrational horror almost of incest added to shame, defilement, and loss.

But he must still be withered. She closed her eyes, trying to ignore his expression of fear, and of lust aroused despite his terror. Thirty or fifty years . . . old age was not an injury. No, not when it came in its own time—but when the body's age came in a moment, without the mind's experience that should have grown gradually with it throughout the seasons . . . it might kill him, might drive him mad.

And she, was *she* not close to madness?

"Keep it up, you horny peddler!" shouted one of the warriors. A warm, heavy body fell on top of the sorceress. She opened her eyes, glimpsed his face close to hers—a face twisted beyond recognition, almost as disgusting as the hardness between—she closed her eyes at once, turning her face. But she had glimpsed something else in that instant—the terror beneath the lust. "Sorceress!" he whispered, fumbling at her breasts and pleading with her in the same moment, "forgive—do not spellcast me—I did not want . . ."

She knew then that she could not hurt him. He was hurting her—hastily, clumsily—the pain was such that for a few moments she almost forgot it was also robbing her of her powers forever. She choked back a scream, tried to concentrate on the sweaty hairs of his chest—they must have torn off *his* tunic, also the pressure of his fingers on her arms—anything but her lower body. . . .

It was over with a haste as painful as the earlier prodding. He was off her, away from her, leaving her alone and naked, with no sense of relief, only of pain and shame and blood . . . had she bitten through her tongue? No, Maldron had cut it. She lay sobbing and exhausted, her mouth filling with the taste of blood, her nose

with the slime she could not clear from it. Dowl was whining.
The sound was almost as painful as her . . . she listened to the
voices of the warriors.

"Not one demon-damned gray hair!"

"Good pricking, peddler. You free tonight?"

"Must've liked it, the stinking bitch."

"Say, sorceress, how is he? Pretty damn good, is he?" This
last came with a kick to her hip. They were no longer afraid of
her.

"Silence!" said the priest. "Away from her with your foul
tongue, Snaste. Spendwell, you wish to take a warrior now for
your refreshment? No? Into your clothes, then. You will return
with us to my hall for your wagon and your pay."

The merchant mumbled something. Frostflower thought it was
a question about payment, although she had no reason to
listen . . . except that any point of concentration was preferable,
now, to her own body. "Fifty more goldens for every year?" said
Maldron. "She did not add a hen's-hatching to your age, merchant!
Accept your two hundred goldens and safe-passage token, and
show some gratitude. . . . Very well, you shall look into the mirror
in my hall, and search for gray hairs and wrinkles yourself, but
remember that the gods abhor a dishonest merchant. Go and
dress."

The voices were quieter now, and the dog's unhappiness
seemed louder. Starwind began to cry. Someone else was near
Frostflower, touching her cheeks, gently wiping her body, drying
the warm liquid from between her legs, holding a cloth to her
nose. She opened her eyes and saw the old nurse bending above
her.

"Have you all forgotten your duties?" said Maldron. "Unweight
her. Gammerstang, hold the dog or I will choose another to do
it. No . . . no . . . hush, small one, hush . . ."

Maldron had taken Starwind, as if he trusted no one else to
hold him; and the baby had stopped crying again and was resting
quietly in his arms. Young creatures forgot their griefs so readily . . . old creatures not so readily. Dowl was still straining to
come to the sorceress, although she was no longer screaming or
sobbing, not even trembling so violently as before.

They removed the weights and unchained her ankles from the
sprunging-stick. Cradlelap helped her to sit up so that the warriors
could free her arms and pull off the remnants of her clothes.

Perhaps she should feel grateful that they had stopped jeering her, but she felt only a numb wonder that she was still alive.

The old nurse finished wiping her and dropped a long, straight garment over her, with slits for head and arms. She rubbed salve into the wounds on her cheeks and ears, and gave her a large, clean kerchief for her eyes and nose. Numbly, Frostflower noticed that the cloth was soft, the salve sweet-smelling.

Maldron helped the old woman to her feet and returned Starwind to her care. "I rejoice that one of my people, at least, is not a fool." Then he pulled the sorceress up and knotted a cord around her wrists, not tightly enough to cause pain.

She stared at him in confusion. "Starwind's parents are a warrior who did not want him and a father who does not know of him," she repeated.

"I hope you will choose to tell the truth before tomorrow." His voice, at least, did not baffle her. It was hard, uncompromising.

She had come alone through Beldrise Forest in the night and darkness; she was led back in the night, but no longer in darkness. Warriors carrying torches came first and last in the procession. Maldron led the sorceress on a longish rope and her dog on a short one, close to his side. She could not have Dowl nearer; but, since she no longer moaned, he trotted contentedly beside the priest. Cradlelap followed, humming to Starwind. From time to time the little part of Frostflower's body that still cared about comfort noticed gratefully that they had left her her own sandals, with thick soles of many layers of cloth stiffened with tree-gum. Indeed, these had been left on her feet all the time she was otherwise stripped naked; and the part of her mind that had once responded to humor recognized the incongruity.

Had she been less miserable, she realized, she would have felt terror at passing through the high, dark stone walls of Maldron's Farm.

Once inside the walls, with the gate bolted behind them, the party stopped to rest while Maldron sent a young watch-girl ahead. Frostflower was allowed to sit on a wooden bench, not quite near enough to the old nurse to touch Starwind. Someone held a cup of wine to her lips; and when a wagon came, she was lifted into it, to ride with Cradlelap and Maldron—although he still prevented her from touching her child or her dog.

Perhaps it had been merely exhaustion that numbed her. During the ride, through several moonlit fields and a small orchard, many of the old terrors returned. She was captured and powerless, already trapped inside the walls of a farm, and soon to be locked in the dungeons of a farmer.

.There were tales of the dungeons beneath farmers' halls, tales of what was done to power-stripped sorceri before their public scaffoldings and hangings . . . but she found that hitherto, whenever she had contemplated rape as a thing that might happen to herself, her imaginings had stopped just short of the actual loss and had never gone on to what would follow—as if she had expected to die at once.

Maldron intended torture—why had he not done it there at the Rockroots? The thought of rats and cesspools, stale sunless dungeons and strange, blood-encrusted instruments glimpsed by the light of burning coals, still could make her cringe. She was quivering again, although still able to walk unaided, when the wagon reached the hall.

The front doorway was covered only by a loosely-woven curtain, weighted at the bottom with small stones that clicked as Maldron pulled the cloth aside. They passed through a small entranceway into a great, echoing chamber. Frostflower glimpsed clean mosaic tile beneath her feet, murals in gilt and dark colors that would be bright by daylight, a high ceiling that glinted here and there as if the torchlight were catching polished decorations. But she had always known that farmer-priests lived in splendor.

Two women and a young child, all in farmers' white, were waiting at the far end of the long chamber, sitting on a dais in the light of several thick wax candles. The women seemed to be playing with the child. At Maldron's entrance, they rose and came forward to him, the child running, the women following more slowly. The farmer stooped and let the child run into his arms. It seemed to be a boy of four or five years old.

"Did you catch her, papa? Did you catch the nasty sorceress?" The child looked up and saw Frostflower standing in the shadows behind Maldron. His eyes widened and he huddled out of her sight in his father's embrace. "She won't hurt us, papa, will she?"

"No, no, Nikkon, she won't hurt us. Look—see what I brought you." The farmer put Dowl's leash into his son's hand. The dog, his head on Maldron's knee, had already been sniffing at the child. Nikkon began to pat his head, shyly at first; and soon dog and boy were playing together on the tiled floor, not too far from the light——a single torch-bearing warrior had come into the chamber, standing behind them like a human light-stand; and one of the priestesses carried a small oil lamp.

Maldron kissed the women in turn, the shorter, lamp-bearing one first. He seemed to hold the taller more closely. "Have any come forward to complain of losing their child?"

The taller priestess shook her head, the silver wreath gleaming in her copper-colored hair. Inmara, the farmer-priestess of the glade. "No. Nor have our messengers found any parents mourning such a loss."

"She has stolen him from farther south or west, then. We must send messengers to Eldrommer, Arun, and Imavan. Take him, Inmara. See if he has any birthmark."

The priestess accepted Starwind from the old nurse's arms. For a few moments Inmara and Frostflower looked into one another's eyes. "His name is Starwind, Lady," said Frostflower, "and he has no birthmark, save a red mole exactly on the knuckle of his left middle finger."

"Vile sorceress," said Maldron's other wife. Frostflower lowered her gaze.

"It is not necessary to tonguelash her, Enneald. They have no other way to get children." Taking the lamp from Enneald's hand, the priest led Frostflower down the long chamber and through an arch into a narrow passage. She saw a line of doorways, each one covered by a thin linen curtain weighted at the hem and bulging slightly with the air currents. Only one room, near the end, had a wooden door; and that door stood open. Maldron led the sorceress through it, set the lamp on a table, and turned to untie her hands.

The room was dark, but it was above-ground and seemed dry. The air was fresh and smelling of new-baked bread. At the back and to one side there were windows, thickly latticed but clearly visible as they let in the moonlight; and, by their distance, she guessed the cell was larger than Burningloaf's secret room. The small table on which Maldron had set the lamp was spread with jugs and covered dishes; a high-backed chair waited behind the table; and beyond, by the light of a votive candle in a wall niche, she glimpsed a long, wide bed.

He finished untying her and crossed to the door. Was this to be her prison? She did not understand. "Reverence?" she said.

He paused. "Well?"

"If I could . . . if you would let me hold Starwind again . . . only for a few moments?"

"You do not deserve even to look at the infant, sorceress."

He had admonished his wife Enneald for speaking less harshly to her than this. "Dowl, then? Reverence, if I could at least have my dog with me?"

"He is my son's dog now."

"You cannot think, Reverence, that I stole the dog, too! You accuse me of stealing a child—you will never find Starwind's parents—and yet you yourself will steal Dowl from me?"

"You are hungry and tired, sorceress. Eat and rest. And think, while you are alone, of a father and mother lonely and mourning for their son."

He left her alone, closing the door. She heard a bolt fall into place outside. But for that, she might have been in such a room as a farmer-priest would give to an honored guest, or even sleep in himself. She went to the windows. The latticework was thick and deepset, the interstices barely large enough for her to slip her hand through; and yet, though they served tonight as bars, they were clearly designed for ornament, carved in the shapes of fanciful animals, and supporting vines that grew up on the outside.

It would have been simple, if she still had her powers, to have grown the vines thicker than the season ever allowed in their natural time, until, crowding rapidly through the lattice, they cracked it. Or even to speed time for the lattice itself, rotting away the wood. The lattice gone, she could have crawled through the opening.

She had eaten almost nothing since her supper in Burningloaf's upper room. With a little relaxation of her fears—the calm of despair coupled with the unexpected comfort of her prison—she realized her hunger. Returning to the table, she sat and gazed at the dishes in the light of the oil lamp. Strange. They were not, of course, such silver and gilded pieces as the farmers themselves ate from; but they were of good white clay, well-crafted and finely glazed. The bread-saucer, beneath its small loaf, was painted in symmetrical designs; the goblet was similarly decorated, and had a thin bowl with gracefully rounded rim. Not the pottery a sorceron would expect from a farmer-priest.

One of the jugs held wine, one water, the last and smallest milk. The milk brought back thoughts of Starwind sucking at her nipples. She filled her goblet with wine, drank deeply, tore off a crust of bread, and slowly ate it with some soft cheese. To her surprise, her fondness for cheese, which had developed since she first tasted it at the beginning of her travels this summer, remained in her tongue. She lifted the thin bronze cover from the largest bowl on the table.

The stench of cooked meat rolled out at her. She dropped the lid back over the bowl and gagged.

She must have come to tolerate that odor more easily than she had thought, traveling among farmers' folk and eating near or with them. Eighteen days ago, at the beginning of her journey, not even the bronze lid and the fragrance of hot bread, sweet wine, and aromatic candle and lamp oil could have disguised the stink of cooked meat so long.

She stood up trembling, choking down her nausea—she saw nothing with which she could have washed away vomit, and she had, after all, taken nothing but bread and cheese and wine—all clean and wholesome. But she understood, at last, the mockery of her comfortable surroundings, the insult that lay in the fresh, above-ground air and the fine pottery.

Butchered, cooked flesh! To offer a sorceress the slaughtered, roasted carcass of a farmer's enslaved animal, between the time of raping her and the torture and execution that must follow— what was that but to show her she was nothing to them but more meat to be butchered and cut?

She groped her way to the bed, fell upon it, and lay sobbing. Vaguely, through the images of skinned and scaffolded beasts and chunks of dripping flesh, she realized the wine must have held herbs to make her sleep, or she could not have drifted away like this, so wet, so bloody, so spidery between her legs...

Not until she woke was she aware of the smoothness of the sheets, the thickness of the pillows. The room was filled with the pale blue light of early morning. She turned her head on the pillow and lay watching the wall murals gradually take on their color. Most of them were stylized flowers, green, red, blue, and gold, with here and there two dots and a slash that suggested a face. Someone had removed the offensive food from the table, and only a single jug and the goblet remained.

She rose and found the close-stool, in a small corner closet shut off from the rest of the bedchamber by a door with only the

simplest latch, and ventilated by several high, tiny windows to
the outside, hung about with small baskets of fragrant herbs. She
used it cautiously, somewhat afraid of new bleeding. Then she
returned and lay again on the bed.

The herbs in last night's wine had been good herbs, leaving
her with no headache, only a feeling of torpor. The Farm was
quiet, more quiet than she had expected. She could hear the faint
sounds of the morning's work beginning, but far in the distance.
The farmers, then, lived secluded by space and thick walls from
the noise of their own farms. Within the hall itself, she heard now
and then a thump, a footfall, a muffled voice; but generally the
farmer-priests and their household servants seemed, by the silence,
to move with quiet dignity even in their homes. As her own people
moved in their retreats—that comparison made her thankful for
the times she had scrambled as a child, shouting and jerky, with
Puffball, Dreamberry, and Dawnstar in the rocks above Windslope.

Now she heard pattering on the tiled floor, a child's squeals
and a dog's yipping—Dowl's yipping. Maldron's son was playing
with Dowl in the long chamber. She listened so intently to their
play that she hardly heard the nearer sounds of the bolt being
drawn up from her door.

The door opened. Maldron came into the room. The sorceress
sat, moved to the edge of the bed, and swung her legs so that her
feet touched the floor, ready to stand. She waited warily, feeling
covered but insecure in the loose, draping garment they had put
on her last night.

"You did not eat," said the priest.

She gave him no reply. Had he expected her to eat his foul,
cooked flesh?

"Have you thought of the mother who labored to give her child
birth, only days before you stole him?"

"I have thought of her." The quick-tongued warrior who had
been so thirsty for life and so afraid of the farmers' mythical
Hellbog, and who now was lost in the real bogs. "But I did not
steal her child. She gave him gladly."

"You will not hold him again, sorceress. Is it not better he
should be returned to the parents who waited twelve hen's-hatchings for him?"

"I have told you how little his parents wanted him."

Maldron closed the door. He could not secure it from the inside, but no doubt he had warriors in the passageway; and even if he did not, how could she have fled, by daylight, from a farmer's hall, through his fields and the midst of his workers, and gain the other side of his distant, fortified, guarded walls?

"I do not know your name, sorceress. Is it against your superstitions that I should know it?"

"We have no superstitions, Reverence. My name is Frostflower."

"Cold. It does not fit you." He approached her...began to brush his hand down her long, tangled hair.

Shuddering, she rose and went quickly to the far window. "You have taken my power already.

"What power your kind pretends to wield against us, I have taken."

"We do not pretend."

"Perhaps some of you do not."

She had not aged his young merchant; probably Maldron had never guessed how near the lightning had come to his silver dagger, nor who had aimed it away from him to save his wife from Thorn's threats—he had never seen any other evidence of her power, and now he thought she never had it. She turned once more to the window. "But you feared to rob me yourself. You forced your poor hireling to the work."

"I did not fear. A priest's body is sacred, not to be defiled with that of a sorceress."

He had followed her to the window. He stroked her hair again, and again she cringed away. "Then do not defile yourself now, when your people are not looking on," she said.

"You do not understand what I have given you in exchange for what you thought of as power? You desire children, Frostflower, or you would not have stolen the infant you call Starwind. I have freed you from your superstitions, so that you can bear children of your own."

"Don't touch me, farmer!"

"You need no longer be a sorceress, Frostflower. Purified, you could become wife to a farmer."

Purified! Part of her brain laughed, though the smile did not reach her lips. "I have had enough of your rites of purification, farmer-priest."

He laid his hands on her shoulders, holding her with her back to him. She stiffened and tried to break away, but this time he held firm. She stopped pulling and stood quietly, weak with lack of food and return of fear.

He stepped closer, relaxing his grip and rubbing his hands up and down her upper arms. "I regret the need to hurt you the first time. I regret the clumsiness of that terrified fool. But it need not be like that, Frostflower; not on smooth sheets, with the freedom of your limbs and with a skilled lover. Even last night, in your fear and discomfort beneath that mewling idiot, I could see how you responded—"

His hold was loosened—she broke away with a sob. "You are cruel, farmer!"

His voice grew hard again. "You have not yet felt my cruelty, sorceress." She heard him return to the door and open it. "But I show you two last kindnesses. I do not ask you to name any who may have helped or befriended you or listened to your sacrilegious teachings—I ask you only to name the child's parents. And I will send you no food this morning."

He left, bolting the door again. Although she could not have looked at another bowl of butchered meat, this promise to send her none seemed the greatest threat he could have offered her—as much as to tell her she must expect great pain this same day, as if he had forbidden her to soil his property with her vomit. Or . . . perhaps by the afternoon he meant to have her on the scaffold, her stomach empty so that it could be filled with the small, sharpened stones. Perhaps before evening she would be hanging from a gibbet, with insects eating her flesh and the stones working their way into her bowels. . . .

She crept back to the bed and covered her face with her hands. Searching for other thoughts than scaffold and gibbet, she remembered she had never entered the trance of cool breathing, which would have restored the time she forfeited from her life when she identified with Burningloaf's iron nails in order to rust them. Stripped of her power, she could not now have recovered that time, even if there had been any purpose in seeking it. But to go through the old exercises for a few moments, perhaps to enter something like the trance, might at least help her gain some measure of detachment-in-unity.

She lay slowly flexing and relaxing her muscles. For a long time this continued to remind her that soon her body would be injured and bleeding, no longer responsive to her control. The dull sense of hunger, too, made her muscles seem already weak and sluggish.

But at last her mind began to empty of fear. Whatever was to happen eventually, she was slipping for now into the state of timelessness, when the past was one small circle of all events both recent and long ago, the empty future seemed suspended forever, and the present was an all-encompassing blanket floating in noth- ingness. Gratefully, just before her mind took the branching off into normal sleep, she began to vary the rhythm of her breaths in the pattern that would have carried her, if she still had her power, into the trance . . . and she entered something much like it, al- though without its restoring quality; for, as her mind slid the last few rungs into unconsciousness, she felt . . . or dreamed she felt . . . a coolness as of soft snow in her lungs.

Had she entered the trance of cool breathing in earnest, and not as a nostalgic exercise to make her wait more endurable, she would have chosen a time beforehand for her awakening, or set a small loop of the outer senses to act as a warning snare and pull her back to consciousness at any disturbance in her surroundings. But she had neglected both these precautions as being pointless and, indeed, no longer possible for her. She had hardly expected to achieve something so like the real trance. She did not wake until she felt a sharp prodding on her cheek.

Opening her eyes, she found Maldron's yellow-haired wife, Enneald, bending above her, prodding her cheek with one long fingernail. "Ah!" said Enneald. "You see, she is alive."

Two others were in the room: a yellow-haired girl just emerg- ing from childhood, and a slender dark-haired youth not much older. Both wore farmers' white. The girl, by her sharp features and light hair, would likely be Enneald's daughter. The boy did not resemble Maldron, or either of the wives Frostflower had seen. Perhaps he was a nephew, or the visiting son of some other priest.

"Is she strong enough?" said the boy.

Enneald pulled Frostflower's wrist, and the sorceress obedi- ently sat. "I say she is strong enough," remarked the priestess. "Inmara will have the final judgment."

"I never knew they could sleep so soundly. Are you sure she's power-stripped?" The girl who appeared to be Enneald's daughter pinched Frostflower on the arm and then pulled back her hand and stood waiting as if to see what would happen.

"I am quite sure, Kalda. Your father saw to that as soon as he caught her."

"We should not be speaking," said the boy in a voice that must only recently have turned deep.

Kalda giggled. "Oh, that's not until we get into the Passage, Daseron!"

Daseron glanced at her with disgust. "Thank the gods you're not old enough to come into the Truth Grove."

Kalda made a face at him, then pinched Frostflower's arm again. "Look at her! Oh, look at her, she's afraid of the Truth Grove! You're afraid, aren't you, sorceress?"

Had her expression shown fear, then? Frostflower was surprised. The calm of her sleep had not yet worn off, and she felt not so much frightened as bemused by the girl's prattle. "Take your enjoyment teasing me now," she said, looking steadily at Kalda. "It seems you must remain curious about this Grove, while I am to know its truth."

"Now see what you've done?" said Daseron. "Aunt Enneald, if you don't keep her quiet—"

"Hush, all of you!" Enneald seemed to relish the chance to claim authority. "Sorceress, you will not speak except to tell us from whom you stole the child. Daseron, think of your own tongue before you scold your cousin." And to Kalda the sorceress heard Enneald say softly, "Prove to them how nearly grown you are, dear."

So had Silverflake and old Moonscar used to admonish Frostflower and Puffball when they were children. So, perhaps, might Frostflower herself someday have admonished Starwind. Silverflake at her sharpest-tongued had not been as unpleasant as Enneald; nor, Frostflower hoped, had she and her sib been so dislikable as Kalda . . . yet it was strange to see farmers behaving among themselves so nearly like sorceri, so nearly like those few common folk whose family life sorceri could sometimes witness. Perhaps, to one another, Enneald, Kalda, and Daseron seemed as affectionate in their bickering as Silverflake, Moonscar, and Puffball had been at Windslope; or Brightweave, Yarn, and Small Spider in their home at Frog-in-the-Millstone. No doubt it was to keep Frostflower from seeing this that silence had been enjoined on them.

Daseron bound a leather cord around her wrists, pulling it until it pressed down on the bones and caused a tingling to spread towards her fingers. She wondered if he were inexperienced and clumsy, or if her torture had already been begun.

Looping another cord between her bound wrists, he led her out through the passageway and into the long, echoing hall. Enneald walked ahead of them, Kalda behind, and two warriors who had been waiting in the passage walked one at each side of her. Had they expected a power-stripped and unfed sorceress to overcome Enneald and Daseron?

Behind the dais at the end of the long hall, they came to a curtained doorway, carved with gilded symbols from the farmers' mythology. At either side of the door stood an oil lamp on a stand. Kalda stepped forward, silent now, but not quite able to repress a smile of anticipation. Taking one of the lamps, she pulled the curtain aside until the rest of the procession should pass through. Enneald took the other lamp and led the way into a narrow, tiled passage.

Frostflower kept her gaze straight ahead and tried to let no muscle of her face move as she passed close to Kalda, but out of the corner of her eye she saw the child grin. Both warriors followed immediately behind the sorceress. The passage grew dusky as the young farmer-priestess let the curtain swing down.

Ten paces from the doorway, they began to descend a long flight of stairs. So at last they were taking her into their dungeons. The remnants of Frostflower's sleep-calm were long dispelled. Now and again she shivered and could hardly stop; and she guessed that her pale skin must be even more pale. She was glad of the semidarkness, glad that not one of her escorters could see her face and that only the swordswoman directly behind her might notice the quivering of her shoulders. Soon she would lose even that degree of solitude.

Yet the descent was not unlovely. The wall mosaics continued the entire way, clean and glistening, with numerous metallic tiles which glanced in the lamplight. The steps, which Frostflower thought to be granite, were worn but easy to descend, dry, shallow, and broad. The air, though close, was fragrant, the incense growing stronger as they went deeper.

Sorceri who had actually seen farmers' dungeons rarely survived. Frostflower and her people had never guessed, speculating in Windslope Retreat, that farmers might design their underground places for their own delectation rather than for the discomfort and disgust of their prisoners. At first the unexpected beauty was vaguely reassuring, but soon Frostflower understood from it how much beneath consideration the farmers held her people. Far from being the focal point against which all their torments of mind as well as body must be aimed, she seemed a passing intruder in their home, worth little special effort to break her will.

The stairs widened into a circular chamber, perhaps twelve paces across. Inmara waited near the center of this room, arranging cloths and brushes on two marble tables. Beyond her was a second arched doorway. Many large hanging lamps illumined the tiled walls and floor, while the air was heavy with incense smoke that curled from braziers and moved only slightly with the slow draft between the doorways. Steam rose from basins around the walls. The ceiling was crossed with thick, gilded beams, and appeared to rise in a high dome above them.

Enneald went to Inmara and spoke softly with her for a few moments, nodding back towards the sorceress. Inmara approached, took Frostflower's leash from the youth Daseron, and untied her bonds, feeling her wrists carefully. Then with the soft pads of her fingertips she touched the prisoner's cheek. It was not so objectionable, somehow, to let this woman see her fear, and Frostflower lifted her gaze to Inmara's large, gray eyes.

"We are to cleanse you thoroughly here," murmured the priestess. "It is no more than what all of us undergo every season and before our greatest ceremonials, except that we are not lifted from the floor."

She led Frostflower to the middle of the room and lifted away the single cloaklike garment which had been her only covering since the old nurse put it on her last night. Here the floor sloped gently downwards on all sides to a copper grating. Inmara stationed her almost upon this drain and fitted silver (or silver-coated) gauntlets about her wrists, tightening each bracelet in turn with an attached screw.

The warriors came forward and hooked chains into the hinges at the back of each gauntlet. They drew the ends of the chains up over metal grooves embedded in the beam above, and continued to pull, jerking a little, until Frostflower's toes no longer brushed against the floor.

"Except that we are not lifted.... Except..." Ah, Lady, you have never been hung by your wrists!

The warriors secured the chains on the other side of the beam, and the priestesses began to scrub her with cloths and brushes. They worked thoroughly and methodically, beginning with her arms and elbows, moving downwards to her scalp, hair, face and ears, throat, shoulders . . . and so on, little by little. She was dimly aware, from the few directions muttered by Enneald, that Kalda must be handing the women their various brushes, hard- or soft-bristled, thin or large and flat, as needed; and from time to time Daseron or one of the warriors dashed a basin of cold or steaming water over her. Soap stung her eyes and her reopened prick-wounds; and even the less tender areas of her skin burned with the pressure of the bristles. If farmers themselves indeed under-went this harsh cleansing several times yearly, she might almost have pitied them. Her feet remained so near the floor that only through an effort of her overstrained will could she keep herself, once satisfied it was impossible, from straining further to reach a footing and take a little of the pressure from her upper body. The bracelets that had seemed merely snug when Inmara first adjusted them, were now unbearably tight; her arms and shoulders, her very ribs and breasts, ached tensely in their dislocation; her hands felt at once numb and about to burst. Her fingertips were nearly on a level with the bottom of the ceiling beam—when she pressed them against the wood, it sent a sharp pricking through her hands; but she continued to press upwards, seeking some forgetfulness of her other pains by inflicting on herself what new pangs she could.

The rasping of hard bristles over the soles of her lifted feet, which would otherwise have been a torment in its own right, was welcome as a sign that the cleansing was almost done and she might hope soon to be let down.

They combed and braided her hair and bound it up on top of her head. They tied some kind of soft cloth slippers upon her feet, and then at last the warriors unfastened the chains from behind the beam and lowered her again to the floor. The cloth slippers soaked up water that had not yet drained through the copper grat-ing; and, as her arms were let down, nausea filled her stomach and a sharp throbbing her head. The smell of incense had become close and stifling, the steam wetly smothering. When Enneald unhooked the chains from the gauntlets, Frostflower swayed and and would have fallen, but Daseron caught her. One of the pries-tesses threw another garment over her, soft and thick and dun-colored instead of brown.

Handling her through the cloth, the warriors took her to the wall and sat her on a bench. Another table stood near, with its basins and brushes. Inmara came, drew Frostflower's arms through the sleeve-slits in the garment, and unscrewed the bracelets. The sorceress glanced at her own whitened wrists between swollen, discolored hands and arms, and looked away again. Touching the skin gently, Inmara eased left hand and wrist into a basin of warm water. The sorceress winced as a brush struck her palm.

"Tell us now," murmured Inmara. "Who are his parents?"

"I have told you."

"You have named a warrior who could not have been pregnant long enough to have borne him. Frostflower . . . we have only prepared you, here, for a Ritual of Truth."

The others—Enneald, the youth, Kalda with her grin, the two warriors—were putting away the rest of the cleansing implements. They did not seem to be listening. Perhaps Inmara had been instructed to press the weary questions again . . . or perhaps she sincerely pitied the sorceress.

"Lady," Frostflower murmured, "have you never thought that a sorceron who can turn a young person old might also . . . might also grow a newborn thing quickly into a youth?"

Inmara's brush faltered. "What do you mean?"

Almost the sorceress had betrayed Starwind to those who might abhor a child grown by time manipulation in the mother's womb. "If . . . if I were to tell you, Lady, that Dowl . . . my companion dog . . . five days ago was a newborn pup?" It was not true—Dowl had lived five years, growing in his own time; but, as Frostflower had chosen her words, it was not a lie, either; and it might show her how farmers would accept the truth of Starwind's birth.

Inmara put down her brush and massaged Frostflower's fingers in the warm water. "We do not question you about Dowl, Frostflower. Nor will I speak of what you have told me. If . . . if Maldron knew the dog to be sorcer-grown, he would decide it must be killed."

Thank God I did not barter Starwind's life to escape a few moments of pain! Thank the priestess for warning me!

Inmara finished washing her hands and wrists, looped a braided cloth cord loosely about them, and helped her to her feet. *They have not been clever*, thought the sorceress; *they have left me already too weak to endure much more.*

She did not notice the order of the procession as they led her out. She did not at first realize they were ascending the second stairway, not the one down which they had come. Vaguely she remembered that Kalda was to be left behind and that a while ago she would have been glad the mocking girl should witness no more; but now she did not turn to see how far Kalda might follow.

At the top of the passageway, fresh air cleared her head a little, and she looked around. They had emerged in a garden. The flowers were not oppressively fragrant, as the incense had been; the splashing of a fountain might have been pleasant if it had not reminded her of basins of water dashing over her. She glimpsed gray, enclosing walls far to right and left, and blue sky above. This was hardly the dark torture chamber of her own people's imaginings; yet its menace was all the keener, as if she alone were forbidden to enjoy such beauty while in the very midst of it.

A small grove of fruit trees waited . . . she could no longer judge how many paces distant, but the trees looked small enough to hold in her hand. She heard a faint chanting, a farmers' chanting, and realized it came from the grove. She shivered and tried to concentrate instead on the birds' calls. The birds—robins and thrushes, swallows and wrens—they might look on, but they could not understand, could not care, perhaps did not realize how some human creatures were hurting another. If they noticed, they must think it some silly human game. The birds, the insects, the small animals that must be hiding even in a farmer's private garden—all these would continue their own lives unconcerned with what happened to her or with what the farmer-priest who claimed to own their land did on it today.

As she walked, her feet unsteady in the wet slippers and parts of her body still damp beneath the cloth, a wasp lighted on her garment and crawled unconcernedly toward her arm. She watched it until one of the warriors noticed it and lifted a hand. "Don't kill it," said Frostflower.

"You're not to talk, sorceress." But the warrior only brushed the insect away. Go, small creature, thought Frostflower, gazing after it until her eyes lost their focus. The small creatures were all she had left to help her achieve some kind of detachment-in-unity.

The procession reached the grove of fruit trees, Inmara supporting rather than leading the sorceress.

Maldron waited in the grove, standing at a black marble altar; and eight or nine young people, all in farmers' white, stood behind it, chanting. The priestesses and Daseron joined them, and that made . . . why should Frostflower count them? She had not realized

he had so many children ... or nieces and nephews ... or wives
and sisters and younger brothers. . . .

He came around the altar. He alone seemed not to be chanting.
Looking down at her, he unbound her hands (will they never have
done tying me and untying me as if they feared I could spread my
arms and fly from them?) and lifted off her garment. She began
to shudder and could not stop, dared not glance up again, dared
not glance at any part of his body beneath his long white tunic.
She closed her eyes.

Someone bound her legs together just below the knees.
Tightly—she almost fell from the bite of the cord—but, thank
God! they had bound them together. Then they took her wrists
and corded each one separately, pulling the loops tight into flesh
still aching from the metal gauntlets. She groaned, but the priests
and priestesses did not stop chanting.

They crossed her arms over her stomach and tied the cords in
back, pulling them until her wrists were pressed, fingers up, at
her sides. Then they lifted her and laid her on the altar face down.
The stone was cold, hard. The sun was not yet high enough to
shine into the grove, and the winds chilled her, striking her wet
hair and her skin where it was still damp. She turned her head to
rest her right cheek against the marble, and smelled incense again.

Opening her eyes, she saw that they were censing the altar,
or perhaps herself, with an incense-burner on a swinging, clicking
silver chain. And still their chant went on ... after the silence of
the underground chamber, this must be a full ceremonial, a farmers' ritual in all its trappings, and she less a withholder of infor-
mation than a sacrificial victim on their altar. Again they had
made her a participant in their superstitious rites. At least the
incense was not so stifling here in the open air. She closed her
eyes and tried once more to hear the free chattering of the birds,
the humming of the insects.

She felt the slippers drawn off her feet. For a moment the
chorus paused while Maldron's deep voice chanted a few words
in the priests' secret language. Then Maldron fell silent, the chorus
rose again, and a lash struck sharp against the soles of her bare
feet.

She guessed it was Maldron himself who swung the lash
... again ... and again. Soon she no longer cared. The leather that
struck her feet was a disembodied force, and she was conscious

of little, between the blows and her screams, except the constant chanting.

After the lash, he began to use some kind of rod or thin club. She was aware of only one clear thought: that if he broke her feet he could no longer make her walk. But he did not break them.

The blows stopped. She lay panting, absorbing the pains that still echoed through her body, feeling her own arm bones pressing into her stomach, and smelling incense and perspiration. Then a sharp blade began an incision in the small of her back.

I will tell them! I will tell them all! All—but what? He would kill Starwind! Or he would not believe it—he would think it another lie. It would do no good. God! It would do no good.

She could no longer hear the birds. She tried to concentrate on the pain instead—old Moonscar had told her there was a way, somewhere, of using pain as a ladder to climb above pain. It was a very dark way ... she could tell only that the blade seemed to be cutting an angle. Then her skin seemed pulled up and something burning struck the raw wound. She did not comprehend until the next incision started, seemingly very close to the first, that only a tiny corner of her skin had been cut away and the place rubbed with vinegar or salt or wine.

Perhaps three such incisions ... perhaps many. Perhaps she was nearing detachment. She could hardly remember the shape of her own body, and whenever she opened her eyes she saw only meaningless forms and colors. Then another hand grasped hers and pain came into her thumb between nail and flesh.

If I told him—if I named anyone—who would not love such an infant?—Who can I name? Names? My mother's old friend ... has no wife!—The weavers—who are they, where are they? Farmers' folk ... Thorn—

Twice during the time he stabbed her fingers she fainted. Once she awakened with the smell of vinegar in her nostrils and wet cloths patting her face. A tube was put into her mouth and she sucked up wine, unthinkingly as a child. Her mind came back sufficiently to realize Maldron had tortured all the fingers on her left hand and one or two on the right. "His mother was a warrior who did not want him," she said. "No one knows his father."

The priest took another finger. Soon she fainted again.

She awakened the second time of herself. She lay on her side between smooth sheets. They were pleasant, although they did not

ease the pain. Her fingers were burning and stiff. The soles of her
feet throbbed. She had dreamed someone was doing embroidery
in her skin, across her back; and a belt of pain lay there beneath
a bandage just tight enough to feel when she breathed in. Still,
it was good to lie quietly, being given no new hurts, with a pillow
beneath her ear and the warmth of a light blanket surrounding her.

She opened her eyes. Red sunlight was slanting through a
lattice and falling on a woman with coppery hair and a white
garment. The room was the same one where Frostflower had first
been imprisoned, and the woman was Inmara. Inmara sat sewing
pale green cloth. The air smelled strongly of incense and faintly
of cooking meat . . . farmers' halls were not so large, after all, if
the smells of their kitchens penetrated even here.

After a moment Inmara looked up and saw that Frostflower
had awakened. The priestess rose and laid down her sewing. She
lifted a cup from the table; she brought the cup to Frostflower.
It was glazed white pottery, with a bronze lid and a thin silver
tube in the lid.

Vaguely remembering that some while ago she had been given
wine through such a tube, the sorceress sucked. The liquid was
warm and oily, with a strange, salty taste. . . .

Not until she had swallowed several mouthfuls did she realize
she was drinking meat-broth.

She choked, spitting out the tube, coughing and spewing the
stuff from her mouth. She tried to sit, fell on to her back—awakened the line of pain—rolled to her other side and lay retching
and gasping.

"Frostflower!" The priestess' voice was not loud. Mock concern—trick concern. Of all farmers, she had almost been ready
to trust Inmara.

"Frostflower, what is it? What's wrong?" A hand was pressing
on her forehead—a soft, warm hand, dry, uninjured. . . .

"His mother was a warrior who did not want him—I do not
know his father."

"You must not repeat that lie. You will not be tortured again."

"You . . . will not force me to . . . to drink meat?"

"Nothing. Rest now." Inmara's hands were busy wiping, wiping Frostflower's face, wiping the sheets where the broth had wet
them. "I should have known you would not want anything immediately on waking. Later—"

"You will bring it back?" The sobs shook Frostflower's body and rekindled her sores, but she could not stop them.

"You ate so little last night . . . Will you have a little hot mintwater, then, to soothe your stomach?"

Was it really possible such a voice cloaked so much malice? "You did not know . . . you did not know we do not eat butchered animals?"

"You do not . . . ? Oh, sorceress, I am sorry!"

They had not known! Last night's bowl of cooked flesh, today's warm, greasy broth—she could almost have laughed. Yet they had known how to take her power.

"Will you eat eggs, then? Milk? Fruit?"

She needed food. Hunger was a dull awareness rather than a healthy craving, but she knew it was there within her. "A little wine . . . if I could have a little wine? And . . . perhaps a few carrots? Or asparagus . . . lentils . . . anything but flesh, Lady."

"Rest." Inmara wiped Frostflower's cheeks and held a cloth to her nose. Then she left the bedside. Her footsteps moved across the tiled floor, her voice called softly. There were murmurings, more footfalls. Frostflower was exhausted and drowsed once more.

The room was twilight when next she opened her eyes. The faint stench of meat was gone, replaced by a stronger fragrance of mint. She stared at her hand, lying near her face on the pillow. Her fingers were thick and white, as thick and stiff as they had felt. She realized at last that each finger was encased in bandages. She began to thump them unthinkingly on the pillow, playing with them—playing with the pain—as if they were new toys.

Inmara came, helped her to sit, and propped pillows behind her carefully, so as not to press against the small of her back, where the pain was. She noticed she was wearing another loose garment, this one of smooth, heavy silk. The priestess gave her a small warm cup and she found she could balance it on her right palm, steadying it with the three fingers left whole and unbandaged, and sipping the warm, mint-flavored water through another thin silver tube.

The sky was still translucent blue behind the black lattice and vines. Inmara lit three oil lamps to keep the chamber light. Then she came and sat beside the bed, feeding the sorceress boiled carrots, tender young asparagus, fine wheat porridge cooked with raisins and peaches.

And suddenly Frostflower understood the full bitterness of farmers' cruelty. If she were imprisoned in a stinking cell underground, lying on bare wet straw, her wounds left to fester, and only moldy bread and stale water set out for her if she could feed herself in the darkness—then she could have looked forward even to scaffolding and hanging as a release. But surrounded with reminders that life could still have comforts, even after rape and torture . . .

Yes, they are clever, they are cruel beyond anything we have imagined of them.

"Lady," she said, "when am I to be hung?"

Inmara tucked the sheets and blanket closer about her arms and waist, smoothed the pillow and cushioned her hands on her lap. "You need not be hung, Frostflower. If you will tell us who are the child's parents . . ."

Here it was, then—the offer of life, the last temptation a sorceron in her place would ever have thought to fear. Inmara offered not only life, but conversion to farmers' ways, adoption into a farmer's household.

". . . Maldron is a good husband, Frostflower—gentle, loving. He has given Enneald children, he gave Wilvara children . . . with the help of the goddess, he will yet give me a child. You could bear babes of your own. . . ."

What else could she have hoped, now? And what sorcerer could she have found willing to sacrifice his own power for her? Wonderhope of Mildrock Retreat? Even if she could bear to have any man touch her again in that way . . . yet she had suffered perhaps even greater pain of the flesh in other parts of her body since . . . and in order to bear a child . . . Wonderhope? No, not Wonderhope—not even Wonderhope, especially not Wonderhope. They had decided so easily, years ago; they had never regretted. . . . To approach him now, to tempt him, to beg him, and then perhaps not to be able to bear even his touch—that would have been crueller than any priest's trick.

". . . You have been through pain enough already for a purification," Inmara went on; and in the lamplight Frostflower saw that the silk garment they had put on her this last time was either white or very pale bluish-gray. "The remaining rites will be mild, only a little sprinkling with water, and putting on the wreath and necklace. You will need to chant in the public ceremonials, of course; but we will not insist you have a statue in your own chamber. You will have your own food—you need never eat flesh..."

It should have disgusted her. It did not. Had she stolen Starwind as the farmers believed, she knew she would have revealed his parents in that moment—and the knowledge was as bitter as what had been done to her in the Rockroots. She put the heels of her palms to her wet cheeks. "You said you would not torture me again, Lady!"

Again the priestess arranged Frostflower's hands in her lap, wiped her face, held a cloth to her nose. "You do not believe that we...enjoy torturing?"

"You surround it with your ceremonies—as if I were—as if I were a piece of butcher's meat for your gods, the gods of your mythology!" Ah, God! How could I have thought of joining the farmer-priests in their superstitions?

Inmara began to massage Frostflower's forehead. The sorceress might have jerked away from the priestess' touch, but not without reawakening the wounds in her back.

"It is because we find the need distasteful," said Inmara, "that we surround it with solemnity."

"Do you always...All your ceremonies are to cover some distasteful need?"

Inmara's fingers moved to the back of Frostflower's neck...gentle, unbandaged fingers rubbing between pillow and skin; and Frostflower must now accept kindness as she had accepted pain: helplessly.

"The ceremony you witnessed at our woodland altar...did that seem ugly to you, Frostflower?"

"I am permitted to remember it?"

"To remember it, among ourselves. Not to reveal it to common folk."

The pride of the farmer-priests. "Not ugly, but...disproportionate. So much ritual to clothe your simple lovemaking."

"It was our prayer, our consecration to Aeronu, the Goddess of Birth. I have never been able to conceive. With the help of Aeronu, Maldron was trying to give me a child at last."

Even the thing that had been done to her in the Rockroots—even that had been meant to be good, a compensation in itself for loss, not a bloody sacrifice that must be made for the sake of children. Otherwise, two sorceri who sacrificed their power and yet did not succeed in getting offspring would have been even more pitiable than a sorceron raped. "It was . . . Lady, it had a kind of beauty."

Inmara's hands moved to her shoulders. The massaging of a priestess was not so different from that of a fellow sorceron.

"Is it so painful to return the boy to his true parents? Frostflower, you cannot watch him grow. We will send word through all the Tanglelands, to the eastern and western mountains, if need be, until we find them."

"You will search for his parents with your messengers . . . yet it was necessary to torture me?"

"Oh, gods!" Inmara's fingers faltered. She regained her self-control and continued massaging for a moment, then rose and removed the small table with its tray of half-empty dishes from the bedside to the door. She did not return to sit by Frostflower. She went instead to the window and stood gazing out through lattice and vines at the dark. Almost as Frostflower herself had stood last night, a prisoner gazing out.

"Yes, it was necessary. As it will be necessary to hang you."

Perhaps I could name the weavers of Frog-in-the-Millstone? They would accept Starwind—Yarn and Brightweave would pretend to be his mother and father, if warned—but how to warn them? How tell them to claim Starwind, so that confusion and surprise will not betray them? And even if it were possible to warn them, there would be neighbors to testify that Yarn had not been pregnant, had not grieved for a stolen infant.

"When?"

"Soon. Perhaps tomorrow."

If they had hung her at once, immediately after the Rockroots, before she had learned that great bodily pain and some measure of comfort were still possible afterwards . . . "And when you do not find his parents in all the Tanglelands?"

"If that were possible . . . I would raise him as my own."

He would not grow up learning of the One God, or knowing the joys of sorcery and study—he would learn farmers' superstitions and how to wield them . . . but he would have comfort in the farmers' halls, and, with such a mother as Inmara, perhaps even a measure of kindness. Perhaps he would follow the example of Maldron's nameless ancestor and drain more of the marshlands, perhaps even find the mud-clotted body of his mother.

"Let me live until you have searched all the Tanglelands. Someone may try to claim him who has no right."

"I will speak of it to Maldron. But I do not think . . . Frostflower, you must tell us quickly!"

So there was nothing more to hope except that her scaffolding would be disembowelment, for the quickest death. Her face was wet and sticky again, tears beginning to drop from jaw to throat, nose filling. She wished Inmara would return with a kerchief, but the priestess was blowing her own nose. God of power! Thorn had not wept even when convinced she must end in the farmers' Hellbog forever. "Lady . . . will you . . . will you bring him to me one more time? Let me hold him one last time?"

Chapter 5

Again tonight Maldron had wept before falling asleep in Inmara's arms. Despite his tears, despite the pity he allowed only Inmara to see, she knew he would have forbidden her to take the infant one last time to the sorceress. No one else, however—not even Enneald or Varin, and surely none of the servants—could question the elder wife, who held highest authority in Maldron's absence. When he rolled from her in his sleep, she rose softly and took the child from his cradle.

From the old cradle that had been made six generations ago and held most of the family's sons and a few of the daughters since Terndasen's time. If the gods permitted her to keep this child, she would name him Terndasen, after that ancestor of her husband. . . . It had been a mistake to give the babe this cradle, and a place in her own room. She would have all the more pain restoring him to his right parents. The nurse should have kept him during their wait.

The child began to cry on being lifted. If Maldron heard or woke, he would think Inmara had left her chamber to walk with the infant and still him. Soon the babe quieted, gurgling drowsily in her arms. Raes and Aeronu had meant her for a mother—why had they kept her womb closed so long? She was in her thirty-fifth year—had Aeronu meant this child for her adoption?

There was no guard at Frostflower's door this night. The sorceress was too weak, too injured. Would she even be able to walk up the scaffold steps tomorrow? Setting the babe safely to one side, Inmara lifted the bolt and opened the door.

The sorceress made no sound. Perhaps she was in such another trancelike state as Enneald, Kalda, and Daseron had spoken of finding her in when they came to bring her to the cleansing. Without putting down the baby again, Inmara groped for a candle, held it to the tiny blue constant-wick that burned in Jehandru's niche before the statue.

The priestess stood for a few moments, holding the candle and looking down, wondering if the sorceress had died. These atheists from the mountains and edges of the Tanglelands had strange, evil arts; perhaps, even power-stripped, they retained an ability to suicide without weapons. Aye, and would that have been so evil a deed, for a woman in Frostflower's place? Ointments and bandages could ease only partially the inflamed knife slits in back and fingers or the bruises on feet and wrists. Nothing—except, perhaps, sleep—could ease the thought of scaffold and gibbet. Had Frostflower's skin seemed so extremely white that first evening, when she was led into the hall? Had her long hair looked so very fine and black, framing her thin, triangular face?

The eyelids trembled and lifted. The eyes no longer shocked so greatly, when their unmatched colors were softened in the candlelight and when one was prepared for them. In a strange way, they almost added to the appeal of the face. But the lines of suffering returned, even before the sorceress tried to raise herself on her pillows.

Planting the candle in one of the bedpost holders, Inmara bent and transferred the child to Frostflower. The sorceress bundled him eagerly and gently into her arms, careful not to bump him with her fingers that had been bandaged into pegs. It was almost like watching a mother whose hands had been cut off, fondling her babe with the stumps.

Then, stroking the tiny head with the three uninjured fingers of her right hand, Frostflower gazed up with gratitude beyond words; and Inmara wondered how her eyes could once have seemed grotesque and menacing. She understood the beauty her husband found in this sorceress—she desired Frostflower for a sister as much as he desired her for another wife. She could not imagine feeling the same jealousy toward Frostflower that she felt towards Enneald on the few nights when Maldron chose the younger wife's bedchamber.

If a mortal could question Jehandru's plan, Inmara would say the gods had been cruel to give Frostflower to the sorceri to raise. Or had it been her own choice? Could this young woman, who might have been so useful, so fertile—could she have chosen of her own will to follow one of those accursed sorceri who slunk about the towns teaching their unclean superstitions? Or could she have been one of the unliving, unnatural children they sorcered together out of snow and mud? No; her pain was too clearly real. She was flesh . . . surely she was herself another child stolen in infancy and nursed on corruption. Had she been saved from her kidnapper, as Maldron had saved the boy from her . . .

"Lady," murmured the sorceress, "you will help me bare my breast?"

"What?"

"To let him suck . . . one last time?" Holding him curled in her left arm, Frostflower began pulling at the cloth of her garment.

For a moment the priestess felt horror. Did stolen babes, then, suck their first poison from the nipples of barren sorceresses? "You . . . have milk?"

"Not yet. I might have had, in a few more days." A look of appeal from those large, sad eyes. "It is useless now, but still, to feel him once more . . ."

"You— What kind of milk?" Inmara should have snatched him at once from the sorceress, before disgust had melted again in confusion and pity.

Frostflower smiled and sighed. "It is not sorcerous, Lady. If it were, I could not have hoped to produce it now, even if I were to live. When a baby sucks long enough and often enough, the breast will fill at last for it."

Sorceri were treacherous; but none of them, not even those who had blasted into senility and death the men or warriors who stripped their power, had afterwards been able to harm anyone. "This is no sorcerous power?"

"We are flesh. Is my body so different from yours?"

I should not have come, thought the priestess. She will corrupt me. Has she corrupted us already, that even now Maldron would forgive her treachery and come to her bed, for the names of the child's parents?

Even as she thought this, Inmara was stooping to help Frostflower pull up the garment. She watched in fascination and longing as the infant nuzzled patiently. "But you are—you were virginal."

The blue and brown eyes glanced up at Inmara, then back to the baby. "His warrior mother, who did not want him, used to grow impatient when I stopped to suckle him."

Why did she persist in the lie that would kill her? "We know Thorn could not have mothered him."

"You will have as much hope of giving him milk as I had. You will have more. You can sit with him in safety."

"I am no sorceress."

Frostflower moved the child to her other breast. "Tomorrow . . . Lady, tomorrow I stand before a crowd of folk who . . . hate us, think us monsters, who will rejoice that they can shout at me unafraid. Lady—what will my scaffolding be?"

Inmara shrugged helplessly. "I think he has not yet decided."

"I hope it will not be the stones. I hope it will be disemboweling—if I could ask for disemboweling? Lady, I do not want to hang too long alive, with them . . . enjoying themselves around the gibbet. There, there! Hush, hush, my Starwind, all is well. It is nothing, Lady. I have disturbed him a little with my fears, that is all."

The baby had started to cry. Stroking his head again, Frostflower hummed some soft melody, weird yet soothing. Gradually her hand stopped trembling, her humming grew steadier, and the babe quieted and returned to his sucking.

If we could find some man and woman in one of the towns, Inmara thought—some man and woman who would take the child, so that Frostflower could name them . . . but there is no time, I know none of the townsfolk well enough, we cannot confide in anyone else, and if the true parents were found—and I am considering a lie! Gods forgive me, Raes and Aeronu forgive me, Ontarac of the Harvest Gate forgive me, all gods and goddesses forgive me, Jehandru of the Seven Secret Names forgive me, I was considering a lie to save a sorceress.

"We will have warriors to guard you," the priestess said. "To keep off the common folk."

"If I could have one . . . one person tomorrow who understood that we are not so different, not so . . . vile. Lady, it will be nothing unclean for you to try to nurse him. It will not displease your gods. You have your own wetnurses sometimes?"

Inmara took the sorceress' free hand, the hand not needed to support the child. She held it long, pressing it just enough for affection, careful not to press the fingertips. We do not hate you, Frostflower, she thought. If you will only give us honesty, we will give you love, a pure home, children—even Enneald and her daughter will accept you in time. She did not say this aloud; it had already been said very often, and a farmer should not beg a sorceron; but she thought it as if the sorceress could somehow hear it in her brain.

At length the infant slept soundly again. Inmara gave Frostflower the wine she should have given her earlier. Probably the sorceress understood it contained herbs to bring sleep. Condemned persons sometimes preferred to spend their last hours awake, but Frostflower drank obediently, without protest.

"Teach him mercy, Lady," she said as Inmara wiped her lips.

"It is for his parents to teach him."

"You will not find them. Only let no one take him who cannot tell you of the small mole on the knuckle of his middle finger."

Frostflower slept. The priestess left with the infant, closing the door softly. Yes, she thought, old Cradlelap has always had full breasts when a child needed suckling. I will ask her tomorrow. To feel him at my own nipple, my little adopted Terndasen...

Gods! If we do not find his parents, then perhaps Frostflower told the truth—I will not be able to keep the child without guilt for what we have done to the sorceress!

He was awake and crying again. He must have sensed her anxiety, as he had sensed Frostflower's a short time ago. She would have to walk a while in the dark hall, to calm him and herself, before returning to her chamber and Maldron in her bed.

Chapter 6

Meat! Good, red butcher's meat roasting somewhere to the south-east of her.

Foraging off the wildlands was not all that damn simple, not for a lone swordswoman who had spent her twenty-four years in hand-to-hand bladeplay, organized raids, and gambling or finding men to milk in her spare hours. That other time Thorn had been in the woods, after the bloody farce of a raid on what-was-his-name, there were two spearwomen in the party, and one of them had worked some time as a townwarrior in Five Roads Crossing, where she learned to bring down thieves. A warrior who knew how to throw a spear could get stags, does, wolves, rabbits, even squirrels—though the squirrels might end up pretty well splattered. With a sword—damn it, the deer and rabbits could smell her somehow before she got close enough; and it was her damn luck, not one boar or wolf had tried to charge her, not even a mangy bear. The first thing she was going to do when she reached Nedge-bottom was get a spear and learn how to throw it, one of those nice light screw-apart spears she could carry around with no extra trouble. The next thing, maybe, find someone who could show her how to set snares and make traps. Three bloody days farting around alone in these stinking woods had given Thorn a little more perspective on death and Hellbog, but the experience had not done one damn thing to fill her stomach.

Frostflower could at least have grown vegetables, pointed out which weeds and berries and mushrooms were poisonous—gods! the fluttering nightmares that one batch of toadstools had given Thorn, or maybe it had been those purplish berries. Damn things had been sour, anyway. Maybe it was the empty belly and the

103

bloody nightmares two days ago that had taught her a few new
ways to think about death and afterwards. Or maybe it was just
the damn loneliness. Smardon's fleshhooks, even a few horny
demons would be better than nobody but the flies and bugs! Even
that damn little sorceress for company ... how was Frostflower
doing by now? Halfway back to her bloody retreat, if she had
been smart and lucky. Well, if it was just being alone that had
given Thorn a different view on Hellbog, then, damn it! she could
at least have thought things over on a full stomach.

Meanwhile, she was getting closer to the roasting meat. She
could glimpse the wagon now, through the trees: a merchant's
wagon, six wheels and a bright green cloth tent over a high frame-
work. A pretty damn prosperous merchant to risk camping in the
woods instead of heading for the nearest town. Well, he was still
in south Beldrise, or maybe north Weldervrise by now; and, since
he could not have made either Frog-in-the-Millstone or Gammer's
Oak (depending on which direction he was headed) before twilight,
he was better off fairly close to Maldron's Farm than on the road
after dark.

Maldron's Farm. Yes. Still have to be careful, Thorn. After
three days of working your way around the farmer's wall, like a
lost turtle with a cracked shell, stopping to hide for five or six
hundred heartbeats at every suspicious noise, it would be a bloody
waste to let yourself get caught now. A damn bad bargain to sell
your life for a full belly before you have a fighting chance to get
the Warriors' God and maybe a few others back on your side.

She worked her way around the camp, looking over the situation. Merchant apparently in his wagon-tent—the bastard had
better come out and turn his meat pretty soon. Six—no, seven
donkeys tethered out to graze. Maybe she could slip in and untether
one, make it look as if the beast had broken loose and run away.
And then what? Eat it, or ride it? Probably eat it; she was no
stablewoman—she could make maybe one out of twenty animals
obey her. But she could not eat the whole damn carcass, and if
she left part of it ... well, the wolves and birds would get to it
and make it look like some animal's kill.

Hellbog! She would have to wait for night, for the merchant
to go to sleep, and meanwhile smell his roasting beef. Unless she
could slip close enough now—no, here he came, sauntering out
of the wagon. Damn cock of a merchant, wearing his green—was
it velvet? Hard to tell from this distance. And carrying a copper-

covered wine flask. Maybe if she jumped in and—no, she was no bloody thief!

Too bad she had taken a bath in the river a few hours ago. Stupid thing to do; but when she found the old Glant slugging its way through the forest, she was in it and scrubbing the stink and itch out of her hair and skin before she even stopped to think that a good, thick layer of dirt made a fairly decent disguise. Maybe she could rub more dirt into her hair and over her face? Well, before she went out of her way to get that itching back, she was going to move a little closer and see whether the merchant was worth it. But, gods! she was hungry for meat and a good pricking, preferably in that order. And that merchant might have a pretty long tool under his fancy green tunic.

She had not yet learned to move quietly enough to slip up on wild game, but at least her rumbling stomach and her brushing over leaves and humus did not alert the merchant or his donkeys. She got to within six or seven paces, approaching him from the side, and then squatted behind some kind of bush to be sure of what she saw. Hellbog, yes—she could handle *him*! Already the Warriors' God seemed to be back on her side.

"Spendwell, you damn pricking bastard!" she said cheerfully, standing up and striding out from behind the bush.

He looked up, his copper-covered flask still at his mouth, and half-choked. She walked over and thumped him once or twice on the back.

"Thorn! You—you're alive?"

"If that last thwack didn't feel solid, I can thump you again. Got another cushion or two for a guest?"

"In my wagon. I'll get them. Here." Wiping his mouth, he tried to give her the flask.

She glanced at a dark red drop left in the corner of his mouth. A few swallows of wine might be pleasant for a change, after what she had been through these last few days. But, damn it, she was still a hunted woman. "You know I never touch the stuff, merchant. I hope you've got a good supply of milk in that wagon of yours. Or water." Some good, clean, tasteless, civilized water from a filterer's shop would be like tingling snow in her mouth after the raw, creature-infested stuff she had been drinking from the forest streams.

"I can give you honeymilk, rosewater, or mintwater." From his tone, she wondered if he was offering the stuff or trying to sell it. From his selection, it was obvious he was a cloth merchant and not a beverage merchant.

"Gah! No plain charcoal-water? All right, bring out your damn honeymilk." Added sweetness was more palatable in milk than in water.

While waiting for Spendwell to return, Thorn settled on his cushions and cut off a hunk of beef straight from the spit. She balanced it on Stabber's point and took a bite. It was still red and dripping; but the one rabbit she had been able to kill she had chewed up raw rather than risk a fire; and, even when only half-done, beef smacked of towns and comfort.

Spendwell, coming back from the wagon, put a skin of honey-milk at her side and then had the sense to sit on the new cushions he had brought out and to keep quiet for a few minutes while she ate. There was some hope for the pricker, after all.

With an effort, Thorn stopped eating before her appetite was satisfied. Gorging after a three-day fast could be worse than getting drunk. "So that's your wagon," she remarked, looking it over. She had known he was well off, by his clothes, when she met him in Three Bridges; but this was the first time she had seen his property. "Pretty fancy stuff, merchant. Aren't you afraid of robbers, camped out here in the woods?"

"I have a safe-passage from Maldron. Ultimate payment for anyone who attacks me." Spendwell fumbled at the traders' permits hanging on the chain around his neck and finally held up a medallion in the form of three golden wheat-heads surrounding an apple.

Thorn laughed. Ultimate payment was pretty strong—hardly enough left of a poor bastard to hang up after the scaffolding was over, and Hellbog guaranteed—but death was death and Hellbog went down only so deep. "A farmer's threat is good when and if he catches whoever murdered you. And you can be sure, if they find that token around your neck after they attack, they'll hack you into so many pieces your parents wouldn't know you, and melt down your cute little safe-passage token into the measure."

Spendwell fingered the token nervously. "No . . . they wouldn't dare hurt me once they saw—"

"Then you'd better get all your other tokens off your chest and into your purse so Maldron's trinket shows up bright and clear. And paint the symbol all over your tent. Make sure they see it *before* they decide to attack. And then pray the Merchants' God nobody sees you who doesn't have anything to lose."

"What could be worse than—"

"I don't know about that, but it couldn't be so much worse than whatever Maldron already has planned for me." Thorn swallowed a few more mouthfuls of honeymilk and wiped her mouth on the back of her hand, her sleeve being too dirty to touch her lips.

"You— *You* wouldn't hurt me, Thorn?"

"Not if you're a good boy, Spendwell." She grinned. Maybe later on she would scare him out of any ideas he might hatch about betraying her; but she saw no use in shaking his guts loose now, especially if she hoped to get a good tumble out of him tonight. "Eat your dinner. It should be brown enough even for you by now."

He cut a few thin slices from the end of the roast and scooped them into his silver-plated bowl. Despite his efforts at daintiness, he slopped some juice over the edge; but otherwise he seemed to be relaxing a little. "You can depend on me, Thorn. I wouldn't mention to a stable cat that I saw you."

"Merchant's honor." She had not intended sarcasm, but he must have heard it in her voice, because he bristled in spite of his nervousness.

"Yes, I *am* an honest merchant, Thorn. You can trust me."

"I never said you weren't." Was this herself—Thorn—being conciliatory? I must be more tired than I thought, she mused. Or more desperate. Four or five days ago I would have jumped at the chance for a quarrel. "Look, I've probably ruined your cushions with this three days of forest dirt on my pants. I'll pay you someday when I've got the money."

"No—no. My gift. Nobody's likely to ask me if I saw you, anyway. Maldron's pretty well stopped looking for you."

"He *has*?"

"Oh, he still has a few spearwomen patrolling the marshlands here and there, but nobody really expects... How did you get out of those marshes, anyway?"

The swordswoman laughed. Damn baker, she had taken his measure pretty well. Maybe she should go back and put Slicer through his guts a couple of times, but the old bastard had done her a good turn when he thought he was betraying her. "I never went into the stinking marshes, my boy."

"Oh. Oh, I see." The merchant grinned. "How about some good, strong brown dye for your hair, warrior?"

"To run all over my shoulders the first damn rain I get into?"

"Thorn!" She had stung him in the merchant's honor again. "Every dye in my stock is guaranteed fast. At least, fast in cloth," he confessed. "I'm guessing it'd be fast in hair, too. You'll probably have to let the color grow out."

"Not till I'm about as far south as I can go."

"Too bad you warriors don't have beards to grow, or cut off. But with brown hair and a new tunic . . . I have some nice crimson broadcloth tunics already sewn up . . . and maybe you'd better cover up those jewels in your sword and dagger somehow . . ." Then he ruined it by adding, "You'll be able to walk all the way to the southern edgelands without anyone guessing who you are."

"I'll ride all the way to the southern edgelands with you, you bastard." She had been planning on riding with him only as far south as he was going anyway, and probably she would still cut loose from him in Nedgebottom if not before; but stone the bugger if he thought he was going to get rid of her whenever *he* wanted!

Helping herself to another small slice of beef, she sat back for a few minutes and enjoyed watching him try to find polite ways to explain how dangerous her company would be. At last she said, "If they wouldn't recognize me as a brown-haired swordswoman, you can be damn sure they won't take three looks at me as a brown-haired cooking-wench. You'll sew up some kind of skirt I can tear off the same time I draw Slicer, and I'll be your secret bodyguard and kill off the robbers for you. Now hurry up and eat." Grinning, she leaned over and squeezed his thigh. "Get some meat into you, and maybe you can get it up good for me tonight."

It was not his merchant's honor that she stung this time. "Gods!" he said. "I'll show you a few things, warrior. Tonight it's going to be you who cries off first."

"Unh?" Gods and goddesses, he'd been cocky in Three Bridges, but not this cocky. Good. "Had a couple of lessons since the Golden Rye Inn?" she asked, leaning back and picking her teeth with Stabber's point.

"Since tumbling with you, Thorn, I have pricked a sorceress."

"Careful, merchant. The goddesses don't have any use for a bloody braggart." Not until she had said this did the suspicion creep in. How many sorceresses had she seen between Gammer's Oak and Three Bridges?

"I'm not boasting, Thorn. Two days ago I pricked a sorceress."

"Either you're lying, or you got drunk and dreamed it. There isn't a gray hair on your bloody head, you damn bastard."

"Ask Maldron if I'm lying."

"Pretty damn safe witness for you as far as I'm concerned." But that silly smirk on the merchant's face was too blasted cocksure; and if anyone ever did dare screw a sorceron, sixty to one it was at a farmer's command.

"They're not all that deadly, swordswoman. You should pick yourself out a sorcerer and try it sometime. I wouldn't mind doing it myself again some day, now I know the way in."

This time he *was* boasting. That was fake satisfaction in his voice, or she had never gambled. Maybe he had done it, but Thorn would have staked the sheen-amber in Slicer's pommel he had not enjoyed it. "What was she like, Spendwell?"

"Small. A lot smaller than you, Thorn. Almost the smallest woman I ever had—no, there was that seamstress in Five Roads Crossing—"

He was talking too fast, getting too far off the subject. By the gods, he was not going to squirm off the barb. "Damn the seamstress in Five Roads Crossing. What else?"

"Soft. White. If I had her in a decent bed, she'd be perfect. . . ." His voice seemed to break a little.

"I'll show you perfection," said Thorn, thinking at that moment she would like to squeeze his neck until the windpipe cracked between her naked elbows. "I suppose she liked you as much as you liked her?"

"She—oh, gods, Thorn, she shook—I never felt a woman shake like that under me, not like . . . like a wet, frightened chicken. Even before I touched her."

"You damn motherpricker." Thorn got up and began to pace around the fire. "You can't even decide if you liked it or didn't."

"I—I *did* give her a good rhythm! As good as I gave you . . . but it took so . . . gods, if she hadn't trembled so much, if I could have gotten a better start . . . if she hadn't been clamped down—"

"I guessed that. I suppose you kept your eyes screwed up the whole bloody time? Or did you get a look at her face?"

"Her eyes . . . weren't . . . right. One blue eye, one brown eye. Maybe if they'd been right, she wouldn't have looked . . . I could have—"

"You wouldn't have been so scared and you could have hurt her more. What else did they do to her?"

"Questioned her, I think . . . and hung her. I—" He tried to swallow a bite of meat, choked, and spat it out.

"Gods!" Thorn sat again, staring into the fire. "Poor little sorceress. Poor little bitch of a sorceress."

"She—deserved it, warrior." Was he telling her, or reminding himself? Either way, she hated the damn motherpricker for it.

"What do *you* know about what she deserved, merchant?"

"She had stolen a child."

The swordswoman laughed. "She didn't steal the damn grub. She took it off my hands for me."

The silver-plated bowl began to slide from Spendwell's lap. He caught it just in time. "You? Thorn, not your . . . ?"

So he was just now remembering, eh? So that was all she had been to him, an evening's tumble and not worth remembering she had had a problem about a brat in her belly. "Yes, it was my bloody grub and I gave it to her."

"It couldn't have been! How—"

"She sorcered it out of my stomach, that's bloody how!" The warrior laughed again. Better than sniveling. "You should have seen me, merchant. Swelling up like a damn bullfrog's throat, and just about as fast." No, damn him, she was glad he had not been there. But, gods! It would have reduced him to snail-slime before he dared touch Frostflower.

Yes, now it was sinking in. This time his bowl slid all the way and upset on the ground. "Then she could have . . ." He put his hands to his hair. Maybe he was trying to feel its color, make sure it was still brown.

"I suppose she felt sorry for you, you pitiable slob."

He picked up his bowl, looked at the spilled meat, and got up to carry it away from camp and throw it out for the crows or something. If he had a dog, like Frostflower's damn mongrel . . . or did sorceri's dogs eat nothing but vegetables, too? Poor little bitch of a sorceress. If I had stuck with her . . .

Spendwell came back, sat again, examined the grease splashes on his long green velvet tunic, and began to cut himself a few more slices of meat. "Maybe she did not age me through pity," he said, "but it was because I was kind to her and because I had no more choice than she had."

"Kind to her! Next time I hear you bragging about how kind

you are to sorceresses, I'll lance your bloody balls. Oh, forget it," she added wearily, as he began to make some hot answer. "Maybe I'll let you do something rotten to me tonight. Why didn't she tell Maldron it was my brat?"

"She did tell him it was a warrior's who didn't want it. Wait, did she say it was you? Yes—because I wondered how she knew you. No, it was Maldron who mentioned your name. First he told her you were lost in the marshlands, and then asked if you were the mother—that was how it was. So that when she agreed, he could catch her lying, tell her he knew you were pulling your belt too tightly just a few hen's-hatchings ago."

That damn cow Clopmule must have told him. "She should have explained about sorcering it out of me. He might have let her off easier."

"But he would have killed the baby."

Yes. Frost would have cared more about the damn grub than about herself.

Spendwell cut off a bite of meat, but did not put it into his mouth. "Maldron himself spoke on the scaffold, just before . . . Told the crowd to spread the news. He's sending messengers all through the Tanglelands, looking for the parents."

"He won't find them." Especially when he probably intended to keep the grub himself, damn sneaking priest. So my brat's going to grow up a farmer, is he? she thought. I might as well have milked Eldrommer when he brought it up. Any other time, she would have been amused. "What about that mangy dog?"

"Dog? Oh, yes, the sorceress' dog. Maldron kept it, I think . . . yes, I know he did."

Not that it mattered. But, gods! Frostflower had loved the silly mutt. The grub, too. And maybe me, thought the warrior. And what I did to her up there beneath the baker's roofbeams . . . "You're sure she never mentioned my name until the farmer told her I was dead?"

He nodded. "I remember now. I thought she was grabbing the first name he offered her. That was it. I never thought you'd have taken up with a sorceress."

Quite a memory the bastard had. Seemed to work by suggestion and by figuring out what he must have thought at the time. Well, he had known Thorn only one night, Frostflower probably only long enough for a scared prick. And most of what he said made sense. Not justice, but sense. "When did they hang her?"

"This afternoon."

"Gods!" Maybe still alive, then . . . with bloody rags stuffed in where her guts had been, or the stones grinding their way down through her insides. At least I can sneak up and—what? Send her from the gibbet to Hellbog quicker? Well, if there was any mild spot in Hellbog, Frostflower would get it. "What gibbet?"

"The one just this side of the marshlands. They took down Flutterblade yesterday."

Flutterblade. So that was the name of the poor bugger Frost had put out of her misery on that same gibbet. Maybe the merchant could tell why Flutterblade had been hung, but Thorn was no longer much interested. "About how far from here—from where we are now?" She had a general idea, but after three days in the woods a person could begin to lose her exact bearings.

"Far enough. We don't have to worry about the gibbet-jeerers seeing you."

"I don't give a rotten damn about gibbet-jeerers." The bastards never stuck around after dark of the first evening, anyway. "Can we get there by dusk?"

"Thorn, you're not thinking—? It won't work. Maldron has two warriors watching her until the end."

"What? Damn! Why?"

"In case she confesses, names the parents."

"What was the scaffolding? Stones or gutting?"

"Neither . . . ritual disembowelment."

"*Ritual!*" Thorn jumped up and drew her dagger—not to menace Spendwell, just to get a weapon into her hand to steady the shaking. Ritual gutting—the last time she had heard of that being done was at least ten or twelve years ago, when she was still learning swordplay from old Bloodrust in All Roads West. "Ritual disemboweling! Is that what I think it is?"

"I don't know what you think it is, warrior. But it's not all that pricktickling."

"Who the Hellbog cares about your bloody prick? All it is, is branding a couple of times on the belly, isn't it?"

"Twice. In a big cross. Hip to hip." The merchant put down his bowl of meat as if there were roaches crawling in it. "I can watch a stone-swallowing with the best of them, but that . . . There was some fat landworker beside me who kept yelling and chewing a piece of stinking sausage the whole time."

"Then you'd better keep away from *real* guttings!" Thorn

grabbed a piece of firewood and began whittling it in long, hard strokes, for sheer excitement. Ritual gutting! That was supposed to be the worst scaffolding of all—took a poor bugger almost as long to die on the gibbet afterwards as if there had been no scaffolding at all, and in extra pain meanwhile. But it left a chance—Warriors' God! It left a chance for survival!

If Frost is still alive, the swordswoman thought, if I can go in there and cut her down . . . Warriors' God! Are you back on my side?

"Ritual gutting!" she repeated. "You're sure—a couple of brandings on the belly, that's all? No skin sliced, no slitting, just a couple of burns?"

"Maybe you'd like a hot sword laid flat on your bare skin?"

"Hellbog, I've had it done! Didn't I show you my thigh, where they had to burn out a crawling infection where somebody's spear gashed me?" But the reproach in his question showed he was sympathizing with Frostflower, and for that she could forgive him a lot. "Why ritual gutting?"

"There's a rumor Maldron wants her for a pricking-slave, if she confesses in time."

"Smardon's fingernails he does!"

"Maybe he only wants to make her confess so that the warriors will kill her quickly. But I saw how he looked at her, Thorn. I think the rumor—"

"Then we'll give the motherpricker a little surprise!" Later on, she would allow herself the pleasure of thinking over all the sweet, bloody things she would do to Maldron if she could. Right now, the sorceress was more important. "We want to get her down as soon as we can. Damn, we'll probably have to wait for dark. If we start now, how dark will it be when we get there?"

She looked—really looked—at Spendwell for the first time in several minutes, and almost laughed at his gape-mouthed face. "Thorn—you're not planning to—"

"You're damn right we're planning to. What the Hellbog did you think?"

"Oh, no, warrior! Not me—I'm not going back there with you!"

Damn squirming bastard, just when she was beginning to warm to him! "Merchant," she said, almost reflectively, looking at him as she picked her teeth with her dagger, "we should have another

body to hang up so people won't notice for awhile that Frostflower
is gone."

"I could make you a dummy," he said.

Thorn could not quite tell from his voice and manner, but she
hoped that he was really eager to do what he could, that he had
not yet caught the threat in her words. After all, she reminded
herself, you could not expect a man to take the chances a warrior
took. Men were not brought up with the idea that they could
always be replaced—that their services were more important than
their lives. A woman learned early that she had to take care of
herself, that her work could be taken by someone else and even
the few folk who had enjoyed her company would soon forget—
a woman's life, especially a warrior's, was her own concern, to
guard or risk as she chose. A man grew up with the idea that all
decent people, including strangers, cared for him for his own sake,
that no one else, not even another man, could ever take exactly
his place in the world, and that therefore he had a duty to the
whole futtering Tanglelands to keep his guts safe inside his body
and his body safe inside his skin. So if Thorn wanted Spendwell's
help, she had better reassure him, not scare him.

At least his bloody brains had been working. "But if you leave
the guards dead, Thorn," he went on, "even if their bodies dis-
appear . . ."

"I'm not going to kill the bitches unless they make me. Frostflower wouldn't like it." So what *was* she going to do about them?
Hellbog and stink! She threw away the stick she had whittled
down to nothing, got out her small whetstone, and began sharp-
ening Stabber as she walked around the camp. "I can dye my hair
while you're making that dummy—no, maybe I'll just wrap a
damn kerchief around my head and pretend I'm a soft little work-
woman. Just give me a length of cloth for a skirt and I'll wrap
it around loose. They'll never know the difference in the dark,
and I can shake it off any time I want."

"You're going to walk there in a skirt?"

"I'm going to ride there in your bloody wagon. How the Hell
do you think we're going to get the dummy there and bring Frostflower back?"

"I don't like—"

"Look, merchant, you'll get a chance to prick two warriors—
they're probably bored as snails, sitting out there on the edge of
the marsh, and itchy enough to milk a demon." Get the damn

guards into a drunken stupor and let the merchant prick them silly, then get a little more wine into their slimy bellies and hold their mouths and nostrils for a minute if they still aren't out. . . . Damn it, all that extra time, with the poor little sorceress dangling above them—but a scuffle, trying to pound them on the head until they conked out and maybe died—anything like that, and she might as well not bother with hanging Spendwell's dummy; the hunt would be on as soon as the guards woke up or were found.

But give them a chance to milk a good, strong, young merchant, throw a few games of dice, drink themselves to sleep on Spendwell's wine; and there was a decent chance they would keep quiet about it afterwards.

Even if the story did come out, who could say for sure that Spendwell, with his safe-passage token from Maldron himself, was the one who had cut the sorceress down, and not some sorceri-lover who came by when the guards were sleeping on duty?

The swordswoman's glance fell on a patch of purplish berries. Same rotten things she had eaten two days ago after convincing herself they were not dreamberries because they were not spotted. She snapped off a stem of the things, looked them over again, and grinned. If it had been these damn berries and not the toad-stools that gave her the bloody nightmares, Maldron's bitches were in for a bad night.

It was almost dark when they came to the gibbet. The last of the rabble was gone—maybe well before dusk, maybe only a few moments ago, but long enough so that there was no sign of them. The two warriors were coughing, grumbling, and throwing dice in the light of a smoke-fire. Better put a few cakes of smudge-incense on the flames and cough, than get chewed up by the marsh bugs.

Two blobs of orange glow, just bright enough to show the smoke rising from them, stood on barely visible tripods near the gibbet. Someone had set up smudge-incense pots to keep the bugs off the sorceress. Thorn squeezed Slicer's pommel, feeling the sheen-amber beneath the cloth of her clumsy, improvised skirt. For the first time in maybe years, her jaw ached with emotion. Then she thought of Maldron having the smoke-pots set out because he hoped to cut Frost down to be his pricking-slave.

"Hey! Merchant?" Maldron's bitches were already hailing the wagon, even before Spendwell slowed it.

"And an honest merchant." Spendwell pulled his donkeys to a stop and leaned forward, resting his elbows on his knees.

"Pretty damn late for an honest merchant to be out on the road. Sure you're not a bloody robber?"

"If honest merchants were never caught on the road after dark, who would the robbers attack?" he replied.

Thorn leaned forward and put one hand on Spendwell's arm. That was the kind of thing a merchant's woman would do if she got nervous. She could feel his muscles shaking. "Who are you?" she called. "How do we know *you're* not robbers?" Bad. She was supposed to be some rabbity merchant's woman. Her voice should have shaken like Spendwell's muscles.

"Do robbers wait around beside gibbets to get eaten by marsh bugs?" The speaker came forward, a medium-tall spearwoman with an ordinary face (but all faces were ordinary in bad light) and a voice that sounded as if she should clear her throat. "We're Maldron's women, watching a damn sorceress to death for him."

Frostflower was just a black shape above and between the smoke-pots, high enough so that she could have been hanging by wrists instead of shoulders and her feet would not have touched ground. Either the hood had fallen over her face or she hung with her back to the road, because the only whiteness was her hands tied together across belly or buttocks. She hung still, motionless—not a twitch, not a moan. Maybe it was the bad light—but Thorn had seen enough poor buggers dangling from the gibbet to know how each jerk swayed when a person was off the ground.

"How do you know she's not already dead?" This time, damn it, Thorn's voice seemed to shake a little. No honest woman's voice should shake when she asked a question like that about a sorceron.

Maldron's bitch laughed and slapped at bugs. "Come have a look."

"Can I bring my wagon off the road?" asked Spendwell.

"Not unless you want to get mired. Cutbone and me aren't here to help push you out if your bloody wheels get stuck."

The merchant stopped his wagon on the edge of the road, got down, and hobbled the lead donkeys. Thorn forced herself to wait for him to come back and help her down. She swatted savagely at the bugs and itched in her wimple and skirt, thinking a steady stream of curses.

Spendwell came back and handed her down. They followed

Maldron's spearwoman over the spongy earth to the gibbet. From this angle, Thorn could make out the little white blot of Frostflower's chin beneath the draping of her hood. Still no sign of life.

Maldron's warrior twirled her spear and poked the butt into Frostflower's stomach. Spendwell clutched Thorn's arm to keep her from grabbing the sword beneath her skirt.

"That's not dead meat," said the spearwoman, although after quivering with the blow Frostflower again hung still. "Want to try it yourself?"

"I wouldn't know the difference," said Thorn, with Spendwell squeezing her arm to remind her not to smash her sword into Maldron's fathermilking bitch.

"Hey, Clist!" shouted the other warrior, Cutbone, who had stuck to the smoke-fire instead of coming out where the bugs were thicker. "His Reverence said weapons off the bitch."

"Who's going to tell his Reverence? Especially if we can get the demon's-turd to talk." Clist raised her spear again and struck the shaft across Frostflower's back. This time the head jerked up slightly, with a low moan.

"How about it, sorceress? Ready to name the brat's parents?"

Frostflower's head had fallen forward and the victim was silent again, as if only her body and not her mind had reacted. You damn fathermilker! Thorn thought at the spearwoman; and then, switching the voice in her brain to the sorceress—Hold on, Frost! Just hold on a few bloody moments and we'll have you down!

She did not know if she was glad or sorry for Spendwell's hand cringing on her arm to keep her from putting Slicer through Maldron's rotten bitches.

"Come on back to the fire, damn you!" shouted Cutbone in a bored voice. "No sense standing out there getting chewed up."

"We're not, you lazy cow. The damn sorceress has it better than we do at the fire—her Ladyship's incense pots are better than the stinking smudge-cakes his Reverence gave us."

"Unh? Maybe you'd rather hang up there with her than roll a few more games?"

"All right, all right, coming." Clist wiped her arm across the bottom of her nose and turned back to the merchant and his supposed woman. "Well, had your bellyfill of gawking? No sense gawking at a damn sorceress if you're not going to poke her around a little."

They followed the spearwoman to the fire. "You're sure she's power-stripped?" said Thorn, looking for something to say that would both explain her staring up at Frostflower and keep her from cursing Clist and Cutbone aloud.

"If she wasn't power-stripped, you think she'd be hanging there? Pricker who did the job even looked a little like you, merchant," said Clist.

"Na," said Cutbone, "that poor slob didn't have a woman to travel with him. Too stinking tight-pursed even to hire a swordswoman. Who are you, merchant?"

"From the south," Spendwell replied, as if he had misunderstood the question. "On our way up from Middle Lorn. Let me get you a sample of my Southvines purple."

He hurried back to the wagon. Damn cringing bastard. Thorn thought she had convinced him it would be safer to use his own name, take advantage of Maldron's favor and the little suspicion that would attach to the man who pricked the sorceress. Instead, he had shied out on her, gone back to his own idea of trying to stay anonymous and hoping they would not recognize him. And there was not a damn thing she could do about it now except play along. She heaped up a pile of faggots at a little distance from the fire and sat, trying to go down gingerly, like a damn dainty craftswoman.

"Hey, merchant's woman! You play dice?"

"No." She refused without thinking, because for once in her life she did not want to play. Only after she spoke did she realize that by refusing she had both kept herself in the shadows on the other side of the smoke and helped insure that Maldron's warriors would not later connect her with the ever-gambling Thorn.

"Come on in closer to the fire anyway. Don't sit out there for the bugs."

"I'd rather face the bugs than—the smoke." Where the Hellbog was that bloody Spendwell? Gods, if he dawdled around much longer, she was going to slip back into cursing aloud. How long did it take to find the damn flask? They had left it handy, between two bolts of cloth near the seat—Thorn could have found it quicker herself.

Well, maybe it only seemed long to her. Cutbone and Clist were not complaining yet.

Clist threw the dice, cursed a bad roll, and looked at Thorn again. "Hey, merchant's woman! How's your man for milking?"

So they were going to claim warriors' privilege on her? Good; that was one way she had planned to help get them woozy and drunk . . . but how the Hell would they expect a good little common wife to react? Proud of the honor? Jealous? She had always been on the taking end of warriors' privilege before—and not too often at that, preferring unattached males, especially ones who had not been milked for several days. "Always has plenty for me," she said.

"Throw you cow's eyes for first go at him, Clist," said Cutbone.

Thorn stared from the quiet figure barely visible on the gibbet to the swearing, grunting, stinking warriors, squatting like rutty toads over their dice, so much alike in their bloody filth that sometimes she was not sure which was Clist and which was Cutbone. Warriors' God! she thought, suddenly disgusted with her whole way of life. *She* might be sitting there dicing instead of either Clist or Cutbone, and anybody else looking on would hardly know the difference.

Her hands twitched on the hilts of Slicer and Stabber beneath her skirt. She could almost have gutted Maldron's women for no other excuse than their likeness to herself.

Spendwell reached the fire just as Cutbone was crowing over a successful toss. "Ready for a tumble, merchant?"

"Honored." Spendwell went around to their side of the fire. "Delighted. I'm always ready to roll a warrior—two at a time, if you like." As he bent to give them the flask of wine, Thorn saw his grin in the firelight and thought, Gods! The greedy bastard means it.

"Fine with me," said Clist, who had lost the throw for first tumble.

"Na," said Cutbone. "One of us has to stay on guard."

"Who the Hellbog's going to come and take the bloody sorceress down?"

"Just in case she talks, you damn quarter-wit."

"Why don't you warriors drink some of my fine wine," said Spendwell, "and settle the question while I bring a blanket?"

That was Spendwell—too damn fastidious to roll a couple of warriors on the bare ground, even if the bitches were almost as dirty as the ground themselves. "I can keep an ear on her for you," said Thorn.

"Thanks, merchant's woman. We'll even leave enough of him to grow back for you in a couple of days."

One of Maldron's warriors took a noisy swig of wine and tossed the flask to the other. "Hey, merchant! How much are you going to charge us for your bloody wine?"

Already more than halfway to the wagon, Spendwell paused. "For that flask," he shouted back, "nothing but your own pleasure and mine. For a second flask, three coppers."

They would not get a second flask like the first. Thorn had squeezed the berries only into the one. Warriors' God—no. No, God of the Sorceri, make their throats nice and dry so they drink it all, and let it be those same bloody berries that gave me the fluttering nightmares!

"Fair enough at the price. Let's have it again before you drink the blasted thing dry, damn you, Clist."

"Hey, merchant's woman, want a swig?"

"Quiet, quarter-brain. Let her and her man drink up their own bloody stock."

Thorn smiled grimly. All the gods, Warriors' God, Sorceri's God, even the half-demon Goddess of Greed seemed to be on her side. She watched Clist and Cutbone guzzle down their free wine as if each was afraid that unless she drank fast her comrade would get more.

The merchant strolled back, wandered around to find a suitable patch of ground, spread out his blanket with dainty care, doing everything slowly, giving them plenty of time to finish the flask. Even if the purplish berries were not dream-poison, the wine itself was strong—Spendwell's best Southvines purple, boiled down a little to make it even more potent. Clist and Cutbone were swaying when they got up and began to fumble with their belts. Damn fools! Swizzling themselves silly. At least Thorn did not share that habit with them.

"Hey! Bring it here!" shouted the spearwoman, her voice slurring. "Naked out there an' the buggers'll eat us raw."

"Stay in the fire an' get seen milking when we should be washing?" said Cutbone.

"Who's going to come by, you damn bish?"

"Some honest mershant, some robber . . . never know. Take th' smudge-pots over there. Few buggers on her face'll do the damn sorceress good."

"Good. Hey, merchant's woman. Get those smudge-pots an' bring 'em over to th' blanket."

"Carry your own damn smudge-pots," said Thorn.

It was a stupid slip to make, but Maldron's warriors only laughed, no doubt thinking she was simply jealous. "Better tell your rutty woman we'll leave enough of you for her!" one of them called to Spendwell.

"The question is what I'll leave of you," the merchant called back. His jollity was strained. If he were close enough, Thorn knew he would squeeze her arm again or mutter some warning in her ear. Watch it yourself, merchant, she thought. Make sure you don't get too bloody nervous to show them a good time until the wine gets them. Or until I have to pinch their mouths and nostrils to make them black out.

She watched Spendwell carry over the smudge-pots and arrange them on either side of the blanket, leaving Frostflower to the bugs. Maldron's bitches stripped and began rolling each other, wine and exertion keeping them warm as they waited for Spendwell.

Completely disgusted, Thorn located a faggot that still had one end unburning and picked it out of the fire to hold like a torch. She found a couple cakes of smudge-incense, crumbled one onto the burning end of her faggot, put the other into her tunic pocket, and walked over to the gibbet.

"Hey, mershant's woman! Going to tickle her toes?"

Damn it, Spendwell, hurry up and start screwing them! If I hear "Hey, merchant's woman!" once more I'll ram this torch down their bloody throats. "I'm just going to keep watch for you."

"Sure you wouldn't rather wash us? Maybe learn something!" They laughed again. It was a big, drunken joke to them. Hellbog, Thorn had tumbled in groups of four and five. She even remembered with dull wonder that she had enjoyed it at the time. Now all that seemed important was how aware or unaware Frostflower might be of the things going on below.

Spendwell got himself stripped and then lunged in between Maldron's bitches. They grunted like pigs, and, from that distance, looked more like white grubs wiggling together on an overturned log than like humans. Turning her back on them, Thorn lifted the torch higher, trying to hold it so the smudge would protect Frostflower without choking or singeing her.

Nearly beneath the sorceress, Thorn could now make out most of her face. It was paler than ever, the eyes closed, the mouth slightly open, the upper lip clotted with dry mucus. The smudge-pots had not kept all the bugs away. A score of bite-welts stood up plain and ugly.

The sorceress hung like a plummet, the long ends of the ropes binding her wrists criss-crossed down around her legs. Unless their bound hands were so anchored, hanging folk had been known to writhe until the rope slipped from beneath their armpits and tangled around their arms and wrists. But Frostflower was not writhing, not moving at all. Thorn could not even see any rise and fall of the chest beneath the dark robe.

All but three of Frostflower's fingers were stiff with bandages, but the backs of her hands were bare above the knuckles. The flesh felt cold and slightly leathery. Thorn pressed harder, searching for the pulse. She seemed to feel something—but it might be only the echo of blood in her own fingertips.

She stretched her arm still higher and forced herself to feel what she could of Frostflower's belly, dreading to find the hard little knots of stones, after all. The skin was covered by layers of cloth, but the stomach seemed flat and empty. It also seemed to have a very slight movement upwards and downwards, but Thorn could feel this only when she pressed as hard as she dared.

She could reach no higher. She took comfort in the fact that the eyes were closed. People usually died with their eyes open and staring. She could not remember which of Frostflower's eyes was blue and which was brown, but she was glad they were closed. Even had they been open in a dead woman's stare, Thorn would not have liked to see them fixed on the scene she could hear behind her—Spendwell and the two bitches thrashing around on their bloody blanket.

The grunts finally subsided. Eventually a few wet snores began to replace them. Thorn glanced around. One white form was stirring, beginning to pull on its dark clothes again. "Spendwell?" she whispered.

"Shhh!" He got his clothes back on, turned the edges of the blanket up over the sleeping warriors, then picked his way toward the gibbet. "One of them could have been awake," he whispered angrily. "You could have given us away, calling my name like that."

"You heard it because it's your own damn silly name. Those drunken cows would've thought it was anything." Thorn had intended to climb up the gibbet and untie Frostflower, letting the merchant catch her; but, watching his arms tremble as he refastened his belt and slapped at bugs, she changed her plan. "All right, get up there and untie her."

"Me? I thought you were going to—"

"I'm going to catch her. I don't want you dropping her, you damn bugger. Or running away if a bloody owl hoots."

"I'm exhausted, Thorn! Those randy warriors—"

"*You're* exhausted, you horny bastard!"

"At least give them a little while longer, make sure they're not going to wake up."

Frostflower had not moved since Maldron's fathermilking bitch struck her across the back, and Spendwell wanted to wait some more. "Get up there, you motherpricker!"

"All right, all right." Backing away from her torch, he hurried to the left-hand ladder and climbed it almost fast enough to satisfy the swordswoman. He hesitated, however, before climbing over onto the top, crosspiece ladder. "Heights make me dizzy."

"I'll burn the damn thing down with you on it."

He edged out along the crosspiece, trying to keep in the dead center of a ladder barely wider than his hips. Midway to the sorceress, he paused. "How are you going to catch her with that torch in your hand?"

Thorn took a few steps to one side and jabbed the bottom of the faggot into the mucky ground. By the time she returned, he had nearly reached the rope. Thorn clasped Frostflower's knees.

On the blanket, one of the warriors groaned loudly. Spendwell's jerk sent a vibration through the solidly-planted gibbet. "Fall off and I'll kick your kneecaps in," said Thorn. "Now hurry up."

"I need light."

"You think I'm going to climb up there and hold the bloody torch for you?"

There was a shriek from one of the drugged warriors. Thank the gods, Spendwell stayed on the ladder. Thorn listened for a few moments, holding her breath. Hearing only a few grunts and a couple of moans, she turned her head and looked toward the blanket. Maldron's warriors were hunched up beneath the cloth— dark blots with only a whitish leg showing. One of the blots bunched together and thrashed another limb out from beneath its covering.

Thorn chuckled. "Looks like those were the nightmare-berries, all right. Hurry it up, you turd."

"Damn it, Thorn, these knots are tight."

"You've got a knife?"

"I thought you wanted to save the rope to hang the dummy."

"We'll splice it together." Maldron's women were safe, not likely to wake up out of their nightmares for a while; and Thorn was able to hold Frostflower up a little and take the strain from her armpits—but she still wanted the sorceress down as soon as possible. Besides, the gods alone knew how long Spendwell with his damn fear of everything from heights to his own heartbeat could stay up there.

One end loosened. The body seemed to shudder before Thorn could adjust her grip. Carefully she eased Frost downwards, holding her now at a slant, one arm still round her knees, the other shifting to her small hips.

"Do I have to cut the other side, too?"

"Yes, damn it, what did you think?" That they were going to give the sorceress ropeburns unstringing her like a bloody bead? Thorn braced her feet as wide as the damn skirt would allow and tightened her grip, trying not to think of how limp Frostflower seemed. Maldron's warriors had more or less subsided, but an occasional groan, scream, or few seconds of panting showed they were only sinking a bit deeper. It was almost worth having had the nightmares herself, to know what those bitches were going through now.

The body of the sorceress flopped forward across Thorn's shoulder. At least she was not stiff—better limp than stiff! A small object hit the marsh weeds near them. "I dropped my knife," the merchant called weakly.

"You can find it when you get down." Mercilessly, Thorn left him to make his own way off the gibbet, while she knelt and lowered Frostflower to the ground.

The sorceress' black robe had been wrapped and belted around her naked body with no undersmock. Thorn was able to work her hand beneath the cloth directly to Frostflower's chest. Pressing her fingers to the skin above the sternum, she felt, at last, a heartbeat—weak and slow, but a heartbeat she knew was Frost's and not the thud of her own blood beating through her fingertips.

"If she's dead—" began Spendwell, halfway down the side ladder.

"No, you damn idiot, she's still alive!"

"Then get her into the wagon."

Thorn scowled at him, then gathered up her friend. Her make-shift skirt ripped off as she stood. She kicked it away and left it for Spendwell to pick up and bring along. Bloody bastard, so damn nervous about his own guts, all he cared about was getting the sorceress out of sight. . . . No, she admitted sullenly to herself, the real reason she was angry at him this time was because for once he had seemed to have Frostflower's welfare more at heart than she—get the sorceress inside and make her comfortable right away. Thorn should have thought of it first.

By feel and memory she deposited Frostflower on the bed of cushions and blankets they had arranged in the wagon. She groped for one of Spendwell's expensive candles, with its wide-lipped holder to keep wax from dripping on the merchandise. She lit it as quickly as she could, annoyed that her flint, iron, and punk were so small and hard to hold.

She was not going to hurt Frost's hands and wrists any more by working at the knots—she cut the cord. The sorceress moaned as it loosened, leaving grainy, blood-speckled impressions on her skin. Thorn swore softly as she unwound the cord from hands and legs before easing the sorceress out of her muddy, sweaty robe. Hearing Spendwell climb into the wagon behind her, she said, "Stay out of here, you turd."

"I'm exhausted, Thorn—I couldn't even get it up for *you* right now." He dropped her skirt beside her and looked over her shoulder. "Gods!"

Thorn had uncovered Frostflower's belly, with the two long, blistering burn-welts across it. "You shouldn't have sneaked a look," said the warrior. "Where's that damn water and salve? Warriors' God! They padded her armpits." Underneath the robe, wads of linen cloth had kept the rope from pressing as deeply as it might have into the flesh. Whether this had been meant as a strange kind of mercy or as a means to prolong death Thorn could not tell, but maybe it had cushioned the veins a little.

Spendwell put the water, salve, and a pile of rags torn from his cheapest cloth within Thorn's reach. She handed him Frost-flower's black robe. It had been torn top and bottom and mended carelessly, big, sloppy stitches just good enough for gibbet-bait. "Put it on your dummy," she said, bending to take off Frost-flower's sandals.

Spendwell had strapped the waterskin beneath the belly of one of his donkeys so that the water would not be ice-cold when Thorn needed it. Remembering how the sorceress had washed her off after getting the grub out of her, Thorn wiped her own fingers thoroughly with the tepid water before wetting a new rag to begin on Frostflower. She swore again, not so softly, when she rolled her over and found the line of livid three-cornered incisions in the small of her back.

The wounds on Frostflower's torso cleaned and rubbed with salve, Thorn covered her partially with a smooth blanket, wiped her face clean and salved her lips, cuts and insect bites, then tackled her hands. The swelling and blotching had already pretty well gone of itself, with the blood flowing more freely again. After a little more rubbing of palms, wrists, and back surfaces, Thorn gingerly began working the bandages off Frostflower's fingers, one by one. The sight of the first fingertip made her stomach churn with rage. She would not dare touch the nails yet—maybe swish the fingertips gently through a bowl of warm water and prop Frostflower's hands on a cushion to dry before rebandaging. "Here," she told Spendwell, thrusting the bandage casing back to him. "Start getting 'em on the dummy's hands."

"It's not going to look right. They'll see they're stuffed gloves as soon as they look." Spendwell had not stuck around to watch the hanging. He and Thorn had hoped Frostflower's hands would be mittened or so corded around as to leave little flesh visible. Thorn shrugged. It could not be helped, and the dummy had been a stupid idea anyway—who the Hellbog thought it up?—but the more time before the substitution was discovered, the more chance they would have.

"Splash 'em with a little wine." That should make the kidskin look blotchy, a little like blood-staled flesh. "Now. Before you get the damn bandages on the fingers. And cord them up tight." That should make the stuffed gloves bulge as if bloated.

"It still won't work, Thorn."

"Damn you, merchant, just do it and let me alone a blasted moment!"

Every fingernail beneath its bandage was caked with dry blood; carefully as Thorn worked off the cloth sheaths, a couple of nails started to bleed again. But . . . Hellbog, they must have been washed before the damn farmers' bandages were put on—washing them again could wait a while longer. Thorn wound a clean rag mittenlike around each hand and slipped Frost's arms beneath the blanket.

Then she turned to Spendwell, who had the dummy robed and its fingers bandaged and was now trussing the cord around its legs, glancing nervously at its glove hands. "All right, it's about the right size," he said, "and all right, the hood covers its head and the hem hangs down far enough—" The soles of Frostflower's sandals showed and that was all you could see of the feet. "—but the *hands*, Thorn, the hands!"

"They look fine to me."

"In this light—maybe. But in the morning . . ."

"All right, let me think." Damn silly dummy, what the Hell-stink was the bloody use fussing around with it? "Get me some flour. And a little dirt."

With flour, mud, and spit, after a few attempts she made an imitation of bird shit and dribbled it onto the dummy's hands. In the candlelight it looked fairly convincing, enough for her to re-assure Spendwell that Maldron's women were not likely to haul the body down for too close a look. They splashed some of the fake bird droppings elsewhere on the robe. If the warriors noticed at all, and if they did not look too closely, they would thank the birds for a good joke; and meanwhile it made Spendwell a little calmer. Thorn did not remind him that the first time one of the fathermilkers whacked the dummy, even if it had fooled them up until then, all this work would be so much donkey shit.

The merchant had done a good job of splicing the ropes. They carried out the dummy and this time Thorn climbed the gibbet, letting Spendwell stay on the ground. Maldron's bitches were hardly groaning at all by now, sweating deep in their well-deserved nightmares. On the way back to the wagon, Thorn chuckled. The smudge-pots would not burn much longer without feeding. Those two cows would wake up in the morning too itchy with bug bites to think about Frostflower for awhile.

Spendwell unhobbled the donkeys while Thorn climbed back into the wagon. The merchant had insisted on pinching out the candle before they left to hang the dummy; Spendwell listened to too many stories about merchants' goods turning into ashes because someone left a lighted candle or lamp inside the wagon and a donkey stamped and jolted it off its stand. Thorn kindled the light again, her fire-striking equipment not quite so hard to get hold of this time.

Frostflower's head was turned toward the sound and light. Her eyes were open, blue and brown, bloodshot but calm. No, not calm—hopeless. Not hopeless, either . . . expressionless. Gods and demons! Had they cracked her mind?

The warrior knelt, holding the candlestick in her left hand, and laid her right palm gently on the sorceress' forehead. A vague puzzlement came into Frostflower's face. "Thorn?" she whispered.

"Yes. Thorn." Feeling an ache in her own jaw, the swordswoman put the candlestick on its stand and patted Frostflower's face with a dampened cloth. Puzzlement was emotion, and recognition was a sign of sanity. "You're safe now, Frost. They're not going to hurt you any more."

"Douse the light, Thorn!" called Spendwell, shaking the wagon as he climbed to the seat. "I'm not driving with a burning candle inside."

At the sound of his voice Frostflower suddenly shuddered and a look of fear crossed her face. Of course—Spendwell was the bastard who had pricked her. "He's helping us," said Thorn. "He's on our side this time, Frost. He's not going to hurt you again."

The sorceress sighed and closed her eyes. Thorn pinched out the candle flame and climbed back through the wagon to the driver's seat. "Slow and easy," she muttered to Spendwell. "And stay out of her sight and hearing until I tell you otherwise."

He chucked to the animals and they began moving stupidly down the road, leaving gibbet, marsh bugs, and Maldron's bitches behind. For several moments Spendwell guided his beasts in silence. Then he said, "I've done a lot more to save her tonight than I did to hurt her. And if Maldron catches us . . ."

"If Maldron catches us, he'll take back his safe-passage token. Then you can tell him I forced you and he'll probably let you off with two or three lashes."

"You *did* force me, warrior."

"Cheer up, merchant. Maybe by the time you leave us, she'll be able to look at you." Spendwell was not such a bad companion, after all. With a little bullying, he made a fairly reliable helper; he kept a good supply of sweet salve for cuts and burns; and that had been a pretty damn clever idea of his to warm the skin of water by strapping it beneath the donkey.

Thorn reached out and gave Spendwell's knee a friendly squeeze. She felt full of guts and ready to slice Maldron down with his whole damn barracksful of fighting bitches. The Warriors' God was on her side again, and Frostflower was going to be all right.

There was no reason she should not be all right. Her mind was still good—she had emotion and recognition in there, and spirits would come back with health. The padding beneath her armpits had kept the blood from stagnating too badly, and it was flowing again in her arms and hands. The burns on her belly, the cuts on her back, were ugly but not dangerous; Thorn had undergone worse in getting treated for battle injuries. With careful bandaging, her fingernails should heal and tighten smoothly. When the swordswoman, judging the shock had worn off sufficiently, began to feed her, Frostflower obediently swallowed a cupful of wine and almost a bowlful of breadsops in milk; and she kept it all down.

The signs should have been good, but something was wrong. More and more often Thorn left the seat beside Spendwell and crawled back to feel Frostflower's face and, if she seemed to be awake, try to get some response out of her. Quit pestering the poor bitch, the warrior kept repeating to herself. Wouldn't *you* want a little undisturbed rest? You're like a damn brat poking a sick bird to death. There's nothing wrong with Frost that wouldn't be wrong with anyone who'd gone through what she's gone through.

Nevertheless, about midnight Thorn made Spendwell stop the wagon completely. "We have to keep going," he protested. "If I fall asleep now, I won't wake up until daylight."

"I'll wake you up." The swordswoman crawled into the wagon. She had not lit the candle since they left the gibbet, not even to mix the breadsops and milk—warriors could always get around in the dark—but she lit it now.

Frostflower did not open her eyes at the light. She did not open them until Thorn felt her cheeks. The whites of her eyes were beginning to clear, and there was little pain in her gaze—too little, considering her wounds—but there was too damn much . . . *patience*.

"It is you," the sorceress whispered. Her lips were dry and cracking again. Thorn rubbed more salve on them.

"How are you feeling, Frost?"

"I am grateful you escaped from the marshlands." The sorceress closed her eyes once more.

Had the poor little innocent guessed how Burningloaf betrayed them both? Probably not, and now was no time to tell her, to blow out her faith in an old family friend. "Hellbog, it'll take more than a few stinking marshes to keep me down. Look, can I get you anything? Another cup of wine?"

The sorceress lay without replying. For a moment Thorn half-feared she had stopped breathing. She bent forward and felt Frost-flower's chest for the heartbeat. Frostflower did not move at her touch, but she opened her eyes again and gazed up Thorn's arm to her face.

"How about it, Frost? You have to say this for the blasted merchant, he only gets the best. Another cup of wine?"

"Thorn. You made me promise, once, that if I found you . . . hanging . . . I would speed your death."

Thorn shivered. The night was getting cold. She put a second blanket over the sorceress. "That was if you found me with my guts full of stones or dropping out. Not if I got hung up whole."

The sorceress made a movement beneath her coverings, as if trying to lift her arm, but gave up in weakness. "Hold my hand. Only a moment."

Gingerly, Thorn pushed away the blankets and took her friend's hand.

"Hold it tighter."

"I don't want to hurt your fingers."

"It doesn't matter. Hold tighter."

Thorn squeezed as hard as she dared, holding Frostflower's hand below the knuckles. After a few moments Frostflower sighed and closed her eyes. "Thank you, Thorn."

The warrior lowered the sorceress' arm again to her side and tucked the blankets around her once more. She could not hear Frostflower's breathing; she could only see her chest moving slightly. Thorn pinched out the candle flame and returned to Spendwell. He was snoring. She poked him in the ribs—hard—and he awoke with a grunt.

"Turn around."

"Unh?"

"Turn around. We're heading back south."

"Thorn, are you crazy? We can't—She's dead? You want to hang her up again?"

"Damn your guts, keep your voice down. She's not dead yet

and even if she were that's the last thing I'd do to her. We're taking her to Frog-in-the-Millstone."

"What? I thought you wanted to get her back up to her retreat?"

"That's ten days away, maybe seven or eight if you smear acid on your damn donkeys' rumps. It's too long. Besides, I've never been there—Windslant or Windhaven or whatever the Hellbog they call it. I know where her friends are in Frog-in-the-Millstone."

"Doesn't she have any friends in Gammer's Oak?"

"She thought she had, and if I see the motherpricker again I'll probably cut out his rotten bladder. Now turn around and we can be there before daybreak."

Spendwell turned around with no more argument. Thorn knew he had never much liked the original plan of getting Frostflower all the way to her retreat in the mountains. Once they had her safely hidden in the weavers' house, Thorn could send him on his way south, looking innocent as a peapod.

It was a big gamble, but the swordswoman was gambling now whatever she did. She was reasonably sure she could trust the weavers, while eight or ten days—assuming they got all the way to the mountains without trouble—was just too damn long to wait before getting someone else's opinion, some older friends' help.

They sat around the table: Thorn, Spendwell, Yarn and Bright-weave. Small Spider, the girl, was sitting beside Frostflower down in the grain cellar, where six days ago the sorceress had gotten the brat out of Thorn's belly.

The swordswoman remembered that Brightweave had a crooked nose and a scar on his lip where a spindle had caught him in a freak accident thirty years ago; and that, although she was ten or twelve years younger than her husband, Yarn had graying hair. No one could have told it by the light, which was one tiny flame on a wick in a bull's horn half-full of oil, set in the middle of the table. They were making sure nobody outside saw the light through the windows. They might as well not have had any light at all. They talked in murmurs.

"You're sure she's lost her powers?" It was the third or fourth time Thorn had said this; but she still could not quite believe the ability to grow a grub like that, and to grab a bolt of lightning in the air, could just vanish after one pricking. Gods, it had not even been Frostflower's fault!

"It's never happened that a sorceron kept any power afterwards," said Brightweave wearily. "The final blasting, and that is the end of it for them."

"Hellstink, Frost didn't even get in her final blast."

"A few sorceri have escaped after blasting their attackers," said Yarn, "but only right afterwards, only if there were no more than two or three folk trying to recapture them. I have never heard of any others who were saved from the gibbet."

"Damn it, getting off the bloody gibbet should be worth something to her!" Next they'll be telling me I shouldn't have cut her down, thought Thorn.

The weaver-woman sighed. "Those who escape to their retreats after losing their power are always pitiable men and women. They seem to age very quickly, and die soon."

"How do you know so much about them?" asked Spendwell.

"Frostflower is not the only sorceron we have befriended," said Yarn. "One of my own childhood friends went to join them."

"At first I let my wife keep up the friendship because I thought it would be better to be at peace with powers like theirs," said Brightweave. "Now I know the sorceri for kindly, peaceable folk. If our daughter were to fall sick again—gods forbid!—I'd trust her to a sorceron before I'd trust her to a farmer's own physician."

"Yes, but why the Hellbog do they shrivel up and die? Gods, I wouldn't mind having a little power like that myself, but the rest of us don't mope ourselves to death because we don't have it."

The craftsman heaved his elbows onto the table and leaned forward. "Warrior, suppose you were to lose your hands?"

"If it means so much to them," said Spendwell, "why do they come out into the Tanglelands? Why not stay in their retreats where they're safe?"

"Why do I fight in raids and risk getting myself cut to pieces, merchant?" said Thorn. Brightweave had made his point. "Why do you go traveling from town to bloody town and risk losing everything to robbers?"

"There is more to it than that." Yarn moved her hand around the table in front of her as if she were drawing circles in the shadows. "They have a third power—a sort of ability to send their minds—their spirits—I don't quite understand it—to other places. But they must spend some time in real travel among other folk before they can learn to do this. Frostflower was traveling in order to learn the third power."

Why would anyone who could grow a mess of vegetables in a few moments and grab a bolt of lightning to cook them want to send her brain off somewhere sightseeing? "And she queered her chances in order to get that bloody grub out of me," said Thorn. "Look, you're sure they all just mope away and die?"

"I've heard of one who didn't," said the weaver. "Sometimes, you see, a pair of them will decide to marry and give up their powers so that they can have children. This young sorcerer, it seems, had already been considering mating with a sorceress. After the warriors forced him, he escaped and went back to his sorceress."

"That's it, then!"

"No," said Yarn. "He already had a woman inclined to sacrifice her powers and bear his children. Frostflower has no one."

"Impossible!" Spendwell sounded genuinely surprised. "You mean all those sorcerers—can't they see what's under their noses?"

"There aren't so many sorcerers as that, merchant," replied the weaver.

"And Frostflower would not ask any of them to give up his powers for her sake," said his wife.

"Then I'll bloody well find one for her myself!"

"She would not thank you, warrior. I have talked of it with her, before . . . all this happened." Yarn rubbed her palm on the table. "Several years ago she felt much drawn to a sorcerer who came to her retreat to study with old Moonscar."

"And he wasn't drawn to her?" said Spendwell.

"He was, but each was more strongly drawn to the study of their powers. He returned to his own place in the western mountains, and neither of them has regretted their decision."

Thorn was not often jealous, but it seemed Frostflower had done a damn lot more confiding in the weaver-woman than in her. "How the Hellbog do you know all about it?"

"My childhood friend. Silverflake she became when she went to the sorceri. She is at Windslope, Frostflower's retreat. I met Frostflower there."

All right, that was a little better. The swordswoman had not realized Yarn was quite that long-standing a friend. But it did not solve Frost's problem. "Look, is there any chance that maybe our horny merchant here put a baby into her?"

"No," said Yarn. "Her flow of blood was only ending the day

she left us to go on to Three Bridges—the day before she met you, warrior."

Thorn sighed. One time only, and in those conditions . . . well, it would have been about as long a chance as throwing a perfect score at Falling Doubles on the first try. All the same, give Frost another little bugger to play with her tits and dirty its breechcloths for her to change, and maybe . . .

"Thorn!" said Spendwell. "Maybe I could . . . try again?"

"Smardon's fleshhook! Try it and I'll twist your balls off for you, merchant."

His head seemed to droop a little. "Just a thought," he muttered. "If having a baby will bring her out of it . . ."

"Not *your* baby, you turd." Thorn turned her head in Yarn's direction. "How do you know this idiot sorcerer hasn't regretted it? What's his name and where's his retreat?"

"He has developed the third power, swordswoman. He visits with old Moonscar and other sorceri in Windslope who also have it."

"Unh. Well, maybe Frost wouldn't be able to stand him touching her now anyway, any more than she could stand our slimy bastard of a—"

"Thorn! I was forced into it, too!" His voice was quivering. "After all I've done tonight, I think I deserve—"

"All right, forget it." Maybe she *was* riding him a little too hard. "I'll give you a good milking myself once this is over. The milking of your life." Meanwhile, the warrior could see only one thing left to do. Maybe it would not be that much more dangerous, after all, than cutting over to the mountains and trying to haul some stupid sorcerer out of his bloody retreat.

Besides, the brat was her own grub and the motherpricking farmer had no right taking it. Thorn stood up. "Get me that brown dye of yours, Spendwell. I'm going into Maldron's Farm and bringing that damn baby back for her."

Brown hair did a surprising lot to make her look different. A red patch over her left eye helped, too. It also laid her open to attack on that side; but if warriors like Bloodrust and Dartglance used to get along with one good eye and a red patch over the other, then by the Warriors' God, Thorn could do it, too, for a while.

Her skin was already dark. Try to stain it any darker with dye or nut juice, and she would only draw attention. But she could go in with a dirty face. After playing around for a while, she made a fake scar across her left eyebrow and cheek, using some weavers' glue that puckered up her skin. The scar was uncomfortable and would probably sting like Azkor's claws to take off; but it stuck, it looked good as long as nobody got close enough to kiss, it would explain the eye patch, and it helped distort her appearance a little more. Spendwell, grumbling that the rescue had already cost him more than three silvers and he was not likely ever to collect the money from Thorn, provided some dark crimson- and purple-striped wool from the southlands; and Yarn and Small Spider set to work sewing it into tunic and trousers for the swordswoman.

Her biggest worry was the gems in her weapons. Trying to get another set of blades in a hurry would stir up curiosity; besides, strange weapons never felt quite right. It always took a while for the hand and the weapon to get acquainted. This was going to be tricky business, and she would rather have dependable old Slicer and Stabber hanging at her belt. All the same, if Maldron or Inmara had gotten a good look at either of the jewels, or if that damn Clopmule, who already knew Slicer's sheen-amber and Stabber's garnet, was up and limping around again, they might screw the whole damn business.

At last, adopting an idea of Small Spider's, Thorn dipped both pommels in hot wax and then pressed caps of blue cloth over the wax before it hardened. She had seen weirder pommel decorations: snakeskins, squirrels' tails, even lizards' heads and eagles' claws. Sober little blue wool caps should not draw a second glance.

She could not use Spendwell. Too bad, in a way—but Maldron would have been curious about what brought Spendwell back so soon to his Farm. Almost silly with relief, the cloth merchant headed south, after making a big show of loading eleven lengths of the weavers' cloth into his wagon to let the town see what he had been doing in Brightweave's house.

"Stop in again on your way back north, you damn screwpicker, and find out what's happened to me," Thorn told him just before he left the house for the last time that day.

"Don't worry, swordswoman. You owe me three and a half silvers and a good tumble." Then he added, tugging her sleeve, "You owe me the milking of my life. Make it back, you dirty-mouthed warrior."

Small Spider put her face to the window and watched the merchant drive away. Thorn went to sleep on the weaver's bed. If she was going to be any help to anyone, she needed some rest now while she had the chance.

She woke in the middle of the night, put on the crimson and purple clothes the weavers had finished for her, and ate a good dinner. When she thought about it, they had done a Hell of a lot in less than a day—finished her disguise, got Spendwell out of town, kept their looms going for the benefit of the neighbors, and still managed to have someone down beside Frostflower the whole time.

The sorceress seemed to be asleep again. She was too pale and quiet for Thorn's liking. The swordswoman would have been happier to see her awake and talking, cursing, sobbing, thrashing—anything to show she was still reluctant to give up. Well, Frost had always been a quiet one anyway. Too damn dignified. How could a person ever be sure whether she was eager about anything . . . except a stupid grub?

The weaver-woman assured Thorn that Frostflower's heartbeat was steadier and her breathing deeper now than earlier this afternoon. Warriors' God! thought the swordswoman. Frost, if you're going to decide to pull through without that bloody brat, I sure as Hellbog wish you could tell me so!

But there was no way of asking the sorceress without waking her up and letting her know what Thorn was about to do.

The warrior sneaked out of town in the dark, lay down in the middle of some bushes to roll and doze awhile and help take the look of newness off her clothes, and then swaggered into Three Bridges shortly after dawn. Three Bridges was a little further from Maldron's Farm, but she was more likely to find a suitable merchant here than in Frog-in-the-Millstone. Frog-in-the-Millstone was just another unwalled village, while Three Bridges had some ideas of rivaling Five Roads Crossing as the trade center of the northeast Tanglelands, and there was talk of enlarging the town walls.

Avoiding the Golden Rye Inn, Thorn used one of the coppers Brightweave had loaned her to buy a decent breakfast at the Upturned Cup. She took her time with her beef, bread, and garlic-water, listening to a couple of stonecutters at a nearby table.

"Azkor himself, all slimy and dripping from Hellbog."

"And never touched the guards, eh?"

"Made the Quit-Sign, they did, and kept down out of his way."

"Unh. Well, Maldron's warriors can thank the gods Azkor didn't touch them as he went past."

"Came close enough. One of 'em almost got his claw across her belly, and the wind it made ripped open her tunic and left a raw welt on the skin. But it wasn't them the demon was after—it was the sorceress he came for."

Thorn half-turned her head. "What's that you're talking about, friend?"

"The bloody sorceress Maldron hung up near the marshlands day before yesterday, warrior. Azkor came to take her that same night. Stretched up tall as the gibbet itself, he did, glowing in his own bog-light, and closed his big flabby chest around the bitch—just folded it around her like he was a big, empty, green bladder. And in the morning there was nothing left of the body except a little, shrivelled-up thing with the skin gone dry as dead leaves, and when they touched it, it split open and a mess of rotten blood and bones spilled out, smelling like Hellbog itself."

Thorn repressed a chuckle and made the Quit-Sign with the stonecutters, all three touching left fist to forehead at almost the same time. "Well, I hope the farmer paid his women extra for guarding a hung sorceress all night," said the warrior, turning back to her food.

"It was a judgment on his Reverence for not stoning her," said the second stonecutter. "I tell you, scorching a sorceron's belly isn't enough. They have to be filled up with stones, or the gods are angered."

"Shut up, Hardedge," said his friend. "The priests know more about it than you do."

The stonecutters finished their meal and left. Thorn bought another cup of hot garlic-water, as a little added precaution against anyone getting close enough to see her scar was fake.

So the berries had made Clist and Cutbone see Azkor, hey? A few spotted berries and a dummy hung up in place of a sorceress, and you had a new tale. What was Maldron thinking about it? That depended on whether his warriors had taken back the dummy to him or buried it first—and on whether Clist and Cutbone actually believed Spendwell's dummy was Frostflower's body after the touch of a demon, or whether they had dumped the thing in the nearest bog and embroidered their story to cover up their own sloppy job of guarding.

Finishing her breakfast, the warrior left the inn and began scouting the streets. Time was important. If she could not find a suitable merchant before afternoon, she would have to trust her disguise even further and go in like a strange swordswoman trying to hire her services to the farmer.

The gods smiled, and Thorn found an old wine peddler named Purplefumes who planned to head north to Elvannon's Farm, then circle around west and south to Five Roads Crossing, and back to Nedgebottom. Purplefumes had left his regular swordswoman in the flesh-mending house in Nedgebottom, with four broken ribs from a tavern brawl; and driving alone along the Roads-West Wheelpath to Straight Road North and up to Three Bridges had put him in a ready mood to hire the first fighting woman who was willing to ride along for two or three hen's-hatchings until he could get his old warrior back.

They rode out of Three Bridges by mid-morning, and stopped at Frog-in-the-Millstone to sell wine to the town's only tavern and eat an early dinner. "The gods smiling," said Purplefumes, wiping his flabby mouth with a patched kerchief that had once been expensive, "we'll have a good munching from Maldron. Always feeds us well whenever I come up with my almond-kissed and sweetmusk, he does. A glass or two of my sweetmusk wouldn't hurt you now, Fleshfly."

That was a bad name, but Thorn had been in a self-punishing mood when she chose it. "You hired me to guard your bloody wines, not get drunk on them."

"Not so much worry in the daytime, not so close to Maldron's Farm. My Cicatrice never screws up her lips at a glass or two of good wine."

"And your Cicatrice is lying in the Nedgebottom flesh-mending house with four cracked ribs."

The merchant shook his grizzled head. "For drinking Glant straw-yellow. I told her to stay away from the Roaring Gleeds. Bad inn. Keeper never could choose his wines. Thin Glant straw-yellow."

Thorn let him babble on through the meal about his wines, which kinds were drinkable and which kinds he would have been ashamed to stock. Wine was wine to her and all of it was dangerous; but it was a good way to keep Purplefumes' mind dithering instead of thinking.

Maldron was a regular customer of the old man's. That would

get them in with no trouble. But these farmers who made a habit of feeding their favorite merchants almost always extended the courtesy of a table in the porch or outer garden to the merchants' hired guards, and Thorn had no desire to sit around eating where Maldron or Inmara or maybe that cow Clopmule could scrutinize her. "I never eat a munching," she said at last.

Purplefumes blinked. "You'd better eat one today, Fleshfly. There's only one tavern in Gammer's Oak and the food there is not good, not good at all. Wine's excellent—he buys from me—but the food is not good."

"I've eaten plenty of bad food, but never between dinner and supper. I'll sleep in the wagon."

"You'll regret it." The wine merchant slapped the table in perplexity, then cheered up. "Lady Inmara will pack you a basket. Lovely priestess, her Ladyship. Nothing she likes better than a little glass of almond-kissed. His Reverence always buys her three casks of it. Lady Enneald wouldn't do it for you, not her. Snatty one she is—saving her priestesshood. Good tongue, though. Maldron buys her four casks of Southvines white and a bottle of slow amber every time I come north."

When they came in sight of Maldron's wall, Thorn yawned and climbed back into the wagon, supposedly to begin her nap. No merchant was ever attacked by daylight within sight of a farmer's walls; and Purplefumes was used to the idea that warriors were like cats in their sleeping habits, dozing off and waking up with equal ease at any time, so he did not question her.

Maldron's gate guards hailed Purplefumes by name, but did not question him as to where Cicatrice was. Apparently his usual swordswoman, also, had a habit of riding inside the wagon with the wine. All the better, especially since the old man neglected to mention to them that Cicatrice was wounded and he had a new warrior for the time being. If he kept on forgetting to mention that, Thorn's cover was better than she deserved.

Purplefumes did try to question Maldron's women about the sorceress' disappearance from the gibbet, but they were close-mouthed.

"Body completely disappeared," said one.

"His Reverence peeled the guards yesterday morning," said the other.

"Eh? Sorry I missed that."

"You wouldn't have seen it anyway, old Purplefumes. He did

it in his own garden—only the family and the raidleaders to watch
it."

"Wasn't all that bloody much to see, anyway," added the second guard. "Longest strip was hardly the length of a beanpod."

Purplefumes' voice again. "Glad to hear it. Can't blame any
poor warrior too much for not chasing away a demon, can you
now?"

"Don't worry about them, merchant. They'll be back on duty
in a day or two. Now go on and peddle your stock. They're in
a bloody good mood for buying wine, his Reverence and her
Ladyship."

Purplefumes drove on toward the hall, while Thorn lay inside
the wagon and thought things over. So Maldron had peeled the
bloody fathermilkers, had he? Good! All the same, getting strips
of skin the length of a beanpod peeled off some part of your body
was no mild punishment, no little pat with a ceremonial whip.
Maybe Maldron had ordered the rest of his warriors to talk as if
Clist and Cutbone had been given a token grinding only, but it
sounded to Thorn more as if he was taking out a blistering rage
on them. No, it was not quite that, either, or why not have it out
where all his people could watch? He must have been trying to
get the truth out of them. That would probably mean that they
had not told him the truth at first—maybe that they had indeed
pushed Spendwell's silly dummy into a bog before the farmer saw
it—but that he suspected something. They must have told him
what he wanted to hear or he would not have stopped with a few
strips of skin the length of a beanpod.

Well, then, how much could the bitches tell him? That they
had drunk themselves woozy on a passing merchant's wine, tumbled the merchant while they left his woman to watch the gibbet
for them, then fallen asleep on duty and found a dummy on the
gibbet when they woke up. Maybe that they guessed the wine had
been drugged with some kind of nightmare-syrup. But they could
not have been sure it was that same merchant and his woman who
took the sorceress away. Thorn thought they had not recognized
Spendwell (though they had seemed close for awhile), and she
was pretty confident they had not suspected her of so much as
being a swordswoman. All Maldron could have learned from them,
assuming they had told him what they knew and not a batch of
lies, was that someone had taken down the sorceress and she might
still be alive.

Nevertheless, if he knew even this much, what the Hellstink kept him from acting on it? All the gossip in Three Bridges and Frog-in-the-Millstone was about the demon or demons (sometimes Smardon or Vuck came instead of or along with Azkor), about whether they had rotted, dried up, burned, mashed, or eaten the sorceress, and whether she had still been alive when they did it. If the priest knew any of the truth at all—even if he thought Clist and Cutbone had taken a little fun with Frostflower against his orders and then buried the evidence—why was he allowing the demon story to go around unchecked? Why in the names of all the gods wasn't he sending out messengers to tell people it was all a pile of donkey turds about Frostflower being snatched by demons?

Because it was another hate tale to keep commoners hot against sorceri, that was the reason!

Thorn let out a string of curses in her mind and twisted Stabber's pommel until the cloth cap and wax loosened from the garnet. Then she sat trying to push it all back together with the heat and pressure of her hands, and remembering how Frostflower had more than hinted that sorceri, too, did their damnedest to encourage the stories—those bloody stories that kept up the fear of their powers.

Damn them all, then! Farmers and sorcerers both—bloody motherprickers, between them mangling poor bastards' minds into gulping down the whole big bloody lie. Damn them all to the deepest pits of Hellbog! But damn the bloody farmers deeper— the sorcerers were only trying to stay alive, after all. . . .

But the sorceri had more than just their reputation to help them stay alive. Smardon's fleshhooks! The way Frost had grabbed that lightning—

The way Frost had grabbed the lightning . . . but sorceri were blasphemers! Where was the Goddess of the Lightning when Frost-flower grabbed it away from her?

Gods! Was it *all* lies, then? Hellbog and Glorious Harvest, gods, goddesses, and demons, Lightning Goddess, Warriors' God, Smardon with his fleshhooks, the Great God of the Seven Secret Names—all farmers' lies? All bloody stories to make us do what the damn priests want us to do?

But no, the tales aren't all false. This bloody lunacy about Frostflower's rescue is one thing—but I saw for myself what the sorcerer did to that poor bitch of a warrior in West-of-the-Marsh.

And if there's no Warriors' God, then Who the Hellstink got me through the woods to Spendwell? Who's been straightening out all the little kinks for me?

Here I am, snug in Purplefumes' wagon, inside Maldron's walls with not a suspicious glance . . . damn sacrilegious to start doubting the Warriors' God now! All right, so some of the stories about sorceri *are* dog-vomit and donkey-farts—that doesn't make it *all* false. So maybe some of the farmers do deserve getting sunk in deepest Hellbog if the Great Giver is really just—that doesn't mean everything every priest ever says is a damn lie.

Remembering uneasily that, while she had disobeyed Maldron, it had been the guiltless Inmara whom she had actually threatened and on whose account she faced the worst Hell-tortures, Thorn made the Quit-Sign and settled down to work the wax and cloth back firmly on her dagger's pommel and to keep her mind on what was happening outside the wagon. The surest way to lose the help of the Warriors' God was to expect Him to do all the work Himself. She had better give the God of the Sorceri some thanks, too; and she guessed he might use pretty much the same rule as the Warriors' God about expecting you to move your own two legs along the way he cleared for you.

When the wagon stopped, Thorn lay down on her side with her face half buried between the greasy pillow and her arm. If any of Maldron's people sneaked a look into the merchant's wagon and saw her sitting up awake and doing nothing, at worst they would think it was pretty damn suspicious and at best they would want her coming out to drink or gamble. If they peeked in and saw her sleeping, they would leave her alone, might even mistake her for Purplefumes' regular swordswoman.

Her right eye was almost covered by a mound of pillow and her left eye by the bloody red patch and her arm on top of it, so she could not have seen much even if she opened her eyes; but she did not hear anything suspicious, although she was ready to fake a couple of snores at the first sound of somebody looking in. Eventually she dozed off in earnest, waking with a snort of surprise after a dream about some bloody old warrior who had been trying to show her how to put a wick in the tip of her sword and keep it lighted.

She heard voices coming nearer, and the wagon started shaking. Purplefumes was climbing back into the driving seat. About time, damn the pricking guzzler. What was he fumbling around with? Oh, yes—putting in the damn basket of food he had gotten

Lady Inmara to pack for his warrior. Now he was climbing back onto the seat and starting the bloody donkeys at last.

She could no longer put off the next big decision: Slip out without telling Purplefumes, or tell him first and then slip out? Either way was a bad gamble. Slip out without telling the old bugger, and he might come back looking for her as soon as he noticed she was gone. Quite a mess that would make at the gates! But if she told him first—no matter what threats she used, since she was not going to be there to hold Stabber at his kidneys, he might just betray her to the gate-warriors. She could hardly tell him the reason she was hiding somewhere in Maldron's Farm: "I'm doing it to steal back a bratty grub to give it to a sorceress and keep her from dying." That sounded idiotic even to Thorn herself, when she thought about it; and to anyone who did not know Frostflower— And even suppose she could make up a story to persuade the dull-brained old drunkard to go along, she could see him giving it away by stammering and doddering at the gates.

So she had better not give him the chance to betray her through his greed or bumbling. If he did not know what was going on, he could not tell anyone much, except that she had disappeared somewhere.

Good. Purplefumes had begun to sing. It was a rowdy old drinking song, and the old sot did not have the words right; but between the noise of his voice, the creaks of his wagon, and the slightly tipsy way he seemed to be driving, he was not likely to hear or feel Thorn's departure. If this was not another sign the Warriors' God was on her side, what was? Practising the woodcat crawl, she worked her way to the back of the wagon, undid a few of the tent toggles, pulled back a finger's length of cloth, and peered out.

She could not go yet. Three workers were only half a field off, cutting hay. Alert for any break in the lazy, steady pace of the donkeys or any catch in the silly song that would warn her Purplefumes was aware of her movement, she continued peering out until they had passed the hay fields and entered an orchard.

Nobody seemed to be around here. Thorn pulled the cloth back a little more and managed a wider view. Still seeing no one, she put her head halfway out. She was tempted to flip up her eyepatch for a better look; but no matter what she did, she would not be able to see anyone in front of the wagon. At least she could see that nobody was behind or to either side. With the fruit trees stretching around the wheelpath, she would probably not get a better chance than now. Undoing the rest of the lower tent toggles, she swung her legs out, aimed her feet downward, and wiggled the rest of the way like a fish flipping through a hole in the net.

Landing lightly on her feet, she turned and glanced around. Nobody was in sight. The wagon was less than halfway through the orchard, and going slowly enough that by walking behind it for a few moments she was able to fasten up the toggles again, covering all outward sign of her departure.

Then she struck off the path and in among the trees. She tried to walk boldly, as if she had nothing to hide. If Purplefumes or anyone else saw her at this point, she would say she was just looking for a good place to shit and was going to catch up with the wagon again before it reached the gates.

In fact, she was looking for a good place to hole up the rest of the day without being found. Getting found would mean a death to make burning alive from a torch in your hair look cozy. If anyone found her, her only chance would be to kill the poor bugger—swordswoman or haymaker—without anyone else noticing, hide the body, and then probably have to find a new hole for herself. Gods and demons, was the damn grub worth it? Was Frost worth it? Was this the way to get the gods back on her side? The God of the Sorceri, maybe—well, if the farmer-priests were right, the real gods and goddesses probably could not keep her nose above the surface of Hellbog whatever she did, and the Sorceri's God might be her only chance.

Of course, her success so far might be a big, divine trap to clamp down on her like a bloody axe.

When, near the edge of a barley-field, she found some kind of animal burrow big enough for her to squeeze inside and pull a couple handfuls of stubble and root-clods over the entrance, she muttered several prayers of thanks to the Warriors' God, promising to burn nine drops of her blood on a piece of bread at the first statue of Him she found. She had no idea what, if anything, she could offer to the God of the Sorceri.

The ground was dampish around her; it had a sour stink; and now and then she thought she could feel the damn worms crawling in it. Once she felt something moving beneath her feet, and kicked down savagely, causing a few squeaks and a scuffle, and bruising her own knee on the side of the tunnel. A couple of times she dozed off and started slipping—or dreamed she was slipping— down to the bottom of the burrow. Another time, something started chewing her heel and when she kicked downwards she dislodged the earth so that the whole bloody burrow began to cave in on her, until she woke with a curse. Later yet, she suddenly panicked for no reason, tried to climb out, found her feet were stuck in slime and the slime was oozing up to her knees and thighs, tried to shout for help, and woke up again with the scream quobbing at the back of her throat. Hellstink! she thought; one more nightmare and I'll be screaming aloud and bringing them over to find me. And I haven't even eaten any nightmare-berries.

Through the holes in stubble and root-clods, she watched the sky get dark. When it was dark enough to show the first stars, she dug her knees and elbows into the earth and began wiggling upwards. She made it out easier than she had half-feared, after the nightmares. All the same—gods! she had been lucky so far. She had been much safer from discovery here than in some haystack or field shed where landworkers might come during their daily chores, but if they *had* stumbled on her in that hole—Smardon's fingernails, she would not have had a chance!

Squatting in the barley, glad to be out in the open air again, she removed her eyepatch and stuffed it into her pocket, then ate her sausage and raisins, working up her saliva to swallow instead of water. She thought of the basket Inmara had packed for Purplefumes' warrior, and wondered if the wine merchant was eating its contents himself, in the inn at Gammer's Oak. What had the old bastard done when he found her gone? She had not heard any sounds of a hunt inside the Farm; she hoped he had not even looked until long after leaving Maldron's gate. Maybe he thought she was some other farmer's spy, and was keeping quiet about her so that he would not be drawn into a quarrel between priests.

After a while, still flipping raisins into her mouth, she got up and began to prowl around the fields, circling towards the hall while keeping away from the wheelpath.

She saw the lights of the workers' cottages to the southwest, and beyond them the dim outlines of the animal barns and stables. The warriors' barracks were to the north, well removed from both the workers' dwellings and the farmers' hall. Thorn was too far away to hear the usual noises of singing, drinking and gambling that went on in the barracks until whatever hour the priest had laid down for curfew. If it were not for their lights and their distance from the cottages, the barracks would have looked pretty much like another big stable.

She had never thought much about it before, but what the Hell were warriors except another kind of stock animal for the priests? Some time so long ago nobody gave a damn anymore, warriors had been priestesses, farmers' second-wives, the fighting body-guard of their husbands and families. At least, that was the story a farmer told you when he wanted to screw you. Now the holy bastards gave you a stable to live in, and kept you downwind from their own scented living quarters.

Well, at least the warriors were free, could move around and hire out to any bloody farmer or merchant or townmaster they chose. Landworkers were farmers' animals too, and they stayed put like damn cows. Maybe they *could* go out and find another farmer or a place in some town, but how many of the clods ever *did*?

Then again, this farmer, that town, what was the difference? Farmers' herds, all of them, doing the priests' work, or carrying goods from one farmer to another, or fighting raids and getting killed so the farmers could swap around their lands like squares on a bloody gameboard. Gods! The only people who were free of the damn priests were the outlaws and the sorceri! That must be why farmers picked their brains out of their snotty noses think-ing up ways and excuses to kill sorceri.

Meanwhile, Thorn had to locate the grub. One of the nurses would have it. Maldron probably intended to keep the brat, but not even Maldron would be so obvious as to give it to one of his wives for safekeeping while they were still supposedly looking for the parents.

Maldron had a smallish family for a priest: three wives, one dead and one barren; two sons and a couple of daughters; two younger sisters, one never married and one widowed and back home again with a brat or two of her own—so much Thorn had picked up from local gossip. Depending on how spaced out the brats had been born, one nurse, the one Spendwell had seen at the rape-party, could have handled them all. Even if the chief nurse had two or three helpers for show, or training, or whatever farmers' nurses did, chances were the old biddy would have Frost-flower's grub in her own room.

Nurses were favored servants. If they did not have bedroom alcoves in the same row as the priestesses and unmarried priests, then they usually stayed in cute little nursery cottages near the farmers' hall.

Maldron had only two such cottages beside his hall, both dark

and one seemingly used for storage; a light shining out from an
alcove bedroom onto this cottage showed Thorn a stack of farmers'
bedroom doors taken off their hinges for the summer and piled
up behind the window lattice. The warrior slunk up to the hall
itself and crawled slowly around, listening at each bedchamber
for a few moments. At one of them she ought to hear the grub
crying. Grubs were always crying, weren't they?

She went all the way down the west row of alcoves, crawling
on hands and knees. She heard a couple of itchy young priestlings
in one bedroom bragging to each other about the women they were
going to prick, and the ways they were going to purify them first,
as soon as they got some stubble on their chins. In the rest of the
alcoves she heard nothing, not even snores. Bloody family must
have finished their supper by now, and the nurse ought to have
the grub in her room with her; but it looked as if the rest of the
farmers were still in the long hall. Crouching near the front doorway, by the priest's offices, Thorn could see light and hear voices
filtering through the loosely-woven summer doorcurtain. Someone
was singing, a slow tear-jerking ballad about a blighted harvest
and a young priest who cut himself up to fertilize the fields. Damn
priestesses had no right to have such lovely singing voices.

The first farmer for whom Thorn ever worked, his Reverence
Ablamar, used to set a pair of warriors at his alcove every night
on guard. Nobody else ever did it. Raiding parties never attacked
the farmers themselves—in fact, just about the safest place a warrior could be during a raid would be the entrance to the farmers'
hall. But his Reverence Ablamar had a good, deep, mellow singing
voice, and he wanted to make sure his favorite young swordswomen got a chance to hear it.

Probably, by crawling on her belly like a grubby caterpillar,
Thorn could have gotten past Maldron's threshold. But there was
always the chance one of the farmers would come out for a starlight
stroll. Deciding to go the long way, around the garden wall, Thorn
started crawling back, past the boastful priestlings and the nine
silent alcoves.

When she reached the garden wall, she stopped crawling. Even
on her feet, it took a pretty good while to get all the way around.
Maldron might not have the biggest hall she had ever seen—Hell,
she had worked for a priest with twenty-one alcoves on each side
of his hall—but Maldron made up for it with the size of his private

garden. The bastard must have room to pasture cows in there around his Truth Grove.

She reached the end of the curve, squatted down on hands and knees again, and started her crawl along the eastern alcoves. The farmers' after-supper entertainments must have ended while she was on her way around the garden, because now she heard voices in almost every alcove. In the sixth, she finally heard what she wanted—not the brat squalling, but something almost as good: a lullaby.

The singer did not sound like an old woman, but how the Hellbog could you tell from a soft, gushy lullaby? The nurse whom Spendwell had mentioned could not have been decrepit, or she would not have been along at the capture. Or the singer might be one of the old biddy's assistants. Strange thing, priests' chants were different from all other music, and usually you could tell farmers' ballads from the kind of songs other folk enjoyed, but lullabies all sounded pretty much alike. The swordswoman crouched outside the alcove listening to bunkum about bees, lambs, and golden pears until she heard a couple of silly gurgles and a few murmurs which satisfied her that the brat really was in there, that it was not just some beginning nurse or sappy farmer-girl practicing.

Sixth room on the east side from the garden wall, fifth from the front door. Thorn was getting itchy to retreat and wait at a safer distance until everyone was snoring, but she sat tight a while longer to make sure they were not going to move the brat to some other room. Damn stupid planning if they did, but what did the swordswoman know about how farmers—or anyone else except warriors in their barracks—raised babies? She could not remember anything about her own life before she was about four or five, already housebroken, and tumbling up somehow or other with half a score other baby bitches toward adult life in the townwarriors' barracks of All Roads West. She sure as Hellstink had never bothered about how grubs got to be four or five years old.

Putting her ear to the wall, she heard soft footsteps, the burr of rockers, another drippy lullaby. Then the rockers gradually seemed to stop. That clinched it. Surely nobody would rock a brat to sleep if she did not intend to leave it in the same room for a while.

The warrior crawled away from the building and lay on her belly about forty paces distant, waiting. The nurse's window-

lattice darkened soon enough. So did the room to the right of hers;
the room to the left had not been lit all evening, so far as Thorn
could tell. She got up. Only two alcoves on this side still showed
lights. She slipped around to the other side, this time crawling
past the front door on her belly, and saw the boastful priestlings
still had their lamp or candle lit, alone in this row of alcoves. She
wandered around the inner farm, keeping her muscles limber and
checking the lay of the land. The workers were all sleeping like
good little cows, their cottages completely dark. The lower floor
of the warriors' barracks was dark, too, but the upper floor was
still lighted and noisy. Too many lazy bitches used being warriors
as an excuse for snoring in bed half the morning.

She approached the farmers' hall again, slipped into the nursery
cottage that was not being used as a storehouse, and took a nap.
She guessed she would not oversleep, not after dozing the afternoon away in the rotten burrow; but she tied a cord around her
left little toe just to make sure the throbbing would get her up
before too long.

The moon was rising above the hall, and heading for a bank
of clouds a little way up, when she awoke. The priestlings were
still giggling in their now-darkened alcove. Thorn cursed them
softly and went to take another look at the barracks. This time
they were completely dark. If it was after Maldron's curfew for
the warriors, it was bloody well time for the farmers themselves
to be asleep. Thorn returned to the hall and listened at the priestlings' bedroom. It was quiet now, but she waited to hear snoring
before she made her rounds of the rest of the building.

Everything was dark, and all seemed quiet—nothing but snores
and other sleep-noises. Thorn made her way to the front door.
Absurdly, before lifting the curtain, she stopped, groped for one
of the pieces of sheepskin hanging on the side of the steps, and
wiped her boots clean.

Well, maybe it was not so absurd, after all. She would do
better not to leave dirty tracks all over the farmers' tiled floors.
She assumed Maldron had tiled floors. Most farmers she had
worked for did. When she got inside she could feel, by the slight
unevenness beneath her soft leather soles, that she was right.

Only twice had she ever been farther into a farmer's hall than
the entranceway. If she could have had enough light to see it,
what a spectacle Maldron's long room must be! Ask warriors and
commoners how they pictured the Glorious Harvest, and five out

of seven said they thought it was like the great hall of a very rich farmer. Maldron might not be especially rich as farmers went, but he had one of the most ancient halls. Some of his mosaics might even have been plastered up in the days when warriors were priestesses—pity Thorn could not get a look at them. Even in the dark, she felt a heady temptation to swagger a little down the middle of the long chamber.

The long hall was not completely dark. A little nightglow sneaked in through the front doorcurtain and the high windows beneath the rafters, while Thorn could glimpse dim blue constant-wicks at the dais-end of the hall and on the corridor walls behind the inner archways. It was just dark enough so that what light there was seemed bloody little, even for a warrior. The interior darkness was thicker than the night outside.

Thorn would have felt happier with weapon in hand; but the farmers, if they came, would not come at her with swords, and her own blades were more likely to clatter against something if they were drawn, so she left them in their sheaths. At first she held her hands out in front of her, and probed the emptiness with her toe before each step . . . but if you were going to swagger, you might as well swagger, not grope like a blasted fool. Just five strides, she promised herself, lowering her arms and letting them swing free. Just five strides across a farmer's hall for once in my bloody life, and then I'll get over to an archway and find the nurse's room.

Four strides she took free and loose, not looking down—then her foot hit something clumpy that wiggled and yelped.

She caught herself and crouched rather than fell, drawing Stabber with her left hand and grabbing with her right. Damn dog! Damn farmers, letting their mangy animals sprawl out on their fancy tile floors!

She got her right arm around some thick part of the mutt's body. Her left arm was raised and taut—a second yelp, anything that felt like a bark or growl beginning, and the mongrel was dead. But it did not bark, or even thrash around. The damn thing whined and wagged its tail—she could feel the tip of it hitting her backbone, up and down.

How the Hellstink did you ask a lousy mutt if it was an old friend? What the Hell was the bugger's name? Dowl. "Dowl?" she whispered. The dog whined again, threw back its head, and somehow connected its sloppy tongue with her face.

She got her right hand around its slimy muzzle and squeezed the jaws together. Returning her knife to his sheath, she reached back to catch the dog's tail and hold it down, stop its blasted tapping against the floor. To her surprise—and the mongrel's own good luck—it kept quiet and let her listen. For about twenty heartbeats something seemed wrong ... someone must be awake somewhere, the air was not moving right, the whole feel of the sleeping hall had been upset. But where? If somebody was up and stirring, in which bedroom ... on which side of the hall? There were no sounds of anyone being awake, unless somebody had stopped snoring. Damn! The snores were not all that loud anyway, not out here in the middle of the hall. And people could stop snoring without waking up.

Hell of a stupid way to get caught, sprawling out in the middle of a tiled floor with one hand around a slimy set of dog-jaws and the other holding down a fool tail, and your own butt squatting on the dog's behind. Maybe if they found her, she could say she had only come to screw a dog! Hellstink, she did not even remember whether Frost's mutt was a he or a she.

Well, when she could sit here thinking nonsense like this, she could guess none of the farmers had awakened. Slowly the warrior straightened her legs until she was bending over the dog instead of squatting astraddle its rump. "Quiet!" she whispered—as if Dowl could understand her—and unclamped her hand from its muzzle, wiping the snot off her palm onto her trousers.

Maybe the damn mutt did understand. It made one more puzzled little whine, but so softly that even she hardly heard it. She lifted her other hand off its tail. It wagged once. She held it down again, then released it for good. She could not stand here all night holding down a dog's tail.

The animal got to its feet and walked out between her legs. She felt its tail hitting her calves as it wagged happily in the unthumping air.

The warrior turned and relocated herself. She could still make out the front door, its curtain vaguely gray in the nightglow. The farther, dais-end of the hall was a big shadow with one constant-wick in the darkness. Thorn was only a few paces from the first archway to the alcoves.

She headed for it without wasting any more time, stepping carefully to make sure she did not come down on any more sleeping dogs' tails. The mongrel she had already roused padded along behind her; but, as long as it was not barking and had quit whining, she was not going to risk kicking it away or whispering anything else at its stupid ears.

Maybe all I really need to take back to Frost is her silly mutt? Na. I don't even know if this is the right one. Damn thing might have slobbered just as much if I'd called it Frogface or Stinkfly. And why risk my guts to bring out nothing but a mangy dog?

Slipping through the archway, the warrior counted the small blue constant-wicks burning outside each bedchamber. Sixth from the garden-end, fifth from the front entrance. Through the thin summer curtain of the nurse's room Thorn could see the tiny vigil candle—a little incense to please a favorite god and keep out the bugs—a few shapes, a few shadows, nothing else. She could not even hear the nurse's snores. Slowly, careful not to let any of the curtain-weights click, Thorn began to lift the cloth.

Chapter 7

Maldron was sleeping tonight in Enneald's bed. He had not spent a night with his second wife since before the afternoon when he and Inmara consecrated their love to Aeronu Goddess of Birth, and, in the turmoil that followed the holy rite, he had received the wound in his shoulder. Night by night, as he retreated to Inmara's chamber for easing of the pain in his body and spirit, Enneald had grown more impatient; day by day, her words became more spiteful. At last this evening Inmara, struggling with her own need, had begged Maldron to sleep with the younger woman. Enneald had been lonely for six nights; Maldron would displease Jehandru if he stayed away any longer from her. Inmara had the child in her chamber to help bring comfort.

The child was at once comfort, fear, and guilt. Her little Terndasen, for so Inmara had begun to call him in her own mind, might on any day be claimed by his real parents. In the meantime he was an innocent reminder of the price the sorceress had paid for stealing him. Sometimes, especially after the scaffolding and hanging two days ago, Inmara wondered how Maldron was able to look at the infant, to penetrate his wife so gently in the same room with the child. She had thought the night after the hanging, even in her own great need for comfort (coupled as it was with her need to forget the frail, wounded woman awaiting death on the gibbet), that it was strange Maldron had not fled to his younger wife's alcove to escape the infant, or at least banished little Terndasen to Cradlelap's care. Yet Inmara knew her husband shared her own longing for the child who seemed sometimes a gift from Aeronu, sometimes a test sent by Great Jehandru to prove their own justice when the real parents were found.

The priestess would let no woman or man claim Terndasen who could not tell her of the small red mole on the knuckle of his left middle finger. Inmara would surely have devised the test herself if Frostflower had not given it to her. But . . . was it still valid? The sorceress had disappeared.

Oh, it had been pitifully clear that the first tale the guards brought was false. Enneald and her daughter had believed, or pretended to believe, their garbled visions of demons; but Maldron, Inmara, even young Daseron and old Cradlelap had agreed that though Frostflower's crime merited the strictest mortal judgment, it should not have brought the most feared demons of Hellbog up for her, not when so many sorceri of far greater wickedness had hung undisturbed by the immortals. Also, Ena the unmarried, Maldron's sister, who had made the demons her particular study, scoffed at the warriors' descriptions as inaccurate and foolish. Taken separately to the Truth Grove, Cutbone had confessed to beating the sorceress as she hung and then to burying the body in the marshes; but Clist had talked of a wine merchant who gave them drugged liquor and must have taken down the sorceress.

Probably Frostflower was dead, but possibly . . . possibly she had been rescued by friends. The sorceri did have friends in the towns, misguided folk half-seduced by their blasphemies—as Inmara herself might almost have been, listening to Frostflower. Maldron and Inmara had decided not to renew the search. If the sorceress were dead, searching again would be lost effort; if she were alive . . . they were weary, body, mind and even conscience, of the need to punish her; and they had the child.

Was it the right decision? If any came now and told them of the small red mole, could Inmara be sure they knew of it because they were Terndasen's true parents, and not because they were friends of the sorceress? No: she could not give him up. If anyone came who could describe the birthmark, Maldron had said they must give up the babe and have the claimant or claimants followed, watched . . . but if they led back to Frostflower, then there must be another scaffolding, a complete disembowelment this time for the sorceress, and probably stoning for her accomplices. Jehandru of the Seven Secret Names!—would it not be better—even though You are the Great Giver of Justice—to withhold my Terndasen from all claimants than to place Frostflower naked on the scaffold once more, tied to the wheel and her entrails being drawn out?

Yet not to return him to his parents, if they were indeed his true—

Who was walking in the long hall?

No one. It was only a summer wind blowing softly through the curtains. But it had called her thoughts from herself for a moment, and for that she was grateful. She closed her eyes, hoping for sleep...

The dog yelped. The sorceress' dog scuffled with something in the long hall. At once Inmara's eyes were open. She held her breath and listened, staring at her candle to Aeronu as if by straining her eyes she could aid her hearing.

Had it been merely a prick of her own conscience? No. Dowl had yelped and thrashed. She was sure of it. But now all was silent once more. Perhaps some small creature, a mouse or beetle, had wakened the dog for a moment. Or perhaps Dowl had only yelped and twitched in a sad dream of his own. Turning her head on the silken pillow, Inmara gazed at the shadow that was their family cradle, Terndasen's cradle now. The child had not awakened. The priestess sighed and closed her eyes.

Someone *was* in the long hall! Someone who walked softly...softly as a spirit? Had the sorceress come back, her strangely-colored eyes now glowing with disembodied afterlife, to gaze at her child? Even such a gentle woman as Frostflower, if crazed with the pain of Hellbog—

No, a spirit would make no footfalls. It was Maldron coming to her chamber. Enneald had fallen asleep and the priest was returning to Inmara.

But could Maldron walk so softly? Why would any of us walk so softly? Only to avoid waking the others? When have any of us feared waking another in our own household? Does the babe not cry loudly every night? Why should footsteps disturb any sleeper more than Terndasen's wails?

The footfalls had stopped for a moment, as if unsure of their way. Now they began again, coming closer. One of the ancient tales went through Inmara's brain, one of the tales never told to common folk, because it came from days when the bodies of farmers were not known to be as sacred as their functions, when doors were not taken off their hinges but kept closed and barred at night even in the summer, because a priest or priestess was still liable to be slain during a raid.

Such things had not happened for generations, not since before most priestly lines could name their ancestors. There were still assassinations sometimes, farmer killing farmer by stealth, matters kept hidden from the common folk . . . but not in her own family! Ah, Aeronu, Raes, and Ontaraec, Great Jehandru—not in Maldron's family! Which of them . . . Daseron, who was visiting with them for half a year? Jehandru, no! It cannot be young Daseron—not my own nephew, my sister's child! And it would be by poison. When it happens it is almost always by poison—even in the dark hours, a knife is harder to keep from the knowledge of warriors and workers. . . .

The footsteps were coming toward Inmara's chamber.

Should she scream? If whoever came had an honest reason for walking softly, Inmara would wake the others to no purpose. If whoever came were an assassin, he or she would lie; this attempt in the night would be thwarted, but poison would come in the day, on any plate of meat, in any cup of wine. It was almost always poison. Or a silken pillow held over the head in the darkness . . . but why? Why?

I am in nightmare, thought the priestess. This is the worst of all nightmares, when everything seems almost natural, almost real . . . except for that one fine strangeness, that one all-pervading edge of horror.

She stared around the shadows, listened to the footsteps, searching for the note of falsity that would assure her she was asleep and dreaming. Two human feet, walking very softly . . . an animal padding behind . . . otherwise all seemed so natural! The footsteps had stopped at her doorway. Her eyes seemed so truly open—she could feel the air drying them between her blinks.

Aeronu, kind goddess, let me live to watch him grow—the infant you have given me!

The infant? Raes and Aeronu, they cannot mean to harm the infant? Impossible—but to steal him! Aeronu, why have I not thought of it earlier? Raes and Aeronu, Eltassru and Great Jehandru, help me—strengthen me!

Breathing as quietly as she could, the priestess began to edge up to a sitting position, readying herself to spring. One did not have such ready command of one's body in a nightmare. She swallowed carefully. Yes, she would be able to scream if the need came.

She could see the doorcurtain moving, being pulled aside. The loosely-woven cloth had almost a sheen, like a shadow that was

gray-white rather than black. Forcing herself to breathe deeply
and quietly, Inmara watched one side of the linen moving inward,
slowed by the clay weights along the bottom and by the stealth
of the dark arm drawing it back . . . slowed also, the priestess dimly
understood, by her own suspense.

The intruder looked into her room. Inmara could see the face,
an oval darker than the curtain but lighter than the shadows behind.
For a heartbeat their two faces seemed turned towards one another,
as the priestess realized the intruder saw she was awake and sitting,
rather than asleep and prone.

The intruder sprang. Inmara leaped forward to meet the
threat—was borne back by greater strength, greater speed and
agility—a strong arm around her waist to prevent her falling, a
hand over her face to prevent her screaming.

She heard the swish of the curtain, the helpless clicking of the
small clay weights, the padding of the dog's paws. She tried to
open her mouth, to find the attacker's hand with her teeth. In an
instant the hand slipped down and grasped her throat. "Scream
and you're dead," the intruder whispered.

It was a horror lived through a second time—the forest outside
the holy glade, the baby in Inmara's arms and a cursed, crazed
warrior threatening her with a bloodied sword. Inmara could not
scream, could hardly lower her jaw against the pressure squeezing
inward and upward.

Her right elbow was caught in the grip around her waist, but
her left arm was still free. She snatched at the intruder's face.

The intruder's hand tightened on her throat, choking her and
pushing her head back until her neck seemed about to crack. One
leg whipped around behind her, catching her knees between her
attacker's legs like a rope in a pair of tongs. The tongs closed
slowly, forcing her knees to buckle beneath her as the intruder,
crouching gradually, lowered her to the floor without a sound,
with pitifully little struggle. She must not faint. She could do
nothing for the moment except cling to consciousness in spite of
the hand held so tightly around her throat.

It could not be Thorn—that miserable, damned warrior had
gone alone into the marshlands! Yet who but a warrior could strike
so quickly and force so surely? And what warrior but Thorn would
dare outrage a priestess?

Holding Inmara to the floor with legs and one hand, the attacker
freed her own other arm from the captive's waist. The dog ap-

proached, whimpering softly. The priestess wondered if he would try to lick her, but the intruder pushed him away, muttering, "Damn you, dog!" Then Inmara felt a blade between her lower ribs and her right breast, pressing so closely that when she breathed she could sense the sharp edge fraying the threads of her night-dress.

"I don't want to kill you, nurseling," whispered the attacker, "but by the gods, if you don't keep quiet and let me tie you with no bloody fuss, you're dead!"

So this stranger thought she was attacking a mere nurse? The hand on Inmara's throat loosened slightly. She gasped, caught her breath, and spoke in a low compressed voice. "I am no nurse. Warrior, I am Inmara, priestess and Maldron's eldest wife."

The hand on her throat seemed to shake, then tightened again. The knife drew away slightly, then pushed back inward. Was the blade actually through the cloth and into her flesh?

"I still mean it, Lady!" The attacker *was* Thorn.

"Why have you come?"

"To get my grub, Lady."

"Grub?"

"The brat—the baby."

Inmara shuddered, driving her own breast tighter against the knife. Even when Frostflower had stopped naming Thorn as Tern-dasen's mother, she had persisted in the claim of a warrior who did not want him.

Even in her confusion, Inmara remembered the test. "De-scribe—the child's birthmark—or marks!"

"Hellbog! It's a he-brat. Lady, keep still."

"You cannot describe his marks."

"Gods, what difference does it make? You want to hear all the bloody details of pushing it out—"

"You could not have carried him in the time!"

"Frostflower sorcered him out of me, damn it! She used to be able to do that, before you damn—Look, don't talk. I don't want to kill you, Lady."

Thorn began to work the priestess across the floor, sliding her slowly, in little half-cushioned jerking movements. What was she doing? Ah, moving closer to the bed. Inmara lay limp, offering no resistance, hardly even feeling the tiles through her thin robe.

Thorn spoke truth. Frostflower's insistence . . . Frostflower's statement about growing her dog with sorcery, which Inmara had suspected from the first to be a hint about the child, though she had quickly smothered the suspicion. . . . Her small Terndasen was the son of this brutish woman, and Thorn—not Inmara—held mother's right over him.

"I can still choke you, Lady." The warrior took her knife from Inmara's rib and twisted around to reach for the sheet and begin pulling it off the bed.

Thorn does not deserve mother's right—Thorn has forfeited mother's right! He is mine now—I deserve him—he is mine and I will keep him, I will not let her bind me and take him, this warrior who deserves death and Hell twenty times over! I can keep him now and keep him without fear of his true parents. . . .

But how could a priestess, who had never needed or learned to fight with her body even in sport, overpower a trained warrior who would not recognize the sacredness of a farmer's person?

One farmer could not, but many farmers—Maldron, acting with Daseron, Varin, Lilm, Enneald with her long fingernails, even young Wendrina, and Erithi who runs and climbs like a boy—they can circle her. Let this warrior claim mother's right when she is hanging from the gibbet with every limb broken and her own stone-filled entrails stuffed down her throat, as is less than she deserves for bruising and threatening me, a priestess!

The room beside Inmara's to the south was the study alcove, empty of sleepers, used in the day for reading and sewing. Young Erithi had taken the room to the north for the very reason that Terndasen's loudest wails never woke her. The noises of scuffling and whispering alone were not likely to bring help.

Inmara had waited unresisting very long now. Thorn seemed busy with the sheet. The priestess suddenly opened her mouth wide and tightened her throat for a scream—

The warrior's hand shoved her jaws closed. Her teeth smashed together, her head struck against the floor, her breath stopped completely. Dazed, her lungs stagnating, she began to struggle unthinkingly until Thorn loosened her grip to allow the passage of air.

"Don't try that again, Lady!"

The priestess lay quiet, her throat, teeth, and skull aching, a taste of blood in her mouth. She could hardly believe that the impact of her head on the floor, or even of her teeth striking together, had not wakened the baby; but the only sounds were

Thorn's harsh breathing above her and the dog's thin whine some-where near.

Even if Inmara could wake the others, even if Maldron, En-neald, Kalda, and Lilm had not been on the other side of the hall, Thorn could still murder her like a common tradeswoman before help came.

Jehandru forgive me, what is it to me that Thorn should meet my husband's justice, if I am no longer alive?

"Why do you wish him now, warrior?"

At Inmara's words, Thorn began to squeeze her throat once more. But the priestess hurried on, whispering desperately through the pressure and the thick fluid rising towards her mouth, "What do you want with him now?"

Thorn's fingers faltered—only a little, but they did not close off Inmara's breathing this time. The swordswoman jerked at the sheet.

"Answer me, warrior!" Inmara tried to summon all her priestlihood, to whisper the command as if the priestlihood were still a weapon this warrior would respect. "I am a priestess! By Great Jehandru, answer me! Why have you come?"

"Azkor's claws, Lady, I gave him to Frostflower!"

"The sorceress is dead! What will you—"

"Hellstink, keep quiet!"

The warrior finally succeeded in pulling the sheet from the bed. "Sit up and don't scream." Still kneeling on Inmara's legs, Thorn took her hand from the priestess' throat and began to twist the sheet.

Inmara did not scream, but neither did she sit. *What was a warrior, to command a priestess?* "You did not care for him when the sorceress lived. Why do you want him now she is dead?"

Thorn pulled her halfway up and threw the twisted sheet rope-like around her shoulders, pulling it tightly in a large knot.

"I love him, warrior! Leave him with me and I will tell no one you have escaped the marshlands."

The warrior thrust a corner of sheet into the priestess' mouth. Inmara spat it out easily while Thorn tried to bind her wrists; but the warrior's silence gave her a new and different alarm.

"Thorn! She is alive?"

"How the Hellstink would she be alive? Wasn't she almost dead when you hung her up on your demon-damned gibbet?"

Thorn was fumbling in the near-darkness, and sheets had never

been woven for binding wrists. Inmara thought she could pull her
hands apart—even, if she were quick enough, catch the swordswoman's hair or ears or throat now, while both Thorn's hands
were occupied with the cloth. Instead, she sat meekly. The struggle
had not gone out of her spirit, but it had turned inward upon
herself . . . and Inmara was weary. Weary not of fighting Thorn—
if there had been nothing left but her emotion toward this warrior,
she now thought she could have fought on, savagely and hope-
lessly, waking the hall and insuring Thorn's capture with her own
death. Aye, her body was only beginning to feel the stir of blood-
lust; her aches and bruises were lending her a fierce energy,
awakening her limbs to thirst for battle, crumbling the ancient
difference between priestess and warrior. It was the struggle within
her own conscience that left Inmara weary.

She had been beaten down, pinioned helpless and unable to
move; but she had not been stripped and raped. All the pains
Thorn had caused Inmara were very slight compared with the
tortures Maldron had so delicately inflicted on the sorceress. Inmara had been shamed, humiliated, desecrated—suffered as it was
unheard-of a priestess should suffer—but she had been violated
only in darkness and quiet. She had not, like Frostflower, been
chained naked to the wheel in the full light of day, raised on a
scaffold, her suffering and shame exposed to a crowd of gaping
commoners who jeered as they watched the burning sword laid
twice across her skin. . . . and all this they had done, Maldron and
his family, to an innocent woman, a woman who could not save
herself with the truth, could not manufacture a lie.

Thorn was indeed the child's mother, and did not deserve him;
but Frostflower still lived. The swordswoman's words and manner
confirmed it more surely than if she had spoken it forthright.

"Thorn!" whispered the priestess. "If you would be her friend,
do not take her the child!"

"Damn sheet," muttered the warrior.

"If she is captured with him again, it will be death!"

"And if you catch her without him, you'll just bathe her in
perfume and send her home in a nice silk robe?"

"Listen to me, warrior! We are not searching for her—but if
you take the child, then we must search, we must disembowel."

Thorn lifted Inmara's bulkily-bound hands to her face, pushed
the knot into her mouth, and tied the ends of the sheet behind her

head. Then she lifted her, laid her on the bed, and tied something around her ankles.

"Lady," said Thorn, speaking in a voice more quiet than a whisper, "I'll give her a quick death myself before I let you gut her and hang her up again. But if you keep that damn brat away from her, you're killing her slowly just as sure as if you stoned her."

The warrior moved away from the bed. Inmara could see little. Her hands, tied up against her face, blocked half her vision. Her breath gathered warm, thick, and moist on her thumbs and the cloth pushing against her nostrils. Still, Thorn had tied her clumsily. A warrior should be ashamed to tie anyone so clumsily. Did they not bind criminals for questioning and execution?

I am still a priestess, thought Inmara. She did not dare bind me well—she is still at least a little in awe of my holiness. Then came the more humbling thought: she was working in haste and with a sheet of polished linen.

Meanwhile, as she thought these things, Inmara was quietly and desperately pulling, twisting, sliding the smooth cloth out of her mouth. For a few moments she feared Thorn had bound her more securely than she had thought at first. But once the knot was out of her mouth and the sheet pulled from the back of her head to around her neck, she was able to stretch her arms apart a little and twist her right hand down out of its loop. The rest of the network fell apart almost at once. The sheet remained around her neck like a battered cloak, but her hands and arms were free.

Thorn was standing above the cradle, apparently looking down at Terndasen by the dim light of the votive candle. Amazing that all their struggles, all their whispers and mutterings, had not wakened the child. Raes and Aeronu! If he should be dead—quietly as young babes sometimes died in their sleep— Why was Thorn studying him so . . . intently?

Inmara bent to her ankles. They were tied only with the hem of her own night-dress, pulled up at the edges and twisted crudely into strands. It was a moment's work to undo the knot—less firmly tied, and she could have kicked free.

The infant started crying—a hoarse, healthy, beautiful wail. But Inmara's relief shattered when she saw Thorn had picked him up.

The warrior turned and saw that Inmara had freed herself. For a moment they stared at each other in the shadows, the swordswoman holding the infant clumsily and confusedly, the priestess poised ready to spring from the bed, while the child wailed loudly. Somewhere, in the deeper shadows, the dog was wagging his tail against something.

She cares nothing for the babe, thought Inmara. If I move, she will throw him to the floor. "I could have screamed long ago," the priestess said in a low voice. It sounded like a promise, but it was not—and even if Inmara had stated that she would not scream, a priestess owed no faith to a warrior.

"What's the bloody difference now?"

"Do you think the babe never cries in the night? He will bring no one, if you continue to speak softly." Inmara rose and crossed the room, holding out her arms.

Thorn looked at her suspiciously, then shifted the infant into one arm and drew her dagger. Inmara jumped forward. The warrior held up the blade, pointed at her. The priestess stopped, horrified but wary, watching for Thorn's next move.

Slowly the warrior edged close enough to allow Inmara to take the child. As soon as she had him secure in her arms, the priestess backed away.

"Go now," she said. "I will tell no one that either you or she is still alive." It rankled to permit the warrior's escape; but, if caught and questioned, Thorn might lead them despite themselves to Frostflower. Moreover, if Inmara were to scream now, the warrior might yet stab both the babe and herself.

"Lady," said Thorn, "if Frostflower didn't need that brat, do you think I'd be here risking my guts?"

Frostflower was not completely innocent. She had used sorcery to bring the child to birth. Even that much guilt merited death. But Inmara was aware of what happened to babes who came unwanted into the wombs of creatures like Thorn. Was it justice to kill a woman for saving a child, by whatever means?

"The longer you remain," said Inmara, "the more likely you are to be caught."

"I gave him to you so you could bounce him back to sleep, Lady. I'm going to take him with me, or stay and kill half a score of you, priests or not."

"Silence your blaspheming tongue!" Deliberately turning her back on the warrior, Inmara walked to the bed and sat. She would open her bodice and try again to suckle him. Frostflower had told her she could, perhaps, do it . . . and old Cradlelap had agreed it was possible. Indeed, today the priestess had thought, for awhile, her milk was about to come.

Thorn followed her. She would not open her bodice with the swordswoman looking on.

"Get him back to sleep," said Thorn, "or I'll take him squalling."

Inmara glanced from the knife to the warrior's face. The priestess was in control of herself once more. She could not have conquered Thorn by struggling; her weapons were pride, dignity, and the detachment that would enable her, now, to scream when she chose, even knowing that the next moment she would feel a blade in some organ. "Who are you, a creature who should have been sterile, a mother with no love for your own son, to judge which of two natural women should mother this child?"

"Damn it, Lady, the bloody thing came out of *my* guts!"

A little more, thought Inmara, and I will cause her to shout instead of whispering. "Perhaps he came out of your body, but he brought no piece of your heart out with him."

The warrior shrugged, almost helplessly. "Gods, I don't understand it. If you don't understand it, how the Hell can I get it across to you? But you'll go on living without the damn grub, Lady, and Frostflower won't."

Why did she not remain angry? Inmara closed her eyes. How can I fight her when she pleads? But Frostflower was not completely guiltless—Inmara clung to that thought—and Frostflower merited death for sorcering the baby.

Sorcered! My little Terndasen... sorcered! No, it does not matter, I love him as dearly—Aeronu! I have held him, nursed him, tried to suckle him these four days—I know there is no difference, sorcered babes are not monsters, they are as sweet and as messy as natural babes.... Did it make any difference to me when I but suspected?

"Take back her dog to her," the priestess whispered.

"I'm going to. But would *you* come back to life for a whining mongrel, Lady?"

Raes, Aeronu! Is he not the sorceress's child? Has she not risked her life to give him birth? What laboring mother would exchange her childbed for Frostflower's sufferings?

Never since the child began crying tonight had he stopped. Despite her successes with him during four days, suddenly it seemed to Inmara that she could not comfort him because she was not his mother, because the little, sorcered infant was screaming for the sorceress. Inmara closed her eyes again, and the tears spilled down her cheeks. "Take him," she whispered. "Take him now. His crying will cover your sounds. Walk softly, and anyone who hears will think you are me, walking with the child."

"Until I get to the door and they start wondering why you're taking him outside on a cloudy night."

True. Though comfortable in the hall, it would be chill outside, and might storm again before Thorn reached . . . wherever Frostflower was. Inmara stood. "I will get his blankets."

"What about my guts?"

The priestess stared at her in contempt "You are not worthy to carry this child.

Thorn shrugged again. "Lady, please, just tell me how to keep him quiet."

How distasteful that this swordswoman must be the means of restoring the child to Frostflower! For a moment, now she held him in her arms, Inmara considered not giving him up, after all. But he was more nearly Frostflower's than hers; the justice of Aeronu and Great Jehandru, it seemed, did not always favor their own priests and priestesses. Inmara changed the infant's breech-cloth for the last time, wrapped him in his soft blanket from the cradle and in a tightly-woven, oiled outer blanket to keep off the rain if it fell. Then she made her final decision.

"At the dais-end of the long hall," she whispered, "is the beginning of an ancient tunnel. You will descend and pass through a round chamber. Walk reverently: it is our place of ablutive purification. On the other side of the chamber the tunnel branches. One branch leads up into the garden, from which you could not escape. The other passage leads beneath the length of the Farm, and will bring you up in Beldrise Forest, beyond the outer wall to the east, an hour's walk from the river Glant. You will see the garden passage at once. The safe passage begins far to the right. The entrance is narrow—you may not see it at first in the mosaic design—and you will know you are in the right passage when you see bare places where tiles have fallen and roots pushed through."

"But you know it's clear all the way to the outside, Lady?"

"I walked it twice, when I came here as Maldron's bride. Several of the children have walked it often, and the warriors keep a few shrines in it and sometimes, I think, use it to leave the Farm for a short while."

Thorn grunted. "So I might run into someone down there."

"You would prefer to leave by the open wheelpath and the guarded gate? Warrior, if I did not mean to return this child safely to the sorceress, I would not give him to you."

The warrior nodded, sheathed her dagger, and touched fist to lips in a salute more respectful than Inmara would have expected from her. Then she held out her arms.

"You will need a candle," said the priestess. "They are in the chest beneath my bed." She could more easily have gotten the candle herself, but she clung to the excuse for holding the babe a few moments longer.

Thorn found a candle, thrust it knifelike through her belt, and came for the child. He had almost stopped crying, but started again at the transfer. "Go quickly," whispered Inmara. "Do not light your candle until you reach the dais."

The warrior seemed about to speak, but did not. Inmara hoped she had wanted to say something grateful, for which her rough tongue could not find words. "Thorn," the priestess added, "do not let her be captured again with him."

"I won't let his Reverence take any one of us alive." Thorn glanced downwards. "Come on, you damn dog."

The warrior left, pushing the curtain aside with her elbow. Inmara sat on the bed. Dowl came, looked up at her face, whined, sat, and put one front paw on her lap. The priestess fondled his shaggy ears for a moment, then patted him once and lifted his paw from her lap. He stood, shook himself, and padded out, pushing aside the curtain in his turn and following the swordswoman.

Inmara lay on her bed, clenched her fists, and sobbed into her pillow. She must think of what to say to Maldron. But first she must offer up prayers for the safety of her little Terndasen . . . no, he was Frostflower's Starwind. Ah, Aeronu and Jehandru, had she acted well? And she must rest—must try, despite her aches, to sleep for a while, to sleep and forget.

Chapter 8

How the Hell did you hold a baby with one arm? And how in Azkor's name did you shut the brat up? Gods, thought Thorn, you'd think it would squall its damn throat raw. Every bloody farmer in the hall must be awake by now, and getting impatient for Inmara to shut him up. Any moment the old nurse or somebody else would be coming out to help.

At least Thorn had made it to the dais. "Shut up or maybe I'll bite your damn nose off," she muttered. Amazingly, the grub left off squalling and began to whimper. "All right. Now hold still, Smardon gut you," the warrior added, hoping the trick would work again. It did not. The grub kept on squirming. Apparently Smardon didn't scare it so much as mother.

Now Thorn could hear four paws padding up behind her. So the mutt had finally decided to come along, eh? Squeezing her right arm tighter around the brat's middle, trying to ignore the wiggling arms and legs, half-wondering if she was still holding it right-side-up, she managed to free her left hand, pull the candle from her belt, and light it at the constant-wick.

She had never been all the way to a farmer's dais before and might never be again. She had serious doubts about following Inmara's advice—at every step down the hall she had been ready to turn around and head for the front door and the open fields— but even if the priestess was setting a trap, it had almost been worth it just to get a glimpse at these mosaics. There was the Sheaf of the Wheat God, the Dripping Comb of the Bee Goddess, the Blossom Wreath of the Apple God, all glistering with the patina of years, cleanliness, and new gilding. Gods! thought the swordswoman, I'd like to see this by daylight.

"Well, come on, dog. Time to get the Hellbog out of here."
Ducking behind the dais-wall, she came to an archway of ancient
wood. Her left hand trembled slightly as she moved the candle
up and around to view the work more closely. The mosaics had
been beautiful, but this was awesome. Even in the candlelight,
she could see the darkness of age in the wood grain. The gilding
had been renewed not long ago, so that the carvings themselves
shone as if they were new, against the background of wood cut
lifetimes ago. The carving . . . you never found carving like this
in anything less than two lifetimes old. Even the small wooden
cloak-toggle carved in a similar style, which Thorn had seen on
her one trip to Five Roads Crossing, had been priced at two
hundred goldens, more than Slicer's sheen-amber. And here was
an entire doorway of such carvings—strong, clean lines forming
ancient, mysterious, sometimes unrecognizable versions of the
holy symbols—and the farmers were on everyday terms with it
as part of their dwelling! If she had not had a baby in one arm
and a candle in the other, Thorn would have liked to trace her
fingertip through one or two of the ancient symbols; but she knew
she would not quite have dared touch the wood.

Warriors' God! It was not worth losing her guts for. Pushing
aside the linen doorcurtain with one elbow, she went through into
the tunnel. The tunnel walls were completely covered with mosaics. Fortunately, after seeing the carved wood, she was no longer
so much tempted to stop and gawk. Besides, if the grub started
wailing again before she got out of the farmers' hearing, they
would think it pretty damn suspicious that the priestess was taking
him down into the tunnel.

By the time she got to the circular room, she judged she was
pretty well out of their earshot. The grub was being unbelievably
good, and the dog was padding along without so much as its usual
silly whine, so Thorn allowed herself a glance around. This time
she was more curious than impressed. The drain in the floor and
the assorted basins and fancy brushes waiting around amused her,
and that was all. More than one farmer had told her a ritual ablution
was the only purification a warrior needed to be fit for the touch
of a priest, but none of them had ever gotten her down to the
ablution-room. Now she finally had a look at one, and she decided
a person could get just as clean in a good river, or even in a
barracks bath-house.

She moved through the round chamber, listening for sounds

of pursuit and wondering what the Hellbog she could do down here if the priestess were betraying her. This was a good place for a trap. She found where Inmara had told her to go: a narrow opening partially camouflaged between two long, vertical stripes of tile symbolizing justice and mercy. She almost turned up the other passage instead, with ideas of hiding in the garden until the chase went by. But... Warriors' God! she had been around the garden wall, and she knew the garden would be a dead end. At least there was a chance of the other tunnel's coming up outside the Farm.

She slipped between the vertical stripes. Only three strides in, she noticed a bare patch in the wall where some of the tile had fallen. Large flagstones replaced tile on the floor. The passage was clean, floor and all; but the wall mosaic had not been repaired.

In the days when farmers could be killed during raids, every hall was supposed to have had one or two escape tunnels. Thorn wondered if Maldron's tunnel had been tiled from the beginning, or if the mosaics had been added after priests' bodies became sacred (and warriors' bodies did not).

The tunnel was getting rougher now. More and more patches of mosaic had fallen. Once or twice she saw broken tile that had never been swept from the floor. Every so often there was a root poking down through the ceiling. Inmara had told the truth about that, at least. A nice, safe mock-wilderness for the farmer brats to pretend they were brave and in some kind of danger. Well, maybe they were at that; one of these tunnels was supposed to have caved in once, somewhere near the middle.

In places the flagstones ended for anywhere from two to thirty strides. If the decorations were put in between the time the priests stopped needing the tunnel and the time they stopped using it completely, maybe the floor had never been finished. More likely some of the stones had been pulled up and carted off for use elsewhere, or covered by dirt washing down from breaks in the wall and secondary entrances. Thorn could spot a secondary entrance, or what might have been an entrance, somewhere around most of the major disappearances of floor stones. Originally, the various ways into and out of the tunnel would have been carefully hidden, so that attacking warriors would not get in and stop the priestly family's escape. Now, many of the entrances were either clogged entirely by the dirtfalls and debris of years, or completely open and letting in nightglow and fresh air. They had to keep some of the secondary entrances open, if the warriors had shrines down here; you could be damn sure Maldron did not let his cattle use the priests' entrance in the hall.

At one of the openings, a sudden draft blew out Thorn's candle. The grub, who seemed finally to be asleep, took it in stride; but Dowl yelped and started whimpering. "Shut up, dog," said Thorn. "You're not burned."

The swordswoman climbed up the narrow steps, cut long ago in the earth and now matted with grass and moss. Feeling at once free and exposed, she took a careful look around. The moon was a white smudge behind the clouds, and the night was too dark to make out how far she had gotten from the unlighted hall. She thought she could glimpse a dark barrier to the east, that might be the outer wall—if it was not a stretch of fruit trees.

Maldron had taken over his neighboring farmers' land to the south and enlarged his walls in that direction. Maybe he had taken over some of Beldrise Forest and enlarged his wall to the east as well, making the end of the ancient tunnel useless. Well, Thorn would go on trusting Inmara for now.

She descended again, sitting on the middle steps to fish out her firebox and relight her candle. The dog huddled around her, whining and getting its floppy head in her way. She had just room on the stairs to push him down and try to hold him with one foot. Then, remembering how Frost had left the mutt with the baby, she put it on the step beside her and said, "Earn your damn food, dog. Watch the brat."

Dowl moved into position on the step below the grub and sat still. When Thorn got her candle relit, she saw the dog was taking her command in earnest, hunching close as a protective barrier in case the brat tried to roll off the step, and looking up at the warrior expectantly. "Good mutt," said Thorn. She put away her fire-making equipment one-handed, managed to gather up the little bugger again, and went down the rest of the steps.

Seven or eight score paces farther along, she came to one of the warriors' shrines the priestess had mentioned. An alcove about six paces deep and maybe eight across had been hollowed out along the right-hand side of the tunnel. It seemed to date at least from the time the mosaics were first put in. It was tiled like the rest of the tunnel wall; but, where along the rest of the wall patches had been left broken, in the alcove they had been mended. Even by candlelight, you could tell where the tiles in mended places did not quite match those of the original design. Thorn guessed that fallen tiles from other parts of the tunnel had been brought here for the repair work. In a couple of spots, a whole symbol seemed to have been knocked out on purpose and a new one put in, as if the shrine had first been made for some other god or goddess than the one who now occupied it.

It was a shrine to the Warriors' God now. The new patches were the Crossed Swords, the Bloody Spear, and the Flaming Shroud. The statue was tiny, dwarfed by its own niche at the back of the alcove; but even before Thorn approached for a closer look, she knew whose image it would be.

It was ancient. That explained why Maldron's women used a statue too small for the niche—its venerability made up for its size. It was dark wood, carved in the same style as the door to the tunnel, and probably rubbed with blood to finish it off. The nose and the tip of the spear had broken off and been replaced with wax.

A brazier stood in front of the God's niche, a basket of kindling and charcoal waited to the right, and a basket of bread to the left.

Damn! thought the swordswoman. Warriors' God, I know I promised You a sacrifice at the first statue I found of You, but I meant after this whole mess was done with and Frostflower had the brat safe.

But she could not remember making that qualification in so many words. She had just promised the first statue of the Warriors' God she found. Damn it to Hellbog, why couldn't the baskets have been empty? Well, He could not expect her to stop in the middle of her escape, could He? Buy why had the damn shrine been put here in the first place, if not so that priestly families could stop and burn a sacrifice on their way out? If they could risk it, with a raid going on above them, what excuse did Thorn have for cheating on her word? Besides, she had already wasted a few moments here, a few moments there, gawking at the doorway, staring around at the ablution chamber and the bloody mosaics, climbing all the way up to take a look at the bloody clouds . . . Hellstink, if she had been walking straight ahead keeping her addled wits on escaping, she would not even have known whose statue this was.

No, that was not just, either. Inmara had told her the warriors kept shrines down here, and who else would warriors have in their shrines? She should have known this would happen when she decided to trust the priestess. Well, if Inmara was cheating her, she had already wasted too much time; and if the priestess was playing her true, she had the time to waste. Besides, if she wanted to keep the Warriors' God on her side the rest of the way, she had damn well better not cheat on her promise to Him now.

There was a thick marble sacrifice-ledge jutting out about waist-high on each side of the curving wall of the shrine, but Thorn decided the grub would be safer on the floor. She put it down on the left-hand side and told Dowl to watch it again. Satisfied the mutt was at his post, she returned to the statue and made a fire in the brazing-pan, lighting it with her candle.

The bread was in sacrifice-sized loaves almost as big as a fist. It was maybe half a hen's-hatching old; but the basket was almost empty. That meant warriors came down here pretty often to sacrifice. She dug Stabber's point a little way into the pad of her left fourth finger, squeezed nine drops of blood onto the bread, and put it on the brazier at once. She should have stood with her fist to her lips in a salute until the bread was unrecognizable; instead, she stood only for the length of two hundred heartbeats, not counting the times she broke the salute to poke up the fire and add another few pieces of kindling. When most of the bread's surface was pretty well singed, when the dog was yapping and the brat fussing—probably at the sacred stench of burning bread and blood—Thorn guessed the God would understand if she left early.

She turned and saw the mongrel was no longer lying beside the grub, but standing over it, looking toward the opening of the alcove. Well, you could hardly blame him for turning his nose toward the fresher air.

As soon as Thorn picked up the brat, Dowl loped out into the tunnel and stood there, looking down it, yipping and wagging his silly tail. "Shut up, grub," Thorn muttered. She shoved her cut finger into its mouth, giving it a chance to suck blood. It fell quiet and she stood listening. Someone was coming.

There was no sense trying to run. The footsteps were too close—a lopsided thumping. If it had not been for the dog and the brat, she would have heard it sooner. Maybe she had, and assumed without thinking that it was the dog banging its fool tail again, out of rhythm.

The first of Inmara's bitches appeared at the alcove entrance. *Clopmule? I just put iron into Clopmule six days ago! Why the Hell would the priestess send Clopmule—why would the limping* cow outdistance all the others? Thorn could not even hear any more footsteps behind.

Clopmule stopped, held up her short torch, squinted in Thorn's direction, and grinned. Keeping her torch ready and her face toward Thorn, she leaned to one side and patted Dowl. "Good mutt. Hey! Good mutt."

It was a trap, of course. The other warriors were waiting in the tunnel. Maybe they had come down one of the entrances remaining between here and the outer wall, to take her from both directions, make sure she could not run out. (Did the blasted tunnel even come up beyond the wall, or had her damn Ladyship lied about that, too?) Clopmule was the bait for the trap, and—Smardon's hooks! what did Thorn do but take the bait?

Inmara's warrior straightened, leering at Thorn. "Who the Hellbog sent you spying, comrade?"

Clopmule did not recognize her? Thorn remembered she was wearing dyed hair, a fake scar, and a dirty face, but—Hellstink, the priestess had known her almost at once, and in thicker shadows than these.

"Arun? Inraven?" Clopmule began the list of the neighboring farmers. "Not Duneron? Na, he married her Ladyship's sister. Well, don't worry, comrade. His Reverence will blister it out of you."

Warriors' God! Inmara had not sent the cow— Clopmule had just come limping down here alone to sacrifice. And if she thought Thorn had slipped in through the tunnel to spy for a raid, that meant the other end was still open. Pulling her finger out of the grub's mouth, Thorn shifted him into her left arm. He lost no time screaming again where he had left off.

"What the Hellstink do you have there?" said Clopmule. "A grub? Vuck's claws, what're you doing with a grub?"

"I'm nobody's damn spy." Thorn tried to hoarsen her voice. Did Maldron allow his workers to buy and sell babies? "I'm bringing the brat in for a friend."

"Unh. That stableman's sickly brat die at last? Well, you picked a Hell of a time to come messing around here with strange grubs to sell." Clopmule seemed disappointed at missing a chance to catch a spy.

Gods, thought Thorn, is the stupid bitch going to fall for it? Is there really some worker trying to replace a dead grub, or is this cow setting up another trap? "Grubs always pick a Hell of a time to come pushing out," she said, stepping forward.

Clopmule grunted again and stepped in front of her. "Well, let's have a look at the little bugger." She bent forward and pushed back the blanket with her crooked forefinger. "Damn, it's ugly."

"Takes after its mother." Thorn was easing Stabber out of his sheath. Now, while Clopmule was bending over the brat, would be the perfect time to punch a hole in her stomach.

"Gods, that's good stuff in the blankets," said Clopmule. "Where the Hellbog did you steal blankets like—" She broke off and stepped back without warning, staring down again at the dog. "Hey! That the mutt—?"

Thorn lunged, knife arm extended. Clopmule sidestepped and parried with the torch. Thorn retreated into the alcove, cursing. The brat squalled and wiggled in her left arm. The dog yelped and danced—it was anybody's guess whether he would get in the way or keep clear.

Clopmule planted herself medium-wide stance in the alcove entrance, transferred the torch to her left hand, and drew her sword. "Thorn, hey?"

"Look, you bloody cow, I know you got it six days ago. I know you're in no shape to—"

"Wasp got it. Takes more than a greasefingers like you to get me in a vital spot."

Thorn studied Clopmule's chest, the bustline smaller than she remembered, not bouncing . . . the damn cow was strapped in tight—she had to be hurting a Hell of a lot more than she let on. Give Clopmule this: the bitch was no whiner. "No, I guess it'd take a pretty damn long sword to get through all that fat."

Clopmule chuckled. "And that's her Ladyship's new brat, is it? Gods, his Reverence should give me a chance to put a couple of wires through you for what you did to me and Wasp."

Damn! thought Thorn. I need Slicer in my right hand, not Stabber. How do I change without giving Maldron's cow an opening? Then she grinned. Clopmule would not dare rush her as long as she held the baby. Maybe the grub had its uses, after all! "And what's his Reverence going to do to you if you hurt this brat while you're trying to get me, Clopmule?"

"If that stinking brat gets cut, it'll be your trouble, not mine."

Probably the bitch was right. With everything else against her, Thorn would get the blame for anything that happened to the grub.

But, for all that, not even Clopmule might really be ready to see a baby slashed open. "Not that much extra skin off my lips," said Thorn, "but how are you going to take her Ladyship's look when you bring her baby back dead?"

Thorn edged around slowly, aiming for the gap between Clopmule and the right-hand wall, keeping the grub between herself and Maldron's warrior. She stayed as far back as she could, but the only way out was finally going to put her within easy reach of Clopmule's sword. The most dangerous place would be at the opening; if Clopmule waited until just the right moment, she could crunch Thorn against the corner where tunnel and alcove walls joined. So far, Maldron's cow had not made a move; but Thorn did not like the shape of her lips, and she might not be able to tell what Clopmule was planning until too late. . . .

Fortunately, Clopmule lunged early. Thorn was not quite far enough to get rammed against the corner—she still had room to jump backwards. Her right elbow hit the sacrifice-ledge, going numb against the hard marble, but she held on to Stabber. The baby was yelling its guts out and the dog was barking its damn throat bloody, but for a moment Thorn had to keep her mind on Clopmule. Not until she was sure Maldron's warrior was not going to follow up at once could she glance down at the brat. It wasn't bleeding, and it couldn't be squalling like this if it had connected with Clopmule's sword. Maybe Maldron's bitch did not give a damn whether or not the brat got hurt, but at least she did not seem to be aiming at it on purpose.

Of course not. As long as Thorn held it, the grub was hampering her own movements, while Clopmule stayed free. Let the brat get killed, and Clopmule must know Thorn would fight like Bloodrastor First of Warriors. "Look, you bloody bitch, I'm going to put the grub down. No use letting him get hurt."

Clopmule leered. "Go right ahead, comrade."

She agreed too easily. Clopmule had never been any match for Thorn with a sword—especially now, when she was walking around with a half-healed slit in her breast and Thorn was desperate. "Truce until I get him down and stand clear of him?"

"You're a damn blasphemer and the gods sent me down here to catch you, Thorn. I'm not promising anything. But go ahead and put the grub down."

"Smardon's fingernails up your bloodly slot."

"Up yours." Clopmule chuckled again. "I'm on the gods' business. I think I'll cut off your thumbs for my sacrifice tonight."

Maybe the damn cow *was* in favor with the gods—she had been keeping up her private sacrifices, probably nightly. Maybe this *was* a big divine trap being sprung on Thorn. Warriors' God, thought the swordswoman, couldn't You have found a better bitch to spring Your trap than this stinking cow?

But you did not worry about such things in the middle of a fight. You just fought and hoped. Besides, if there was a God of the Sorceri, Thorn should have someone on her side. And..."Look, Clopmule, what happens between you and me is one thing, but how do you think the Birth Gods will like you if you slash a baby?"

"How do you think they like you for getting the grub in my way?"

Thorn adjusted her grip on Stabber. "I know you're still hurting, Clopmule. You know and I know I can slice you to catfood in a fair fight. Let me go and save your slimy guts."

"Azkor's claws in your eyes." Clopmule did not shout it. She said it with a grin. "I told you, Thorn, the Warriors' God is making me a gift of you. Now put the damn grub down." She waved her torch. Thorn remembered, uselessly, her dream about fighting with a flame on the tip of her sword. Hellstink, she would settle for having Slicer in her right hand.

"All right, Thorn, go on holding the damn grub if you want," Clopmule went on, "and we'll stand here until Snaste and Redbone come down to sacrifice at dawn."

Maybe it was as well Clopmule had not let her walk out. The cow would have limped off for reinforcements. Thorn backed up slowly. She had to go ahead and risk putting the brat down. Where would be the safest place? Right beneath the God's niche? Too close to the bloody brazier—if it got knocked over, she would smell roasted baby. Gods, it was hard to concentrate with that bloody cow grinning at her! Right beneath the sacrifice ledge, that would be best. The ledge to her right, so if she got Clopmule she could grab him up again on the way out.

She squatted slowly, keeping her gaze on Clopmule. Fourteen to thirteen Maldron's cow would jump before Thorn had a chance to get Slicer into her fist.

The dog trotted over, sniffing at the grub. Maybe it was not all that stupid. It seemed to realize the brat needed protection. Too

bad the mongrel was more likely to get in the way than protect
it.

Clopmule did not seem to be getting ready for a lunge. Maybe
she was so confident in the God's favor that she really did intend
to let Thorn put the brat down and move away. Thorn dropped
her glance for about a heartbeat to make sure she had the grub
safely on the floor.

Dowl yelped. Thorn looked up and saw Clopmule springing
at her.

She pulled her arm out from under the grub and rolled. Clopmule didn't change direction—coming too fast. Damn! How to
reach her before—

There was a crash and something hot hit Thorn's leg. She
struck it away—it was the torch—and rolled again, sat, and
slapped the last sparks out of her trousers. The dog was howling . . . or was it the baby . . . or both?

The torch was on the floor, still rolling a little, still burning.
Clopmule had fallen full length beneath the sacrifice ledge. She
lay quiet—Gods! Right on top of dog and baby! But Thorn could
see no movement. Might be a trick. Thorn got the torch and
crawled slowly over on hands and knees.

It was no trick. Clopmule might be alive, but not by much.
Thorn poked her lower leg with the torch, and there was no
reaction.

Thorn put Stabber back in his sheath, slapped out the sparks
that were taking hold in Clopmule's pants, and crawled on. She
still could not tell who was howling . . . maybe it was only in her
own brain . . . and she was not sure she wanted to look.

She looked.

The brat was yowling full force, its grubby face nothing but
open mouth and little screwed-up red wrinkles. Clopmule's arm
had fallen across its body . . . gods! Only a hand's-length closer,
and her sword, still clutched in her hand, would have hit the grub.
It had pushed one of its arms out from the blankets and was hitting
its tiny hand up and down against Clopmule's arm.

"Make a fist, you stupid grub, a fist," muttered Thorn, reaching
down and trying to curl its fingers up against its palm.

Maybe the dog had been howling before, but he was whining
now. He was caught somehow between Clopmule's shoulder and
the wall, looking at Thorn as if she could tell him how to get out
without stepping on the baby. "All right, just a moment, you damn

mutt," said Thorn. "Like this, grub. Watch." Making a fist, she
pounded Clopmule's hand until it let go the sword, then lifted
Clopmule's arm off the baby. "Just a little bit longer, dog." She
scooped up the grub and scuffled backwards with it, until she
could stand without hitting the ledge. "Now."

Dowl was already wiggling out. He shook himself, padded
over to Thorn, and stood looking up at her and whining. She
glanced at him, stooped, and held the torch closer. The dog's left
side had a splotch of blood as big around as a melon.

Gods! But what was the mongrel doing walking around, then?
Thorn could not see anything falling out, and Clopmule's sword
had landed far enough away from the dog, unless it swiped him
on the way past.

Thorn stepped forward and had a look at the ledge. Blood. Not
a lot, but enough. She turned Clopmule over with her foot. More
blood, a lot more. The bitch must have knocked her head against
the ledge. Her breast wound had popped open again, too, to judge
by the dark stain spreading on her tunic.

"I guess that tells us whose damn side the Warriors' God is
on," muttered Thorn.

After putting the grub down again at a safe distance, she rubbed
her hand over Dowl's side. He did not flinch, and she did not feel
any raw flesh or new blood leaking up from beneath the hair . . . no,
the wetness was all on the surface, all right. She wiped her hand
on Clopmule's trousers.

It seemed impious to leave so much blood on the sacrifice
ledge, the shrine mosaics, and floor. But Maldron's warriors
would be able to clean it up more thoroughly than Thorn could
do the job now. Her candle was still burning where she had left
it on the floor near the brazier. She picked it up, shook it out, and
stuck it through her belt. It would be useful if Clopmule's torch
burned low.

The grub had stopped crying and seemed half asleep, but he
batted his arm again when she bent over him. She tucked the arm
back beneath the blankets. She could not get them folded the way
Inmara had, but she guessed they would be snug enough for a
feisty brat like hers.

"You little bugger," she said, scooping him up again. "Too
bad you weren't a she. Quite a warrior we could have made out
of you."

Maybe Frost had arranged the damn thing's sex somehow,

when she grew it that afternoon, to make sure it could not be a warrior. Poor, sneaky little bitch of a sorceress . . . would she still be alive by the time Thorn got back?

The dog was licking Clopmule's face. "Come on, you stinking mutt," said Thorn. She had not cared all that much when Dowl took his time following her out of Inmara's room, but it disgusted her to watch the stupid animal fuss with Clopmule. "Come on, you bloody turd. Don't you want to see your sorceress again? Frostflower?"

Whether he recognized the name, or whether he just wanted to keep close to the light, he padded after Thorn immediately. She studied no more wall mosaics; when they passed another alcove, she did not even turn her head. When she guessed she should be getting close to the wall, she went up another side opening. The clouds seemed to have blown over, but the stars were faint. It was getting close to dawn. For a moment Thorn considered setting fire to the nearest grain field, giving Maldron something else to worry about besides chasing her. But some things you did not think of doing even if you were the slimiest of the scum—to burn a field, to destroy food, would be to outrage all the gods and goddesses and a few of the demons. Thorn returned to the tunnel and did not surface again until it narrowed, slanted up, and led her out into the woods forty or fifty paces on the other side of the wall.

The opening was hidden in the middle of a thicket. While Thorn extinguished the last efforts of the torch by rolling it on the tunnel's earth-covered ramp, Dowl snuffled around and located a space between two bushes. Pulling the blankets down over the grub's face to protect it from prickles, Thorn shoved her way out, paused to make sure of her bearings, and hurled the dead torch to the north. She heard it clunk against a tree somewhere; she hoped, if the searchers came through the tunnel, they would find it and think she was heading for Gammer's Oak, the Rockroots, or All Roads West.

Keeping the sun ahead of her, she headed for the river. She had learned how to avoid leaving a trail—she would be rotting off a gibbet by now otherwise—but if the sky clouded over she still risked going in circles in the damn woods. Following the Glant would take longer than cutting southwest across Beldrise and Weldervrise, but only if she could keep from getting lost. She would not be able to sneak into town before dark, anyway.

The brat was leaking through its damn blankets. Why the Hell had the priestess forgotten to give Thorn a few score extra breech-cloths? Maybe she was afraid the swordswoman could not have wrapped them around the grub's stinking butt without breaking one of its legs. For a long time in the middle of the day the little bugger howled—good thing nobody else was travelling the Giant Wheelpath. Thorn found a few wild strawberries and tried mashing them and putting them into the grub's mouth, but all she got was messy fingers. She would not risk drugging it with any other wild berries, and she was damned if she was going to let it suck *her* tit. Nothing there, anyway. So it would have to go hungry for a while. That gave it something in common with its mother. At last Thorn put her sword away and stuck the tip of her right little finger into the grub's mouth, holding it there as she walked along. If it was fooled, it was stupider than a pair of blank dice; but eventually it seemed to accept the situation of empty stomach, wet blankets, and mouth full of mother's finger. It squirmed itself into a knot it apparently found comfortable, stopped sucking and tried to cough out the fingertip and went to sleep. "You tough little bastard," muttered the warrior, glad to get back the use of her hand.

The western sky was still glowing when they came in sight of Straight Road. Thorn crouched at the edge of the forest until the first stars were out, then made her way to the road, feeling each step before she put her foot down. She carried the grub in both arms now. Like the mongrel, she was too damn tired to do anything but keep putting one foot down in front of the other. It was more darkness and luck, or maybe the favor of the gods, that got them the rest of the way to Frog-in-the-Millstone unobserved.

She went down the outside stone steps almost carelessly and tapped at the cellar door. Would Frostflower be awake? She tapped again, more loudly, and leaned against the door. Dowl started to whine.

Eventually Thorn felt the wood shake, heard the bolt being drawn back. Coming out of a dozing stupor, she stood away from the door. Yarn opened it cautiously and scrutinized her for a moment, then stepped aside to let her come in. Except for the small lamp in the weaver-woman's hand, the cellar was unlit. Thorn looked at the place where Frostflower had been bedded. The shadows seemed empty.

Yarn closed the door and rebolted it before speaking. "She is upstairs. She is resting quietly, and seems no weaker."

Somewhere on the floor above, a dog was barking. Dowl thrashed his tail and replied. "Shhh!" said Yarn, bending to catch his muzzle.

"Take the grub," said Thorn. "I'll keep him still."

Yarn put down her lamp and held out her arms. Thorn let the baby half-roll into them. It was painful to lower her own arms again. She squatted and put one hand around Dowl's jaws, rubbing his dirty hair with the other. The dog above quieted down.

"We got Golt yesterday," said Yarn, "to account for any strange noises."

"What happened here?"

"Maldron's warriors came, about midday. They were searching all the houses. We put Frostflower in Small Spider's bed with her face to the wall, and told them our daughter had taken very ill. They poked beneath the bed and in the close-room, but did not look at her face."

"What about Small Spider?"

"She hid in the cellar while they searched the first two floors. When they went to the loft-rooms, she slipped up and hid beneath Frostflower's bed. The gods have been kind to us." Yarn carried the grub to the table and started unwrapping him.

"Good." Thorn could have given them the praise they deserved if she herself was less tired and if Yarn were not taking the whole thing so damn . . . phlegmatically. Smart of them to get that other dog, too. Its bark sounded pretty much like Dowl's. "How did you know I was going to bring back this bloody mutt?"

Yarn smiled. "A dog new to a house can be used to explain many noises besides barking."

Chumming with sorceri was making sneaks out of them all. "Now the only thing we've got to do is keep them from barking at the same time."

"My husband will have muzzled Golt by now."

The weaver started bringing things down: table scraps for Dowl, kettles of steaming water. Thorn washed herself while Yarn washed the baby and Brightweave poked its dirty blankets down the close-stool. That was a waste, but they could hardly risk keeping the farmers' baby blankets around. They had better get rid of Thorn's purple-and-red clothes, too.

Yarn lent her a night-dress. Except for the makeshift skirt she had wrapped around her trousers a few nights ago, Thorn had never worn a skirted robe. It felt strange—luxurious but danger-

ous—like wine rubbed on her skin to slow her muscles from the
outside rather than the inside. Well, if Maldron's warriors had
already searched the place this afternoon, she ought to be safe
here for a while.

Yarn spooned goatmilk into the baby and the weaver washed
the dog in the water Thorn had used, while the swordswoman ate
ravenously: warmed-over stew, bread, cheese, raspberries, cool
charcoal-filtered water. All this was delay, but there would have
been less joy in waking Frost to see them when they were smelly,
blood-stained, and hungry.

There was something else, too. All Thorn's weariness had
dissolved in tension. She had brought back the baby and the dog;
but it had not been a clean rescue. She had battered a priestess
and left a fellow warrior bleeding and maybe dead. The gods
seemed to have been on her side tonight, but they might have been
handing her chances to make Hellbog even nastier for herself. For
two nights and two days she had been working toward the moment
when she could put the grub back into Frostflower's arms, and
now she was half afraid the moment would not repay her.

She could let the weaver-woman give it to Frostflower instead,
but then she would miss . . . what?

She wiped her mouth and tried walking up the stairs in her
night-dress. How the Hell did people get around in skirts? "You'd
better take him up the damn steps," she told Yarn. "But I'm taking
him in to her."

Brightweave stayed in the kitchen, holding his own whining
mutt. Dowl sniffed at the other dog for a moment, but soon he
was bumping around the women's legs again.

Small Spider met them at her bedroom doorway. "You're safe!"
she whispered. "You did it! Oh, swordswoman, praise the gods,
you're all safe!"

Thorn grinned. This was what had been missing. Finally, after
all the damn efficiency and self-restraint, someone was showing
a little honest enthusiasm.

"Is she awake yet?" whispered Yarn.

"No, but—"

"Go wake her up," said Thorn.

The older woman shook her head. "It may not be wise. Sometimes her sleep is like a trance."

"Damn it, go wake her up!" Small Spider's reception had made
Thorn feel for almost the first time that she had done something

worth swaggering about, and she wanted to go in to Frostflower
before the weaver-woman's everlasting prudence weighed her
down again. "She's been resting for two bloody days—she needs
some excitement."

Small Spider glanced at her mother eagerly. "I will wake her,"
said Yarn, handing the grub back to Thorn.

When Yarn had gone into the bedroom, Small Spider brushed
the baby's cheeks with her finger. "Oh, isn't he darling! How did
you ever *do* it, Thorn? Isn't it wonderful?" Without the girl's
praise to help her through the wait, Thorn would have gone in
herself to hurry things up.

At last Yarn returned. "You can go in now, warrior." She held
back the curtain with one arm and folded the other around her
daughter's shoulder. "We will be here."

Thorn entered the room. It was lighted by a candle in the god's
niche above the bed. Frostflower lay propped up on several pillows. She was looking toward the door, and she seemed to have
some expression in her face . . . not hope, not fear, not eagerness . . .
curiosity, maybe, but not as if anything concerned her. More as
if she was watching a newly-hatched chick and wondering if its
down would dry out brown or yellow. Thorn wished she knew
what the weaver-woman had told her.

"Who is it?" said Frostflower. The warrior realized her hair
was still dyed and she might look as strange as she felt in a faded
night-dress. How much did the sorceress know of what had been
going on around her? Did she even know Thorn had been gone
for two days?

As Thorn hesitated, the dog pushed past her and ran toward
the bed, barking and wagging its back end loose.

"Dowl!" The sorceress tried to raise herself a little higher on
the pillows. She winced, but smiled immediately afterwards and
held out her arms. "Hush, Dowl, hush." The dog stopped barking
and began trying to scramble up onto the bed, while Frostflower
patted him with her bandaged hands. She was not laughing, not
exclaiming as Thorn had seen her do before when she played with
the mutt; but at least there was a hint of pleasure in her face.

By the gods, soon there was going to be more! If the damn
dog could do that much . . .

Frostflower looked up again. "Thorn? How . . . What . . . ?"

The swordswoman walked quickly across the room. Halfway

to the bed she gave the grub a surreptitious poke with one finger. For once, she wanted him to yowl. He obliged.

Frostflower stopped petting Dowl. The dog licked her arm and then sat with his front paws on the bed, watching the women and thumping his tail. Thorn knelt and held the baby so the sorceress could get a good look at its yelling face.

The sorceress held out her arms, not practically, as Yarn had done, but reverently. Thorn put the baby into them, keeping her own arms beneath it until it was safely lowered to Frostflower's lap. Almost at once it stopped crying, blew a spit bubble, and went back to sleep.

Using one of her good fingers, Frostflower wiped the drool from the corner of its mouth. "How large he's grown," she said softly.

Thorn was glad she had brought him in herself. The weaver-woman would not have known how to enjoy this moment.

Chapter 9

The sorceress had lain too long in deep slumber; she did not know how long. From time to time she had wakened, and one of her friends had put food and wine into her mouth and attended to her needs before she began again on some technique of the mind . . . never of the body, her body was too weak and full of hurts . . . and achieved a dreamless rest that would have honed her power in the old days, but that she valued now only for the forgetfulness it brought. Once, attempting the first, elementary technique with which she might have been able to enter free travel, she had dreamed she felt her body divide in two . . . she had seemed to be in the upper shadows looking down on herself and on the bed looking up at herself at the same time, and she had wondered if it would have been like that . . . when she woke, whoever gave her food had been weeping. That was the only time she had dreamed, before Thorn brought Starwind back to her.

That night, after Thorn brought him back, Frostflower's blood flowed too quickly for her to use a technique. She no longer wanted to forget, but to be healed. In the old days, she could have gone into a healing trance, speeding her own body's time; now, she could only wait for her body to mend in its normal time. By breathing slowly, she would manage to drift into a natural sleep; she would dream; she would wake, turn her head, see the infant sleeping in the weavers' old cradle, Small Spider dozing or Yarn watching beside both cradle and bed, and Dowl sleeping curled on the floor or standing, his head on a level with hers, watching her. Then she would sleep and dream again.

Sometimes she dreamed of sliding rocks, of golden beetles with crimson marks like writing on their backs, of icy water trickling over her feet, of a dark cave which was either a loose memory or an old dream she had first dreamed in early childhood, of Windslope Retreat and the various cottages in which she had lived, but in the dreams they were mixed together—stone walls and wooden beams at once—and different, sometimes small and dungeonlike, sometimes as luxurious as the dwelling of the farmer-priest. Once she and a companion had to carry a pail of unbaked bread over a wide field of gray grass that turned into mud beneath their feet; they were carrying the bread to Thorn, who was sleeping in the grain cellar so that the infant would not wake her if it cried—so much remembrance of reality carried over into Frost-flower's dream—and the companion was either Thorn herself, or Small Spider, or Wonderhope, or a stranger. Most of these dreams should have disturbed her, but vaguely comforted her instead.

At other times she dreamed of what she tried to forget or feared to imagine while awake—she was walking through an unknown place when she came to a body dressed in red, twiching on a gibbet, and, going forward to speed its time and hasten its death, she saw her own face beneath the red hood; or she was Thorn carrying Starwind through endless Truth Groves, with priests now closing in from one side, now from another, now firing the trees with their torches, and the demons of farmers' superstition pouring water on the ground to turn it into a Hellbog; or she was on the scaffold again, almost as it had really been, the sword smoking in the brazier while she waited spreadeagled . . . but this time, instead of being tied to the egg-shaped frame, her knees and upper arms were glued with a paste that was causing her flesh to melt into the wood, and the crowd was filled with sorceri, more and more of her own people each time she looked—until at last an old sorceron stood before her on the scaffold, said "I am God," and thrust a testing finger up her. . . .

That was the worst dream; and it came, she thought, more than once. Yet even from this dream she woke strangely calmed, feeling something almost akin to power in the rapid throbbing of her blood. Her loss could never be regained; but she had the child back, and she allowed him to fill all the places where once her own ambitions had been.

So frail a creature on whom to base her entire will to live . . . she recognized the danger—a chill, an accident, any of countless childhood dangers could take him, even were there not ten days' journey between the weavers' home and the safety of Windslope. But he was no more fragile than the entrance to her own body had proven; and, having died over and over in the hands of the priests, she had used up her capacity for despair.

Towards morning, the child woke and began to cry. Yarn changed his breechcloth and helped Frostflower put him first to one breast and then the other before feeding him from a spoon. Poor Starwind! Already seven—no, eight days old (how long had Frostflower lain in the weavers' house?) and he had never yet successfully drunk from a breast . . . unless the farmer's old wet-nurse suckled him.

When Starwind slept again, Frostflower decided to practice a trance technique. The night's dreams had helped her adjust to the idea of living again, but now she judged herself in need of another period of deep, uninterrupted sleep. Starwind's mouth on her nipples being her most vivid recent sensation, she thought of how she might once have speeded time for her breasts, and found herself wondering, in the unclear thought that preceded sleep or trance, whether, now her body had felt man, she could hasten the coming of her milk . . . half-forgetful that the same penetration which was meant to engender new life replaced for all time the power to manipulate time. . . . Passing through the half-dream, she scarcely knew whether she took the branch that led to natural sleep or the one that would have led to trance.

When she woke, her eyelids orange with the full daylight against them, she was surprised at the decrease of pain in her body. She should not have been; she soon realized that her body had been healing itself for however long she had been here, while her mind, having lost almost all sense of the passage of time, still kept the memory of pain fresh. Now that Thorn had brought Starwind to detach her concentration from herself, the memory was no longer juxtaposed upon the actuality.

She opened her eyes and saw Thorn sitting beside her. The swordswoman's hair was indeed brown. It had not been a trick of the shadows last night.

"Your sleep was comfortable?" said Frostflower.

"Too damn comfortable. I slept the morning away like a blasted turtle."

Frostflower smiled. "Or like a sick woman?"

Thorn grinned back and started to put a flask with a copper drinking-tube to the sorceress's lips. Frostflower shook her head

and tried to sit. Suddenly drinking-tubes were repellent to her—
she would drink from a cup.

The warrior helped her into a sitting position, gave her cool
cherry juice, and lifted a pot to a cooking-brazier. Then she returned to sit beside the bed. "Look, Frost," she began, but paused
and took one of the sorceress's hands before going on. "I wish
you'd try to get a little solid meat into you.... All right, don't
worry, it's only porridge cooking. But—damn it, if we had a
tree's age I wouldn't even suggest it, but if we're going to get
you back to your retreat before the bloody farmers decide to search
the town again, we've got to get your strength up."

Even from this friend who had risked everything for her and
the child, it was hard to take the suggestion of meat. "I will be
strong enough very soon. I could almost have sat up by myself."
Frostflower pressed her fingers tightly around Thorn's. "You see?
There is almost no pain in them. I will hold the bowl and spoon
and feed myself."

Thorn shrugged. "I'm slipping out of here tonight to go find
that damn merchant and his bloody wagon. I'm taking Small
Spider and the dog with me."

"Why?"

"Safer. Probably not by much, but still a little safer. You're
supposed to be Small Spider. If Maldron's bitches come again
before I haul Spendwell back here, the weaver or his wife puts
Starwind in with you and you huddle up with him under the
blankets and keep him quiet."

Frostflower nodded. She had been only dimly aware of the
first search, but she realized Small Spider must have experienced
great danger hiding from the warriors. "And the cradle?"

"They're going to bring up a box for him instead, make him
a bed out of sick-room rags. Clean, of course."

"Bring the merchant quickly, Thorn. I will be strong enough."
Strong enough, perhaps, even to look at him and thank him.

As Thorn stirred the porridge, Frostflower began to pick the
bandages from her fingers. Her nails were still tender; but, after
she had dabbed some dry blood away with saliva and the cleaner
strips of bandaging, they looked very well healed. She was proud
of the way she handled her bowl and spoon.

Thorn watched her musingly. "You're really sure you've lost
your powers?"

"Don't hurt me, Thorn."

The warrior tugged at a piece of cloth covering the garnet in the pommel of her dagger. "Look, Frost, your God seems like a pretty good sort. Why would he take away your powers when the damn thing wasn't your fault?"

It was painful to talk of her loss, even to think of it; but Thorn seemed ready to listen and perhaps be convinced. As long as Thorn clings to her superstitious belief in the farmers' gods, thought the sorceress, she will think herself damned to everlasting torture. I can do so little to thank her; if I can persuade her of the truth, free her of that ugly fear... but how to begin? "God did not take away my powers. It was Maldron who took them, using... that unfortunate young man."

Thorn grunted. "I can see why your God doesn't punish that motherpricking farmer—it'd be a couple hundred gods or so to one. But why take it out on you?"

How could she explain without making the Infinite seem cruel? "It is not cruelty, Thorn. It is the order of creation.... God is female and male in the same being, and all things are the offspring of the divine union. Either we can imitate God in the union that creates offspring, or we can imitate to a small degree God's control over creation; but we cannot do both."

"Frostflower, as far as I can see, your God's been working pretty damn well with some of mine to get us through. Most likely yours even did the convincing—I don't know why my gods would have wanted to help me out for my own sake. That doesn't seem as if he's—she's?—angry with you, does it?"

Frostflower sighed and put the half-empty bowl down carefully in her lap. Her fingernails were beginning to ache, and her throat muscles to swell. "It is not anger. The order of creation is for the good of all. If we could imitate the powers of both creation and control, we would grow proud."

"You haven't imitated the powers of creation. It only happened once, and it didn't take any bloody effect."

The sorceress blinked, trying to hold a tear in her eye so that Thorn would not see it. "To imitate control, a person must act alone, individually, as she or he was born. When the individuality is once broken, it can never afterwards be restored."

"That's not much control your God has over creation, if he can't bend one of his own rules sometimes."

The tear rolled down from Frostflower's brown eye. That was

always the eye that filled first, and it was on the side turned toward Thorn.

"Damn my bloody, rotten mouth." Thorn picked up the bowl and spoon. "I'm sorry, Frost. Forget I said anything. What do I know about it? Come on, let's get a little of this mush into you while it's still lukewarm."

The sorceress nodded and opened her mouth, but closed it almost immediately and pushed away the bowl and spoon. Her breasts—perhaps she would have noticed it sooner if she had not been tangled in regrets and explanations—

"Frost, what is it? What the Hell—What's wrong?"

Wrong? Nothing was wrong—she thought nothing was wrong. Her breasts were tingling, and felt..."Thorn! Give me Starwind! Quickly!"

Thorn almost dropped the bowl of porridge in reaching for the infant. Frostflower looked down and saw two small wet spots on her bodice. She touched one spot lightly, then opened the garment.

She was shocked to feel Thorn's arms quivering as the warrior handed her Starwind. Glancing up, she was even more shocked at Thorn's face. The swordswoman looked as if she thought the end had come and her friend called for the babe to tell it good-bye. "No, no, Thorn! Nothing is wrong—my milk has come!"

The swordswoman relaxed, grinned, and settled back to watch the feeding. "Well, I'll be damned! But don't think you're going to get out of finishing your own blasted dinner this way."

Thorn put her hands behind her head and whistled very softly. Dowl sat up and put his front paws on the bed as he watched, head to one side and the sunlight coming through the window to mottle his coat with reddish-gold patches. Starwind sucked con-tentedly, drinking at last, no longer causing her skin the faint, unsatisfying dry soreness. "I had thought we must work as if from the beginning. I had thought these last days... Thorn, my breasts must have been filling all along, as if he were still sucking, all the while the rest of my body and my mind... Perhaps the very pain was stimulation?"

"Unh." Thorn cocked her head, unconsciously achieving ex-actly the same angle at which Dowl was holding his. Seeing the two of them watch her with the same expression, Frostflower chuckled.

Thorn glanced down at the dog and saw the joke. "Damn mongrel," she said, leaning forward and rubbing his head between the ears. "Well, tell the truth, I never really expected it to happen at all. Look, Frost, will you do one thing for me? Sometime, when you're feeling up to it, will you just stick a seed in the ground and do whatever you used to do, and see what happens? All right?"

The suggestion was impious, but clearly Thorn did not realize that. "It would be like questioning the wisdom of God, Thorn."

The swordswoman shrugged. "Well, I guess you know more about it than I do. Tell him I'm sorry if I insulted him, then, will you?"

The sorceress nodded, let her head rest far back on the cushions, closed her eyes, and held Starwind a little more tightly. Soon she would shift him to her other breast . . . having him with her, feeding from her, growing even now, though imperceptibly, in her arms—it did not fill the emptiness of her loss; but . . . ah, God! it went so far to console her for it.

Chapter 10

This time Thorn went disguised as a male charcoal burner, in trousers unlaced around the legs and a dark gray tunic that hung straight to her calves and had slits up both sides—clumsier than warriors' clothing, but not so clumsy as a skirt. Her voice was deep enough to pass for a man's, and she did not intend to talk a lot anyway. Yarn cut about a thumb's length off her hair, so that it barely covered her ears. The disguised swordswoman wore an old, chipped forest knife in plain sight and Stabber beneath her tunic, with the cloth bloused out above the belt to hide the outline of his handle. Slicer she carried rolled in a blanket in the middle of the long bag slung across her back; there was no way she could have worn him at her side without risking detection.

Yarn cropped her daughter's hair even shorter than Thorn's. "When she returns, and our friends see her again, we will say it needed to be cut to reduce her fever," sighed the woman, coiling the long black braids and wrapping them in linen. (Thorn's shorn fringe had gone down the close-stool.) In a gray tunic almost as long as Thorn's, with her face and hands smudged and dirty, Small Spider made a passable boy.

They both rolled their newly-sewn charcoal-burners' clothes in ashes and walked over them several times before putting them on, and they rubbed the dog with mud and soot—not that it helped disguise him much, but there were plenty of mongrels around that looked pretty much like Dowl anyway. They went by the names of Cleansmoke and Ash. There was not a Hell of a lot they could do about the mutt's name, but they tried dropping the "D" and calling him Owl, and he seemed to respond pretty well.

Small Spider cried a little when her hair was cut, but otherwise she seemed to love it all. Thorn shrugged and told her, "Don't act like a damn nervous pussy or I'll get a stick and thrash your muscles loose from your stupid bones." She herself would have no trouble imitating a charcoal burner's weariness with life and work. She was sick of traveling around in disguise. Gods and demons! Was this going to be her life from now on? Better turn sorceress and grow moss in the mountains than keep hopping around from one disguise to another until she no longer much cared whether or not anyone recognized her and trussed her up to cart back to Maldron.

Their story was that their old donkey had broken a leg in the forest and had to be killed and left for the wolves. That gave them an excuse to hunt through towns and farms, supposedly looking for a new donkey. It also gave them an excuse for being charcoal burners with no charcoal to sell. Since they needed a reasonably strong donkey and could not afford—either actually (Brightweave's purse could not stand too many extra expenses) or as poor burners—to pay a fair price for one, they also had an excuse for not buying the animals they were offered.

They got through Three Bridges fairly well; it was a large enough town that a pair of strange burners drew only a few glances, and their occasional haggling for a donkey they could not afford earned nothing more than an exasperated shrug from the would-be seller. But at Arun's Farm they encountered a stableman who was ready to sell a good animal for a silver and a half, because it had been his dead grandson's pet and he did not want the reminder. "You won't find a donkey cheaper that still has any work left in it," he remarked; and even Thorn could see the beast was worth at least three silvers. When Arun's stableman went down to a single silver, Thorn had to tell him she would try to borrow the money in Nedgebottom and return with it. "If you can't get one silver together without borrowing from the Nedgebottom skinners," he said, "you'll have to leave them your son as security, burner."

"Maybe I'll put a donkey hide on the young rascal and get some work out of him for once," said Thorn. "Come on, Ash."

The swordswoman had not planned on going to Nedgebottom, since she guessed that even when he had Maldron's safe-passage token, Spendwell would be a little too fastidious to go into that town. Nevertheless, after the experience at Arun's Farm, they went. If someone told the stableman they had taken the turn for

White Orchard instead of Nedgebottom, he would be more likely to wonder and remember them clearly than if they headed for Nedgebottom and simply never came back to Arun's Farm.

Once out of sight of the farm, they could perhaps have doubled back; but in the long run it would take less time and likely be safer to go on into the unsavory town than to roam around after dark in its neighborhood. As down-on-their-luck charcoal burners, they could hardly rent a room in one of the town's two respectable inns—folk would remember. They found a cramped alcove with a torn curtain in a stinking greasetrap called Bottom of the Flask. Thorn had slept soundly in even worse places; and had she been alone she would have felt safer here, in this disguise, than she had felt anywhere else for half a hen's-hatching. But with Small Spider to take care of, she sat up against the wall the whole bloody night, her hand on the pommel of her sword, listening to the young girl's snores. Gods, was Thorn only nine or ten years older than Spider? She felt old as Bloodrust that night.

She felt even older next morning. After a quick check around Nedgebottom, as long as they were there anyway, they headed on for White Orchard. Spider kept whistling the same damn tunes—if it wasn't "The Lovers in the Stable," it was "Silverpalm's Lament" or something that sounded like "The Drunken Thatcher." Thorn was too tired to fight off gloomy thoughts of hiding out in Nedgebottom or in the woods with Frostflower and the grub and Dowl—what the Hell would they eat, if Frost refused meat and could no longer grow vegetables?—or trying to herd them all in disguise to the mountains on foot . . . the eastern mountains were a few days closer than the northern, and the mountains were lousy with sorcerous retreats all the way around, weren't they?

By afternoon the swordswoman was almost dozing on her feet, and her thoughts had become repetitive nightmares. She was as groggy as if she had wine in her muscles, and she was ready to peel Spider for whistling. Maybe she should have told the damn merchant to wait somewhere for news of her. She had had a pretty shrewd suspicion, even before Spendwell left the weavers, that she would need a way to get Frostflower and the brat back up to the mountains. But she had feared that if she told him, instead of waiting for her he might travel away as far and fast as he could.

They finally had another kiss from the gods when they reached White Orchard. Small Spider glimpsed Spendwell through an open tavern door. The bastard was eating beef slices in carrot sauce and drinking red wine from a glass horn.

A pair of dirty, impoverished charcoal burners could hardly go in and sit down at the same table with a prosperous merchant taking his dinner in one of the town's most expensive taverns. Thorn and Spider walked on to the wagon-field and sat on the grass outside, chewing stale bread, cheese, and peaches from the cheaper foodsellers, keeping watch on the wagon-field gate.

When Spendwell came sauntering back after dinner, Thorn approached him and said, "Extra donkey to sell, merchant?"

He gave her a quick glance and wrinkled his nose very slightly. "I'm sorry, brother, not one I can spare."

She grunted and looked around. The wagon-field guards were busy with their dice and nobody else except Spider was within forty strides. She sidled nearer and muttered, "Spendwell, you bloody liar, you had seven of the stupid animals last time I counted."

He took a closer look and started, but kept his wits. After glancing around and seeing the weaver girl in her boy's tunic waiting several paces away with Dowl, he turned back to Thorn and said, "I do have one that's getting old, brother. I might be able to sell it at a price you could pay."

One of the guards was a gray-haired old spearwoman with a face like a dried apricot. The other was a lazy-looking young bitch with a scar over her nose. Maybe an early case of battleshock had left her content to rust her life away as daytime guard at the wagon-field gate of a quiet town like White Orchard.

"Don't remember your face, burner," said the old guard as Thorn followed Spendwell through the gate.

"Need a donkey. None around my usual towns," muttered Thorn.

The younger guard laughed. "Better not let that smutty charcoal burner near your cloth, merchant."

Laughing at their rotten joke, the bitches went back to their game—Fives after Twos. Thorn followed Spendwell to the donkey pen in the middle of the field. Here and there another merchant was fussing around with his wagon; but the field was half empty, and the noises of the animals in the pen would help cover their conversation.

"That one, with his left ear laid back," said Spendwell in a fairly loud voice. Pointing at an unusually glassy-eyed beast, he added, barely loud enough for Thorn to hear, "Where's the baby?"

"Snug with the sorceress."

"I didn't see—that's not the sorceress with you?"

"That's the weaver's brat. . . . What do you call that donkeyskin stuffed with flab, merchant?"

"Dillseed. Carries more for his age than any other donkey I've ever had. . . . But she's safe?"

"For the time being."

"Thank the gods!"

"Quiet, Spendwell. You're getting loud. . . . Thirty-four kips."

"I thought you wanted a donkey, burner! This time next year, Dillseed will still be worth a silver and a half."

Yes, the damn donkey probably had a better chance than any of them to still be around next year. "Looks like it'd bite my fingers off."

"Any donkey will try to bite if you mistreat him. . . . We can't talk here."

"Shrewd merchant." They certainly could not talk here much longer. A pen of donkeys stank even worse than a warriors' barracks after fighting practice in the winter. "Thirty-six coppers, then. . . . Any woods near the road south of town?"

"South? Why not north?"

"Why not south?"

Keeping up a surface haggle that Thorn hoped would convince any casual listener, they arranged to meet in Glandron Forest to the south of White Orchard. Small Spider would watch for the merchant and whistle him into the woods with "The Lovers in the Stable." To make it sound as if money changed hands—Thorn insisted on keeping Brightweave's funds in her own possession—they clicked coins in the shadow of Spendwell's wagon, and so ended the mock purchase of the donkey.

"If that's an old animal, I'm a dairy wench," remarked the gray-haired guard at the gate.

"Not old. Cantankerous," replied Thorn. "Come on, you four-legged turd." She had so much trouble with the beast that the town warrior ought to be convinced Spendwell had sold it cheaply because of its evil temper. All the same, the old bitch had a sharp memory for niggling details, and that worried Thorn.

Once she got Dillseed out to Small Spider, the girl managed to coax him along more easily. They found a weedy clearing in the woods south of town, between the road and the river, and waited. Thorn had told neither the merchant nor Spider the real reason she wanted to wait south of town. If they waited north, on the way back to Frog-in-the-Millstone, Spendwell might think again about rejoining them. They stood in the shadow of the gibbet; simply meeting them here could be dangerous. Even though Thorn had kept the money, the merchant might consider losing a donkey a reasonable price for heading south to safety. He was not so likely to try avoiding them if, in order to do so, he would have to head back north into Maldron's neighborhood.

It was almost evening before Small Spider glimpsed the cloth merchant's wagon and started whistling. Nobody else was around; Thorn had spent most of the afternoon checking on that. The gods still seemed to be on their side. Nevertheless, she did not quite believe Spendwell intended to join them until his wagon was actually turning off the road.

Small Spider met him near the edge of the woods and guided him back to the clearing. "Take back your son of a bastard donkey," Thorn told him when he arrived. She jerked her thumb at Dillseed, who was disgustedly trying to chew his tether loose from a tree on the bank of the river.

"Gods! Were you trying to drown him, Thorn?"

"I wasn't about to lead the bloody animal back and forth every time it acted as if it wanted a drink." Thorn noticed that Spendwell had a wine flask on the seat beside him. Well, at least his tongue was not slurring yet. She herself had not felt so greatly tempted for years to sit down and drink a few mouthfuls of wine.

"So you did it! You're quite a warrior, Thorn."

"Unh." She enjoyed his admiration, but she was not going to encourage it and get bogged down in flattery. "So you thought Small Spider was Frostflower, eh?"

"I am about the same size," said the girl eagerly. "And my hair is almost as black. That was how we got the idea to hide her in my bed."

"And you don't look a Hell of a lot like Small Spider, either, in that disguise," said Thorn.

Beneath the dirt on her face, the girl turned pink. "I'll go untie Dillseed."

As Spider ran toward the donkey, Thorn turned back to Spendwell. "You should have known I wouldn't let the sorceress outside without a patch over one eye."

"I should have known she wouldn't be strong enough to travel yet."

"Don't bet on that. She's already got both dugs full of milk for the brat." Thorn had not yet told Spendwell outright that she wanted him and his wagon to smuggle Frostflower back to the mountains. How much he had guessed she was not sure, but she might as well learn right away whether he would come willingly or whether she would have to drag him. "She'll be strong enough to ride by the time we get back to Frog-in-the-Millstone."

Spendwell nodded and tied his reins to the stay-post on the driver's seat. "I thought she might need me again. I didn't think you found me just to tell me you were all safe."

"Maybe there's hope for you after all, merchant." Thorn would not mention her doubts of him—the bugger needed encouragement. "We're not safe yet, but we should be better off with you than without."

"You will be. As safe in my wagon as if you were already in the mountains. I've been making plans, Thorn." He jumped down from the wagon and approached her. He walked pretty steadily, but she could smell the wine on his breath.

"You and your Southvines white have been making plans."

"Na. Southvines purple. You should try some tonight."

She no longer much wanted it. "You damn bastard, you think I haven't been making plans?"

"I thought you might like help." Was he boasting again . . . or begging? "Why do you think I waited around here? Why do you think it was so easy to find me?"

"Easy, you bastard?" Thorn thought of the curious stares here and there in Three Bridges, of the stinking stableman at Arun's Farm trying to give them his donkey, of her sleepless night guarding Small Spider in Nedgebottom. Well, maybe Spendwell really had waited, tried to keep himself available. Probably he would not have traveled much faster at his normal trading pace; but this was not a normal situation—and if he had wanted to disinvolve himself, he could have been in Nearmidnorth by now. "Tell me one thing, Spendwell," she said, putting her hands on his shoulders. "Did you wait around to help me, or the sorceress?"

"If she didn't need help, you could have made it better alone, couldn't you, warrior?"

"Smart, merchant. I'd have gutted you if you said anything

else. Just don't tell me why you want to help a sorceress so much,
or maybe I'll peel and boil you."

He wiggled his fingers under her palms. "You're the one who
owes me a good milking, Thorn."

She glanced at Small Spider, who had the donkey untied and
was letting it drink before leading it back to tether it someplace
safer. The merchant and the warrior both deserved a good screwing. They would deserve it more, and maybe enjoy it more, after
they had everyone safe, including themselves—but in a few days
they might be dead, not safe. They had better take the chance
while they had it; it would help keep the merchant's courage up,
and she could always give him another couple if they made it
through this mess with their guts still on the inside. "Wait until
Spider's asleep. We'll bed her down in the wagon and spread a
few blankets out here for us. Meanwhile, you get us a decent
supper—I'm sick of poor workers' slop—and I'm going to sleep
until it's cooked."

They left the following morning before light. Thorn let Spendwell keep himself awake on the driver's seat, while she slept much
of the way in the wagon. They reached Frog-in-the-Millstone very
late in the afternoon. Thorn, Small Spider, and the dog remained
in the wagon until almost midnight. It was a good thing Frog-in-
the-Millstone was too small to have a wagon-field for traveling
merchants; Brightweave had his own little pen for the donkeys,
while the wagon waited between his house and the spinner's next
door. It was also a good thing that no one had looked inside
Spendwell's wagon between White Orchard and Frog-in-the-Millstone—they would have had a hard time explaining the presence
of two charcoal burners and a muddy dog in the middle of Spendwell's expensive cloth.

For the ten days from the weavers' home to the mountains they
would have a better explanation. Thorn would be a laboring man
(another change of disguise, this time to a landworker's short
tunic), Frostflower his wife, and the brat their son. They would
all ride inside the wagon; and if nobody looked inside, fine. If
somebody did see them, they were a family who had lost their
work when their old priest's farm in the south was raided by a
neighbor who had too many workers for his own land. They had
come as far as Glantfork without finding another place. Hearing
that Elvannon was a bighearted priest with poor land that needed

good, hard workers and that did not attract raids, they had paid
Spendwell most of what remained of their savings for a ride to
Elvannon's Farm in the shadow of the northern mountains. To
explain why the laboring man was riding inside instead of reducing
the price of their ride by helping the merchant, Thorn, or "Pitchfast" (as she had renamed herself this time), would be recovering
from a sudden fever. She would lie on the wagon floor with her
sword and dagger hidden under her blanket. Nobody would question the presence of a baby with two parents in evidence; and,
while they would not attempt to hide the dog, with luck Frostflower
would be able to keep it quiet and unobtrusive, visible but not
memorable.

All of them helped devise the story, and by the time it was
settled, Thorn was no longer completely sure which details had
been hers originally, which Spendwell's, and which the weavers'.
Even Frostflower, who otherwise sat silent, testified to Elvannon's
character.

Frostflower still had a slightly bleak expression in her face.
It worried Thorn, but it would fit in with their story. The sorceress
was strong enough to travel, anyway. She was almost as strong
as when the swordswoman had first met her. Well, who would
not look bleak, with a return to the gibbet constantly threatening
her? Thorn probably looked pretty damn bleak herself.

They put Frostflower into a landworker's trousers and a nursing
mother's worktunic, almost as short as Thorn's; they curled her
hair in a braid around her head (Thorn thought it had been stupid
of the weaver-woman not to cut it as short as she had cut Small
Spider's; but, now the sorceress was no longer taking Spider's
place, it was better to leave it long); they wrapped her head with
a kerchief that Spendwell folded in the style of the southlands;
and they took the warrior-red eyepatch Thorn had used earlier,
dyed it dark brown, and adjusted it over Frostflower's right eye.

Only once did Frostflower demur. "This is lying, isn't it?"

"We can't stroll up Straight Road North as ourselves," Thorn
replied.

"You said, once, that my people live lies, that we would not
know how to tell the truth."

"When the Hellbog did I ever say that?"

"In Burningloaf's upper room."

"I was a damn stupid bitch. Anyway, it's different when you're
fighting for your life."

Frostflower played with the lacings of her tunic. "Yes," she said.

Yes, scorch my guts, thought Thorn. The sorceri know all about dissimulating to save their lives—except that they have to do it somehow without downright lying. "Look, Frost," she said aloud, "I know what the bloody priests do to you if they catch you wearing anything besides those damn black robes, but you don't have your own rules about it, too, do you? I mean, your God doesn't make it a sin for you to wear anything else?"

Frostflower looked up with something like her old smile. "In our retreats, we wear bright colors, embroideries, the loveliest clothes we can make."

The warrior had not expected quite that revelation. The thought of sorceri walking around their retreats dressed like butterflies was irreconcilable with the gloom-ridden, menacing places of the tales she had always believed. But so was Frostflower irreconcilable with everything she had always believed of the sorceri. Thorn grinned. "All right. You're not lying, you're just wearing the clothes your friends have given you. Sorry they're not brighter. All you have to do, if anyone asks, is just sit quiet—don't say yes, don't say no, don't say anything—if they think you're dumb, fine, you don't even have to open your mouth to deny it. Leave all the lying to the merchant and me."

"Thank you, Thorn." Frostflower looked down again. "It is good of you. But it does not matter so much, now, whether I help you to lie or not." She began to play with her lacings once more. They went down to her waist, the tunic being made so that a mother could undo the front and pop her breasts out quickly and easily when feeding time came for the brat. After a moment she smiled again. "How will you say I lost my blue eye?"

"The bloody brat poked it with his little finger."

The sorceress chuckled. "Would anyone believe it?"

"Of course they'll believe it. That's a damn strong grub and he'll poke their own eyes out if they don't believe it. All right, you got hit by a flying chip of wood one day when your father was chopping logs for the fire."

Spendwell and Brightweave spent much of the afternoon putting still more of the weavers' cloth into the merchant's wagon. A couple of townsfolk, visiting to ask about Small Spider's health and seeing such a prosperous young merchant as Spendwell back again so soon for more of Yarn and Brightweave's cloth, con-

gratulated them on their success and asked how they could keep
up with the demand for their weaving. Brightweave pointed to the
length presently on Yarn's loom and remarked that she had to
finish it before morning, since Spendwell wanted it, too.

Late that night, Thorn and Frostflower came up from the cellar
where they had spent the day hiding and adjusting their disguises,
and Small Spider came down from the supposed sickbed on which
she had taken her own place. Frostflower climbed alone, with the
baby and Dowl, to the uppermost floor to make whatever prayers
sorceri made to their God. The rest gathered all the household's
statues into Brightweave's bedchamber.

It was a very simple ceremony. They could not chant, both
because they had no priest and because they could not risk being
overheard. Brightweave, Spendwell, and Yarn took turns muttering prayers as nearly as they could remember the priestly words,
pausing sometimes to leave out phrases they had forgotten, rather
than missay them too badly or risk making up their own words.
Very few priests would have sanctioned such a ceremony at all;
many would have said the petitioners were worsening instead of
bettering their chances. A private, wordless sacrifice of praise or
gratitude was one thing—a gathering of petition was another. Less
than a hen's-hatching ago, Thorn would have considered such a
gathering, without priest or chant, blasphemous. *We've all been
corrupted,* the swordswoman thought as she stood in the back with
fist to lips, wishing the weavers had a statue of the Warriors' God.
*We're all getting sloppy, even the damn merchant. Frostflower's
making us all irreligious, and she's not even down here with the
rest of us bastards!*

Afterwards they had a small supper, hushed but groundlessly
cheerful. Yarn finished her length of cloth and Brightweave loaded
it into the wagon at the same time Thorn and Frostflower, with
the baby and the dog, slipped out to it. Thorn slept the rest of the
night on the wagon's floor, not waking until it jerked and she
heard Spendwell explaining to some early riser that Brightweave
had loaded the last length of cloth during the night, before he
went to bed.

Frostflower could not have slept so uninterruptedly as Thorn.
She had to keep the brat dry, fed, and quiet the whole time until
they were well out of Frog-in-the-Millstone.

Chapter 11

"The cloth merchant has passed our Farm," said Maldron, "driving north."

"You are sure it was the same merchant?"

"Snaste saw his wagon from the gate."

"Snaste." Despite herself, Inmara felt her cheeks tighten, narrowing her eyes slightly. Why could it not have been Snaste, rather than the limping, jolly Clopmule, to find Thorn in the tunnel and be left almost dead? Was it only six nights ago? Why could it not have been Snaste, rather than Wasp, to be killed six days before that, in Beldrise Wood near the New Altar? No, the priestess realized; Snaste could not have been killed that day, because they would never have permitted such a woman to guard the grove where she and her husband were trying, with Aeronu's help, to join fruitfully at last.

"Whatever you think of her," said Maldron, "she is no muddlehead. She saw a green wagon with my own safe-passage symbol painted on it. She would have recognized the wagon even without the symbol—she was the scout who first suggested using Spendwell."

Inmara glanced at the book she had laid down when Maldron came to join her in the herb garden. She had neglected to mark her place by moving the applewood chip, and the parchment had rolled up again. It hardly mattered; Esimir's sayings did not give the comfort folk pretended they gave. "The merchant has your safe-passage. Why should he not travel where he wishes?"

"He turned south after leaving us. Cloth merchants do not often sell their stock within half a hen's-hatching after they leave us here. And if they do, they fill their wagons again at Five Roads Crossing."

"Or at Three Bridges."

"Or at Three Bridges. But they do not drive north again to restock at Elderbarren or All Roads South. And they continue on south from Three Bridges or Five Roads—they do not return to sell more northern cloth to folk they have just left."

Inmara sighed and rubbed her hands over her upper arms. It was no longer right between her husband and herself. He tried to trust in her as always; had he not come to her instead of Enneald with this latest news? She tried in all matters except one to share her thoughts with him. But the untruth . . . no, not even untruth, merely a few matters left untold—that the babe had been sorcered from the womb, and that at the last she herself had given it into Thorn's arms—lay between their minds and bodies like a new, perverse maidenhead that would not be broken.

"There is something more," said Maldron. "Quickeye returned this morning from White Orchard."

Quickeye. Which of their warriors was Quickeye? Ah, yes—Maldron had given her leave a hen's-hatching or longer ago to visit her father . . . or perhaps it was her brother. Strange that Inmara had not noticed the absence of her face. The gods knew she had been constantly aware of the absence of a cradle from her own chamber. "What of Quickeye?"

"While in White Orchard, she earned a few extra coppers by sitting guard at the wagon-field for a sick townwarrior. Three days ago a pair of strange charcoal burners came to the wagon-field. One was tall, the other short, to appearances a dark-haired boy. They sat outside at a little distance, watching the gate as if waiting for someone in particular; they let at least one merchant come out without approaching him. When Spendwell arrived, the taller workman went to him at once, asking to buy a donkey. At first, Spendwell claimed to have an old animal to sell; but when the burner came out, he had bought an evil-tempered beast, not an old one."

Quickeye would have been in White Orchard since long before they had hunted the sorceress. "And Quickeye knew the merchant to be Spendwell?"

"Quickeye chose her name for a quality she would like to have if she could develop it without effort. Her companion at the wagon-field, a certain Wiltleather, apparently makes it her practice to know the names and wagons of all merchants using the field. Wiltleather also noticed that the supposedly evil-tempered donkey turned gentle enough when the smaller of the two charcoal burners took charge of it. And that they turned south with the animal."

Inmara watched a sticklike insect digging a hole in the nearest patch of herbs, between the thyme and the parsley. "Why should they not turn south?"

"They had come from the north, through the town; and they claimed to have traveled far from their usual rounds in searching for a cheap donkey. That means their usual rounds should have been north of White Orchard. They why did they not return north? And when Spendwell left, later in the afternoon, he also turned south. Why has he now come north?"

The afternoon was quiet, here in the garden near the Truth Grove. The sky had only a few white clouds, and the wind was soft and tentative. Yet the priestess remained ever conscious that such weather could turn to storm within half a day. "The merchant was driving north when you found him, was he not?"

"And he drove south afterwards, when he left us."

"Perhaps he has only now remembered someone he had meant to visit to the north of us."

"Inmara, the man is behaving like an ant that has forgotten the way to its hill! He could not have prospered as he has if he were such a blunderer."

"I doubt he is hired many times a year to strip a sorceress." Inmara was surprised that the phrase came so smoothly out of her mouth.

Maldron rose and walked several paces to the plum tree. Inmara saw its branches shake; and when her husband turned and came back, he was crushing a few leaves in his hands. "Inmara, several persons can ride unseen in a merchant's wagon, all the more safely if a priest's safe-passage symbol is painted on the wagon-tent."

She could no longer pretend to herself that she had not guessed where his conversation was tending. But perhaps she could pretend for awhile longer to him. "Will you hire spies, now, to keep watch on all whom we have ever paid to do our work?"

"Shall I send messages to all our neighboring farmers and townmasters that they are no longer to watch for the swordswoman who mauled you and stole our child?"

"Why should farmers and townmasters watch? All the news we have yet gotten comes from a wagon-field guard—and it seems she did not consider it sufficiently important to report to her own townmaster."

"No, not to Easylife of White Orchard, not when the merchant was bearing my own safe-passage. She could have known that Easylife would do nothing. But she glimpsed the same merchant, or a wagon like his, traveling north early the following morning, back into my own territory; and she knew Quickeye would soon return here, and could bring me the news. It seems that Wiltleather was able to impress Quickeye with the possible importance of the matter."

"Perhaps you should hire this Wiltleather away from Easylife."

"Perhaps I will. A pair of eyes that absorbent are worth something, even in a wrinkled head."

Inmara shook the parsley, and the sticklike insect scurried away, leaving its hole unfinished. She had dissembled again, pretended not to understand Maldron's drift; and it was leading them to another quarrel. Already his voice was growing harsh, even more harsh than his penetrations had been these last nights . . . he had never been harsh before. "Maldron," she said, "I . . . Husband, someone may have hired him to go to Elderbarren for some of old Tatterpenda's lace."

"Anyone who could afford to pay Spendwell for so much of his time could more easily have paid a small wagoner to do the errand. And what of those two charcoal burners?"

She could use sarcasm again; she could ask whether they were now to set spies on all common laborers whose faces some town-warrior did not instantly recognize. She could tell him that she herself had difficulty in remembering Quickeye's face. And then? How long did she have left before he left her and went to Enneald? "Maldron," said Inmara, "husband . . . let them go."

He sat down next to her, with only the book between them. Dropping his crushed leaves, he picked up the sayings of Esimir and began to roll the parchment more and more tightly. "Let them go, Inmara?"

"Let them go. Have we not done all that Justice requires to the sorceress? Maldron, she has suffered everything but death itself—she must have suffered even that in her mind. To hang her a second time . . . would be too much."

"Too much by far. We have more than satisfied Jehandru, or He would not have let her be rescued from the gibbet; and the common folk still believe her dead and taken by demons. We will make an arbor for her between the Truth Grove and the wall, with a small chamber in the tunnel for winter and foul weather. We will not hurt her again, even if she still refuses to name the babe's parents."

Gods! Did he still hope, even now.... "Maldron, she will never be able to bear your penetration. If you force her, you will—"

He threw the book to the ground and took his wife's shoulders. "Have I been such a crude lover, Inmara?"

Raes and Aeronu! If she could only accept his strength—willingly, responsively, as always before—and afterwards hold his head and give him comfort and the reassurances he needed that, when he went forth again, he would act in accordance with the will of the gods . . . but what she had left unsaid stiffened her arms and fingers . . . and there was the sorceress and the baby—Inmara must keep her wits and her will, must somehow prevent him from hunting them down again.

"I will not force myself upon her," he was saying. "But with time, with gentleness . . . and what of Thorn? Are we to leave that blaspheming wretch unpunished?"

"Seize her later, husband!" Yes—let Thorn get Frostflower and little Terndasen to the mountains. The sorceress would keep the babe in her own retreat, and as for the warrior . . . "We will set spies to watch for her return, seize her when she comes back alone."

"And if she stays in the mountains? She has laid hands on you, Inmara. She had bruised you, stolen your child—are we to permit her escape? And the merchant? Are we to leave his treachery unpunished?"

"Thorn must be forcing him." The priestess moved closer to her husband, trying to embrace him. Over his shoulder, she saw the book where it lay on the ground, unrolling by jerks.

Maldron had called the babe "your child." A few moments before, he had called it "ours." He did not know—Inmara had never told him—the truth about its birth, but he no longer intended to seek its parents. Believing it a natural, stolen child, he meant to keep it for himself and her . . . and perhaps for the sorceress also, as an offering to make her quiet and contented in her life as their caged, secret pet. "We cannot keep him," she whispered. "Maldron, we cannot keep him. He is not ours, and the sorceress will never tell more than she has told already."

"Better that we should keep him than allow him to grow up among the sorceri. Inmara, it is an act of piety to keep him from their retreats!"

Aye, and to hold him again . . . an image passed through her mind, of herself and Frostflower sitting together on this same bench, watching Terndasen take his first steps along the path through the spring herbs. Would that be so distasteful to the gods? Inmara had taken it upon herself to allow a sorcered child to live and grow up in the sorceress' care—could it be so much worse to share in raising him?

Ah, gods, they would make a priest of a sorcered child! A man of unnatural birth to lead the ceremonies and handle the holy things! Yet the blame would be hers alone, not Maldron's—while if Maldron knew the manner of Terndasen's birth, he must kill the child.

Or perhaps he would let them go, allow them to reach the mountains. Yes—perhaps, for the sake of those few days the babe had been almost theirs, he would allow it to grow up, even though it became a sorcerer. But if he hunted them and caught them now, he would be guilty of keeping a child whom he thought to belong to other folk. Which of them was worth more to her: the husband she had loved and lived with so long, or the sorcered babe she had known only a few days? And then, if Maldron brought them back, the lie would remain between them always, hovering in her mind and body for the rest of their lives, threatening to force its way from her lips, or to surface in some chance remark of Frostflower's. She saw Maldron learning the truth twenty years from now; she saw Terndasen as a tall young priest lying dead on the altar, bleeding from the silver knife that Justice had required her husband to drive, overlate, into their adopted son's throat—

"Maldron," she whispered quickly, before the image could fade, "Frostflower told us the truth. He is Thorn's own son, and he was sorcered out of her womb."

Maldron slowly released her, turned, and leaned forward, sitting with his face in his hands.

If she had only had time to think, to determine whether he were the more likely to allow Terndasen to live among the sorceri, or to chase them all down and obliterate Frostflower's sin . . . gods! that a woman could live fifteen years with a man and foretell so imperfectly what he would do! "Maldron," she said timidly, "it was really nothing more than speeding the child's growth. It could not have been so unnatural."

"What do we know of their sorcerous rites?"

She sat rebuked, waiting. The book had unrolled to the circumference of a small cup, and was blowing back and forth slightly on the ground. The sticklike insect, or another like it, had returned to finish its hole between the parsley and thyme.

At last Maldron lifted his head from his hands and sat upright again. "You do not think the warrior lied to you?"

"I think she told the truth." Inmara left the rest of her confession unspoken. Her husband would understand now, without her telling him, that she herself had given Thorn the child.

"Yes. I suspected it." He stood. "Even so, the sorceress has been punished enough."

"And the child? Maldron, the child?"

"If he is a monster in the sight of the gods," said the priest, "let the gods kill him before I bring him back to you."

He helped her to her feet and kissed her several times, in several places. "I must leave you. We will trap them between Gammer's Oak and Duneron's Farm. Wait for me—I'll have the child in your arms again before morning." He kissed her one last time. "Enneald may wait also, if she chooses."

When Maldron had left the garden, Inmara fled to the altar in the east wall, her own private alcove behind the peach trees. The wind was chill here in the shade, and she had left her short cape on the bench in the sun; she stood for a few moments shivering before her marble statues: her own old Ontaraec and Eltassru from childhood years, the Raes which had been her father's gift at her marriage and the Aeronu which had been her mother's—all flanking Maldron's own gift to her, the Tree with seven spheres in its branches, which was the nearest any human, even a priest, dared represent Great Jehandru, God of Justice.

Maldron had given her the Jehandru which had been made for his grandmother Arrana, that priestess who was strong as any priest. Now Maldron was turning from the gods—refusing to act first as their instrument, defying them to do their own work if Maldron's human will did not happen to coincide with the Justice of Jehandru.

Inmara knelt, bending almost double, her right hand reaching up to hold the roots of Jehandru's image in a grasp of supplication.

Chapter 12

The merchant had made a rattle of acorns, knotting them together in a bracelet that clicked when Frostflower shook it above the infant's head. Starwind blinked and finally tried once to grab the acorns. Despite the rapid growth that had given him no time for normal experience in the womb, his mind seemed to be developing well.

When had Spendwell found the chance to gather acorns and knot them together? Perhaps yesterday, at the weavers' house; perhaps several days ago, while he waited for Thorn to meet him again. Frostflower had not quite been able to look at him long enough to ask; but she had been able to thank him, and even to accept the acorn rattle from his hand without jerking when their fingers touched. For that she was a little proud of herself.

It was irrational that she needed so much conscious effort to overcome her revulsion for Spendwell, who was comparatively innocent, when the hatred she should have felt toward the priest who had forced them both had dissipated somehow of itself even while he was further torturing and tempting her.

That last day, when Maldron had unbound her hands on the scaffold, lifted off her one, loose garment, and murmured, "It is still not too late"—even then she had felt no more anger, only shame, terror, and an unbearable grief.

"You could not explain to them," she had whispered, conscious of the wooden frame behind her, the swords and braziers in front of her, and the crowd of farmers' folk beyond and below.

"The rabble! I have all the reason a priest need give them ready on my tongue."

"If I could tell you his parents, do you think I would not have told you before now?" Her head bowed, her eyes closed, she had felt her hands twitch, as if wanting to hold him there a few moments longer between her nakedness and the eyes of the mob, as if he were her only protector instead of her chief executioner. One who had no friends within reach clung to the nearest enemy who spoke with a gentle voice.

Then, afterwards . . . long afterwards as it had seemed, when he stood in front of her again, at the gibbet, his hands had felt gentle, feeling through the cloth of her sleeves to be sure the padding had not been displaced when his warriors adjusted the rope beneath her armpits. "You cannot now live as a free priestess," he had whispered, "but you can live quietly and peacefully in a private corner of my hall."

Being clothed again, she could look up at him; but she could not speak. Vaguely she had realized that some passer-by, who could have looked at both their faces and then traveled on to home and supper, might have seen as much to pity in Maldron's face as in her own—perhaps more, since he was a farmer and she a sorceron, hated by all farmers' folk. She had not pitied Maldron— she had pitied only herself; but she had not hated him, either. He had wiped the tears and perspiration of pain from her face, and held the cloth to her nose before stepping away so that his warriors could pull her off the ground and secure the rope. She had felt no gratitude to him—her face was wet again too quickly, and her nose choked and dripping; but his hand had been gentle, and she had remembered Inmara saying that he was a tender bedfellow . . . if such a thing could be.

She could not remember feeling, even when she dangled on the gibbet, the eagerness for death that pain like hers was supposed to bring, nor the hope for afterdeath that, believing in the One God, she should have felt. She wondered if that was because Maldron had left her body that faint, unreasoning hope. The horror she had felt on learning she was to be neither stoned nor disemboweled, but hung whole, must have become an inability to desire death. She thought she had hung quietly, her struggle closed into her mind except when one of the guards struck her against the orders she had heard the priest give them. She had felt anger neither at them for striking her nor at him for leaving her alone with them. She had felt only fear—the fear one sometimes feels before falling asleep, magnified into terror by the certain knowledge that this time she would indeed fall asleep forever—and that

vast, empty grief. In effect, she had died there on the gibbet, for
she had reached no vision of hope. . . . she had finally, with a great
effort, begun a trance exercise, but she did not know whether she
had completed it or broken it off in fear, slipping at last into a
natural unconsciousness preceding death. Her last recollections
before awakening in the wagon with Thorn above her were of
panic, pain, and increasing confusion.

During that period of imprisonment and death, the more self-
centered emotions had squeezed out of her all hatred for Maldron
and his people; and she was so thoroughly drained that it would
not come back, even now. But she had not seen Spendwell since
before entering the farmer's great hall, when there had still been
room in her for the emotions of life and hope (although she had
not believed it at the time). She had forgotten the merchant; and
so her dislike for him must have lain dormant in some corner that
escaped the purging, to come back now with life. Or with partial
life. Spendwell was a constant reminder of what she had lost.
Maldron's tool though he had been, it was Spendwell's flesh that
had taken her power. His youth was a reminder, too, of her
weakness. For the sake of other sorceri after her, she should have
withered the merchant . . . and because she could not regret her
mercy, Spendwell had even become a reflection of her own guilt.

Well, all memories eventually grew dim. After a while, these
thoughts of scaffold, sprunging-stick, and priests' altar would no
longer flash unbidden into her waking mind; A while after that,
and she would die.

The wagon jolted again. Thorn cursed and sat up, rubbing her
head. "Straight Road North, hah! Some damn fool's been digging
rabbit traps all over the bloody pavement."

"It is smoother walking," said Frostflower.

"It'd be smoother riding, too, if the blasted merchant would
use round wheels instead of rectangular ones. Gods, I wish we
could see what's going on outside. Feels like— Get your damn
dog off me."

Odd, how the variations of infancy remained in the adult voice.
Even having Starwind so short a time, and needing, for so much
of that time, to quiet his sounds, Frostflower had begun to learn
the difference between wails of anger or demand, cries that were
simply testing the lungs for the joy of making noise, and fussy
cries like muttered complaints. Thorn's complaints were the equivalent of Starwind's fussy crying.

"Dowl has been very careful to lie here beside me all the while you slept," said Frostflower, speaking to the warrior much as she spoke to the baby when he merely fussed.

"Unh? Just lonely, is he? I should've gone on pretending to be asleep. What's your trouble, mutt? Brat pushing you out of her lap, hey? Well, all right, come on."

The swordswoman settled back against one of the tent posts, holding Dowl clumsily on her lap, rubbing his ears, and slapping his face away when he tried to lick hers. Frostflower chuckled. Thorn looked up with an inquiring grin, and Dowl managed to flick his tongue across her cheek.

"I was thinking," said Frostflower, "that you would not have been able to sit with him so quietly when he was a pup."

"Quietly? Lick your own self, mutt. Get a mouthful of your own hair." Thorn tried to push his nose down towards his shoulder, but he wiggled out from under her hand. "Oh, come here!" Space was cramped, and the warrior obviously had never played with a dog before; but Dowl seemed overjoyed to have won her at last.

I have thought only of myself for too long, mused the sorceress. I have accepted their efforts for me without considering that none of them have ever stopped caring about their own survival. Thorn has run the greatest risks, and I have never noticed it in her face until now, when it is eased a little.

Her own left eye hidden by the patch, Frostflower turned her head to see them better. Thorn and Dowl had begun a small tug-of-war with a knotted rag. The wagon jolted again, and Thorn let go. Dowl sat down suddenly, the rag all his and stuck in his teeth. Looking puzzled, he snapped his jaws a few times, then ducked his head to offer the cloth back to Thorn. It was good to see the warrior relaxing. Hoping to encourage the game, Frostflower chuckled again.

"That's what I like to hear," said Thorn. "Score two. Warriors' God, I wish I could be so lucky at dice."

From time to time during the day Spendwell's whistling of a tune farmers' folk called "Turnip Cake" warned the group inside of another traveler on the road. Then Thorn would stretch out under her blanket and Frostflower would call the dog to sit beside her and the baby until another tune told them their wagon was once more alone. All these other travelers either went on south or overtook and outdistanced them heading north without stopping to look inside Spendwell's wagon; but Thorn's restiveness often burst out after the danger was past. "Gods, I wish I could see what goes on out there! Watch them going by, not just lie here listening like a rotten fish with its fins bitten off! I feel like a roach in a damn trap." Once, near midday, she asked, "Suppose we took to the woods, Frost? You think you could at least try to grow us some food again?"

To attempt that would be to doubt the very source of her people's power. If Thorn understood, thought Frostflower, she would stop tormenting me with such questions; perhaps I could make her understand how serious it would be by telling her it would displease our God almost as much as she believes threatening a priestess displeases her gods. But the comparison would be hard to explain, since the One God had made no Hellbog. Moreover, this was no time to remind Thorn of her own sin and fear of torment. Frostflower only smiled and shook her head slightly.

They stopped for a while at midday. Thorn had wanted to eat cold dinners; but Spendwell insisted it would save no time in the long run, since if the donkeys did not have their midday rest they would walk more slowly in the afternoon. As long as the donkeys had to rest, Spendwell made a fire outside and cooked. However, he cooked only a stew of vegetables.

They ate together inside the wagon. "You could have roasted a few slices of beef, too," said Thorn, "as long as you had to build the damn fire."

Spendwell shoved one of the food baskets over to her. "You can eat your cooked meat cold as well as hot, warrior."

Thorn took out a brownish piece of cooked flesh still on its bone. In Elderbarren, three days south of Windslope, a townboy had stood at a safe distance from the sorceress and waved such a piece at her mockingly, saying it was the leg of a chicken. Hard to recognize it as such; but cold cooked meat did not stink so overpoweringly as hot, and the sorceress found she was once again able to see a friend eating flesh without losing all her own hunger.

"You must not avoid cooking your usual food for my sake," said Frostflower. "I can eat most vegetables raw as well as cooked. If others see you cooking no meat, they may ask questions."

"I'll tell them I cook to suit myself." Unlike the warrior, Spendwell did not reach into the basket of cold flesh. Frostflower smiled at him, wishing she could look into his eyes and smile more sincerely.

While the sun was high, the tent cloth was a bright, almost luminous green inside; and the air grew uncomfortably warm. Thorn dozed, Starwind fussed, and Dowl panted for much of the afternoon. Now and again Spendwell's whistle warned them to even greater stillness, and they heard some foot-traveler or wagoner pass them on one side or the other. The tent cloth had faded to somber green and the interior was dusky when Spendwell stopped again and climbed back into the wagon.

"It's too early to stop," said Thorn.

"Clouding up in the northwest," said Spendwell. "I think we'll be in a storm before morning."

"Damn! I hope your blasted wagon doesn't leak."

"I have five hundred goldens' worth of cloth in here, warrior."

Thorn grunted. "All right, get back out and keep going till the storm breaks."

He hesitated. "Thorn . . . we'll have to spend the night in Gammer's Oak."

"Steamy Hellbog we will!"

"It's the safest way. It'll be almost dark when we get there, and folk will gossip if we try to go on."

"Let them build a wagon-field and put a wall around their lousy flyspeck of a town before they gossip about merchants driving on by."

Frostflower listened to the argument in surprise. The merchant was clearly right. The best way to avert suspicion would be to spend the night in Gammer's Oak. Why was Thorn, who had done so much and planned so carefully to avert suspicion, now protesting?

"I can at least get the wagon between two houses," said Spendwell, "and the donkeys into somebody's pen."

"And your own bloody carcass into a nice warm bed, while we huddle in here waiting for the damn tent to leak."

Squatting, because the tent was not high enough to stand upright, the merchant shifted his weight from one leg to the other. The wagon swayed slightly, as always when anyone moved. "I know you'd rather travel all night, Thorn, but the donkeys need rest; and it'd look strange not to take the first good shelter, with a storm building up."

"Find a place around here and stop."

"We're already too close to Gammer's Oak."

"Who the Hell is going to know? All right, then, drive on to
Duneron's Farm. That's not all that bloody far beyond Gammer's
Oak, is it?"

To drive willingly into another farm! They would probably
have to shelter in farms farther north, where towns were fewer;
but to seek a farm already tonight—to stay within the walls of
Maldron's nearest neighbor . . . "Thorn," whispered the sorceress,
"would it not be safer to stay in the town? I will not try to visit—"

"All right, damn you both to Hellbog! Hurry up and get us to
the bloody, stinking town."

Spendwell returned to the driver's seat. The remaining distance
seemed longer than it should have, for the mood had changed;
instead of fellowship, there was now strain and division. Thorn
sat sullenly picking at the wax that covered the garnet in her
dagger's handle, while Frostflower sat not quite daring to ask her
friend why this great aversion to Gammer's Oak? Perhaps it was
Thorn's superstition again, fear that the town was unlucky for
them because of what had happened in it before. Or perhaps the
warrior only feared the shadow of memory would be too painful
for them there. The sorceress wished it were time for her breasts
to fill again and give her something else to do than think of this.

They knew the wagon was in sight of Gammer's Oak when
a town dog barked. Dowl lifted his head and ears, but remained
quiet, obedient to Frostflower's hand on his fur. They felt the
turn, the downward slope, and the mixture of loose cinders and
crushed hard refuse, grittier than the ancient, dust-covered paving
stones of Straight Road beneath their wheels. The town dog barked
again and they heard it run past the wagon, perhaps chasing a cat.
Otherwise the town was quiet. Gammer's Oak was not large
enough for much coming and going during the supper hour.

The wagon stopped. After a moment, Spendwell came inside
again. "I'm going to buy a few loaves of bread and see if I can
keep my animals behind the baker's house."

Thorn snatched his arm, and he gasped a little. "You turd!"
whispered the warrior. "You sneaking, bloody—"

"Listen to me, Thorn! It's the best—"

She pulled him closer to her and muttered a few angry sentences
into his ear. Frostflower could not understand Thorn's words and
forced herself not to try, because they were clearly not intended

for her; but she wondered. Part of Spendwell's reply, at least, was easy to overhear:

"Blast you, Thorn, get it into your head it's the best place for us! No one will suspect the man who . . ."

Thorn shook him and muttered something more.

Then Spendwell again: "If you don't trust me by now . . ." His words became inaudible to the sorceress, but after a moment Thorn replied,

"All right, go on in before somebody sees the wagon and gets suspicious."

When Spendwell had gone, Frostflower crawled nearer to Thorn. She had seen, when they hid in his upper room together so long ago, that there had been some antipathy between the swordswoman and the baker; but she had never suspected how much. "Thorn," she whispered, "we will sleep in the wagon. You need not see Burningloaf again at all."

"I'd damn well better not see him again. Let's just hope that bloody merchant knows enough not to tell the bastard we're in here. Blasted sneak—never telling me what he had in his rotten brain until I can't do anything about it!"

"Shhh."

"Unh. You're right, I'm worse than the damn dog. Better gag me or something." Now the warrior was forcing her voice to be soft and calm. but her fingers were clawing audibly over the wax on her garnet.

Frostflower sighed. Although she understood they must be completely cautious, she would have liked to let her grandmother's old friend know somehow that she was safe. "Thorn . . . why do you hate him so much?"

"Gods! You don't even suspect?" It was almost too dark to see one another clearly, but Thorn turned her head and stared at her companion.

"What?" Had something happened between them that Frostflower did not know of? But when?

Thorn laid down her dagger and put one hand on the sorceress' shoulder. "Look, Frost, forget I said anything. You know I'm a foul-tempered bitch. Go nurse the baby before you forget where you put him down."

Frostflower crawled back to her side of the wagon. Starwind was sleeping peacefully in the nest of silk and linen she had made for him. Feeling ashamed of the curiosity that had made her probe

at Thorn's secret grievance, she sat and began to fondle Dowl's
ears. The wagon grew darker yet.

"What the Hell's taking him so long?" muttered Thorn. "Gods,
suppose someone hears us snoring in here tonight?"

"We can sleep in turns."

"You sleep. I've been snoozing all—shh!"

A door opened and shut, and someone walked quickly to the
wagon and climbed up to the seat. Next moment he slipped inside.
It was Spendwell.

"What took you so damn long?"

"The baker's sick."

"Burningloaf?" whispered the sorceress. "What's wrong?"

"Food-poisoning. Something he ate this morning. Rancid duck,
he thinks."

"You took your bloody time finding out the bastard's breakfast
went bad!"

"I had trouble getting him to talk, Thorn! I had to be sure it
wasn't quickfever or plague."

"Oh, noble merchant! Rather than bring the plague out here
to us, you'd have stayed inside and left us here in your bloody
wagon for the damn farmers to find!"

"Spendwell!" Frostflower put her hand on his arm, then pulled
it back as she felt him turn. "How sick is the baker? He will live?"

"I don't know. I haven't seen that much—"

"He has vomited?"

"I don't . . . yes, the place smelled like it."

But the odor could not have been strong, or Spendwell would
not have hesitated before remembering it. Burningloaf must have
vomited earlier and cleaned it up himself, then become weaker.
So the poison had already gotten into his blood . . . and he was an
old man. . . .

"I must go to him," said Frostflower.

"No!"

"Shh, Thorn! Spendwell can drive between the houses, and I
will slip around in the shadows to the back door."

"Damn it, let his stinking neighbors take care of the bastard!"

"There was nobody with him," said Spendwell.

"Somebody must know about it! The whole damn town must
know about it!"

"Burningloaf has suffered for years from a delicate stomach,"
said Frostflower, "and he is proud. His neighbors will think it is

only another of his attacks. Perhaps he thought so himself until—"

"Then how the Hellbog does our damn merchant know it's not just another attack of queasy stomach?"

"I must see him, Thorn."

"Damn it, Frost, think! If we're caught, what happens to the baby?"

"They will make him a priest." The sorceress had faced that knowledge before, and reconciled her mind to it.

"And us? Gods and demons, it's not worth risking our guts for a horny old bastard with a cud of acid in his belly!"

"He was the friend of my grandmother and mother before me."

"He sold you out, Frost!"

"What?"

"He sold us both out! How do you think the damn farmer found you?"

For a moment Frostflower said nothing. She hardly realized how the energy had gone out of her body until she felt Thorn's hand on her arm. The warrior's grasp was not hard, yet fingers seemed to displace flesh as if it were watery dough.

"You are mistaken, Thorn. He did not like you, but dislike is not—"

"I never went near the damn marshes, Frostflower. When I left here, I turned east and headed straight for Beldrise. But I told Burningloaf—and nobody else except Burningloaf—that I was going to the marshlands, and now every bloody commoner between here and Gladron thinks I'm at the bottom of a stinking hog."

"No one else? You told no one else?"

"I didn't even meet anyone else between your stinking baker and the merchant here! Gut you, Spendwell, get her some wine!"

They poured wine. Frostflower hardly realized which of them put the cup into her hand. "Someone must have seen . . ."

"Seen what? Nobody saw me—they'd have seen me heading for Beldrise, not the bloody marshes! Spendwell, get on your seat and start driving."

"No!" The sorceress caught at his hand. "No!" How could she say the rest? There was no way to say it—no way to lessen Burningloaf's guilt—but he had not known the swordswoman long. He had disliked Thorn and she him. "Thorn, perhaps he told them only about you, not about me."

"Did you tell him where you were going?"

"I . . . I . . ." She had told him she would go north through Maldron's own forest—but it must have been coincidence, the farmer's shrewdness! "Maldron knew I would go north! How many places—"

"How did he know? Did you ever tell Maldron where your retreat is? Why north? Why not east?"

And the farmer had come prepared, so well prepared—the sprunging-stick and a man to force—that would be only farmers' precaution against any sorceron—but the wine and the goblet and all those things for his damnable ceremony to "purify" her eyes and ears . . . the old nurse to hold the baby. . . .

"He expected to find you in Beldrise, Frostflower," said the merchant softly. "He was surprised to find you had gotten as far as the Rockroots."

"Get back to your damn seat and drive, merchant," said the warrior.

"No! Thorn, I must see him! He is sick—"

The swordswoman smashed her fist into something—her own arm, perhaps, or a pile of Spendwell's cloth. "Damn the dirty, motherpricking—all right, merchant, make sure nobody's looking and let her go in, damn it!"

Spendwell hesitated. "Should I go in with her, or . . ."

"How the Hell do I know? Do what you like, damn the pair of you! You will anyway. I can sit outside and watch—what's one more bloody risk. No, damn it, you'd better stay here and make sure I don't get out and cut somebody's belly open."

"I will hurry, Thorn." The sorceress crawled to the back of the wagon, unfastened the toggles, and peered cautiously out. The street was dark and seemed deserted. Someone might be walking in the shadows between and beyond the lighted windows, but Frostflower thought not. The small town was so quiet that she heard Dowl's soft whine clearly from the middle of the wagon, Thorn's breathing, the donkeys' occasional stamping and snorting, then at last Spendwell's whispered assurance that all was clear at the front of the wagon. She hoped that, from the driver's seat, he could lean around and see to right and left also.

"Go in the front," muttered Thorn. "Don't waste any more time slinking around to the damn back."

Pushing the tent flaps aside, Frostflower jumped out. She did not land lightly—she was trembling and felt weak, and she twisted her right ankle a little, although not enough to lame her for longer than a few steps. She glanced around once more; but how would it help her, now, to see anyone who might walk by? If someone came, she must trust Thorn and Spendwell to tell the story they had prepared, of being landworkers from the south. She hurried across the few paces between the wagon and Burningloaf's door, opened it, entered, closed it again behind her, and leaned against it for a moment, panting. She blew out one of the lamps, then remembered her friends waiting outside and left the other burning.

"Who's there? Merchant?" God, how feeble his voice sounded from the inner room! Pushing the curtain aside, Frostflower went in quickly.

The old man lay in a rumple of blankets halfway between wall and oven. Apparently he had tried to move his pallet near the oven, as if the season were winter and not summer. Although his face was flushed, he was shivering.

"Fernlet!" he cried, pushing himself up and then falling back. It was her grandmother's child name, the common-folks' name he had known her by when they were both children, before Fernlet joined the sorceri and became Silkenfern.

"No, not Fernlet." She hurried across the room to kneel beside him and put her palm on his forehead.

"Frostflower." He reached toward her hand. On the second attempt, he got his fingers round her wrist. "I thought you were your grandmother come to spellcast me for . . . gods forgive me, they took your eye!"

With her free hand, she twisted the brown patch around to the side of her head. "No, not my eye, old friend. They left me both my eyes."

He grasped her hand more tightly and closed his eyes as a paroxysm went through his body. Then his fingers loosened, he sighed, and his eyelids relaxed. Freeing her hand, the sorceress began to straighten his bedclothes. Frostflower's people did not fall sick from the food they ate; but from what she knew of illnesses, she thought Burningloaf would survive.

She judged that he would recover in his body's own time, even without anyone here to nurse him . . . but did she so judge only because she was eager to leave him for her own and Thorn's safety . . . or because in her soul she did not care whether or not he lived?

"Frostflower," he murmured, "they lied."

"Why, Burningloaf?" Why had he betrayed her? Had she frightened him so much that night? Or had she so injured his pride? Even to ask him this in words would be to injure his pride again, so she only asked, "Why?"

"The baby . . . they said you had stolen it, Frostflower. All the tortures of Hellbog—for whoever helped a sorceress steal a baby!"

"But you knew the truth. We told you he was Thorn's."

"Stealing a child . . . I couldn't risk it. I didn't say . . . I didn't tell them your story about sorcering him. Frostflower . . . you're living on the edge of Hell . . . already ankle-deep in the bog, all you sorceri—I couldn't risk going down with you!"

He had grown up with her grandmother. They had all visited him in turn, Silkenfern, Dawncloud, and Frostflower . . . but not often. He should have trusted them, should have known that sorceri told only truth . . . but he had believed the farmers instead. Was that so much his fault, living day by day beneath the farmers' creed? "Old friend, you do not think Silkenfern and Dawncloud are in your Hellbog?"

"And he lied, Frostflower. He said he wouldn't hurt you, only strip your power and give you a good life, a useful life . . . your own children, maybe even make you a priestess. . . ."

Aye. Farmers' folk had different values. Not even Thorn could understand what it was to feel a plant grow beneath your fingers, to ride a clean cold wind, or to seize a bolt of lightning and guide it away from a dwelling or a living thing . . . not Thorn, who would only have considered such powers useful if she could aim them like a sword against her enemies. How could Burningloaf ever have understood the joy that had made Frostflower and Wonder-hope grateful for their decision to remain as brother and sister?

"He lied to me . . . a priest, and he lied. To send you to . . . Frostflower, I dreamed of your grandmother in Hellbog! Gods! The nightmares, over and over!"

"Nightmares deceive, old friend."

"And when he hung you—"

"It is over, Burningloaf. We are safe. Sleep now . . . you will be well again."

He had thought to save her from Hellbog and give her what to him must seem the best of lives possible for her. Could she blame him? Had she not seemed to show him, when she rusted loose his hooks and caused his cords to fall with their silly weights, that honest folk might indeed have something to fear from sorcerous powers?

He should not have betrayed Thorn also; but Thorn had not been his old friend, and he had believed his own salvation endangered. It was Thorn's part to castigate or pardon him for what he had done against her, and Thorn had shown she was more intent on her own escape than on seeing the baker again.

I should leave him some sign, thought Frostflower, so he will know, when he recovers, that I was not another dream. Some sign that will not cast suspicion on him if another finds it by mischance. She looked around the room. A snowflake pattern outlined with flour on his kneading-board?

She thought he was already asleep, but all at once he seized her hand again. "Frostflower—do they know you're safe?"

"Who, Burningloaf?" The farmers must know, or at least suspect, that it was no demon who had taken her from the gibbet; but Thorn, Spendwell, and the weavers had told her the common folk seemed still to believe that she was in Hellbog, the warrior in the marshlands, and the infant in Maldron's hall. The priests had apparently been secretive about Thorn's rescue of the babe.

"Snapperfoot came north this afternoon."

"Snapperfoot?"

"His Reverence's favorite runner."

Was Burningloaf's urgency due to fever, or to a sudden, sane realization of something he must tell her? "Snapperfoot stopped to buy light ale and flatfish from Maltmouth," the baker went on. "He told them at the tavern he was running to Elderbarren to get lace for their Ladyships—but he was dressed as a beggar."

A priest's runner, dressed as a beggar, could have caught up with their wagon, slowed to a walk, and passed Spendwell's donkeys without rousing more alarm than any other traveler on the road, and speed on at a run again once he was far enough ahead. "Did you see him, Burningloaf?"

"Maltmouth's wench came to me for bread afterwards. Maltmouth thinks Snapperfoot was going to Duneron or Allardin . . . some secret message among the priests. I did not listen, my stomach was—"

"You listened well enough, old friend. Now sleep. I cannot stay."

"No—no. Frostflower . . . for your grandmother's sake . . . tell them all."

His last words seemed—not delirium—but the confusion that preceded sleep. Had his talk about Maldron's runner been dreaming, also? They must escape at once—the baker's urgency of moments before had been transferred to the sorceress—but if the priest had indeed sent a secret messenger ahead of them, they must go cautiously or meet a trap ahead.

Perhaps even now the farmers are encircling us! I must get to the wagon and tell the others . . . yet we need caution, not blind haste—we must think, not panic.

She forced herself to sit for a few moments stroking the baker's forehead, until he loosened her hand again and slept. She did not know whether she was right or wrong to wait those few more moments, but they helped calm her thoughts a little; and, when she rose, she knew at least (although she had no time to linger on the thought) that in learning how her oldest friend had helped destroy her, and forgiving him his part, she had also, somehow, finally forgiven Spendwell. Whatever happened, she had that.

Chapter 13

Thorn squatted at the front of the wagon, leaning her elbows on the driver's seat beside Spendwell. "Storm's getting closer," she said.

"Maybe I should drive the wagon between the houses?"

"And then what?"

"We could stay here as I planned. The donkeys will have some shelter, and—"

"And you think you'll be able to get a good night's sleep in there with him sick? You wouldn't be fit to drive tomorrow. And if you slept in the wagon and then missed getting out of here early enough, the whole bloody town would be asking why you slept in the wagon instead of in somebody's house."

"I could ask for shelter next door and pretend I never went into the baker's house."

"And hope the buggers next door haven't been sneaking glances at us out of their windows already."

"If they're doing that, they'll ask why if we drive on tonight."

"Anything we do now, somebody's going to ask questions, merchant! It'll be a dark night, and we'd damn well better travel right on through it, storm and all, and get as far away from this lousy town as we can."

"The donkeys need rest and shelter."

"Damn your rotten donkeys! I want my guts inside me, not strung up on a frame like a bloody spiderweb."

"All right, Thorn, we'll drive on." The merchant subsided. Thorn heard him thumping his fingertips nervously on his leg. The soft, padding rhythm was like the pebble punishments old Bloodrust used to mete out when Thorn was a brat . . . one little pebble after another dribbling down onto your bare backside until you wanted to scream for nine or ten good whacks instead and an end to it. Stone the blasted merchant for giving in with less of an argument! Thorn needed something to talk about, or she might jump down into the street and start shouting and swinging her sword at the muckholes.

"How long do you think it'll be before the damn farmer tells the whole country to watch out for us?" she said.

"He can't admit that a commoner got inside his Farm and took the baby from his own hall."

They had talked it through over and over, and now Spendwell was giving her back her own arguments. Except for one word. "A warrior is not a damn commoner, merchant. We used to be priestesses ourselves."

"Hey? I never heard that. When?"

"Maybe five or six lifetimes ago. Keep it to yourself. It's another rotten priestly secret."

"Hunh. You a priestess." Spendwell began to chuckle, very softly. "I'm trying, Thorn, but I can't picture you as a priestess."

"Then shut up and picture yourself as a piece of gibbet-fruit. Nine bloody days of farmers and spies and warriors between us and the mountains, and you sit chittering like a stupid jay."

"Maybe we're too skitterish. Maldron can save his honor more easily by letting us go than by catching us again and letting the Tanglelands know how you got into his hall." At least the merchant had stopped chuckling; now he was talking to reassure himself.

"What happens when the blasted commoners start wondering what happened to the brat?"

"He can put out word that it died of . . . something."

"Food-poisoning? Has he put out a story like that yet? He's going to try to catch us first, merchant."

"But he won't. . . . He can't scaffold us without everybody knowing—"

"You muckhead, do you think he needs a scaffold and gibbet? He could give us a stretching-out in his private Truth Grove that'd make a public scaffolding look comfortable. Or take us to the scaffold with our tongues skinned and make up his own version about what our crime was." Why am I talking to the merchant like this? Thorn wondered. I should be encouraging him, not trying to scare his guts loose.

"He . . . He wouldn't . . . Then he wouldn't attack us in a town. We could tell the townsfolk. Yes, we're safe in the towns, Thorn."

"We could shout all the way from here to his Farm. Who would the farmers' cattle believe, us or their priest?" Damn it! She hated Spendwell as much for arguing with her as she had for keeping his stupid mouth shut and thumping his fingers. "Well, cheer up, merchant. Farmers tell warriors things they don't tell the rest of you cattle; but farmers don't always tell each other everything. Maybe we're lucky, and Maldron's having some secret feud with Duneron and Allardin. If he can't depend on their help, he's not going to tell them everything, and we may just be able to slip through their neighborhoods."

"Gods. You're worse than a sorcerer, Thorn. Until I met you, I could trust the farmers. Now . . ."

"Now you're beginning to grow a brain. I'm going to have a look behind."

Dowl was whining again, but he was always whining. Frostflower was the only one who could keep him completely quiet. Thorn did not even try to shush him as she crawled back through the wagon.

Frostflower had not refastened the tent toggles. All Thorn had to do was push the flaps a little apart and squint out. The view was about the same as from the front: already dark as midnight, with a clouded sky above, and some half-light filtering out here and there through window lattices into the street.

Spendwell was right about one thing. Maldron might attack them in a town if he was desperate enough, but he was a Hell of a lot likelier to attack in open country. They would probably be safe here for the night. Maybe she should tell Spendwell to go ahead and drive the wagon between houses. She had been a scramblebrained fool to suggest going on to Duneron's Farm—Inmara's brother, wasn't he?—and take the chance that their disguises and the safe-passage Spendwell had for helping Maldron would . . .

Somebody was walking around out there.

Probably a townsman. Even in a flyspeck like Gammer's Oak, people had to go out of their own houses sometimes after supper, to buy something they should have bought earlier, or to join a game of dice or board-pieces at a friend's house. How else could townsfolk sleep so late in the mornings, unless they spent their evenings like warriors, looking for some kind of amusement, instead of bedding down, like good farmworkers, shortly after supper?

She got a few glimpses of the walker, but she could not see much—only a dark figure in a long tunic. Rot the bastard, he seemed to be keeping in the middle of the street, away from the windows. If this was only a townsman, why was he walking so damn slowly?

Smardon's fingernails, Thorn, you're as skittish as the blasted merchant! Why the Hell shouldn't a townsman take his time strolling along the street? It's his own damn town. It's small enough that a turtle could crawl from one end to the other during the time a cook needs to hardboil an egg; and it's still too early in the evening for robbers. Robbers don't often work in towns this size, anyway.

Still, you'd think the bugger would hurry, with a storm coming on.

Na. If he's out on an errand, he has plenty of time to buy three or four of whatever he wants and get back home before the rain. If he's out for dicing or boardgames, he can sit the whole blasted storm through snug at his chum's house.

Was that someone else walking, farther down the street? No, it had stopped. Must have been a cat after a couple of damn mice. Or maybe Thorn's nerves were even more on edge than she had thought. Warriors' God, to be in a plain, honest raid again!

Damn it, they should have gone ahead and driven the wagon between two houses. Here it was, sitting out in the street, with the light from the baker's windows reflecting on it, maybe bright enough to show its color. Frostflower had put out one of the baker's lamps. Why in the names of the gods hadn't she finished the job? Had she thought they needed the light out here? Or was that rotten Burningloaf retching in the outer room instead of the inner one?

Maybe the townsman was turning off before he got to them. . . . No such luck. He had just gone on by the last house before the baker's. Well, it was too late to drive the wagon between houses. At least if he could see it, he wouldn't bump his nose into it; and the common cattle had not been told to keep watch for Spendwell's wagon. This was no worse than all those bloody travelers they had gotten safely past on the road . . . except that it was more normal to see a wagon rolling along Straight Road than sitting lazily in the middle of a town, after dark, with its owner still in the driver's seat. Would Spendwell know enough to slouch down or slip into the tent when he heard the footsteps? Anyway, Thorn's guts had knotted up every time they passed someone on the road, too.

The townsman got out of her angle of vision. She shifted quietly, edging the tent flaps a little farther apart. Gods! He was turning towards Burningloaf's door!

Coming to buy bread? Damn it, why hadn't the sorceress put out all the lamps? Gods! I can't let him find her alone in there with the baker—I can't leave it to her to lie her way out!

The swordswoman thrust aside one of the tent flaps, preparing to jump down and give the townsman some story or other. He turned. For a moment he seemed to be looking at her, and she tried desperately to remember what the Hell name she was using this time. Then she heard footsteps coming around from the front of the wagon, and realized the townsman was looking at Spendwell. Carefully she lowered the tent flap again until the opening was only wide enough for her to see the merchant join the townsman.

"The baker is not selling tonight, friend," said Spendwell.

"Is he not, merchant? I thought you must be waiting here for cake hot from the oven." The newcomer's voice was faintly mocking, but maybe he just considered himself the town wit.

"I've been trying to think who would be best for me to go to."

"For what, merchant? Bread, or a night's shelter?" The newcomer put his hand on the door. "It is not bolted, at least. I do not suggest you go to what passes for an inn, brother; but if you can wait until I exchange a few words with my friend the baker, I'll lead you back to my own house."

"In fact," said Spendwell, moving closer to the door, "the baker is sick. I was wondering who would know best how to help him."

"Sick? How?"

"I'm . . . not sure. But it seems serious. You might be safer not to go near him."

The townsman pushed the door partway open. "You must have been near him, and I've been standing close enough to breathe some of your exhalings. I must see him for myself before I can decide who we should go to."

Spendwell shrugged and went in with him. Thorn dropped the tent flap, crouched in the wagon, and frowned.

The merchant had not done badly, under the circumstances. While not actually betraying Frostflower's existence as long as there was a chance of keeping the meddler out of Burningloaf's house, Spendwell had left it easy enough to explain her. Probably he was even now telling the townsman about the farmwoman who had ridden up from the south and who had been sitting with the sick man while Spendwell himself tried to think what else they could do. No doubt Thorn should stay here in the wagon, pretend to have slept through it all, and leave the talking to the merchant. But . . .

That scuffling again? It sounded closer by a house or two. If she had been on a raid, she would have said it was a few clumsy warriors slipping from one hiding-place to another around the farmer's haystacks and outbuildings. Here . . . Hell, it had to be that stinking town dog after a cat, or the cat after mice or squirrels . . . but they were too quiet for animals chasing each other. And too noisy for competent warriors—Azkor's claws! She had never listened for raid noises in a town. Towns were full of noises. In a big town like All Roads West or Three Bridges she would never had noticed a scuffling like that. She was just skitterish because Gammer's Oak was too bloody quiet. Damn it, if Dowl would just stop his blasted whining!

What worried her most was that neither Spendwell nor the newcomer had called one another by name. Spendwell had been here before. He knew the town, what there was of it to know. At least one of the men should have recognized the other, unless the newcomer had moved into town since Spendwell's last visit. But Spendwell's last visit would have been less than a hen's-hatching ago, and why would anybody want to come and settle in Gammer's Oak?

Anyway, the swordswoman could not squat here like a cheese waiting to go moldy. She had to get out. She had to know what was happening in the baker's house—or at least pace the street and watch the door.

She crawled back to the middle of the wagon and got Slicer. Could she risk taking him with her? Better not; landworkers did not carry swords. But she could leave him near the tent flap. "Dog," she muttered to Dowl, "take care of the brat." Then, reminding herself that she was Pitchfast, a laboring man from the south, and that Frostflower was Pitchfast's wife Sweetpear, she pushed the tent flaps aside and hopped down into the street.

She glanced around and saw nothing, but—damn it!—she *felt* something. She felt as if she was in the middle of a raid. But farmers did not raid flyspeck towns.

She felt for Stabber's pommel under her tunic, and wished she had enough evidence of immediate danger to get Slicer into her right hand, even at the risk of breaking her disguise.

In case anyone was watching, she made a show of yawning and rubbing the back of her neck while she looked around. Her instincts told her to stay out here, close to her sword. Burningloaf's house seemed quiet; Spendwell must be doing a good job in there, and if she went in she might mess it up for him. Especially when she saw the baker again—or when he saw her. Damn! She had almost forgotten, for a moment, what a lousy sneak the bastard was.

Still, if Pitchfast the farmworker had just awakened to find his wife and the merchant both gone—then Pitchfast, as an innocent commoner from another part of the Tanglelands, would go looking for them. So maybe Pitchfast had better act in character. If Burningloaf had not betrayed Frostflower to the new townsman, chances were he wouldn't betray Thorn this time, either. He might not even recognize her; and if she thought he did—Smardon's fingernails! she'd give him a stare that'd keep him quiet.

Glancing around again, she crossed the few paces to the baker's door and pushed it open. Already she regretted leaving Slicer so far away; but the gods knew how many town gossips might be peeking out of their windows. She should never have climbed out of the blasted wagon. But, having come so far, she had to go all the way.

Good. There was nobody in the outer room. She could hear Spendwell and the stranger talking softly in the inner room. All I have to do, thought the swordswoman, is close the door, stand here for a few moments, then go back out and crawl into the wagon again. That will satisfy the town gossips, and the bastard in the oven room will never know I was here.

Easing the door shut so that they could not hear it back there, she listened intently. Their talk sounded safe . . . something about how well the old man was sleeping, and would he thank them for calling in the herb-woman without his permission, when he would have to pay her whether he had really needed her or not? Trust Spendwell to think of that argument! Well, she had stayed long enough.

Gods! Somebody else *was* out there in the street—and that was the sound of warriors sneaking around, or Thorn never deserved to go on another raid.

Probably she would never go on another raid whether she deserved to or not. They were closing in on the baker's door, at least one on each side. Sounded like two on the right . . . or else that was a damn careless—or damn cocksure—bitch on that side.

What now, Thorn? Bar the door? That would be confessing you're no landworker named Pitchfast and the sorceress is not Pearbloom (or was it Pearblossom?). What the Hellbog? They already know who you are, or they wouldn't be closing in! Slam the door, bar it—make a noise, hold them here at the front, and give Spendwell time to get Frostflower out the back way.

And then what? Gods, that townsman! He's one of them—one of Maldron's bloody spies—maybe even a warrior in disguise. A warrior back in that little room with a merchant and a sorceress? Gods, they'll be as helpless as snails with their horns pinched off! And what if they do get out? That merchant will take care of Frost in the woods? More likely she'll take care of him, able to grow food or not—but she'll never leave the damn brat behind, and it's still out in the damn wagon with Maldron's bitches in the way!

All right, then, Thorn, *you* have masterminded this whole bloody plot, *you* have forced the merchant into everything, bullied the sorceress into being rescued—they're both living in stark terror of you; and if you can make Maldron believe that, maybe there's still a chance he'll be a little easier on those two.

Thorn grinned. It was not far from the truth. She *had* bullied Spendwell, rescued Frostflower without asking if she would rather be killed quickly. For a moment, it all seemed amusing; and this might be the last chance Thorn would ever get to enjoy a little humor. Warriors' God, if she only had Slicer in her hand, she could go down happy.

If she had Slicer in her hand, maybe she wouldn't have had to go down at all. Four to one at worst, if there were three outside and the one in the oven room was a warrior. If they had not realized her sword was still in the wagon . . . and the damn dog should at least have barked if they had poked in the wagon to get Slicer, so he should still be safe. . . .

They were going to sneak until the last moment. If they planned to burst in through the door, they should have done it by now. They must think I have my sword, thought Thorn. They're not

quite sure where in the house I am, and they're shy about coming
face to face with me and Slicer. She grinned again. If nothing
else, at least I swung a good sword. Azkor's guts, you'd think
the stinking priest would send braver warriors after me.

She resheathed her knife, put her shoulder against the door,
and waited, breathing softly. With luck, the door would be her
first weapon. Amazing that the voices in the oven room mumbled
on as before, unaware of what was going on. Well, even honest
raids were never as long, or even as loud, as they seemed to the
warriors.

The door began to push inward. At first, the movement was
almost tentative enough to be caused by the wind, or by Thorn's
own muscles echoing her heartbeat. Without actually pushing
back, she held the door steady for a moment. The hands outside
slid around to a new point of leverage. Now Thorn let the door
open easily to about the width of two or three fingers. Then she
braced herself and whammed it shut.

One of the warriors howled in pain. As Thorn had hoped, the
stupid bitch had got her fingers too close to the door frame, or
maybe her blade too close between her body and the door. Thorn
swung the bolt into place, yanked Stabber out of his sheath, and
ran toward the inner room.

The supposed townsman was the first one out of that room.
He stopped and fell back a step when he saw Thorn. Maybe he
knew she was an outlaw warrior; but she was dressed like a landworker with knife in hand, and he looked baffled.

She jumped in close, held the knife at face level, and punched
her other fist between his legs. It was dirty fighting, but it was
the quickest way she could think of to find out whether he was
a male spy or a warrior in disguise. He was a male, so she left him
thrashing on the floor, cursing as if he'd rather have been knifed.

Frostflower and Spendwell were pushing out of the sickroom
behind him. Thorn herded them back in. They retreated word-
lessly—Maldron's bitches outside were pounding on the bolted
door—but Frostflower glanced over Thorn's shoulder at the
twitching townsman. "Maldron's spy," muttered Thorn. "Don't
worry, he'll recover, maybe too soon. What about the baker?"

Burningloaf was trying to prop himself up on one elbow, blinking as if his mind was still asleep, looking bloodless as his own
flour. He saw Thorn and gave a weak scream.

"Thorn, no!" cried Frostflower. "He did not help them—not this time!"

Maybe and maybe not, but Thorn was not going to waste time trying to find out, or even punching him for what he had done before. "Shut up and go back to sleep, you bastard!" she shouted at him while she pulled Frostflower and Spendwell to the back door. Then she spoke quickly and low, not wanting the baker to overhear. "All right, listen! Don't come out with me. Some of them may be sneaking around. But if the front door goes, then get out the back and run like demons."

"Starwind?" said Frostflower.

"Safe in the wagon with your dog. They won't hurt them. If they catch you, merchant, you never did any of this on your own— I made you do it all."

Thorn ducked out the back door. She went to the right—less distance to the corner of the house on that side. She carried Stabber in her left hand. Her right hand felt naked, but her left was better used to the knife. Maybe that was where she had made her mistake with Clopmule down in the priests' tunnel, trying to work with Stabber in her right hand instead of her left where he belonged.

She had guessed right; one of the bitches was sneaking around the house. Either they realized what Thorn was doing, or they were going to try to break in through the back. Maldron's warrior did not seem to be bothering too much about silence any more. *I hear her,* thought Thorn, *but chances are she hasn't heard me yet. Good. I don't have time to be overcautious.*

She slipped up to within a stride and a half of the edge of the wall, then jumped away from the house and turned the corner in a wide part-circle. She timed it perfectly—she would have caught the other warrior flat against the wall, if only she'd had Slicer.

Bad luck and good. The other warrior was an axewoman—no sword for Thorn to win from her—but most axewomen were clumsy sows with arm muscles like stonemasons and brains like the stones. Thorn dodged the first swing, jumped back, and pretended to fall, careful to keep her left leg crooked under her.

The axewoman closed in and heaved up her weapon, laying herself open. Thorn straightened her leg and lunged up, slamming her knife into the axewoman's left shoulder.

Maldron's warrior screamed and tried to swerve her axe around, but it was already in downward momentum and she could not turn it one-handed. Thorn dodged it easily, ducked, levered

Stabber upward in the axewoman's shoulder, pushed against her belly, and let the weight of the swinging axe carry her in a somersault over Thorn's own back. It worked almost every time with axewomen. (And if they were smart enough not to open themselves up by taking a swing when you seemed to have fallen, then they pretty well had to give you a chance to get up again.)

Thorn grabbed the axe, less to use it than to get it out of its owner's reach. The axewoman seemed to be effectively lambasted, cursing and clutching at what was left of her muscles between ribs and shoulder; but sometimes you could not be sure. Thorn raced the length of the house and almost reached the street before Maldron's second warrior, holding a lighted torch, blocked her way. Where the Hell had she gotten the torch? Must have been lighting it while her companion—Thorn could still hear banging in front—was busy at the door. Gods, had they been planning to burn the door, or smoke us out?

This one was a swordswoman. She would be harder, especially with that burning torch . . . but Warriors'God, what a beautiful blade! Nearly as beautiful as Slicer, and a lot closer. And me with nothing but Stabber and a damn clumsy axe that not even the axewoman could manage one-handed. Well, at least she's holding the damn torch stiffly—must be the cow whose fingers I bruised in the door.

The only thing to do with the blasted axe was swing it low. Thorn tried to aim for the swordswoman's shins. Maldron's woman jumped back easily and—bruised fingers or not—made a swoop with the torch that almost caught Thorn's arm. Damn axe! Clumsy, off-balance—all it might be good for was trying a feint so she could get close enough to use Stabber.

Thorn started to swing her arm as if to loft the axe for an overhand stroke. She could see Maldron's bitch grinning, waiting on her guard until the unaccustomed weapon pulled her opponent off-balance. Smardon! thought Thorn, she must think I'm stupid. Now!

Thorn fell into a crouch, dropping the axe and thrusting upward with her knife. Something whirred over her head. Maldron's bitch seemed to drop the torch even before Stabber hit her thigh. Another knife had landed in her chest.

Thorn twisted out of the way and let her fall. Behind them, the axewoman was screaming curses.

"You fathermilker!" Thorn shouted back. "Damn you to Azkor's guts!" What a dirty, stinking—you threw knives at animals in the woods when you were desperate for meat, not when you were fighting another warrior hand-to-hand. And to throw it at my back! Gods, maybe I threw a dirty punch a few moments ago, but that was only to find out...not to murder...I should go back and slice her in half at the navel with her own bloody axe!

But there was no time for revenge. Thorn extricated the fallen woman's sword and turned into the street.

Maldron's third warrior was waiting, sword in right hand, dagger in left. Her stance looked good.

"I'll tell his Reverence what happened to Snaste," she said. "Frankly, she deserved something like that."

"Tell him what you like," said Thorn. "If he adds something else to whatever he already has planned, I probably won't feel it anyway."

"Your fighting deserves a clean death, Thorn. I'll try to give you one."

After the axewoman with her knife-throwing, and that other cow, Snaste, who must have seen what the axewoman was about to do and grinned at it, this last warrior looked like a friend. "Damn your guts," said Thorn. "I think if this were a plain raid, I'd enjoy fighting you."

"And if it were a raid, I could give you a clean fight. As it is, I can only offer you a clean death."

"Idiots!" The voice came from the house. Thorn glanced around. She could make out the head and shoulders of Maldron's spy, outlined at the window lattice. "You idiot, Silverstroke!" he went on. "His Reverence wants her alive!"

Silverstroke turned her face toward the window. "I have never seen the reason in sending anyone to Hellbog with additional tortures beforehand."

Thorn hefted the sword. It was not Slicer, but it had a good balance. Maybe she should lunge now? No; Silverstroke was only pretending her attention was on the spy. Let Maldron's warrior make the first move.

"You're judging your priest, warrior!" said the spy.

"Does Maldron really expect Thorn to surrender while she's still breathing?" On the last word, Silverstroke lunged, not even turning her head until her sword was already aimed—well aimed, too. It would have been a solid hit if Thorn had herself been off-guard instead of pretending.

The street seemed to grow slightly darker. The villagers would be putting out their lamps in order to see more clearly as they squinted through their windows at the street. The people in poor, crummy flyspecks like Gammer's Oak did not see fighting every year. They would be talking about tonight for the rest of their lives. Well, that was fame, of sorts. Meanwhile, you could be sure none of the villagers was going to interfere with warriors. As for the lights going out, warriors were used to fighting in the dark. The warriors' God had the eyes of a cat in the reflecting circular brows of an owl.

Silverstroke was good—one of the best Thorn had fought for years—but not quite good enough. Her reflexes were quick, but her swings were a little too wide, so that it took her too much time to recover and aim again. She tried to get in too many swings and thrusts, wearing herself out while Thorn avoided flamboyance and stayed fresher. Nor did Silverstroke vary her feints often enough or skillfully enough. She usually pretended to swing and turned it into a thrust—and her thrusts were weak because her standard swing threw off her thrusting-aim. When she did start with a thrust and turn it into a swing, Thorn could see it coming right away. None of these faults was very big—only big enough to make the difference. Silverstroke had three scratches to Thorn's one by the time Thorn got her against the wall with the sword point resting on her belly.

Now Thorn had a better chance to study her opponent's face. As she had suspected, Silverstroke was young, probably not long away from her teachers. She had not yet fought many warriors better than herself. "You'll be one of the great swordswomen someday, if you live long enough," said Thorn.

Silverstroke smiled wryly, threw her sword down and sheathed her knife with a gesture of surrender. Thorn nodded. Now to get Spendwell and Frostflower to the wagon without scaring them out the back door into the woods or letting the whole town know Spendwell was a willing accomplice.

"Merchant!" Thorn shouted. "All right, merchant, come out of there. Your wagon's in the street and so is a burning torch!"

She heard the bolt rubbing against the door. So far all right, but he could be moving faster. She glanced at the torch where it lay, still burning, near the body of the warrior Snaste.

Thorn had to be careful what she said—she had better not trap herself into making a threat she would not want to carry out—but a little show for the commoners peeking out through their darkened windows, a little shouting and waving the torch around, might help give Spendwell a townful of witnesses that he had been forced. "Hurry up, merchant! I'm getting that torch."

Silverstroke leaned against the wall, diddling with one of her nicks. If it had been Snaste or the axewoman, Thorn would have made sure she was flat on the ground before turning her back on her; but you could trust these high-minded, clean-mouthed warriors who chose names that sounded like . . . Hell, it sounded almost like a sorceron's name! Silverstroke had warned Thorn she would pull a dirty trick if she could; but that was before she showed an empty palm.

Thorn took about three steps toward the torch, and then Silverstroke fell on her from behind.

She hadn't stopped to pick up sword or draw knife—she used her body, throwing herself against Thorn's backside to lever her own bent knees down on the fallen woman's elbows. Thorn kept her grip on both Stabber and Snaste's sword; and if she were on her back she could have used them—everything else being equal, she judged she was stronger than Maldron's young bitch—but she was not double-jointed. Like this, her arms were pinned; and, with one of Silverstroke's hands clamping down on her neck, she could not twist to her side and up. She tried kicking, but Silverstroke was too far forward for Thorn's heel to connect. She tried humping her back, and Silverstroke's hand damn near broke her neck.

She thought, by the position of thumb and fingers, that it was her attacker's right hand, and it felt as if it had the whole weight of arm and body leaning on it—but she didn't quite believe her attacker was Silverstroke and not yet another of Maldron's warriors until she heard her speak.

"I'm sorry, Thorn."

"You dirty, fathermilking bitch!" It was hard to talk, with a hand and arm bearing down on her neck and one side of her face being pressed into the hard filth of the street. "You gave the surrender!"

"In a normal raid, I would have kept it. You are the better swordswoman."

Thorn heard the door opening. Its scrape echoed through the dirt beneath her ear. You're a little damn late, Spendwell! Thorn relaxed her muscles. If Silverstroke shifted her center of balance too far while getting out her knife and aiming it, Thorn might yet catch her off-guard and roll free. If not, a relaxed body would let the blade go in easier.

"Stop! Silverstroke, you—"

"Keep away, Slapdust!"

The spy, not the merchant, had come out. Thorn felt his running feet thud towards them. He must have grabbed Silverstroke's arm, because her body went off-balance. Thorn jerked, twisted, and rolled free. Her first glimpse was the spy trying to hold back Silverstroke's knife hand.

"Stand clear!" Thorn shouted at the man as she slashed out with her own knife and cut open Silverstroke's arm.

Blood spurted. Thorn had hit a vein. Good.

After a quick glance to be sure Thorn would not strike again, Silverstroke dropped her knife and began groping for the pressure point to hold and choke the bleeding.

Thorn got to her feet. "Thanks, spy."

"Thank him when you're on the scaffold, Thorn," said Silverstroke.

Maldron's warrior should be safe enough now, busy trying to keep her own blood inside her; but Thorn moved well out of her reach anyway. "Spendwell!" She saw them in the doorway, him and Frostflower, but she shouted again for the benefit of the town. "Merchant, get your stinking arse out here!"

He seemed to flush. He opened his mouth, but closed it and pushed his way out past the spy Slapdust. Looking in the other direction, he hurried by Silverstroke. The sorceress, however, paused before Maldron's warrior.

"We were only scouts, Thorn," said Silverstroke. "We were not supposed to attack you, only wait here and keep watch on your movements in case you came into Gammer's Oak."

Frostflower looked at Thorn. Thorn nodded. Maybe the sorceress had decided to try a little sorcery again to close up Silverstroke's wound—that would be worth losing a few more moments.

But Frostflower only pulled off her head kerchief and folded it into a bandage as she knelt in front of the bleeding swordswoman.

"His Reverence is bringing thirty more women up Straight Road North after you." Silverstroke let Frostflower take her arm, suddenly pulled back as if just realizing it was a sorceress who touched her, then shrugged slightly and watched her wrap the bandage. "Maldron is leading them himself, with his nephew Daseron. He's mounted ten of them on horses."

"Hellbog he has!" Horses—the farmers' own animals—even a priest's private messenger had to be specially consecrated if he was going to ride a horse for speed. If Maldron had emptied his horse stables—ten or twelve grown horses was a good number for any farmer to keep—and consecrated the warriors to ride them . . . granted, it took less to consecrate a warrior for horseback than a common messenger or spy . . . but, gods! he was determined to catch them tonight.

"His Reverence will hang you for two days for this, Silverstroke!" said the spy.

"Before I stop bleeding, or afterwards?" The warrior stared him down, then turned her face back to Thorn. "They should have started by now. His Reverence planned to start at dusk, he and the others riding horses in front, the rest following on donkeys or foot."

Frostflower pulled the bandage tight, and the bleeding slowed to almost nothing. "Do not leave it tight too long," she said.

"I know wounds better than you sorceri do!" said Maldron's warrior. Then she glanced at Frostflower and softened her voice. "We think his Reverence intends to let you live in one of the cottages, sorceress."

Frostflower shuddered, rose, and hurried on to the wagon. Thorn threw down Snaste's sword. "Maybe Snaste will survive. Or maybe she's named somebody to get it."

"Don't let them take you alive, Thorn," said Silverstroke.

"Get someone to take you inside before the storm gets here." Thorn sprinted to the wagon and hoisted herself onto the driver's seat beside Spendwell. They had better get out of here before Frostflower thought of the other warriors and wanted to bandage them, too. "All right, merchant, get moving!"

He did whatever it was drivers did with the reins to make their animals go forward. By the time they passed the last building and turned up the slope back to Straight Road, they were going pretty well . . . for donkeys that had already been worked the whole day. Outrunning Maldron and ten warriors on fresh horses was another bloody bowl of mush. Thorn climbed back into the wagon.

"Where are you, Frost?"

"Here."

"Where's the grub?"

"I have him. Dowl is here with me, too."

"Unh," Thorn could imagine them there together, Frostflower hugging the baby to her chest, Dowl hunched up beside her with his head in her lap. Already the swordswoman could see them in outline. She crawled past her friend, found Slicer in his sheath, and belted him around her hips.

"Thorn . . . they will probably be ahead of us as well."

"Unh?"

"One of Maldron's runners passed through Gammer's Oak today. The townsfolk think he was going to a farmer north of here, to Duneron or Allardin."

"Hellbog!" It came as no surprise. "Probably Duneron. He's Inmara's brother, and closer to us." Thorn crawled to the front of the wagon again. "Turn off the road, Spendwell."

"What? I can't turn off."

"Maldron is coming up behind us with ten warriors on horse- back, and Duneron's either coming at us from ahead or blocking Straight Road with gods know how many more."

"I can't turn off here. There's no wheelpath through north Beldrise, and on the other side of the road the ground's still a mudtrap from the last storm."

"Risk going through Beldrise."

"In the dark? How many trees do you want to smash against?"

"Damn your loose guts, would you rather try crashing through Duneron's warriors? How soon can you turn off?"

"When we get to the stretch between Beldrise and the Rock- roots."

"All right. Get us there before Maldron catches up and Duneron comes down, if you have to screw your donkeys to do it."

"Blast you, Thorn, you don't have to talk to me like this! First in Gammer's Oak, now here—"

"I'm going to scream my bloody guts out at you every time we're in anybody's hearing, and if you want to go on peddling cloth after I'm dead, you'd better take it all and act scared green of me." Thorn crawled back inside the wagon, found a candle, discarded it and groped for Spendwell's lamp as easier to balance. Some things even a warrior could not do in the dark.

She unstoppered the lamp and inserted the wick, then hesitated. Having light now would mean extra time afterwards for her eyes to readjust to the night, and heartbeats might count if Maldron caught up with the wagon before they turned off. On the other hand, if Maldron overtook them before they reached the Rock-roots, how much could she do against his warriors, anyway? She got out her firebox and ignited the wick.

Frostflower gasped. "You're hurt—"

"Hey!" shouted Spendwell. "No lights in a moving wagon!"

"It's your squatty lamp, merchant, and I've got it in my lap. It'll burn me before it burns your damn cloth. Just a few nicks, Frost. Most of the blood came out of somebody else."

Frostflower returned the grub, very carefully, to his improvised cradle, got a flask of water and some clean rags, and crawled over to Thorn. "Your face! Is it dirt or..."

"Dirt or bruises. Not the only part of me. You might as well take off your damn eyepatch for a while."

Frostflower took it off and slipped it into her pocket. Her braid of hair, already loosened, slid from its coil around her head and hung over her shoulder, the end unplaiting. She flipped it back out of the way and began to dab at the warrior's face. "Thorn... you would not really have burned the wagon?"

"Did I ever say I'd burn the blasted wagon?"

"No... perhaps not."

Thorn looked at her friend. What is Frostflower thinking? That anything I threaten to do, I'll do—or that now I'm quibbling with words the way I used to sneer at her people for doing? "Well, I wouldn't have burned it until we got Starwind out, anyway," she said. "And Dowl, and my sword."

The wagon lurched and a few drops of hot oil splashed from the lamp onto Thorn's leg. She cursed and blew out the flame. "Hell, what's the use of cleaning a couple damn nicks and bruises now? Azkor's claws!" She restoppered the lamp, pushing the wick down inside as she rammed in the cork. Frostflower found one of Spendwell's jars of ointment and Thorn salved the burns by feel; fortunately they were small. She'd know they were there, but they would not cripple her. "Spendwell! Any signs of that bloody storm?"

"A little lightning. Off to the north."

"Any chance it'll hit us before we get to the Rockroots?"

"I doubt it."

"Hellbog." The storm might have hurt Maldron more than them. They would only have had to drive through it avoiding him; he and his warriors would have had to search with the rain in their eyes and the wagon tracks rinsing away in front of them.

The donkeys seemed to be slowing; but every time Thorn shouted to Spendwell, he replied that, if anything, they were going a little faster. The brat started to cry. While Frostflower fussed with it, Dowl crept over to Thorn and put his head on her leg, whining. The warrior was surprised at herself for rubbing his neck so gently. Good thing he hadn't plopped his jaw down on her burned leg. "When we get to the Rockroots," she said, "we're going to leave the wagon and find someplace to shelter in the rocks."

Frostflower was silent.

"Well, damn it, we can't sit waiting for them in a green silk wagon tent, storm or no storm!"

"I nodded, Thorn. There are many crevices and sheltering boulders in the Rockroots."

At last the wagon swung off the road. Immediately the ride got a lot rougher. If they didn't want to be jounced right through the tent cloth on some bump or other, they would either have to abandon the wagon as soon as possible, or slow the donkeys to a walk. Thorn preferred to abandon the wagon. "Drive it behind the first good rock you find, merchant."

Almost at once he swerved sharply, bringing them to a stop as he finished the turn. They went out the front of the wagon. It was closer, and Spendwell was right there to help Frostflower down with the baby, and to hold the blankets and basket of food that Thorn grabbed on her way out.

"Spendwell," said Thorn, "I probably got blood on some of your cloth. Add it to your other expenses, and pray to the Merchant's God to help get me through this and find you again someday to pay—"

"Later." Spendwell slung the blankets over one shoulder and slid the handle of the food basket over the crook of his elbow. "I'm going with you."

"No, you bloody ass, you're staying here! Go with us now and—Hellbog, what would I do with you now if I'd been forcing you so far?"

"You're wasting time, warrior." The merchant took Frostflower's arm and started off with her. Dowl went a few steps after them, turned back to look at the swordswoman, and whined. Cursing, Thorn cut off the leather reins near the harness and took them along.

More used than the others to getting around in the dark, Thorn took the lead. The large rocks were fairly easy to avoid; but the smaller ones beneath their feet, combined with the patches of mud, made walking hard. They were going deeper into the Rock-roots, and that was something; but if it had been more important to cover ground than to find a hiding place, they might have been better off riding the donkeys.

"I should have a few candles in the basket," said Spendwell.

"One candle would be enough to show them where we are," Thorn replied.

"We could snuff it at the first sound of horses."

"Damn it, merchant, by the time we heard their bloody horses, they could have seen our light! Our only chance is that they don't even notice we've gone off the road until Maldron meets Dune-ron."

But if Maldron stopped in Gammer's Oak, he would learn they knew he was on their track. He would expect them to turn off Straight Road at the first opportunity. Silverstroke might not tell him, but that rotten spy Slapdust would.

"Thorn," said Frostflower a few moments afterwards, "it will soon be time to feed the child."

"Feed him on the walk or let your breasts drip."

"Thorn!" said Spendwell. "We're going to have to rest soon, anyway. You as well as the rest of us."

To their right was a stretch of open space, bare ground with a few knee-high rocks and some low, straggly bushes. To their left was a huge, dark mass of rock. Thorn yielded at last to Spendwell's suggestion of a candle, though she did not light it until they were at the base of the rock formation. Climbing up to explore, she found an overhanging ledge that sheltered a crevice about five paces deep and eight or nine long. The lower rock extended maybe a pace beyond the overhang and then dropped off. The ledge was roughly shoulder-high from the ground. A number of smaller boulders and chunks of broken rock hemmed in the crevice at both sides and along part of the front at both ends, leaving narrow places to climb up. Thorn did not much like the wide stretch of open ground between this rock and its nearest neighbors to south and east; it would let them see the enemy approaching, but it might also give the enemy a better chance of seeing them from a distance. She would also have preferred a crevice completely blocked to view from below. Nevertheless, to go on and hope to find another hole as good just before the storm

broke would be to demand a near-miracle from the Warriors'
God. Thorn stuck the candle on one of the waist-high rocks in
front of the crevice, and let it burn until all her party, with the
blankets and basket, were safely up.

Frostflower settled down on one of the blankets and began to
nurse the baby. Dowl stretched out near her, thumping his tail
slowly against the rock. "All right, Spendwell," said Thorn, feeling very tired, "make yourself comfortable and put your legs
together in front of you."

"What?"

Thorn unrolled the leather reins. "If you had stayed with your
damn wagon, you could have persuaded the priest I had forced
you to take us as far as you did and then abandoned you when
I couldn't use you any more. You insisted on coming with us.
Now, if Maldron finds us, it's going to be pretty blasted hard to
convince him I made you come along."

"Can't you wait? They may not even come close."

"If they do come close, I may not get the chance to make it
look convincing. Damn you, merchant, I'm too tired to argue,
and I want to rest. Would you rather be tied up now, or have the
stones working their way through your guts in a day or two?"

He grumbled, but let her tie him. By tying his ankles with one
strip of leather and looping another round his chest and a con-
venient rock so that he could not bend over and reach his feet,
she was able to leave his hands free and still make it look reasonably convincing. Maybe she ought to gag him or give him a
gag to slip on if Maldron came? No, her mind was getting fuzzy.
With so much done already, she should have time to tie his hands
and gag him if they heard horses coming. Or say she had been
holding his mouth shut.

In the morning, if they were still around, she would have to
figure out some other way of tying him, to make sure he could
get himself loose eventually, but not until she and Frostflower
were out of sight. For now, she said, "You're a good fellow,
merchant," exhanged a kiss and a few squeezes with him, and
then crawled back, stretched out flat near the sorceress, and shut
her eyes.

The brat's sucking sounded loud. "I'm surprised your milk
hasn't gone sour for him after all this," said Thorn.

"No, he is feeding very well." Frostflower paused, then added,
"It would have taken much more than this to sour your milk,

would it not, Thorn? Or would yours have been sour from the first?"

It was a weak attempt at a joke, but at least it was an attempt. The swordswoman chuckled. "He would have gotten pure vinegar if he tried to suck me. . . . Did you smile?"

"I smiled."

The dog got up, turned around, and settled down again with his head on Thorn's ribs. She did not push him off. Frostflower shifted slightly.

"Thorn . . . I'm afraid."

"Good. That means you've come back to life." Thorn rolled out from beneath Dowl's head, turned over, and propped herself up on one elbow, putting her other hand on her friend's knee. "Remember what that swordswoman said back in Gammer's Oak, Frost. His Reverence isn't going to hurt you again. He's going to give you a little cottage to live in. And Spendwell should get off easily enough; all you'll have to do is keep quiet and let him lie his way out."

"And you?"

"My problem will be whether to give the final honors to Stabber or Slicer. Probably Stabber. He's a good size for it."

"To live within Maldron's walls, like a candle in a narrow dish, its wick smothering in its own wax . . . to die quickly or to live on until the memories dull and I might grow resigned . . ."

"Well, why not? Maybe he'll let you keep my jewels. Stabber's garnet might just about cover Spendwell's expenses, and you can keep Slicer's sheen-amber for yourself, pass it on to the grub in time. Maybe Silverstroke would take the rest of Slicer."

"I had thought I could not be frightened again." The sorceress put one hand on Thorn's and pressed tightly.

"Frost, look—our gods, yours and mine, they haven't cleared the way for us so far just to let the damn farmer get us in the end."

"You talk as if there could be such a thing as fate, such a thing as an omen . . . as if the future already existed and we had only to walk from scene to scene as if each moment were a room with only one door. But there is no future, Thorn—there is only an empty void, and not even God knows surely how it will be filled."

"Then I know more than God," said Thorn, "because I know I'm going to spend the next few moments sleeping."

She rolled over again on her back, closed her eyes, put one

hand beneath her head, and rubbed Dowl lazily with the other hand when he curled up to her. She slept.

The first crash of approaching thunder wakened her. Gods, she thought drowsily, no more sleep for the damned. Well, at least the rain's coming. She lay still for a while longer, listening to a few rolls of thunder that sounded more distant than the first, and wondering if the rain was really so close, when Frostflower touched her shoulder.

"Thorn! Listen . . . horses."

Thorn sat up and listened, then tried putting her ear against the rock. Yes; either horses or ambitious donkeys—and Frostflower had heard them first. Gods, a sorceron's senses were even keener than a warrior's. Who else besides Maldron and his bitches would be out here tonight? Duneron and his party? Duneron would stay on Straight Road until Maldron told him otherwise; besides, one farmer would be almost as bad as the other. Thieves looking for shelter at the last moment before the storm? With Maldron, at least Spendwell and Frostflower had a chance of surviving. Thieves might let them all go, but were more likely to slaughter them all, baby and dog included. Odd, that none of them had thought of thieves before now.

Spendwell apparently got the same fear at the same time. "Thorn! I'm helpless—if they're thieves . . ."

"Shush!" The warrior crawled to his corner. "They're not thieves." She listened again. "Too many of them. Too many damn horses for a pack of thieves. Give the bloody farmer this, he keeps down the thieves in his neighborhood." Yes, that was why the fear of thieves had not occurred to them until now. One or two sneaks might get away with a few robberies, but not a whole rotten pack together. Maldron was clean about that, at least—cleaner than some priests Thorn had known.

"Yes. Yes, you're right. Thorn, maybe we could still run before—"

"Where?" Damn it, this was no time to change plans. "We won't find better hiding. Now shut up. I'm going to gag you and tie your hands."

Frostflower crawled over to them. "No, Thorn. Let him hold Starwind."

"You hold Starwind. Make sure they don't kill you."

"I held him once, in the middle of warriors, It did not save me. I would rather die with you, here, tonight."

"Do you want to get Spendwell hung, too? How would it look if they found him half-tied and holding the brat? Get back behind your rocks and let me finish the job."

Frostflower retreated to her corner. Spendwell already had a napkin folded for his own mouth. Thorn finished in a few moments, but not soon enough to get back to Frostflower. The first horses were now so close there was nothing to do but stay quiet and hope the sorceress kept brat and mongrel quiet, too.

They were coming at a slow trot . . . too slow a trot. They were not merely chasing, they were looking. They must have found the wagon; they must also have found tracks. It wasn't likely they had come this close by accident. Thorn was too cramped here to have used her sword without some risk to Spendwell, but she drew her knife, sliding it out with hardly more noise than that of her own breathing.

Now reflections of light, as well as the sounds of hoofbeats, were reaching them clearly. Through a chink in the rocks, Thorn could see Maldron and his warriors approaching. Maldron and a scrawny priestling were in front—yes, Silverstroke had said Maldron was bringing along his nephew, gods knew why, maybe to start training him early in how to track people down. The two priests carried small torches, and leaned down to study the ground as they rode. Only farmers could ride horses well enough to carry torches and lean down like that. Some of the warriors seemed to be having trouble simply staying on the animals' backs.

A wad of something burning thrown in among the horses would give the riders plenty to think about. If Thorn could be sure they might not ride on without finding her party . . . Thin chance of that! Still, there was the chance; and if she tried lighting a fire, Maldron would know where she was even before she could throw it. What could she make it out of, anyway?

Besides, she was thinking like a damn demon's-cud. To throw a weapon at other warriors as if they were common outlaw dung-flies! By the gods, was she a warrior or a . . .

She was an outlaw dungfly herself. Maldron's axewoman had already thrown a knife at her. Smardon's fingernails, she was going to fight back any way she could!

No, she wasn't. It would come to the same thing. Make Maldron's women cut her down, or keep Stabber in her hand so that she could stick him into her own stomach at the end—but fight

honestly. No sense giving Smardon any more holds on her than
he already had.

Maldron stopped his horse and leaned even farther down. Gods,
if only he would fall and crack his own damn skull! But he
straightened up and turned his horse away from the ledge. He
stopped about ten paces distant, motioning his warriors to move
into a semicircle around the boulders. The priestling joined Maldron. Both farmers began to ride slowly back and forth in front of
the rock formation, Maldron to the right, the priestling to the left,
then back again to meet in the center, both holding their torches
high the whole time.

Thorn and Spendwell pressed back between the rocks in their
corner. Frostflower did the same in hers. Some of the torchlight
reflected in on them, and for a moment they could see one another
almost clearly; but Thorn was pretty sure that, even lighted up,
the corners of the ledge were deep enough and the front rocks
extended far enough to hide them from the sight of those below.
Frostflower was doing a damn good job of keeping the dog and
the baby quiet.

Nevertheless, whether he could see them or not, the priest must
have noticed what a likely hiding place this was. Maldron's mind
would be working through the same thoughts Thorn had examined
when she decided to stop here. Smardon's fingernails gut her,
why hadn't she foreseen this and outguessed him—holed up in
some unlikelier place, split up her group and hidden them separately?

Thorn could not see all the warriors, but those she could see
were still on their horses. Although a priest might put his warriors
on horseback for speedy travel, no woman would stay on horseback to fight. Either Maldron was taking his time because he knew
he had his quarry trapped, or he was keeping his women ready
to ride on because he was not sure and he wanted to lose no more
time here than necessary.

After a moment he rode to the warrior on the far left, talked
softly with her, then rode to the far right; and Thorn knew it was
over. She could not see the warriors behind Frostflower's corner
of rocks, but she saw the one on her end dismount and approach
the formation.

The warrior disappeared from sight, but Thorn knew she was
there, close beneath the ledge, waiting for a signal. The warriors
would start climbing at the same time, one on each end. Fortu-

nately—if anything could be fortunate at this point—Frostflower's end was higher and rougher, and would probably take longer to climb.

Thorn pressed her ear against the rock and listened. She heard the warrior start climbing, followed her ascent part of the way . . . now a few pebbles dislodged, now a foot slipping in its toehold and a hand clamping quickly on stone. Then the thunder rolled again, covering the noise of the climber. Thorn glanced at the other end of the ledge. She could not see Frostflower's expression, but the sorceress sat unmoving, one arm extended to the dog's head, with the baby a lump of pale blanket across her chest.

Spendwell's face was closer and clearer. The gag made his mouth an expressionless smear; but, looking at his eyes and brows, Thorn wondered if the waiting might crack him. She squeezed his leg once, sympathetically, before pressing forward as far as she could go and still keep out of sight.

Hunched at the edge of her rock, she could see the warrior who was climbing up on Frostflower's side; she could still only hear the one on her own side. Hurry up, you clumsy cow! Warriors' God, what do I do if that other bitch reaches Frostflower first?

The vein trick had worked on Silverstroke back in town. It ought to work here, put at least one or two warriors out of action. There was no sense in killing when it could not save your own guts; and maybe the bitches would remember the favor and repay it by sharing their last bubbles of surface air whenever they sank into Hellbog themselves.

Maldron's warrior reached the ledge . . . her fingers slid into view around the rock. Stupid cow, sticking in her hand before she looked. Thorn seized it, caught it back against the rock and slashed her knife once across the wrist, then pulled herself partway round the rock, stabbed once, quickly, higher up the arm, and kicked the woman outward, only releasing her in time to keep from falling with her. Maldron's woman gave one scream, and her own struggling helped carry her off the ledge, spurting blood all the way. If she was smart, she would try to check the bleeding as soon as she landed.

Meanwhile, Thorn ran across the ledge. There was no more hope of hiding. The horses were whinnying, the warriors shouting, the priest shouting louder. Thorn drew Slicer as she made her dash. She got to Frost's end with an instant's breathing space.

The other climber was badly balanced on a narrow edge of

rock. Before she could jump forward to better footing, Thorn dodged her spear and drove Slicer's point into her thigh. By the blood this one left behind as she fell, Thorn knew she had again hit a vein.

She turned to make a quick count and see what side the next attackers would come from. Two out of action—or if they returned to action they would soon bleed themselves unconscious. Eight more women, besides Maldron and his nephew—Silverstroke had told her accurately. Three of the remaining warriors had jumped or slipped off their horses; the rest were still mounted and trying to keep the animals calm.

They won't have it easy if they all try to climb up at once, Thorn thought; and if they stagger up a few at a time, by the Warriors' God, I may still have a chance! But—damn! If the priest is smart, he'll just keep a ring around us until the rest of his women get here. How long before the donkey contingent catches up? Even with eight warriors, he could starve us out. Maybe when the storm hits us, and it should be almost here . . .

"Snapstick!" said Maldron, and one of the spearwomen raised her arm and hurled her spear.

Thorn dropped to one knee just in time. The spear went over her and struck the rock, recoiling and slithering off the ledge and back to the ground. "Bitches!" screamed Thorn. "Motherpricking priest!"

"Outlaw and blasphemer," said Maldron. A second spearwoman lifted her weapon to throw it.

Thorn scrambled into Frostflower's corner and crouched there behind the rocks, breathing hard. An axewoman had thrown her knife in Gammer's Oak—maybe that could be charged to the axewoman's own rotten nature. But when a priest ordered a spearwoman to throw at another warrior! Damn his rotten guts to Azkor's gullet, didn't some of his kind even claim the Warriors' God had revealed the rules to a priest in the beginning and not to Bloodraster First of Warriors? Spears were for throwing at thieves, lust-killers, common outlaw turds, animals when you were out in the wilds and needed food—that was why more spearwomen than swordswomen or axewomen became town warriors and wilderness lawkeepers—but a spearwoman fighting another warrior kept her spear in her hands, weapon against weapon!

Damn them all, I was going to fight honestly and die, but if they're going to treat me like outlaw dung! The next one who comes up gets it in the crotch!

But Hellbog! They didn't have to come up.

Thorn found a chink in the rocks on Frostflower's side and peered out again. At least five of the remaining eight warriors were spearwomen. So the farmer had planned this all along. And Thorn had never even learned to throw her knife effectively—not that she would have wanted to let him out of her hand, not even if she could have landed him between Maldron's slimy lungs. Stone her, she might not even get the chance to fight dishonestly! Maybe she could find something to make those wads of fire . . . pieces of Frostflower's skirt and some kind of grease from the food basket? How would she get the chance to throw them, with at least five spears ready to come at her as soon as she ventured out too far from behind the bloody rocks?

The storm, she thought. That's our only chance. Once the rain starts, if it comes down hard enough, I may be able to slip out, if Maldron doesn't make his next move before then.

"Blasphemer!" shouted Maldron. "Come out! Accept the quicker death."

I thought he wanted me alive for his bloody scaffold. Unh. He wants to get in and take Frost right away, and he can't do it as long as I'm here. "Peel your tongue, farmer!"

Beside her, Frostflower trembled. "Thorn . . . it would be a quick death."

"Maybe. And maybe he just wants to get some spears through my arms and legs and save the rest of me for later. Damn him, I'll take a quick death when I choose, not when he chooses, scorch his guts!"

Lightning hit somewhere not far off. The baby started yelling. Outside, the horses whinnied sharply.

"The gods themselves strike at you, blasphemer!" cried the priest. "Come out! Take our spears before Meactira blasts both you and the sorceress with you!"

"Let the Lightning Goddess make her own decisions, farmer!"

Lightning . . . fire-wads . . . wind and rain . . . a bolt that had almost hit Thorn, seeming to knock her guts loose and to melt her brains, leaving her dazed and terrified for the rest of the afternoon . . . If Frostflower still had her damn powers . . . and Thorn thought she did, if only she would admit it to herself.

"Frostflower, show the bloody priest what you can do with lightning."

"Thorn! I can't—"

"Don't snivel! You healed up pretty damn fast once you decided to live, didn't you? You filled up your breasts pretty damn fast for the grub once you got him back, didn't you?"

"Thorn, I . . . I—you must not ask me to—"

"To what? Blaspheme? I've blasphemed my gods for you! Frost, Frost, you've still got your power! Believe me, you've still got your power!"

The sorceress bowed her head, hunched her shoulders, and hugged the squalling brat closer. Her body was shaking a little. Probably she was crying. "You tell me of my God, warrior? You will not let me slander yours. You tell me you know the ways of mine, better than all the sorceri who have ever lived?"

"It's the bloody brat, isn't it? You can't work while you're holding the brat. Put him down, Frostflower. Let Dowl watch him awhile."

"And if you are wrong? If—"

"If what? If you can't quite get the bolt? If some god or other blasts us because you tried? Look, if I get the brat across to Spendwell and out of the way for you—"

"No! No—you would not let me give him to the merchant before!"

Damn, bloody, cringing little bitch of a sorceress! I'll have to—

"Show yourself, outlaw warrior!" shouted the priest.

"Send a few more of your bitches up here to me!"

"I offer you a clean death, and life to the sorceress. Take it now, or we will heat the rocks!"

Thorn looked out again. There was not much wood in this part of Rockroots; but two or three of the warriors, under the direction of the priestling, were pulling a few bushes toward the rocks, and someone was getting down a bag that probably contained charcoal or grease. The rest of the warriors still waited facing the ledge, with their spears ready to lift. Maldron sat on his horse, looking smug, keeping the animal calm somehow with his knees while he drew out his ceremonial dagger.

"Light your damn fire quick or the storm gods will spit it out for you, priest!" As if to agree with Thorn, Meactira obliged with another bolt of lightning and Eajandur with a loud thundercrash.

Thorn turned back to the sorceress. "Frostflower, either you put the brat down and grab the next bolt, or I'll kill—" Kill the grub? Careful, Thorn, don't trap yourself again the way you did when you threatened the priestess! "I'll kill us now, first you and then me!"

Frostflower trembled and closed her eyes. "Yes. Perhaps it is best."

Azkor's claws, I don't even have a good threat left! I'm dead anyway, Frost is the priest's screw-pigeon if she survives, and she knows it. All she cares about now is the damn brat, and if I threaten him I may have to kill...

"Frostflower, I told the priestess how he was born!"

"You..."

"I had to tell her. Inmara knows you sorcered him out of me. Maybe Maldron knows it now, too."

It might work. Frostflower was obviously aware of what priests did to babies they considered unnatural. "No! No, he would not kill—Inmara will not let him kill—"

"But you'll never know. You'll die first. Do you know why I wouldn't let you give him to the merchant? Not for Spendwell's safety, not for your safety—for the brat's safety! Because Starwind had the best chance of staying alive in your arms!" Thorn put her knife against Frostflower's throat. Oh, gods, sorceress, should I have whined and pleaded and begged you? Would you have listened to that better than to a bloody threat? Damn you, sorceress, don't make me..."I'll let you put him down. I won't let either of us fall on him. What the priest does to him afterwards..."

"Let me take him to the merchant," said Frostflower. "If they let me cross the ledge, if they do not strike me down, I...will try."

Was the rock already beginning to get hot under them? Impossible. The stinking priest couldn't get enough fuel to heat so much rock; he was just trying to panic them. Thorn moved her blade away from Frostflower's throat and nodded. "Here. Take Stabber. You'll need to cut Spendwell's hands free." And if they spear you and wound you, or get me before you, I hope you have the sense to use Stabber on yourself.

Frostflower took the knife and got to her feet. Here, the overhang was barely high enough for her to stand upright. "Tell your bitches to hold their spears!" Thorn shouted through the crack. "Unless you want to skewer the sorceress, too."

Dowl whined and began to get up, but sat again when Thorn put her hand on his neck. Thorn did not watch the attackers. If, after all, the priest wanted Frostflower dead, or if one of his bitches broke discipline and threw her spear despite orders, Thorn did not want to know which of them was responsible. In her lust for vengeance, she might lose the opportunity to kill herself before they could disarm her. So she kept watching Frostflower.

The sorceress carried Starwind in her right arm, holding him toward the rock wall, away from the priest and warriors below. Stabber, looking foreign in her hand, would be in plain sight for them; but Frostflower never glanced down at the attackers. Her hair had almost completely unbraided and hung loose and tousled down her back. She walked . . . not slowly, not quickly . . . but tensely, with a nervous self-control that even to Thorn looked almost like pride. A few of Maldron's bitches muttered, but the sorceress seemed not to hear them.

It must be true that the priest meant to take her unharmed. Nobody threw a spear, and the mutters stayed low and under-voiced.

When Frostflower was about two-thirds of the way across, another bolt of lightning struck somewhere to the near north. The sorceress paused for only a moment, glanced up at the stone overhang, and then walked on, while the thunder rolled and faded.

She reached the far side and went into the shadows. Thorn could see her kneel; she would be cutting Spendwell's hands free, giving him the infant. Maybe she was telling him something, too . . . or maybe not. Then the sorceress returned, walking back toward Thorn's corner. She still carried the knife, tightly and stiffly, as if she had clutched her left hand around a sacred trust and then her mind had forgotten it. She was playing with something in her right hand, four fingers and a thumb twisting and turning feverishly while the rest of her body seemed almost paralyzed. Gods, she was playing with that silly acorn bracelet Spendwell had made for the grub—she must have forgotten to leave it with him.

Frostflower stopped midway, turned, and finally looked out at the scene before her. For a moment her head moved slightly as she gazed at the warriors and priests. Then she caught her breath, her fingers stopped twisting the string of acorns, and her left hand jerked outward as if unconsciously pointing. "Your knife! Priest! Drop your knife!"

Thorn peered around the rocks. It was quicker than looking through the chink, and she could pull back if she saw a spear coming. But nobody was watching her.

"Do you tell a priest of the gods to drop the symbol of great Jehandru's justice?" Maldron raised his ceremonial silver dagger above his head, pointing it upwards. "Come down, sorceress! I offer you—"

Lightning. The flash, the noise—the sound that seemed to knock you empty—as when it had struck so close to Thorn herself that time before. Maldron and his horse were lying limp on the ground, his torch on the ground a few paces away. Other horses were screaming, plunging, running . . .

A spear came through the air toward Frostflower, but struck against the rock as the sorceress dropped to her knees with her hands to her face. Thorn dashed out and dragged her back behind the rocks before another spear came. Frostflower was sobbing. The acorn bracelet had slipped halfway down her right hand, catching on her thumb. Stabber was still clutched in her left hand—gods, if her fist had turned differently . . . ! The gods watched an innocent with knives; the blade had left a shallow cut across the back of her right hand, but it had not even scratched her forehead.

They were all in confusion outside—shouts, curses, fear in their curses. It was sinking in that the sorceress had not been stripped of her power, after all. But—Azkor! Thorn had not expected her to kill him. Had hate gotten the best of her at last? Or was her control slipping a little? It was just as well for them that the bastard was dead; but if they did not follow up, finish scaring off the bitches before someone organized a rush—

"Cry later, Frost! There's still enough up there—grab another one!"

"I didn't! Thorn, I couldn't! The knife—it was his silver knife! Silver draws lightning! I couldn't—"

Outside, the young farmer shouted, "Climb! Climb, cowards!"

Thorn pulled Stabber away from the sorceress and pushed her face to the crack in the rocks. If she wouldn't grab lightning to fight back, maybe she'd grab it to save a stinking farmer. "Look there! The priestling has a damn silver dagger, too, doesn't he?"

Frostflower looked. "Young priest! Young priest, throw down your dagger! Far from you—throw it down!"

"Rush them!" The priestling's voice had not been deep for very long, but already he knew how to take charge, damn him. "Your safest place is on the same rock with her! She cannot strike you there without risk to herself! Climb!"

"He'll never drop it, Frost! Shout at him again and he'll lift it higher!"

Frostflower stiffened. Her fingers went tight on the rocks. She stared out through the crack, her mouth slightly open and her breath coming in pants. Thorn turned, Slicer and Stabber ready in her hands, and looked out from around the rocks. A couple of the warriors were either hanging back or running away, but five or six were starting for the ledge. A few drops of rain were beginning to fall, loud and wet. The dog was barking—Warriors' God, keep him back out of my way!—and on the other side of the rocks the brat was screaming in Spendwell's arms.

Another crash. For an instant Thorn thought it had hit the priestling. His horse screamed and reared, and he fell from its back. But he scrambled up, still waving both torch and silver dagger, and Thorn saw a small rock split some paces behind him.

The warriors stopped, looking from the ledge to each other to the young priest. "Climb!" he shouted.

And a third bolt of lightning struck near the edge of the open space and set a small bush bush ablaze.

This was not coincidence! And it was not just the damn silver daggers drawing the bolts now! Not so close together! Thorn jumped out into the open, standing in plain sight and swinging her sword. "You heard your priestling! Come on up, you bitches! Don't you trust your blasted priests any more?"

One of them raised a spear, but before she could throw it, Thorn had jumped down among them. She was reckless, she was no longer thinking more than a few heartbeats ahead, but—Warriors' God! she was fighting like Bloodraster First of Warriors herself! One against five, and they scattered before her. They didn't know where and when the next bolt was coming, and they didn't realize the sorceress was not going to blast any people, only rocks and bushes.

There was an eerie feel in the air, and it was on Thorn's side. The next bolts came, hitting another small rock—then another—then a second bush, almost all at once, one of those series of bolts that come in a crackle like a bloody dance step. The last of the horses had long ago run for safety.

"The rain!" shouted a warrior who was staying clear of the fight; and Thorn realized what caused the eerie feeling around them. After the first large drops, the rain had stopped falling on the rock formation and the clear space . . . but, beyond the torch-light and all around them, they could hear it coming down violently.

One of the spearwomen dashed back away from Thorn and raised her weapon, aiming it above Thorn's head. Thorn turned and shouted a warning. Frostflower had come out from behind the rocks and stood in plain sight on the ledge.

The spear flew towards her. A bolt of lightning caught it in midair.

Thorn yelled and turned back. Nobody was left to fight her. Two were dead or unconscious, two more were clutching their wounds, the one who had just thrown her spear was kneeling in abject surrender, two were still bleeding at the base of the rocks where Thorn had tumbled them on the first assault, and the remaining three had either run away or were huddling somewhere on the edge of the scene. The living horses had all disappeared. Maldron lay dead.

The priestling came forward, clearly scared almost witless but trying not to shake, and handed Thorn his dagger.

"I don't want the blasted thing," she said, and thrust it into the ground. "Break all the spears—you break them, Young Reverence, I don't want your uncle's women handling them again. Leave all the other weapons—"

"I give the sorceress safe passage," the boy said with some attempt to salvage his pride, though he spoke in a trembling voice. "And you, for as long as you travel with her. You have the word of a priest and the heir of a priest. My father and my aunt will honor my pledge." He looked past Thorn and his self-control faltered a little. "What is she doing?"

Thorn turned again and watched. Frostflower had come to the edge of the rock and was sitting, slowly, paying no attention to anything around her. She slid from the ledge and landed lightly on her feet—a warrior would have done it faster, but not better. Dowl padded out on the open ledge, looked down, shook himself and, instead of jumping after her, began making his way down through the rocks at the right.

Frostflower took three or four steps forward, looking at the ground. Then she knelt and began to dig with her fingers. Thorn went forward, arriving near her at about the same time as Dowl,

and they both stood watching silently. Thorn became aware of
blood running down her side, but ignored it.

Frostflower still had Starwind's rattle. Her fingers trembling,
she twisted one acorn loose and dropped it into the hole she had
dug. She covered it with dirt still moist from the storm before this
one and spread out her right hand on top of the tiny mound. Her
fingers stopped shaking; but, as if she could not concentrate in
two directions at once, the rain began coming down in the area
she had kept dry until now.

The priestling ventured close to Thorn. Taking his torch before
the rain put it out completely, the warrior got down on one knee.
Frostflower's eyes were closed, water was dripping from her black
hair, and the rain was washing the cut on her hand and splashing
mud up between her fingers. Then something else appeared between her fingers—a small green shoot. An oak tree in the first
stages of growth.

Frostflower did not open her eyes and look down at it until it
was a finger's-length high and opening its leaves. Then she lifted
both hands to her face and leaned forward sobbing.

Chapter 14

Her power had come back . . . or she had never lost it . . . and she should have lost it forever. She had committed the sin of presumption, and had been answered with such a flow of power as she had rarely experienced in all her life before. First came the drunken, disbelieving glory of seizing charges from every part of the cloud and riding them one after the other into anything that was neither human nor animal, dissipating them harmlessly in the deeper layers of the soil—and then, afterwards, she felt for a time as if, had she not already survived so much, she could not have endured this last, most unexpected bewilderment, this apparant self-betrayal on the part of nature's One God.

Was the mere fact of power worth regaining, when it meant the loss of all certitude in the very creed she had hoped to teach Starwind?

Two of Maldron's warriors were dead. Four were wounded, but still alive; and Frostflower sped their healing, bending above each in turn to manipulate the body's time. The two who were less seriously injured held back for a few moments, scorning to be touched by a sorceress, until, seeing Frostflower insistent, the young farmer Daseron told them to forget their scruples for this night.

Frostflower did not know whether Daseron truly believed what had happened here—that she had saved him from such a self-invited death as his uncle's—or whether he was only cowed into acquiescence by fear of further destruction. All his presumed knowledge of sorcery must have been overturned along with hers, when a sorceress he knew to have been raped, had seen tortured and hung, had yet replied to his threats with a display of full power. He listened meekly to her warning that he should never again offer his ceremonial metal to a lightning-filled sky, and he swore truce with her on the golden wreath he cautiously worked from his uncle's head but did not place on his own, holding it in his hands instead. She hoped he believed at least partly in her good faith, her assurances of harming no one and nothing—she preferred not to think that even a young and very frightened farmer-priest would buy his own safety at the supposed risk to his aunt's farm and people. She remembered his face as being comparatively gentle, that time he came with Enneald and Kalda to prepare her for the Truth Grove; she thought she had guessed, even then, that his words and actions were rough not in malice, but in self-discipline and doubt at his own impulses toward pity. Surely his spirit more nearly resembled that of his aunt, Inmara, than that of her husband.

After Maldron's warriors, Frostflower healed Thorn. Thorn's wounds were not dangerous, but she had a wide, bloody gash in her side, which she had received without realizing it during the last, strange burst of battle.

They carried Maldron's body back in Spendwell's wagon. Daseron rode on the driver's seat beside the merchant. The warriors stayed behind. Frostflower put those she had helped heal into the trance of cool breathing so that their lives would not be shortened; they lay in the shelter of the ledge, guarded by the four who had not been injured. When Spendwell's donkey met those warriors who were coming on donkeys, the young farmer sent them on, one to find the other priest, Duneron, and tell him to take his women home; the rest to help find the horses and bring back the dead. Later, when the wagon met still another group of warriors, coming on foot, Daseron ordered them to return to the Farm.

Inside the wagon, Frostflower put Thorn into the trance. Then she sat, holding Starwind, feeling Dowl against her leg, and gazing toward the dark shape that was Maldron's body, wrapped in a length of Spendwell's best silk. Inmara had said of the priest that he was a kind and gentle husband.

Frostflower kept an oval space clear of the rain around the wagon and donkeys; but sometimes her concentration faltered and a few drops slanted through, patting the tent above or causing one of the donkeys to snort.

As for why she felt she must return to the Farm, even at the price of repeating the oath of truce Daseron had timidly made her swear, she did not fully understand; but Inmara had been kind to her, and her need to speak with the priestess one more time, to explain, if possible, or to...seek forgiveness?...had become a kind of focal point in her confusion, an immediate goal beyond which she could not yet plan. And there was the question of removing Thorn's outlawry among her own people.

The sorceress insisted on stopping in Gammer's Oak to speed Burningloaf's recovery and to heal Silverstroke and the axewoman Thorn had left there wounded. The third warrior, the one called Snaste, was long dead and beyond help. Thorn did not awaken from her own trance until they had left Gammer's Oak behind them again.

Thorn had been apprehensive about returning to Maldron's Farm...Inmara's Farm it would be now, for a few years, by the practice of the farmers; for Varin, Maldron's elder son, was not yet of age to govern, and Varin's mother was dead, leaving Inmara the senior wife. But in such a return lay Thorn's only hope of pardon, and Daseron had promised her safe passage for at least as long as she remained with the sorceress. Daseron was a little older than Varin, and his command held good among the warriors only for this short time, while there were no other farmers present. Perhaps that was another reason he had given in to Frostflower's will——to leave the final decision to his aunt. Had the other wife, the cruel-tongued Enneald, been thrown into command by her husband's death, the sorceress would not have insisted on this return with Maldron's body; but Inmara would confirm her nephew's pledge.

Thorn's nervousness increased from the time she awakened in the wagon until the time, near dawn, when they rode through Maldron's gate. Then she took out her two dice and sat throwing them, sometimes from one hand to the other, sometimes onto a cushion set atop her crossed legs, until the wagon reached the hall.

When at last they came before Inmara, the warrior lay face-downward and extended one hand, trembling slightly, a thumb's-length above the tiled floor.

For a few moments it seemed as if, although looking down at the swordswoman in front of her, Inmara saw only her own long vigil, now closed by the knowledge of her husband's death. Then, finally, she moved her right foot beneath Thorn's fingers and let them rest upon it. Frostflower learned later that had the priestess put her foot on top of the warrior's hand and pressed it to the floor, that would have shown she refused mercy. Even while watching, however, the sorceress understood from the curious farmers' ceremony that her friend was forgiven. Had she thought otherwise, she would have pleaded for her friend, even to the point of displaying her power in a mock threat; but as it was, she could perhaps best help Thorn by staying aloof.

The work of speeding folk to health and of keeping the rain away from her party had helped ward off some of Frostflower's bewilderment; but now she was exhausted—would have been exhausted even had she not spent so much of the night using her powers. The farmers gave her the same room where once they had imprisoned her. For a long time, as she lay there gazing at the curtained doorway in the early morning light, she could not sleep for over-exhaustion and the scars of former fear. Eventually weariness would close her eyes, and then her nerves would gradually grow taut again, and—frequently—a spear would seem to come out of the darkness at her, burst into fire, and yet continue its course, piercing her again and again, painlessly but repeatedly.

When the spear had actually come towards her, sometime during the confusion at the Rockroots, she had seen it not as a thing that threatened her life, but only as a thing to take the bolt she was just seizing. Possibly it had never threatened her life; trying to remember the scene, she thought it had not been aimed quite true. But later, realizing that for a moment she had, perhaps, been in mortal danger, she wondered if it might have been better had that spear found its mark.

She would open her eyes to be sure there was still only a light curtain across the doorway, and not a heavy, closed wooden door. She thought of requesting the farmers to set up a mattress for her in the open hall, but that would betray lack of trust.

At last she slept. She woke in the middle of the day, feeling calmer but still sad and bewildered. Her breasts had spurted during her sleep. She rose and went through the almost-deserted building, found Cradlelap with the children, and fed Starwind while the old nurse brought a light meal for the sorceress herself.

Cradlelap told her that Thorn was undergoing rites of pardon and purification, long and painful, but not dangerous. While the children napped and the old nurse sewed, Frostflower waited in the alcove where the priests kept their scroll books.

She had never known that priests had the skill of writing. Their

symbols, like the form of their books, were entirely different from
those of the sorceri, but beautiful in their own way. Frostflower
unrolled parchment after parchment, gazing at the rows of stylized
figures and angular arrangements of lines, and wondering whether
this was the written form of the common language of the Tanglelands, or of the ancient tongue used by the priests in their
rituals, and of what the parchment was made. Less than a hen's-
hatching ago, she would have considered herself defiled somehow
even to touch these farmers' books; now, she thought wistfully
that here, somewhere in these unknown writings, might—probably
did not, but *might*—lie some hint that could help guide her back
to a certainty . . . if not the same certainty she had lost, then perhaps
to a new groundwork on which to arrange her thoughts.

Now and then she heard the farmers' chanting, faintly, from
the Truth Grove. Twice she heard a scream. The rites must be
harsh, to draw screams from that proud warrior—but Thorn had
wished for them herself. They would wipe away her outlawry, so
that she could again move undisguised, without fear, among the
farmers' folk; and they would free her from the farmers' Hellbog.

At last, late in the afternoon, Thorn and Inmara came to the
door of the alcove. The swordswoman wore a simple garment of
the sort they had put on Frostflower, pure white and hanging to
her knees. Her legs and feet were bare; so was the arm she extended
to steady herself against the doorway. She seemed exhausted, but
well content.

"Look," she said, pulling aside the loose fold of cloth at her
throat and grinning proudly. Just above her left breast was a new
burn, scorched and blistered, in the shape of the safe-passage mark
Spendwell had painted on his wagon tent.

"I think I'm drunk," Thorn went on. "I just drank a cup
of . . . almond-kissed? More wine than I've drunk since . . .
since . . . Last part of the ceremony. No, Frost, no speeding this
time. No trances. I'll sleep it off the old way. See you in the
morning." She gripped Frostflower's shoulder for a moment, then
turned and went back through the hall, very slightly uncertain on
her feet.

"She will sleep tonight in the garden," said Inmara. "Her couch
is ready, near the herbs. If it rains again . . . I do not think that
likely, not tonight . . . you may go out and keep the rain from her."

"Was it necessary to brand her?"

"It was her own choice. Tokens may be lost or stolen. If she comes to any place in the Tanglelands where they have heard only the first part of what happened here, she will have the proof in her own flesh that she is pardoned." The priestess sighed deeply. "Thank the gods I did not have to guide the iron. Thank the gods for Daseron's steady hand."

Inmara paused, as if there were still something to say and she was not sure whether to say it now, or to rest for a while first . . . or whether she would be able to rest before it was said.

"I could have saved him," said Frostflower. "Had I made the attempt a few moments earlier, I could have saved him."

Inmara shook her head. "Do not blame yourself. He . . . When he left here, he knew how the child was born. He knew, and he defied the gods to prevent him from keeping and raising the child. He—" The priestess stopped and covered her face with one hand for a moment before going on. "I do not say the other choice would have been right. For myself, I can no longer believe that a child born as Tern— as your Starwind was born is so unnatural. But I am only a priestess, not a priest. My husband believed the gods would want the child killed, and, believing that, defied them" She shook her head again. "You did not kill him, Frostflower. Jehandru . . . struck him down."

"Not Jehandru. It was the silver dagger. Lady, let none of your people point metal toward the sky during a storm."

"Aye. The sacred dagger . . . pointed toward the gods whom he had challenged to cross his own will."

Inmara paused again, struggling with her emotions. Frostflower waited in silence. Could she remain so confident that it had not been the farmers' gods who struck down their own priest? Had she any right, even if she did know the truth, to argue with the priestess? Inmara seemed to find some pattern, some consolation, in the thought that her husband had died for breaking part of his own creed; take that pattern away from her, and Maldron's death would be a meaningless loss. No, unless Frostflower saw Starwind threatened, she would not argue against Inmara's beliefs. But why did the priestess remain here? It was as if she had meant to say something else, and Frostflower had distracted her with the ill-timed plea for forgiveness.

"Frostflower, if you can grow a child in the womb . . . can you also feel a child in the womb?"

"I felt Starwind, Lady."

"Will you . . . feel my womb?"

"Lady?"

"We had tried for so long. Perhaps I am barren. It seemed I must be barren. But we made our offering to the goddess Aeronu, that day at the forest altar. He had not sinned then; he had done nothing to defy the gods, and I think that I have always... Frostflower, I must know! I must know if I carry his seed!"

Was a farmer requesting sorcery of a sorceron? "Lady, I felt Starwind before I began to speed his growth, but he was already more than a hen's-hatching old. If the child were too small, I might feel nothing unless I first sped the mother's time."

"But could you feel him, if he had been conceived that day on the forest altar?"

That day... it had been fourteen days ago? Fifteen? No more than fifteen. "Yes, if it had been conceived then, I would feel it without further sorcering. But if it were conceived any later... and you will learn very soon in your own time, Lady."

"I must know, Frostflower. I must know at once! Even if you had to grow him to a hen's-hatching old, that could not be so greatly wrong. It could be no worse than your healing of our warriors last night, and Daseron permitted that, did he not?"

Aye, but perhaps the young farmer had been too much in awe of her to forbid it. Last night, Frostflower thought, I must have behaved strangely, speeding time for woman after woman, demanding to return here with Maldron's body. "Rest tonight, Lady. If, in the morning, you still wish it, then I will feel your womb."

"No. In the morning, it may seem sinful. I may fear it, and then I would have to wait." Inmara put her hand on Frostflower's arm. "My thoughts are clear, sorceress. I have thought of this since you returned last night, and I believe my thoughts are clear. Now, tonight, I see no wrong in it. And if I am mistaken, the gods will not blame a poor priestess who weighed her action on a day of grief and strain, with no priest to guide her. Frostflower, will you search my womb?"

Perhaps Inmara wished somehow to associate herself with her dead husband's guilt, to remain joined with him in the judgment of their gods. Perhaps she was only desperate for a certainty to help support her through the days to come. "Very well, priestess, I will do as you request."

"Will you do it in our Truth Grove?"

A place was not good or bad, sacred or fearsome, except as

humankind used it. Frostflower nodded. "Wherever you wish, Lady."

Inmara drew closer and gave one sob, as of relief. "Thank the gods! It was the only sign I asked of them—that if you agreed to return and do it in the Truth Grove, I would know surely there was no wrong in it."

She had asked for an omen. There can be no omens, Frostflower thought; the future does not yet exist; there is only an emptiness waiting to be filled, and not even God knows surely how... but can I be confident even of that, now? Perhaps, after all, the future is already before us and we have only to move into it from hour to hour.

"But we will not go to the Truth Grove," said Inmara. "I could not, not so soon after today. Besides, they will still be scrubbing the altar. We will go to my own private alcove in the garden."

They went. They passed Thorn, already asleep near the herbs, and they glimpsed a few white-robed figures moving in and out of the Truth Grove, carrying censers and brushes. They came to Inmara's alcove, a quiet place, screened from the rest of the garden by curving rows of peach trees and lilac bushes. The thick garden wall was hollowed out to accommodate a polished granite altar and several niches, set into the rougher masonry. The tops of the peach trees and the upper part of the wall were still golden from the late afternoon sun, and the farmers' gods seemed peaceful and beneficent, although mysterious, in their niches.

Inmara lay on the altar. "Must I raise my skirt? Will you need to... put your hand into me?"

She must be thinking of the operations physicians were said to perform. Smiling and shaking her head, Frostflower put one hand lightly on Inmara's abdomen. "No. This is all."

"If you must grow it in order to feel it, do not tell me."

"If I must speed your body's time, I will have to put you into a trance afterwards, or the natural span of your own life will be shortened by the equivalent number of days."

"I will pay that price. Do not tell me."

It was perhaps as well. To put both mother and unborn child into the trance of cool breathing together was very difficult to accomplish without some risk to the infant... if there was an infant. Ah, God, if the priestess has remained barren, how shall I tell her that?

Letting her hand rest a little more heavily on Inmara's robe,

the sorceress closed her eyes and concentrated upon the firmness
of the flesh beneath the cloth, then sent the vibrations of her mind
deeper, gently probing the layers of blood and tissue, so well-
fitting and hallowed when they were joined in living coordination
as nature's God had planned them . . . for a moment, she forgot
her doubts while she found the new nubbin of life within the
priestess.

"Yes," she whispered. "Yes, it is here."

Inmara sighed deeply. Her body had seemed relaxed before,
but that had been the relaxation of a mind willing it so. Now her
mind no longer needed to will away her tension—it went of itself,
and the sorceress felt the difference.

"Is it male or female?"

"I cannot tell." That seemed to Frostflower a very strange
question. "Does it matter?"

She could tell, however, that the child must be at least thirteen
days old, possibly as old as sixteen days. It might well have been
conceived that day of the farmers' fertility rites on their woodland
altar!

"Priestess," she went on, "I did not have to speed your time."
She knew, from the way Inmara pressed her hand, that she had
done right in telling her.

"If he is a boy," said the priestess, "I will name him Maldron.
If a girl, I will name her Arrana. Perhaps she will become as great
and priestly as Maldron's grandmother. I will teach him . . . or
her . . . to respect the sorceri, Frostflower."

Even though she believed Maldron to have been killed by his
gods for sinning against them, Inmara gave him a burial of honor,
according to the farmers' customs. His family cut the body de-
voutly into small pieces, and chosen warriors ploughed the pieces,
still fresh, into one of his fields—the same field in which his
grandmother Arrana was said to have been buried before him. The
thought sickened Frostflower, although she tried not to show it.
Her own people buried their dead whole, or cremated them; and
she was grateful that a sorceron, no matter how uniquely favored
for a time by a ruling priestess, could hardly attend the priestly
ceremony. Nor did Spendwell attend it, being a commoner. They
sat in one of the orchards outside the farmers' hall and cared for
Starwind and small Nikkon, who alone of Maldron's family was
considered too young to join the burial rites. Thorn, however,

witnessed the funeral. For her, it was a signal mark of pardon and restoration to be permitted there.

That evening, learning that Inmara planned to make the swords-woman Clopmule her chief raidleader (the old leader having been killed at the Rockroots), Thorn told the priestess something that had happened during her escape from the Farm—Clopmule had risked the safety of the child in her eagerness to capture Thorn.

Frostflower, who sat near them in the garden, had never heard of this before; and Inmara was as horrified as the sorceress to learn it.

"I thank you, warrior, for telling me this," said the priestess. "I had not guessed the woman's true nature. I will not keep her here."

"She's fairly competent in a fight," said Thorn. "You can't turn out all the warriors who're like Clopmule, Lady Reverence. But you need someone better than that to lead them."

"How am I to find the right woman?" Inmara took the golden wreath from her head and turned it nervously in her hands. "To have been so mistaken in Clopmule . . . I know so little of warriors, so little of ruling a farm. I never expected . . . Thorn, perhaps you . . ."

Thorn stared at her for a moment, then looked down and smiled ruefully. "Not me, Lady Reverence. You women would never accept me, even if you could forget."

"You are right. But I think . . . I could have trusted you, and learned to forget. Who else can I . . ."

"You have one warrior you can trust," said Thorn. "Silver-stroke. She's still young for a raidleader, but if you could find a more experienced woman to work with her, you might have a damn good team of leaders."

"Silverstroke . . . yes, I think she is the one who is said to be the daughter of a priest by a warrior in the western Tanglelands." Inmara nodded, and after a pause went on, "Maldron spoke of hiring an old townwarrior called . . . Wiltleather . . . from White Orchard."

Frostflower rose softly and left them. Her milk had come, and she was not comfortable with talk of raidleaders.

The following day they began the journey north once more, riding in Spendwell's wagon. This time they met no danger; but

Frostflower became nervous at Spendwell's attentions to her, and at his continued refusal to cook meat for himself.

On the sixth afternoon, when Thorn seemed to be asleep after the midday meal, Spendwell brought his cushion and sat near Frostflower, who was nursing the child beneath an elm tree some paces from the fire.

"I've been thinking," said the merchant. "Maybe it really doesn't have anything at all to do with your powers."

"Generations of us have believed otherwise."

"But maybe none of you has ever tried it before. Maybe all sorceri until you have only assumed their powers were lost. If any of them had tried..."

Few of them had survived rape and returned again to their retreats. Yet, of those few...how could Frostflower be sure that none of them had ever made a small experiment, alone, in secret, and afterwards grown morose not for loss of power, but for loss of faith? Perhaps other sorceri had survived rape and never returned to their retreats, living instead as renegades and outlaws, practicing their powers for harm and revenge among the Tanglelanders. Any stories of such women and men would be accepted by the faithful sorceri as still more superstitious exaggerations of the farmers' folk; and any good sorceron who met such a renegade might well keep the knowledge secret in grief and horror.

"Virginity is essential for the practice of power," she said. "This has been taught from the times of the first sorceri."

"Maybe you're...well, not quite mistaken, but...maybe your people haven't made the distinction they should have made between, well, marriage and...the other."

She did not look at him, but she tried to rearrange her robe so as to hide from his view the breast Starwind was sucking.

"Maybe...sorceress, maybe I didn't affect your powers because we were meant to marry, you and I."

Again the half-formed notion of farmers' folk that the future already existed somehow. "You have not heard that sometimes two sorceri wed?" said Frostflower. "They do not practice their old powers after coming together for the sake of children." Yet could she even be sure of that, any more? Could she say certainly that married sorceri never slipped away by themselves to grow a small flower or bathe themselves in a clean wind? Those childhood walks with her own mother...could Frostflower swear, now, that the weather they enjoyed had always been pure coincidence, or that she had never found a plant that had not been there a few moments before? Had they not sometimes found a blossom opened very early for the time of year, or a few berries ripened when all the rest were still green?

Yet if this were so, then her mother and all those other parents were living a lie far more brutal than their mere silence among farmers' folk—they were lying to their own people! No, rather believe that nature had cracked somehow in her own case, than believe her people were lying!

"Frostflower? Frostflower, I wasn't so very. . . . ? I'm ready to convert, Frostflower."

"I do not think you could ever learn the power, merchant. Even if you are right, I do not think . . ."

"No, but you get other converts like me sometimes, don't you?"

Her own grandmother had come to Windslope already carrying a child. That child, Frostflower's mother Dawncloud, had married a convert who was a widower when he joined the sorceri. Could Frostflower be sure that her father, Wintergreen, converted because he came to believe in the One God, and not because he desired Dawncloud?

Frostflower looked at the merchant and blinked, trying to clear her eyes. No, not even if married union did not destroy sorcerous power—not even if, as he had suggested, their marriage was foreknown and she would lose her powers (as well as her faith) unless she accepted him as husband—not even then could she bear the touch of that part of his body upon hers again. She did not even think she could have borne, now, to mate with Wonderhope. But how could she tell the merchant this, so that he would understand and not be hurt?

"I do not think you would enjoy our life, Spendwell. It is very different among us, up in the mountains."

"I would have you."

"If you did not have me? We are mortal, too. We die of disease and accident—we do not always live our full span of time before the body uses itself up."

He was silent. She hoped he was considering his chances for returning and building up his success again as a merchant, after a lapse of years and with the tainted reputation of one who had joined the sorceri.

"If you join us, Spendwell, it must be for more than myself.

You must know what life you will enter, and you must think well
of what you give up."

"I've been thinking about it since—well, since we saved you."

"You cannot have known anything of our life, except in your
own imagination."

"Then teach me. Tell me about your retreats. Tell me about
your God."

She shook her head. She no longer knew anything about the
One God. Moreover, she realized vaguely that, instead of under-
standing her words, he would continue listening to the mere sound
of her voice and watching the movement of her lips. "Think it
through again, merchant. Carefully. If you must, then go to another retreat, in a far distant part of the mountains. Learn from
them. . . . let them teach you for at least a year. Go to Mildrock,
in the western mountains."

Mildrock—Wonderhope's retreat. Perhaps, if she herself could
not make Spendwell understand, Wonderhope could.

"Mildrock," he repeated. At that moment Thorn snorted and
woke up.

Later that afternoon, in the wagon, Thorn slipped close to her
and said softly, "Don't worry, Frost. I'll milk that nonsense out
of the mushhead."

"You were not asleep?"

"Na. Just curious to see how far the idiot would go."

Either the merchant did not try to speak alone with Frostflower
again, or Thorn did not give him the opportunity; but more than
once Frostflower awakened in the night to hear movement and
grunting outside the wagon, and to find Thorn's place on the
wagon floor empty. On one of these occasions, she thought she
heard the swordswoman mutter, "You bastard, you could never
be a bloody merchant again. You think the farmers' cattle
would . . ." (some words Frostflower could not understand)
". . . Besides, where would you find another milker if . . ."

Spendwell still cooked no meat for himself, but he did not ask
how to find Mildrock. When they reached the mountains, even
the prospect of spending a night in Windslope seemed to unnerve
him slightly.

Frostflower and Thorn sat together on a rock that afternoon,
looking north toward Windslope while Spendwell put out the fire
and reharnessed the donkeys. They would be in the Retreat by

nightfall; but as yet only the study-house was visible, looking much like another distant boulder unless one knew what it was.

"You can't see anything from here," said Thorn.

"We do not build our dwellings to be seen easily from below."

"No, I guess not." The warrior cleaned her fingernails and whistled a slow tune.

"Thorn, you need not come the rest of the way. You and Spendwell can turn back here and pass the night at Elvannon's Farm."

"The bloody merchant can turn back if he likes. I want a look at the place. May want to come back here again sometime."

"To watch your son grow?"

"Don't remind me the little bugger's my son." Thorn reached over and pinched Starwind's cheek. He gurgled and raised his arm as if trying to reach her hand. "Unh. I'm getting better—he didn't cry that time. If I get another one inside me, I'll come up and let you get it out."

"We will welcome it. What will you do now?"

Thorn shrugged. "First, I'll work awhile for Spendwell. Ran up quite a debt, cloth and suchlike—no, damn it, don't worry about it, it's my expense. I owe you something for saving me a borter's price."

"I can grow you more dreamberries."

"No, thanks. You've already grown me more than we agreed on back then. Any more would go stale before I could sell them. No, all this has been my bloody scheming and my own damn expense, and the best way to pay Spendwell off will be as his blasted bodyguard. I can try a little matchmaking, too." She grinned. "Me, matchmaking. By this time next year, I think I can have him on a steady diet of beef and Small Spider. She's itching for him already, if I know the signs. After that, maybe I'll see how her Lady Reverence is handling her Farm. And after that . . . Hell, what are *you* going to do now?"

"I must search." Frostflower gazed up at the study-house, its outlines blending in with the mountainside. Whatever other sorceri had done in her place—if any others had indeed found their powers intact when their virginity was broken—she would not keep it secret. She would tell everything. Perhaps old Moonscar could explain to her what had happened. She would listen to his counsel, accept his wisdom . . . but if he told her she must never again use her power, she would not obey him. "I have lost my God,

Thorn . . . or, at least, my certitude in God. I must find it again, or something to replace it."

"Well, if you don't want your God any more, Frost, I'll take him. I think he's—she's?—pretty good. Doesn't seem to mind working along with the Warriors' God, either. In fact, they work pretty damn well together."

Frostflower smiled, envying her friend. "Your world is very simple, Thorn. Perhaps you are right. I think the truth must indeed be simple, if I could find it."

"Hell, you never wanted to milk Spendwell, and so your God just didn't count it. What's the problem? . . . Well, how are you going to search?"

"I must have a year . . . or at least a winter to suckle the infant and to study all I can learn in my old retreat. I will learn the third power, also—the power of free travel, traveling only with the consciousness and not with the body. If they will not teach it to me in Windslope, because of what has happened, then after a year I will leave and find another Retreat where they will teach me. I think I must come out again in any case, to travel through the Tanglelands, to learn from the farmers' folk." To learn from them, not to try to convert them. "Perhaps I can find someone who will teach me the writing of the priests, and allow me to study their books. . . ."

"Gods, you'll need five lifetimes and then some. Are you going to lug the brat around during all this?"

Frostflower gazed down. Starwind was sleeping peacefully, looking as if he knew all the truth she did not. It was the deceptive look of infants, who knew nothing and could only wait to be taught. "No. I will not expose him to danger again. He will grow in safety at Windslope until he is old enough to choose his own life and dangers. But I must find something I can teach him, if only it is something that I can be sure is false, to warn him against it."

Dowl whined and thrust his nose under her hand, impatient of waiting for his share of attention.

Thorn laughed and reached over to rub his fur. "I suppose you'll be taking the mangy mongrel again, though?"

"Yes, unless he finds another sorceron. I didn't take him with me when I began this journey, Thorn. I started down the mountain, and Dowl chose to run after me."

Thorn closed her hand around Dowl's muzzle and tugged-of-war with him for a few moments. "Suppose he decides to come back down now with the merchant and me, hey? All right, dog, all right." She released Dowl and grew serious again. "Wait for me, Frost. I'm not going to let you go chasing around the bloody Tanglelands by yourself again. You wanted a year with the grub? I'll be back for you in a year." She paused and grinned. "Well, the future doesn't exist yet. Give me a year—give or take a couple of hen's-hatchings."

NOTES

"Sheen-amber" is a Tanglelands name for tiger's eye.

The form "hung" is used in preference to "hanged" because the Tanglelands method of execution differs from our method.

For Frostflower's lactation, see MILK: THE MAMMARY GLAND AND ITS SECRETION, edited by S. K. Kon and A. T. Cowie. (New York, London: Academic Press, 1961. 2 vol.) Vol. 1, pp. 289-291.

THE FANTASTIC WORLD OF FANTASY